SOMETHING
LIKE
FATE

SOMETHING LIKE FATE

A NOVEL

Amy Lea

ılılıl SKYSCAPE

Text copyright © 2025 by Amy Lea
All rights reserved.

Published by Skyscape, Seattle

www.apub.com

Amazon, the Amazon logo, and Skyscape are trademarks of Amazon.com, Inc., or its affiliates.

ISBN-13: 9781662517600 (paperback)
ISBN-13: 9781662517617 (digital)

Cover design by Tree Abraham
Cover image: © 279photo Studio, © New Africa / Shutterstock

Printed in the United States of America

For my sweet little C.J.

PROLOGUE

For generations, the women in my family have foreseen their true loves.

That probably sounds bizarre and frankly a tad creepy, but let me explain: I come from a long line of talented Chinese fortune tellers on my mom's side. After coming to America in the early 1900s, the Zhao women began blending ancient methods with Western psychic practices to appeal to more customers. And while Westernizing was hotly contested by my great-aunt, who rightfully feared diluting tradition, a unique power developed—the ability to foresee our soulmates (before ever meeting them).

You might be wondering how this actually works in practice. Can we cross paths on any given gum-pocked street corner and just *know*? Could we identify them among thousands of sweaty, inebriated souls at a music festival? Like most things in this life, it's complicated. In fact, it works differently for everyone.

Take my late grandmother. At only ten years old, the face of my grandfather, a total stranger, came to her mid–math test. His features, particularly his single left dimple, were so clear, it was as though he was standing right in front of her. Personally, I wouldn't take kindly to some stranger's face haunting me at random. But his lopsided smile blanketed her with comfort, like the first ray of sunlight kissing your skin after a harsh northern winter.

My grandfather's face imprinted in her memory so vividly, she instantly recognized him a decade later—in an elevator, of all places. The moment they made eye contact, she emitted a croak reminiscent of an ailing seagull and collapsed face-first into his chest. My grandfather never missed an opportunity to say he "swept her off her feet." They married three months later and the rest is history.

The generations are filled with butterfly-inducing, squeal-into-your-pillow, swoon-worthy love stories that could make even the mushiest romantics skeptical enough to question their authenticity. And it doesn't stop there. In addition to predicting one's soulmate, my relatives have used their abilities to help countless people find themselves, giving them hope, comfort, and direction.

Now, you might be wondering about me. How did I find The One? My Forever? I'd love to dazzle you with a heart-stopping fairy tale woven with sunshine, rainbows, and glittery unicorns. But it would be bullshit.

I haven't foreseen My True Love. I haven't foreseen anything at all, for that matter. Because I'm me, Lo Zhao-Jensen—the extraordinarily ordinary. The only Zhao woman in recorded history with zero—and I mean ZERO—psychic abilities whatsoever.

Until now.

1

I'm on the cusp of hooking up with Mark B. when it overcomes me, fast and furious.

It's more vivid than a recent memory. Crisp and clear as a movie on Dad's prized ultrahigh-def TV. I see an unrecognizable cityscape, made up of slippery-looking glass skyscrapers extending to a cotton candy–blue sky. My nose is engulfed with a rich espresso-like scent that threatens to clear my airways. Barbs of heat prick my neck, as though I'm getting the brunt of a high-noon sun and not sitting in a darkened basement at Pi Kappa Alpha's end-of-finals party. The last big bash before summer. A cluster of red cartoon hearts drifts over the skyline like hot-air balloons expanding fast, getting larger and larger until—

"Lo?" Mark B.'s sour beer breath snaps me back to reality, and his glistening wet lips come into sharp focus. They're hovering dangerously close to mine, and a surge of dread rockets down my spine.

"Sorry, I, uh, I thought I saw . . ."

"You good? You kinda went all bug-eyed. Looked like you were having an allergic reaction or something," he says with his signature bluntness.

"How attractive of me." A catatonic state and the flush of anaphylactic shock is the ultimate recipe for seduction, didn't you know?

I expect him to brush off my self-deprecation, like he usually does. Maybe humor me with a little white lie about how I'm kind of "adorable" or "endearing." But he doesn't say anything at all. Not a thing.

And while this moment will probably haunt my soul for millennia, there are more pressing matters. Like, what the hell did I just see?

Mark B. senses the mood shift, the hard angles of his bewildered expression glowing orange from the lava lamp on the side table.

I consider explaining, but the words don't come. There is no way to explain all of *that* without him thinking I'm a total loon. Besides, what even was "*that*"? A figment of my alcohol-induced imagination? Can't be. I only had two red Solo cups' worth of beer.

Could it be a hallucination from stuffing myself like a sausage into this two-sizes-too-small orange suede skirt? Possibly.

A bizarrely vivid daydream? Marginally more likely. Then again, I've never had daydreams thrust upon me like a chemistry lab partner I didn't choose.

I recall something my grandmother used to say: that visions strike at the most inconvenient times, like a school test in her case, or while on the toilet, like my aunt Mei. Could it really be a vision? I stomp down the hope and kick some dirt over it for good measure. I won't venture down that tunnel. I did not inherit the Zhao abilities. I've already begrudgingly made peace with being the talentless outcast in my family and a smidge below average at, well, everything.

Mark B. clears his throat and gestures at the space between us. "Do you actually wanna hook up or no? Because lately you always seem to have some sort of issue," he says, making air quotes around *issue*, as though it's intentional on my part.

Trust, I wish it were. The past multiple times we've hung out, I've had some . . . complications, to say the least. One time, I fell asleep ten minutes into our movie and snored like a seventy-year-old man with sleep apnea. He recorded me to prove it. The time after, I tried to make up for it by zealously throwing myself on top of him without notice, only to pull a muscle in my inner thigh and keel over in slow motion. And now this.

"Do you want to hook up?" he repeats impatiently over the pulse of the bass and chanting upstairs. The beer pong tournament is in full swing.

I bite my lip. "Um . . ." Do I? That's the million-dollar question. Technically, yes. I didn't wear a matching bra-and-undies set for nothing. It's not like this would be our first hookup, and it's not that I don't enjoy hookups in general. I do, in the moment. But when it's finished and he rolls over with a single grunt, I can't help but feel a swell of disappointment. Is this how it's supposed to be? Hollow? Anticlimactic? Would it be different with someone I really, really like?

Not that I don't like Mark B.

I liked him instantly when we met at, you guessed it, a frat party. It was an ABC-themed party (anything but clothes) before the holidays. I was standing in the kitchen, trying to cut my duct-tape dress off with right-handed scissors so I could actually sit or pee comfortably. He sauntered over in a toga fashioned out of a wiener dog–print bedsheet and offered to help cut me out of it "in a nonsexual way."

He had one of those ultraconfident gaits, a swagger about him, always in command, which in hindsight was a massive part of his allure (and the wiener-dog sheets, of course). I was stunned he was even paying attention to me with his bootleg Hemsworth-brother looks.

After he fetched me a spare T-shirt from upstairs, we bonded over the shared trauma of being left-handed in a right-handed world, our love of cherry Jell-O shots, and watching videos of lost dogs being reunited with their owners. The stuff of substance.

For a frat boy, turns out he's an above-average human who genuinely wants to make sure I'm comfortable. He always pays for my Ubers home and responds with enthusiasm to the baby animal videos I send him. But there's absolutely no lingering eye contact, no zap of electricity when we touch, not even an ease or comfortability from investing so many hours together over the past few months.

I've always wondered what it would feel like with someone who feathers the tips of his fingers across my jaw, stares lovingly into my eyes, and tells me I've "bewitched him heart and soul." Who blesses me with a passionate, toe-curling kiss, altering my body chemistry forevermore. As you can tell, I've put *a lot* of thought into it. Hundreds of hours, actually. But what do you expect when your whole family falls madly in love with their soulmates?

This is nowhere close. So I'm not sure why I'm so fixated on hooking up with Mark B. one last time. Maybe I'm settling, or desperate. Probably both. But it just feels like the right way to mark the end of the semester before flying halfway across the world for a whole month. I must salvage the situation.

"I want to!" I practically yelp, yanking him by the collar of his pilled campus-crested hoodie.

His brow quirks, amused by my sudden enthusiasm and sultry bedroom eyes peeking out from self-cut (okay, hacked) seventies curtain bangs. I'm really selling it here.

His lips are sopping wet when they fuse against mine, like drenched pillows. All my justifications go out the window when he shoves his tongue in my mouth without notice. It's heavy, like a gigantic slug.

My mind knows I'm in desperate need of mental escape, because the image hits again, exactly the same as before. The city skyline, the espresso scent, and the hearts.

I abruptly pull back, shaking the image (and the moisture) away like a wet dog. "Um, be right back. I need to use the bathroom," I mumble, bolting for the nearest exit.

The vision fades when I close the door behind me, but only partially. It's nagging at me, like a scratch that needs to be itched.

I need to talk to my aunts. ASAP. But first, I need to get out of here.

I blink, groping in the darkness for a light switch. There's a soft knock on the door.

"Lo?" Mark B. says.

I should tell him the truth—that I'm having some strange, intrusive vision that won't go away. And that even if I weren't, things between us still don't feel right and never have. But because I'm incapable of intentionally hurting people's feelings (a.k.a. a complete and total coward), all that comes out is a painfully cheery, "I'll be right out! Just finishing up."

"Finishing up what?" He sounds alarmed. "That's not a bathroom."

As soon as my eyes adjust in the darkness, that unfortunate fact becomes clear. I've locked myself in a storage room filled with dusty boxes, broken furniture, bikes that have seen better days, and likely a frat-boy ghost or two.

Another, slightly more urgent knock. "Lo? Please tell me you didn't go to the bathroom in there."

I slap my hand over my mouth, remaining silent. Get. Me. Out. Of. Here.

And that's when I spot it. A window. Bless. Sure, it's barely large enough to squeeze a small toddler through, but desperate times call for desperate measures.

Braving the sticky cobwebs, I comb through the junk in desperate search of a ladder, a step stool, any object tall enough to reach the window. My results yield a rickety end table and a dust-caked Crock-Pot box from the nineties. The table is wobbly, but it gives me just enough height to reach the window. Bangs plastered to my forehead, I contort my limbs through the small space and emerge onto the crowded lawn victorious. And by *victorious*, I mean running-from-a-deranged-chainsaw-wielding-back-country-serial-killer aesthetic.

No one seems to notice, which is both a relief and seriously concerning.

The lawn is a complete zoo. I weave through a group of sorority girls cradling matching bedazzled bottles of strawberry wine like newborns. I narrowly avoid a head-on collision with a very drunk guy in a Cowboys jersey double-fisting two frothy beers.

"Sorry!" I call over my shoulder as I round the front of the house.

My best friend, Bianca Alves, waves me over. She's leaning against the red brick, chatting with a muscly guy in a backward baseball cap who is absolutely not her type.

She beelines it to me. "Did you guys hook up?" Bianca asks, thick, dark brows raised in anticipation. Tonight, she's opted for an argyle miniskirt shorter than mine, paired with a white cropped T-shirt that flaunts her bronze competitive-dancer abs.

"No," I croak. *Why did I flee from Mark B. like that?* I shamefully avoid all eye contact as she swiftly shuttles me inside and upstairs. I feel like a disgraced pop star being ushered into rehab through a pack of ravenous paparazzi.

We filter into a random fraternity bro's room littered with bongs, crumpled papers, dirty laundry, and overturned beer cans.

"Did you do anything? At all?" Bianca asks, the disappointment dripping in her voice. She stands in front of the smudged dresser mirror, retying her hair into her iconic Ariana Grande–esque ponytail—styled the same as the first day we met in Intro to English Lit.

At the request of the TA, we went around the room and told everyone our favorite books. All the die-hard English majors shared some variation of depressing literary fiction or Austen classic. As a science major taking the course as an elective, I shouted *The Great Gatsby* out of panic, despite only having watched the Leonardo DiCaprio film. When it came Bianca's turn, she declared *Twilight* with the unshakable confidence of a middle-aged white man. She's been my hero ever since. So much so that I tried copying her ponytail on multiple occasions, only to more closely resemble a balding US founding father. Hence the curtain bangs.

"I mean . . . he put his tongue in my mouth for about two seconds before I fled through a window," I admit, omitting the crucial details of my strange vision. I really need to get out of here and talk to my aunts.

"Fled through a window," she repeats, wholly unsurprised.

I sidestep to avoid dipping my toe in a puddle of mystery fluid and explain how I announced I was going to the bathroom and instead found myself in the storage room.

"Shut up. He probably thinks you drunkenly took a shit in there and passed out," she says with an aggressive snort.

The thought of Mark B. and his frat bros scouring the storage room in search of human feces has me practically doubled over, gripping the dresser for support. We laugh until we cry, until our abs ache. Once we've semi-recovered, she asks, "But seriously, why are you suddenly so against hooking up with him? You were so into it a few months ago."

I cringe, plunking onto the bed, lamenting the missed opportunity. "Honestly, I ask myself that daily. He's . . . nice. I just don't get soulmate vibes from him." Bianca skewers me with a *not this again* look, so I add, "And he made me feel like a total dumbass for not knowing what the word *perspicacious* means."

Bianca twists her lips. "What does it mean?"

"Exactly. No one knows, except people trying to sound smarter than they actually are. He explained it, but I blacked out and disassociated."

"Ew, what an asshat. You know, I heard he failed prelaw last semester. I bet he's trying to overcompensate," she says.

"That would explain the look on his face when I told him I wanted to drop out of college and be a dog walker," I say. It was a joke—technically. One of those test-the-water jokes that had an edge of seriousness.

He looked at me like I'd announced I was going to live in the forest, wearing a leaf to cover my privates and trading berries and twigs as currency. "Why would you drop out for a minimum-wage job?" He said *minimum wage* like it was a dirty word, which was on brand, coming from a family of highly decorated lawyers. His grandfather was a judge whose name was tossed around for the Supreme Court.

"I don't know if I like my program," I'd told him truthfully, the weight of it lifting off my chest. I'd been grappling with my total disinterest in the program all year, terrified to tell anyone, especially Dad, who was thrilled I was following in his and Mom's footsteps as forensic scientists.

"Why don't you switch majors?" he asked. It was a fair question. But I'd already taken a range of electives, none of which were any more interesting.

Unlike Bianca, who's known she's wanted to study fine art since she was thirteen, I've always had a mild interest in everything and a passion for nothing. In fact, I'm not entirely sure college is for me, which is why I've been tossing around the idea of deferring or dropping out entirely.

Bianca sighs while doing dance stretches on the edge of the dresser. "Okay, so maybe he's a little bit of an elitist prick. Maybe he's not your *soulmate*. But the boy has an eight-pack," she says, winking suggestively.

I avoid her hawk eyes and start picking the thick, Barbie-pink polish off my nails. "Isn't it wrong to use Mark B. for his body?" I ask.

She swats my hand to stop me from stripping my nails—a bad habit of mine. "Men use women for their bodies all the time."

As though the universe is on Bianca's side, my phone pings with a text.

Mark: Where'd you go?

I open a follow-up text, only to be assaulted with a dick pic.

Weary, I fall back onto the lumpy mattress. Why are guys so gross and predictable?

"That's . . . a very unflattering photo." Bianca grits her teeth, tilting her head to examine it from all angles.

"Is genitalia on its own ever attractive?"

"I've seen some striking peen, but this is not one of them."

"See? Romance is officially dead, Bianca," I say through a violent shiver, recalling his wandering hands that felt more like octopus tentacles.

"He's still down to hook up after you ran away like that. I'd say it's more alive than ever," she points out.

"It's on life support. For me, anyways."

Bianca frowns like I'm hopeless.

"Coming from the girl who blubbers on my shoulder during *The Notebook* when Noah declares into the rain that it's still not over. The girl who weeps when celebrities break up because you get so emotionally invested." She hesitates, peeking over her shoulder to ensure no one is within earshot before whispering, "I think your family's gift and all the fairy-tale love stories have given you unrealistic expectations."

I appreciate her guarding my secret, as she has since I invited her to Lunar New Year with my aunts. I don't normally make a habit of telling people about my family's abilities; people get weird about it. Some are terrified, some automatically think you're bonkers, and others are disappointed we can't foretell their futures on demand. Others want us to help them connect with deceased loved ones, even though we aren't mediums (there's a difference). So I hadn't mentioned anything. Funny enough, Bianca recognized Aunt Mei from a psychic fair she went to a few months earlier. She's been fascinated by psychics and mediums ever since her grandma died. She even has her own deck of tarot cards and YouTubes how to do readings.

"That's probably true." She's not wrong. In the car, you can find me listening to my romance playlist while gazing longingly out a rain-flecked window, pretending to be in the music video.

She continues, "Like, if a guy doesn't give you immediate butterflies, you're over him."

"But why waste my time if he's not my soulmate?" I counter. I naively expected college to be a mecca of emotionally mature men with steel-cut bods in search of long-term relationships, maybe an engagement on the horizon. Even my parents paired off young. They met at work, fresh from college, where they bonded over a shared theory about a blood-splatter pattern in a murder investigation. Pure romance, right? On their first date, they watched an episode of *CSI* for shits and laughed at how inaccurate it was. Of course, I only know this from what my aunts tell me. Mom passed away from a sudden brain aneurysm when I was just four.

Instead, I found a thousand Mark B.'s whose definition of romance is sharing a bong hit—and apparently sending dick pics.

"All I'm saying is it doesn't always have to be a universe-bending moment, you know. Sometimes sex is just pointless sex. And that's okay," Bianca points out.

"You're right. But I still can't hook up with Mark B. anymore." I flex my fingers, stressed at the prospect of having to break it to him—not that he'll really care.

"Fair," Bianca says, dark eyes gleaming. "Oh my god. Maybe you'll meet someone new in Italy?"

I tilt my head in consideration. "Italy would be romantic." Excitement bubbles in my gut. Not just at the prospect of an Italian romance, but of spending a whole month backpacking through the country with Bianca. This trip couldn't be coming at a better time. Maybe it'll even give me some perspective, or inspiration to get my life together. Maybe I'll come back with a fresh outlook and a renewed love for my program.

We've been planning this trip since she saw the background photo on my iPad—of my mom and Aunt Mei on a sisters' trip to Italy the summer Mom graduated high school thirty years ago.

Mom and Mei look so full of life. They're linked, arm in arm, on the cobblestoned streets of Florence, gelato in hand. You'd never know they'd battled a nasty bout of food poisoning the night before. Or that they stayed in an endless string of budget, bug-ridden hostels for an entire month. Or that they required months of acupuncture to heal their backs from the weight of their rucksacks. Still, according to Mei, my mom couldn't wait to go on another trip once she had enough money.

I've always known I wanted to follow in Mom's footsteps (literally) and go to Italy. It just always felt out of reach. Not to mention, Italy isn't cheap, especially on a student budget. But Bianca convinced me it was realistic, so long as we embrace the backpacker life: staying in hostels, cooking our own meals, joining free group tours, and taking public transportation. Besides, she's half-Italian and has always wanted to explore her roots.

My phone pings again, and my stomach does a barrel roll. "Oh god. It's another dick pic, isn't it? I feel like this one is going to be worse."

Bianca takes one for the team and checks on my behalf. "It's . . . a picture of a poodle missing a leg."

"Doris?" I snatch my phone. As I suspected, the photo is definitely not from Mark B.

It's from Teller.

A rush of adrenaline floods me.

"Yup. Your *best friend*," she hums with an eye roll. I know it bugs her that she has to share that title with someone else. As close as Bianca and I have gotten this year, she knows she can't compete with years of history.

I examine the photo of Doris, the tripod poodle I'd convinced him to rescue from the local shelter, in a chunky-knit argyle sweater. Despite a strong aversion to dogs (because allergies), he begrudgingly fostered her "temporarily," until he could find her a good home. A shock to everyone, including me, his family fell in love with her and adopted her.

Lo: OMG DORIS

Teller: I'll give her a hug from you.

I stare at Doris's button eyes and tight, old-lady curls, and it finally clicks. If he's with Doris, he's home.

Lo: WAIT WHAT?

Lo: ARE YOU HOME FOR THE SUMMER????

Teller: Damn, I missed being screamed at via text.

Lo: ARE YOU HOME OR NOT

Lo: ??

Teller: Yes, I'm home. Got in yesterday. What are you up to?

Lo: just at a frat party. kind of wanting to leave. WHEN CAN I SEE DORIS??

Lo: and you, too. BUT MOSTLY DORIS.

Admittedly, I have zero chill. We haven't seen each other since he left town last August to go to Northwestern, four whole hours away. Despite promises to reunite during Christmas break, the timing never worked out.

Teller: I'll come pick you up. What's the address?

I giddily send my location, and he texts that he'll be here in fifteen minutes.

"Teller's coming to get you?" Bianca asks knowingly, pulling herself from the bed.

"Yeah. I'm getting kinda tired anyway," I lie, suppressing my massive grin. We leave the relative quiet of the bedroom, and the abrupt chatter of chaos makes my ears ring as we head downstairs. "Want a ride back to your dorm? Teller won't mind."

I feel guilty for leaving her, but Bianca isn't the kind of girl who needs a sidekick. And Teller is also the only person I can talk to about what I saw tonight, aside from my aunts. He's the calm, logical presence I need right now. And no offense to Bianca, but she can get a little *too* into this whole psychic thing. While I love how naturally she accepts (loves!) that aspect of my life, she'd want the vision to be true so badly, it would just get my hopes up.

"As much as I'd love to finally meet this guy, I told Chris I'd head back with him," she yells over the music. Chris is her flavor of the month, a guy she met at the gym with a nipple piercing. He writes his own poetry and makes exaggerated eye contact while reading it, which is a blood-red flag (look, I don't make the rules). Bianca disagrees. She finds his creativity and way with words a turn-on (shudder). Though to be fair, he seems reasonably nice and offered me the rest of his fries when the three of us went to Five Guys last week.

We promise to text each other when we get home, and I head outside to wait for Teller.

I'm cloaked in darkness, sitting on the front step, when he pulls up in his old Toyota Corolla (champagne color) in exactly fifteen minutes. Teller is nothing if not punctual. Before I can stand, he exits the car. Odd. He's never been one to head toward a crowd if he can help it.

It hits different this time, seeing Teller Owens in the flesh after almost a whole year.

Teller is not classically hot. You wouldn't pick him out of a lineup and think, "Wow, that guy should be an Abercrombie model." He's just Teller. A bit nerdy, with ears that stick out slightly and a mouth that appears a little too big for his face. He's the kind of handsome that grows on you once you get to know him better. His contemplative expression (brow quirked and subtly pursed lips) is the same. He always looks deep in thought, lost in the labyrinth of his mind.

But my findings are surprising. First, there's his jawline. Since when did it become so square? And then there's the rude angle I have to crank my neck to absorb his towering height. He's always been tall, but lanky, with limbs too long to be functional. But now, he's grown into his height. He's . . . dare I say, muscly? And not in a bulky, imposing way. He's solidly lean, almost graceful in his movement.

I take in the way his shoulders and biceps fill out his plain T-shirt. The sudden firm broadness of his chest. I blink to ensure I'm not seeing things. It's like he's just stumbled upon this brand-new body. I don't know what to make of him as he sidles up the path, wayward mop of dark hair swaying with each step.

He flicks his caramel eyes, scanning the crowd for me. When our gazes snag, a gentle, earnest smile spreads across his face, lighting him up from the inside out. It reminds me of how much I've missed it. Missed him.

He stops short a couple feet in front of me, absorbing me in totality, and says, "Your hair."

I pat down my tame-resistant hair, which is now both frizzy in some places and flat in others, a result of aggressive layering. It's one of my biggest beefs with the universe—that I did not inherit silky, straight locks from Mom's side of the family. The injustice.

A couple weeks ago, I had an existential crisis while memorizing useless formulas for a chemistry exam. My hair kept falling in my eyes, but instead of waltzing to the nearest hairdresser on Google Maps like a normal person, I gave myself the student equivalent of the Mom Chop, a layered bob just above the shoulders. A far cry from the one-length style I'd had since I was ten.

It was a mistake, particularly the bangs. Little did I know, shorter hair actually requires more styling. Otherwise, I look like a feral child who's joined a pack of wolves. I've taken to pulling it into a messy bun, aside from nights (like tonight) where I felt inclined to make an effort.

Instinctively, I tug a few strands of my wavy bangs, suddenly feeling self-conscious. "I know you hate change, but it'll grow back—"

"I do hate change, but this . . ." He leans back, seeming to appreciate it from another angle. "This is a good change. It suits you. More, actually, than your old hair."

"Because it's somehow more unruly?"

He snickers and conveniently doesn't confirm nor deny. "Get over here."

I do a dramatic slo-mo run to close the distance between us, practically knocking him over with my bear hug. Usually, when I propel myself into him like this, he coughs and shrugs his way out, affronted because personal space and all that. But tonight is different. And it's not just that I can no longer touch my fingers together when I wrap my arms around his torso.

He's actually hugging me back, like he knows how much I need this right now. He pulls me so close, my feet lift off the ground. His familiar scent folds around me, the same as always, laundry hanging on the line of a freshly mowed yard with a dash of existential angst.

It's only when he sets me back down that I draw back to get a good look at his face. There's something up. It's evident in the sag of his shoulders. The droop in his brows. The tenseness in the corners of his mouth. He's holding something in—something big.

Before I can even ask, he blows the air from his cheeks and says, "Sophie broke up with me."

2

"Wait, Sophie broke up with you?" I repeat for the seventh time as I slide into the passenger seat, rocked to my core.

"Yup." He crumples over the steering wheel, head down, wholly distraught before passing me a bright-purple Slurpee (grape) from the gas station and a box of Raisinets from the console between us.

It's *our* snack. We drank Slurpees after every shift, every hangout. He'd complain that they were going to rot our teeth, and I'd be too busy nursing a brain freeze to defend it.

I squeeze the Slurpee cup so hard, the flimsy plastic cap pops off. All I see is red, and my mind floods with ill wishes toward Sophie, like getting the one grocery cart with a squeaky wheel, a harsh sun glare while driving that manages to evade the sun visor, or getting declined from using a one-day-expired coupon.

I'm not a spiteful person by any means, but at the thought of someone knowingly crushing Teller's heart, I go into protective mode. To me, he's like one of those palm-size sea turtle hatchlings that struggles through sand mounds in hopes of making it to sea. Innocent. Pure. Filled with good intentions. And right now, he looks as though Sophie flipped him over, shell-side down, and abandoned him, leaving him helpless.

I'm tempted to plot some light, innocent revenge. But for Teller's sake, I keep my anger at bay and be what he needs: a calm, stable presence. I give him a supportive pat on his shoulder, slow-blinking, staring at the dashboard, which is predictably void of dust and debris.

Here's the thing—Teller and Sophie have been inseparable for three whole years. They met at one of those *Shark Tank*–esque regional competitions for teens pitching business ideas and immediately became a couple.

Despite being long distance for two years before college, Teller fell hard in love. I should know, because I'm the one he confided in. The one he went to for peer review of his text responses. The one he consulted when deciding on a gift (a gold-plated, heart-shaped locket or a custom star map of the day they met) in celebration of their monthly anniversary. I even helped him pick out her promise ring. As his best friend, that's my job.

I raise my brow, and a silent exchange passes between us. *You're kidding me.*

I wish I were kidding. His chest falls in a shaky exhale.

With anyone else, I'd be firing off questions, itching to fill that dead space. But with Teller, that space is alive in the echo of our belly-busting laughter, tears, the murmur of secrets shared, and the quiet in between.

"What happened?" I finally ask.

We take a quiet moment to sip the icy sugar through our obnoxiously large neon straws. He reclines against the headrest and flexes his fingers over the wheel, measuring his response like always, never saying more than he has to. As someone who habitually word vomits before processing my thoughts, I found these few-beats-too-long pauses a little unnerving at first. But I've come to respect that about him.

"*Game of Thrones*," he finally says. "During exams we decided we wanted to binge-watch a series. You know, a break and reward from studying. We both came up with a list of shows and assigned point values to the ones we wanted to watch the most. Typical geek-and-numbers stuff."

"Only you could turn TV-watching into a mathematical puzzle."

The corner of his lip turns up in the briefest smirk as he pulls onto the empty street. "Anyway, when we tallied it all up, we realized we both wanted to watch *Game of Thrones*."

"Isn't that a good thing, wanting to watch the same thing?"

Teller tosses one palm to the ceiling, the other hand still on the steering wheel. "You'd think, but apparently not. She went on this big rant about how we've become too predictable. How we agree on everything all the time, like what takeout to get, what music we want to listen to, our daily routine."

"I thought having things in common was a positive." I think about all the times Teller gushed to me about how they liked all the same movies and music. How they're both introverts who prefer to stay in on Friday nights and do a puzzle. How they share a passion for trivia and big data. How they both make every decision logically, with care and precision, no matter how small, like spending a whole afternoon researching which cutlery set to buy for their apartment.

My grandmother used to tell me that having shared interests is the key to lifelong companionship. That's probably why my parents worked so well with their shared love of science and true crime.

"Same. But Sophie said she felt suffocated and stagnant. Like we were becoming the same person after being together for so long. We both want to go into data science, get the same designations." He pauses and lowers his chin. "Basically, she decided she wanted college to be about discovering herself. Said she wanted to explore her identity without me, to have new experiences so she doesn't regret things down the road. And I get it. I don't want to get in the way of her finding herself. But . . ."

"You wish she would do that with you?" I finish for him.

"Exactly. I told her I'd give her some space and let her grow, but that we didn't need to break up over it. We went back and forth, and she admitted she was bored." By the way he says *bored*, I know that hurt him.

My jaw tightens. He's always been sensitive, even if he tries to mask it with sarcasm.

I pin him with a serious look. "Teller, you're anything but boring. Your favorite song is 'Monster Mash,' for god's sake." It's one of my favorite things about Teller. I only discovered this tidbit when we started sharing a Spotify account last year; it was one of his most-played songs. He was even among the song's top 1 percent of listeners. I probably should have known, given his affinity for Halloween.

"I still don't know why you think that's so weird. It's incredibly catchy and playful." He says it so seriously, it makes me snicker. I can picture it now, him bobbing his head stiffly and mumbling the odd lyric, but only during the loud parts when no one will hear him.

"See? Not boring. You are perfect," I say, tossing him a wink.

"I have no idea what that one is from." He lifts a shoulder, not into the Guess the Rom-Com game we used to play, but I couldn't resist this one.

"Come on! It's *Love, Actually.*"

"Ah, right." He pauses, the right side of his mouth curving into a half smile. "You're sweet, Lo. But you don't have to lie to make me feel better. I already know I'm boring."

I thought he was, too, when we first met.

It was the summer before tenth grade. I was fifteen, and Dad had moved us from suburbia to a trendy downtown neighborhood lined with vegan restaurants and fair-trade coffee shops. He claimed it was to be closer to his work, but I knew his true motive. See, after Mom died, he raised me alone. To his credit, he was the best girl-dad, consulting internet tutorials on how to do hair, watching every rom-com in existence with me (even when they made him sad), and learning the lyrics to Taylor Swift songs so he could sing along in the car. But as I entered my "rebellious teenage years," he needed reinforcements, which was why he wanted to live near Aunt Mei and Aunt Ellen.

My aunts were thrilled; they wanted to mentor the family gift, which they assumed I'd inherited from Mom. She was excellent at all three of our family's key traditional Chinese fortune-telling practices, but ironically found her true passion in science. But after months of rigorous practice, it quickly became clear I had no abilities. Sure, I could study the rules of palmistry and face reading. But without the natural intuition to go along with it, I was hopeless. I couldn't even figure out the math involved in Bazi without error. And if I'm being honest, I was a little impatient with the whole thing, angry over the fact that we weren't also mediums. We couldn't communicate with Mom or dead people in general, so what was even the point?

"Maybe it'll take a little longer than normal to get the hang of," a nervous Ellen suggested. "Our cousin Cece didn't demonstrate her abilities until, what, fifteen?"

"Cece was twelve," Mei mouthed, thinking I wouldn't see. Even twelve was considered *late*, historically speaking.

My aunts tried their best to mask their disappointment, but I was devastated. It meant I was a talentless failure. And the worst part? I'd have to rely on my own poor judgment to find The One—just like everyone else.

I mourned my loneliness, lack of talent, and, by extension, Mom by channeling my angst the only way I knew how—working my way through an ungodly number of rom-coms. Without my parent's relationship as a model, at least I could experience love through Kate Hudson or Sandra Bullock. Dad used to make fun of the cheesy one-liners, priding himself on sniffing out plot points a mile away. But the truth is, I think these movies healed us, in a way.

Sure, some of them hit a little too close to home, like *P.S. I Love You*. Dad had to excuse himself to the bathroom multiple times during that one. But mostly, they made us laugh. All those giddy, fluffy feelings coursing through me when the final credits rolled were addicting. And most of all, they filled me with hope that I could still find happiness like that, even without the family gift.

Admittedly, I got a little too obsessed with experiencing love via the big screen. Once I'd made a perma-body indent in the couch, I decided to apply for a summer job in hopes of meeting new friends before school started.

The Cinema wasn't one of those flashy franchise theaters with reclined leather seating and 3D panoramic screens. It was a small, locally owned business that strictly played films from 2010 or before for five bucks a ticket. It had its own charm, with its red-velvet seats, flickering neon lights, ticket booth with tarnished brass accents, and retro marquee sign with weathered letters displaying the films of the week. Inside was like stepping into a time capsule with its worn merlot carpet that was always flecked with bits of popcorn.

When I limped into the lobby for my first shift with a broken flip-flop, Teller wasn't pleased.

"You're half an hour late," he said from behind the register. Despite his authoritative tone, he looked my age. A mop of thick, dark waves swooped over one eye. He looked deep in concentration as he vigorously scrubbed the counter with a disinfectant wipe. A baggy maroon polo—The Cinema uniform—hung off his thin frame.

"Sorry. They changed the bus schedule and by the time I realized, I had to sprint three blocks to catch it and the thong of my sandal ripped out. It was a whole thing," I explained, reading the perfectly straight name tag on his chest.

His face contorted in alarm. "Did you just say *thong*?"

"Ew, don't be weird. My flip-flop thong, obviously." I brandished my broken flower-power-print sandal for emphasis.

His pale face creased in horror before peering over the counter at my bare foot.

"What?" I asked, hitching my shoulders in defense, catching a whiff of chemicals.

"You're barefoot. In public. You can't do your shift without shoes."

I leaned my elbow on the freshly disinfected counter and whispered, "Are you a germaphobe or something?"

"I wouldn't put my bare skin on a sticky floor covered with dirt, but I don't think most normal people would," he added. "Doesn't mean I'm a germaphobe."

"I think that's the exact definition of a germaphobe," I pointed out, semi-amused. "Did you know germaphobes actually have weaker immune systems?"

"That sounds like a myth to me."

"It's not. I haven't been sick in six years," I bragged. It was a half-truth. I'd gotten a couple colds here and there. Admittedly, I just wanted to ruffle his feathers a little. Based on his wide-eyed expression, it was working splendidly. He was far too serious for my liking.

"Six years? I don't believe you."

"It's true. Here's the secret: I have two dogs, Brandon and Brian, a bonded pair of chocolate Labs. Brian is the chunky one. Brandon is skinnier but lazy. Anyway, I let them lick my face. Every day." I leaned in like I was relaying top-secret information.

"Brandon and Brian? Those are terrible pet names."

"Excuse you, their birth mom named them, and I felt it was only right to respect her wishes."

He eyed me sideways.

"Wait, did you say you let them lick you on the tongue?"

"I said 'face.' But if the moment strikes, they do occasionally lick my tongue. Brandon and Brian are very affectionate boys, especially Brian. Brandon is a bit more temperamental, but when you rub his ears a certain way, he goes cra—"

Teller just shook his head and tossed over a name tag, along with a pair of black Nikes I assumed were his nonwork running shoes. "You're . . . the weirdest person I've ever met."

For that first week of training, I assumed Teller had written me off. We barely talked, aside from communicating the essentials, like how to do certain tasks, or when we'd take our breaks. Whenever I sang along to the radio to fill the dead space, he'd wince. During slow periods, our lack of conversation was awkward, to me at least.

Based on Teller's cordial, yet concise exchanges with customers, I assumed he just didn't talk much in general. I wasn't sure if it was because he was shy or straight-up dull, but I had an urge to find out. To make him like me. Besides, I was in desperate need of someone to talk to other than Dad and my aunts—someone my own age.

"So . . . ," I said one slow Friday night while sweeping trampled popcorn bits into a small pile. We had only a handful of customers for a showing of *Armageddon*. As you can imagine, nineties films that stream for free weren't exactly drawing large crowds.

He eyed me, waiting for me to continue my thought process.

I started rambling about how it's not going to be easy and how we'll need to work hard, every day, in a terrible southern twang, trying to keep a straight face.

He squinted at me over the medium soda cups he was stacking in two neat piles of equal height, trying to figure out what the hell I was talking about.

"*The Notebook*. It's what Noah says to Allie," I explained, copping to my secret. "I've been quoting out-of-context rom-com lines to you all week. Haven't you noticed?"

"I don't watch a lot of rom-coms. But that does explain some things."

"Sorry. I get bored sometimes." I leaned my weight against my broom handle. "Though I'd be less bored if we actually talked. Since we're working together all summer, shouldn't we get to know each other?"

"I already know a lot about you," he said casually, peeling his eyes from his soda-cup pile.

"Like what?"

"You're a sicko who likes to be barefoot in public places and lets animals near your mouth. You also have a penchant for floral patterns and a talent for memorizing movie quotes."

"That's a strangely accurate description of me," I admitted. I respected his assessment. Most guys probably wouldn't remember my name. The bar is truly in hell for boys. "But I still don't know anything about you, aside from the fact that you like Halloween more than is normal." I only knew that last bit because I'd caught him making his costume (a guard from *Squid Game*, sleek black face mask and hot-pink jumpsuit) three months in advance.

"Halloween is superior to any other holiday. I stand by it. And fine. Ask me anything." He sucked in a breath and held it for a couple beats, as though bracing for me to ask him his darkest secrets.

"What's your favorite animal?" It was an easy enough question, yet very revealing all the same.

A shrug. "I don't know."

I furrowed my brow, taken aback and frankly offended on behalf of the animal kingdom. "You don't know your favorite animal?"

"I'm not an animal lover," he said calmly, like that was just a totally normal trait, normal as someone not liking cilantro.

A cough tore its way up my throat. "What? You monster! Why?"

"I'm allergic to most of them. Same with my mom. We don't have pets."

I blinked, watching him as he moved on to refilling the straw dispenser. "Wait, you've never had a pet? Even a hypoallergenic one? A fish?"

"Nope," he said quickly, turning to a group of preteen girls who came to report a clogged toilet in the women's bathroom. "Ugh, not again." Teller let out a long sigh and ushered me to the supply closet.

"All right, this is going to be one of the most important skills you'll learn at this job," he said, handing me a face mask, rubber gloves, and a plunger. We geared up like we were entering a biohazardous site and set forth to the toilet.

"Oh god." I coughed, staring down at the mess, plunger dangling from my limp hand.

"So there's a technique," he said, confidently reaching for the plunger. It occurred to me that he was being brave, particularly for a germaphobe.

"A *technique*? Does this happen . . . often?" I asked, not truly wanting to know the answer.

"A couple times a week, give or take," he said, voice muffled under the mask. He then proceeded to demonstrate the "technique," really putting his back into it.

"I still can't believe you've gone your entire life without the unconditional love of a pet," I said, trying to distract myself from the grossness.

"Is that so weird?" he asked over the gurgle of water.

"Yes, it's very weird," I said bluntly. "You're missing out. There are so many animals that don't have fur. Like those hairless cats."

He faux-gagged, stuffing the plunger into the toilet bowl like it personally offended him. "Those things are wrinkled abominations. They totally negate the cuteness of a cat. And it's not just the fur I'm allergic to. It's the saliva."

I tapped his back to switch places. "Here, let me try," I said, taking the plunger to give it a whirl. "What about a bird?"

"Allergic to feathers. They're also distantly related to dinosaurs, a disturbing fact that's seriously overlooked by the general public."

"A lizard?" I wagered, leaning my full body weight over the plunger.

"Reptiles make me deeply uncomfortable."

"Fair. What about a goldfish?"

"What's the point of a goldfish? They just swim around in a little bowl. You can't hug them or play with them. They give nothing back."

"Excuse you. My childhood goldfish, Scrambled and Egg, were very affectionate," I informed him. I held back a snicker at the image of Teller hugging an animal. I wasn't certain he was capable of being affectionate with anything.

"You had fish named Scrambled and Egg?" he asked, leaning against the stall doorframe.

"Yes," I said, slightly out of breath from plunging. "And they were basically puppies with fins and no fur. Every time I put my face to the glass, their gills would expand and they'd swim up to the side of the bowl. I swear they'd lick the glass."

"Lo, they probably just wanted to be fed," he said, deadpan.

"I like to think it's because they knew I was their mom." He cut me a weird look, which made me feel like a huge loser. So I changed the subject. "When's your birthday?"

He eyed me for a beat longer than normal, like he couldn't quite figure me out. "Why do you want to know my birthday?" My aunts asked everyone their birthdays to determine their zodiac compatibility, so I assumed it was a perfectly normal question.

"So I can steal your identity," I said seriously, coming dangerously close to his leg with the dripping plunger. This toilet was impossible. "I'll take your full name and social security number, too, while I'm at it. Also, I might faint. Can you try again?"

He took over. "Oh, right. Well, just try not to murder anyone. Or do anything too embarrassing to bring shame to my family name."

"It'll just be a little light fraud. No big deal. Might even swing by PetSmart and get a fish or two in your name." I say, watching the rise and fall of the water with each plunge.

"If you get me any animal, I'd like a pony."

I blinked, unsure I'd heard him correctly. Either that, or he was being sarcastic, despite an all-too-serious expression. "A pony?"

And he was. "Ponies are my favorite animal, if you insist I have one."

Who was this guy? "Why ponies of all things? Aren't you allergic to them too?"

"A hundred percent. But I like them in theory. They're adorable and mini."

"Wow," I said. It was the first moment I felt like there was hope that we could actually have some common ground. "Teller Owens, lover of ponies."

He covered his mouth over his mask in a quiet chuckle, stare going rigid again when the plunger splashed water onto his shoe. We spent the rest of the evening taking turns trying to unclog the toilet (unsuccessfully) before deeming it a lost cause and calling our manager to get a plumber. It was revolting, but the smile never left my face all night. Because that day I'd accomplished something huge: I'd made Teller Owens laugh for the first time.

I smile at the memory as we pass a particularly bright streetlight that illuminates Teller's face in dusky gold. I steal a peek at him. His profile is different. His nose is longer, more mature. Even his lips are fuller. It strikes me that he's a full-on adult now, probably with a ceramic plate set. Certainly not a cupboard full of red Solo cups like Bianca and her roommates. He probably even does his own taxes. And while all these changes on their own are slight, taken together, they're a stark reminder of the year that's passed.

"You aren't boring, Tel. But I'm sorry either way," I finally say as we pull into my neighborhood. "Any chance she'll change her mind?"

"I mean, I begged her. Like . . . full-on begged. It's embarrassing to even think about. But she had her mind made up and asked me to move out. So now I'll need to find a place for next year." He left most of his furniture in their apartment, and he isn't sure where he'll live next year since all his friends have their living situations figured out. I feel terrible for him. He was so excited to have his own place that he could organize just the way he likes. And now he's losing it.

"That seems abrupt. Do you think she might have been unhappy for a while?"

He frowns, like he hadn't thought of that before. "Maybe. It's definitely possible. I've tried asking her. You know, for closure. But she isn't really answering me."

"How often are you texting her?"

He sighs and looks down at his phone in the cupholder. "I tried a couple of times. As much as I could without making her feel uncomfortable. I understand she needs some space, but I feel like I deserve an explanation, you know? After everything."

Upon inspection, his conversation with Sophie is entirely one-sided. He's sent her a couple multiparagraph texts, which are, frankly, sad.

I'm always here if you want to talk. I love you and miss you and always will. She's texted him only once in the past week to arrange for sending back his keys.

"If it's any consolation, I'm glad you're back for the summer. I was beginning to think you'd never come home," I admit. It still feels strange, him being here next to me. He wasn't planning on coming home for the summer, and I'd resigned myself to the idea that Teller would probably never be back in town for longer than a few days.

He gifts me with the tiniest smile and it feels like a reward, given how down he is.

"You know what you need?"

He squeezes his eyes shut. "Don't say it."

"Another pet—"

"No."

"Why not? Doris needs a friend. And so do you. There's an adorable white standard doodle at the shelter named Boris. He has the cutest brown nose. You could have a Doris and a Boris."

"That would be sweet," he admits. "But my parents are good with one dog. Besides, I have you." *I have you.* I let the words marinate for a few moments as we curve around a corner.

"Seriously, though. It's been too long. Fill me in on the last year, aside from your breakup. And don't leave out a single detail," I warn, unable to suppress my chill. I feel this bursting urge inside to make up for lost time. I'd spent so many hours wondering what he was up to, wishing we could be hanging out.

"The past year . . ." He whistles and runs his hand through his hair, like he's sorting through where to begin. "You go first."

Embarrassment coils through my gut. Where do I even start? Should I dazzle him with how Dad has switched things up, cooking curly fries instead of crinkled? How Brandon developed a questionable lump on his belly? How I convinced our old manager, Cindy, to give me shifts at The Cinema and that it's the same as it always was, dead slow? Or the fact that I'm questioning my entire life trajectory and maybe-might-have had a vision but I can't be sure? It feels unfair to dump on him after not seeing him for so long, especially after his life just imploded. "I asked you first."

He lets out a resigned sigh. "Fine. What do you want to know?"

"Everything. Like"—I wave my hands around, trying to come up with an easy question—"what grinds your gears these days?"

"What grinds my gears?" he repeats with a snicker. "Am I an old man or something?"

"That's exactly what you are. A grumpy elder who calls bylaw on neighborhood kids playing outside past seven and drives below the speed limit." I nod toward the speedometer to confirm.

He turns his whole body to check his blind spot before taking a right turn. "Hey, safety is cool."

"You sound like my dad."

He places a proud palm over his chest. "The highest honor. Eric is my idol." He's not lying. Teller and Dad get along swimmingly, probably because they're both nerds who live and die by order.

"*Anyway*, current pet peeves. Go."

He strokes his chin, pretending to look deep in thought despite already having an answer locked and loaded, like I knew he would. "Okay, fine. I really hate those news articles that turn out to be slideshows. Why do you have to make me click through to read the whole thing? Or download the app?"

"But they always have the coolest pictures."

"I'm not there for the visual aids. I want the straight-up facts." Quintessential Teller.

"Okay, what else?"

He fires off the next one just as quick. "People who sign off texts with their name. *Yes, Mom, I know it's you.*"

"My dad does the same thing! He also starts each text with 'Hi, Lo.'"

"Oh yeah, I remember that. Even indents each paragraph like a formal email. Does your aunt Ellen still create a new Facebook account every time she forgets the password to her last one?"

"Yes. She's up to about twelve accounts now. How are your parents, anyways?"

"They've been living their best lives since we all left home. Actually, when I told them I needed to crash for the summer, they were kind of put out. My dad made a big deal about hauling my bed frame and mattress back upstairs. They'd already transformed my room into a craft room."

"A craft room?"

"My mom became kind of obsessed with embroidery. Don't ask. It's the bane of my dad's existence. Every time a new package of thread shows up at the door, he loses his mind because he thinks she's wasting money."

"Is she?"

He shrugs. "Not sure. But you know how she is—she gets really into things for a short period of time and then abandons them. Like someone I know." He softly elbows me in the rib.

"*Ha ha.* Very funny." I snicker because it's true. "Do you have any weird new hobbies or interests I should know about?"

"Well, I've taken up kickboxing."

My brows shoot up. I didn't expect him to have a new interest, mostly because Teller is such a creature of habit. "Kickboxing? You?"

He gestures to his torso, mildly offended. "Does it not look like I kickbox?"

"I noticed you got scarily fit. But I guess I just assumed you magically sprouted those muscles overnight," I tease, noting how he looks away bashfully. "How did you find yourself in a kickboxing gym of all places?"

"A guy from my program, Greg. He's pretty into it and convinced me to join a session. I was really stressed about those first midterms, and I guess it became an outlet. Doing it every morning makes a huge difference with my anxiety. It's like a total reset."

"Damn. And here I am sporting the freshman ten."

"You look great, Lo," he says sweetly, his eyes lingering over mine briefly before turning his car into my driveway. "And living at home must be amazing. You get home-cooked meals and your laundry done."

I work down a swallow. "Well, unless I want Dad's frozen specials, I do most of the cooking these days. Though I'm missing out on the whole adulting experience. Dad still keeps close tabs on my where-abouts." My first choice was to live on campus, but given my college of choice is in town and my house is ten minutes away, Dad didn't think it was worth the expense. Plus, I couldn't fathom leaving Brandon and Brian, or Dad—especially Dad. The two of us have been a package deal since Mom died. I've never gone more than a few days without seeing him, with the exception of when Aunt Mei brought me to New York City for a long weekend in eighth grade. Even then, Dad FaceTimed me daily. "Bianca keeps trying to convince me to get an apartment with her next year, but I feel too guilty leaving Dad at home alone."

"Why? Do you think he'd be lonely?"

"A hundred percent. I mean, he's never said it outright, but he wouldn't know what to do without me there. Who would walk the dogs? Or pack his lunch? Watch TV with him in the evenings?" Sadly, Dad's entire life revolves around three things: work, comic books, and me. Oh, and complaining while watching rom-coms with me but secretly loving every second. Dad hasn't dated since Mom died, nor does he really socialize, except with Jones and Arjun, two forensic-nerd colleagues he occasionally sees Marvel movies with.

"Understandable. But I think he'd be happier if you're doing what makes you happy. Besides, you'd only be like, ten minutes away."

I'm not entirely sure about that, given his reaction to my monthlong backpacking trip. I already feel guilty enough about that. So much so, I secretly asked Arjun to arrange a weekly D&D night while I'm gone, in lieu of our father/daughter movie nights. Aunt Ellen also assured me she plans to ask him to fix a bunch of her electronics since she's terrible with technology, which should keep him busy.

I don't take my seat belt off. I'm not ready to end our conversation, and clearly neither is he, because he turns off the ignition. "Speaking of doing things that make me happy, did I tell you I'm going to Italy?"

He raises his brows in surprise. "You're finally going to Italy? When?"

"In two days. For a month, with Bianca. We're gonna backpack around the country and eat our weight in gelato and pasta."

"Backpacking, huh? You better not become one of those *Well, back when I did Europe* people." He mimics an obnoxious British accent.

I snort, knowing exactly who he's mocking. Cindy. She was a manager at The Cinema for about two weeks before jetting off to Thailand. She'd spent a year abroad, returning for a few months to make money before going back again. Cindy was notorious for adopting a fake British accent and always found a way to bring up what countries she "did." Everything was "I've done Egypt," "I've done Scotland. You *have* to go." Teller and I used to laugh about how she'd take pictures with unsuspecting orphans and poor people she met on her travels, treating them like props to get likes. According to her socials, she's now a Reiki healer in the Costa Rican jungle.

"So you'll be gone a whole month?"

I let out a groan. "Of course, the one summer you come home, I'm gone."

"We'll still have half of summer when you get back," he reminds me. "And be careful with the gelato. You are lactose intolerant even if you're in permanent denial." He always reminds me of the time I got violently ill in his car after eating too much ice cream.

Shockingly, he didn't kick me out of his car and banish me from his life entirely. Instead, he reached over the console to hold my hair back. That was probably the moment I knew for sure Teller was a true friend.

He's looked out for my stomach ever since, promptly reminding me I can't eat cheese or ice cream or anything that makes life remotely worth living. Annoying as it may be, I'm grateful.

"So where are you guys staying? In hostels?"

"Exactly. My mom and aunt stayed in hostels when they went, since they had no money. Well—except for one place. My grandparents gifted them a baller agriturismo called Villa Campagna in Tuscany," I explain, recalling a photo Mei has on her mantel. It's of her and Mom, playfully posing with exaggerated confidence, chins and pinkies up, on the balcony of the villa. According to Mei, she and Mom felt laughably out of place among the wealthy, middle-aged guests, so they told everyone they were tobacco heiresses. No one actually believed them, which was the best part.

"What's an agriturismo?"

"Kind of like a farm stay, on a vineyard. Not that it matters. I looked it up on Expedia and it still exists, but it's like a bazillion dollars a night, so hostels it is."

"Hostels with . . . communal showers?" He whispers *communal* like a church boy uttering a swear word. I can't help but chuckle.

"Absolutely. It's the only way we can afford it."

A dramatic shiver. "Make sure you check your bed daily for bedbugs. Under the mattress, around the frame."

I give him a light smack on the bicep. "There won't be bedbugs. They're extremely rare, but it makes the majority of hostels look bad."

"Google reviews don't lie. And it's not necessarily the hostel's fault. The bugs come in off the hundreds of people traveling through who don't even know they're infested."

I smirk. There's no arguing with him. "Well, I'll let you go. I feel like I'm delaying your sacred nighttime ritual."

"I don't have a nighttime ritual."

"I doubt you, Teller Owens, just plop into bed without a bubble bath, brushing your teeth, flossing, sipping some detox tea, meditating—"

"First, I would take a shower. Baths are just soaking in your own filth. Two, everyone brushes and flosses, or at least they should," he informs me. "And don't knock my mindfulness podcasts. I need them to fall asleep. You'd listen to them, too, if you lived in my house. It's chaos."

He's the middle of three boys. And while Teller is impressive on his own, he's convinced he's the invisible middle child next to Kurt, a newly minted foot doctor, and Nick, who's competed on every reality TV game show known to man (*Big Brother, Survivor, The Challenge*) and won zero. He's got this "villain" persona that's made him popular, allowing him to make a whole career of it (and peddling random products on social media).

Teller once told me in jest that he thought he was adopted, or switched at birth, because he was so different from the rest of them. He even looks different. His brothers are fair, with blondish hair and light eyes. Teller inherited his darker features from his grandmother.

The first time I went to his house, his theory of invisibility was confirmed. In all the chaos zigzagging around in the family room, neither brother bothered to acknowledge him, except for Nick, who took the time to ask why "someone like me" would hang out with "someone like him."

I spot Dad peering through a crack in the curtains. Even though I'm nineteen, he still can't sleep until I'm safe at home. As a recovering military child, Dad grew up with strict curfews—not that he went out anyways.

"I better go in. Let's hang out tomorrow? You need to get out of the house before you spiral into a depression." Teller's always curled into his shell when he's sad.

"Who says I'm gonna spiral?"

I dart a knowing look. "If you could, you'd spend days in your room with your galaxy light, sulking and listening to Coldplay or something equally depressing."

"Don't knock Coldplay. They have emotional depth, okay? And I'll have you know I'm keeping busy. I begged my mom to give me some shifts at Roasters. I'm working tomorrow, six to three." His mom's coffee shop is just a couple blocks from my house.

"Perfect, I'll meet you at the end of your shift. Thanks for the ride, Tel," I say, exiting before he can come up with an excuse.

Gooseflesh erupts along my bare arms and stomach from the chilly spring air. Before going inside, I fire off a text to my aunts in the group chat.

Lo: so . . . something interesting happened tonight.

Mei: Define interesting. Do you need me to pick you up somewhere?

Ellen: Hello?

Ellen: Hurry up. Tell us! I can't handle the suspense.

Mei: If you don't respond in 5 min, we'll assume you've been arrested or are in the hospital.

Lo: sryy for the delay, just got home. dad wanted a play-by-play of the night.

Lo: PS. i like how you assume something tragic happened to me.

Ellen: You don't have the best luck or track record, sweetie.

Mei: Yes, your life is kind of a series of unfortunate events.

Lo: true. BUT I think I might have . . . maybe had a vision??

Lo: I THINK

Lo: maybe not. IDK. 📷

Ellen: !!!!!!!!!!!!! FaceTime me in!! Hank is gone this weekend so I'm here with Maisey.

Mei: I'll be over first thing in the morning.

3

When you think of psychics, you probably envision a Cher looka-like with a faux-silk headwrap. Maybe she's draped in an eclectic array of mismatched fabrics, waving long fingernails over a misty crystal ball, excessive jewelry clinking with each wheezy breath.

That's not Aunt Mei. She looks straight off the runway in a stark-white power suit and a pair of four-inch fuchsia pumps (she won't be caught dead in flats), dark, silky hair in a chic, blunt bob. She's a fancy Bay Street stockbroker by day and a psychic by weekends, which means she doesn't sleep or know the pleasure of comfortable clothing. I like to joke that she uses her psychic abilities to predict the stock market. She's never disputed the theory.

"Why is Mei here?" Dad asks, tilting his head toward the window as she struts up the walkway.

It's a fair question. It's 7:15 on Saturday morning—a peculiar time for an aunt drop-in. Then again, I shouldn't be surprised. When I got my first period, she drove to our house in the middle of the night with a bag of pads, jumbo tampons, Tylenol Extra Strength, a heating pad, and a crap-ton of personal anecdotes I'd have preferred not to know.

Before I can explain her presence, Mei waltzes in without knocking, as she always does. "Tell me everything," she instructs, no formal greeting. Part of me feels guilty that she's come all the way here for probably nothing.

"I like your shoes," I tell her, winking at Dad, who chokes down a laugh, fully expecting Mei to launch into a story about where she got them and for how much. And she delivers.

"Twenty dollars at T.J.Maxx. Can you believe it?" She stretches her shoes out, admiring them, face alight at the mention of a bargain. She might be fancy, but she's a Zhao through and through—which means she's obsessed with shopping on the cheap, and even more obsessed with bragging about said deals. "Anyway, make with the details."

I sit on the edge of the coffee table across from Mei, who's perched on the arm of the couch, crossing and uncrossing her legs, unable to stay still. She's always had a frantic energy, always doing five things at once.

"Honestly, it was probably nothing. Just some weird hearts and—"

Mei clasps her chest and lets out a muffled sound reminiscent of an injured pigeon. Before she can get a word out, her phone vibrates in her alligator-skin bag (75 percent off at a Black Friday sale at Nordstrom). "Oh, it's Ellen," she declares, putting her on FaceTime.

Ellen is in bed, satin face mask pulled over her forehead. A bedazzled pink maternity sleepshirt that reads MOMMA NEEDS A NIGHT IN in Curlz font stretches over her seven-months-pregnant belly. "What's going on!?"

Mei, Dad, and I simultaneously wince at the shrillness of her voice. As an elementary school teacher and toddler mom, screaming is her default.

I hide my cringe and lean in. "I was hanging out with Mark B. when—"

"Mark B.? Who is Mark B.?" Ellen sits up, back straight against the headboard, and squints into the camera to get a better view.

"Yes, who is *Mark B.*?" Dad asks with an expression of abject terror. He's usually one to sit back and quietly observe, with the exception of these subjects: science, dad jokes, true crime, Marvel, or my safety.

"No one!" I assure. "Just a guy. I don't like him that way—"

"Anyway, Lo had *the* vision," Mei informs them prematurely.

Weary, he stretches his slender six-foot frame on the couch, pale skin turning a shade of ketchup. I have half a mind to bring him a cool cloth to drape over his forehead.

Ellen sucks in a breath, dark eyes glittering, like she's watching a juicy scene from one of those K-dramas she's obsessed with. "*The vision?*"

Mei nods.

Ellen clutches her chest. "Oh, thank gosh. I was scared she'd end up like Cousin Lin—"

Before she can continue, Mei shoots her a stern look through the camera, instantly shutting her up. "Shhh. We don't talk about her!"

Ellen makes a zipper motion over her lips, like she always does when she's said too much, which is more often than not. It's a running joke in the family that she can't be trusted with secrets.

"What about Cousin Lin?" I demand. I don't remember much about her, aside from her being vaguely mentioned as one of my grandmother's cousins. She died the year after Mom.

"It's nothing for you to worry about. Just some silly lore," she explains, waving it off, but not before arrowing another *Why did you bring that up?* scowl at Ellen.

"Anyway, make with the details! I need to go feed the monster," Ellen says, referring to Maisey, her two-year-old daughter.

I'm tempted to keep pressing, but once Mei has made a decision, she doesn't budge. Besides, I know I can get Ellen to spill the tea at a future date. "Well," I start again as the guilt begins to seep in. They're going to be disappointed in me, just like last time I had a false alarm (a strangely vivid dream where I was riding a Godzilla-size meerkat to school). "I was at a frat party—"

"A frat party?" Dad asks, alarmed by this new information. "You said it was a girls' night with Bianca."

"It was. But we ended up popping in really quick." I have to lie, lest Dad lose his mind. He's under the impression that frat parties are nothing but loud music, alcohol, and orgies (half-true) that inevitably lead to *Dateline*-style crimes. As a self-proclaimed dork, Dad never set foot in a party when he was young. He preferred to have his nose in comics and chemistry textbooks.

I can imagine that having a talkative daughter who parties is like parenting an alien. I've always tried to rectify our personality differences by pretending to share the same interests, like watching gritty true-crime documentaries with him and studying forensic science in college. After disappointing my aunts, I felt an obligation to at least follow in Mom and Dad's footsteps academically. That's why I can't bring myself to admit that I'm hating my program and would rather swallow glass than stick it out another three years.

As expected, Dad looks skeptical, like I was snorting hard drugs off the bathroom sink or something.

I describe the city skyline for my aunts. I detail the hearts, the scent of espresso, and the hot sensation I felt on my neck and back. And how it happened a second time, moments later.

"It's probably nothing," I say, covering my eyes in shame. While my aunts have taught me the logic of Bazi, palmistry, and face reading, I'm unable to read people intuitively. I've tried all the exercises Mei and Ellen taught me, like practicing tarot, meditating, visualizing, focusing on the senses—none of which made a difference. In other words, I'm a complete disappointment to my entire family.

"No. It's definitely not nothing," Mei tells me, drumming her fingers over her chin in thought. "Give me your hand."

I extend it toward her lap and she examines it, the line between her brows deepening before sliding her eyes to meet mine. "Hmm, your fate line is still broken." Go figure.

"Does it mean I'm going to wind up destitute and on the street?" I ask, panicked that she *knows*.

I expect her to confront me about how close I am to dropping out, right in front of Dad. But she just tilts her head. "No . . . just that you may have some instability, which checks out with your sun line. There are quite a few little creases, which means you have too many interests and lack focus."

All true. Nothing I don't already know.

"Anyways, let's check your love line." She runs her hand across my palm. "It's still the same too. You're very passionate, stubborn, and willing to sacrifice. But your marriage lines—" She pauses to examine closer. "These are new."

I zero in on the little lines right below my pinkie. Frankly, I have no idea whether I've always had those or not. But I trust Mei. "What do they mean?"

"See how both lines are equal in length?"

I nod.

She drops my hand and starts pacing between the kitchen and living room. "It could mean a few things. That you're prone to love triangles or generally indecisive when it comes to settling down."

She abruptly turns to Dad. "Did Kim ever tell you her vision?"

My gut tightens at the mention of Mom.

Mei's determined eyes meet mine. "Your mom saw recurring visions of a pair of thick glasses like your dad's. Smelled the heavy scent of Dove soap. And a bunch of hearts exactly like the ones you're describing."

I clutch my stomach, breath hitching.

"Really? What did it mean?"

"She had these visions *before* meeting your dad."

Now I understand why Ellen and Mei kept saying *the* vision.

I dig my nails into my thighs. With each year that passes, I'm terrified I'll forget Mom. As it is, I don't have many memories of her. Most of what I "remember" comes from stories my aunts have told me. Like of her and Dad dipping plain potato chips in ketchup and vinegar instead of buying flavored chips, or staring at the world map in our house, talking about all the places she wanted to travel to. Sometimes, I'm overcome with the suffocating sense that I'm forgetting her entirely.

Whenever I feel like that, I look at the only nondigital photo I have of her. It's a candid shot of her and Dad just sitting on the couch in sweatpants. She has no makeup on, hair in a messy bun, legs in his lap. It's not filtered or posed. There's no overt show of affection like their wedding photos, but there's something about it that just makes my heart thrum. Their love for each other radiates through. Maybe it's the warmth of Mom's sideways grin. This happy, giddy version of Dad I can barely remember. The way Dad's palm rests, snug over Mom's knee. You can just see it in their eyes. Pure love. The kind of love I want one day.

Their connection is so palpable, the pads of my fingers tingle whenever I touch the photo. Dad gave it to me when I was twelve after catching me sneak it out of his wallet one too many times. I keep it tucked safely in my purse as he instructed, to ensure I never lose it.

Keeping her memory alive is all the more difficult given that Dad doesn't like to talk about her. And who could blame him? Losing the literal love of your life is devastating and unbearable enough to destroy the strongest of people. To be fair, he's open to talking to me about literally anything else, like puberty or the grisly details of his current murder cases (against my will). But when it comes to Mom, he withdraws entirely and becomes an iron fortress, which is why I never bring her up.

Case in point: Dad has gone quiet, seemingly fascinated with a thread on his pants. I feel bad that this conversation has clearly upset him. But at the same time, just knowing I've had a vision similar to Mom's sparks something inside me. It's like an invisible magic string that holds us together. A new connection that tethers me to her memory in a way I've never been able to grasp.

"Your mom saw the same vision a couple times. She described it like a riddle she could never unlock, like a cruel game of Pictionary. And then when she met your dad, a forensic scientist, it all made sense," Ellen explains.

I massage my temples, trying to wrap my mind around what this means. "So you're saying I'm . . ."

Mei's eyes light up like jewels under the glow of the living room lamp. "You're going to meet The One."

"But when?"

She presses her lips together and ponders. "I think, if the imagery is literal, on your Italy trip."

"Oh god." Dad audibly groans. He has a hard enough time keeping tabs on me at home, let alone halfway across the world for an entire month.

"Dad, I'm an adult. I'm perfectly capable of taking care of myself," I remind him.

Before Dad can rattle off my long list of indiscretions, Ellen pipes in. "Isn't Venice known as the City of Love?" Venice is the first stop. From there, Bianca and I are planning to visit Rome, Florence, and the Amalfi Coast.

My ears start ringing and my face flushes with heat, as if I've just chugged a bottle of hard liquor. *The City of Love.*

"Isn't Paris the City of Love?" Dad clarifies.

"I thought it was Verona. You know, Romeo and Juliet—" Mei starts.

"There are multiple romantic cities in Europe. Venice is one of them," Ellen informs her. "The City of Love!"

My mind flashes back to the image of the city and the hearts. It all makes sense. I'm going to fall in love in Venice. The most romantic city in the world.

This is going to be the trip of a lifetime.

4

I'm wrestling a stolen pair of socks from Brandon's mouth when Dad clears his throat. He's anxious-tapping a small red spiral notebook on his thigh. Before I can ask what it is, he tosses out one of his famous Dad jokes: "Why did the suitcase go to therapy?"

"Dunno. Why?"

"It had too much emotional baggage!" he says, pulling out the jazz hands.

I can't help but laugh. Dad's jokes never fail to make me smile, no matter how cheesy.

He nods toward my rucksack. "I see you've made some progress."

I give a half-hearted shrug. "If you can call it that. It's just so hard to know what I'll need for a whole month, especially if I'm going to meet my soulmate. I need the perfect outfit for my meet-cute."

He gives me a side-eye, running a hand through his neatly combed hair. "Meet-cute, huh?"

"You know, the scene in the movies—"

"Where the love interests meet. I know. You've always been a romantic," he chides with an affectionate smile.

I let that statement linger. "Was Mom like that?"

"Was Mom like what?"

"Romantic," I repeat. "I must get it from somewhere."

He presses a hand to his chest, feigning offense. "You don't think your old man is a romantic?"

I can't help but snort. "Dad, you're a man of science and all things practical. When I turned thirteen, you printed an infographic of potential diseases or infections for our birds-and-the-bees talk."

"I stand by that chart. It was an excellent visual aid," Dad says, maintaining a straight face. "But to answer your question, yes. Mom was the romantic. She was a hopeless romantic, actually."

He doesn't expand on that, not that I expect him to. But his response also fills me with a fuzzy feeling, followed up by a deep ache in my gut. While it's nice knowing I share my romantic tendencies with Mom, I still can't help but wish she were here. Wish I could talk to her about love. Ask her advice about the vision. About how she navigated things with Dad after they met. Did she know Dad was The One immediately?

It dawns on me that I don't actually know much about how my parents met at all, aside from the fact that they met through work and watched *CSI*. I've never really worked up the courage to press for more details, mostly because I haven't wanted to upset him. But now seems like the perfect opportunity.

"How did you and Mom meet?" I ask, heart pounding as I await his answer.

Dad stiffens, cornflower blue eyes still trained away from mine. "You already know this. We met through work."

"All right, but you must have had a meet-cute."

He swallows nervously. "I don't know if you could call it a meet-cute, per se. We met during a briefing when remains of a suspected missing person were found. Not exactly the most romantic setting, huh?"

I shrug. "The human-remains aspect kind of dampens the mood. But anyway, you must have talked? Clicked during that meeting?"

"I don't remember much about it, to be honest."

I blink. His terse response strikes me as odd. Dad has a wicked memory. He remembers all sorts of things, like all 118 chemical elements, or what outfit I wore on my second birthday. And yet, he doesn't remember the details of his first interaction with his soulmate?

"That's it?" I prod.

"That pretty much sums it up." He averts eye contact. This feels like more than just his typical avoidance, so I let it go. "How's the planning going?"

"I still want to follow Mom's itinerary, but we're allowing for some flexibility. And we both want to do Amalfi at the end," I explain. Mom and Mei never went to the Amalfi Coast.

He squeezes the small spiral notebook in his hands before setting it gently on the floor next to me. "Speaking of, I wanted to give you this. I thought it might help."

I flip it open and my heart patters. It's Mom and Mei's original itinerary, written in Mom's loopy handwriting.

"I know Mei told you all about their trip, but just in case she forgot anything, it should all be here," he says, tapping the notebook.

"Thanks, Dad," I say gently, trying not to burst this bubble as I flip through the pages. She listed everything by day. Just having this with me feels special, like she's guiding me along, showing me where to go.

Day 1, land in Venice—see Doge's Palace and ride gondola, check into Casa Canale Hostel

Day 2—tour Saint Mark's Square and Saint Mark's Basilica

I realize I'm muttering out loud when Dad warns, "Be careful of pickpockets in crowded areas like that. And don't talk to or go off with strangers."

"We'll be safe, I promise. No need to worry."

"I can't help it. It's my job to worry." He also has a bit of a warped perspective of the world, given his line of work and all the true crime he watches.

"Well, I appreciate you being okay with me going. This trip means a lot."

He nods quietly. "I know." He may not want to talk about her, but giving me her notebook shows how much he cares. And that means everything.

Before I can thank him, my phone starts vibrating. A dimly lit photo of Bianca sticking her tongue out while devouring spicy BBQ wings at Wing Night flashes across my screen.

At the sight of her name, my throat tightens. Bianca doesn't like using the phone. And when she does, she'll text me first to tell me she's calling.

"You're going to hate me," Bianca croaks, confirming my gut feeling.

"This can't be good." I grit my teeth and squeeze the slobbery sock tight like a stress ball, bracing myself. Different possibilities flit through my mind. Is our flight canceled? Delayed? Is she gearing up to ask if Chris can come?

"I can't go to Italy."

There's a long pause and my insides all but unhinge, stomach nose-diving. I toss the sock on the floor next to my open suitcase. Wow. I did not expect that.

"What? Why?" All the images of us wandering around Rome, arms linked as we take in the beauty of the Colosseum, flicker through my mind.

"I shattered my foot," she explains, voice quivering. She goes on to detail the drama of her trip to Costco, of all places, and long story short, she had a freak accident involving a bulk tub of coconut oil dropping on her foot, shattering the bone to smithereens. She spent hours in the ER and now has a cast. The doctor says she might even require surgery depending on how it heals. Coming from the girl who danced through a torn ACL and multiple broken toes this year, I know she's in bad shape.

I starfish on the floor and Brandon circles me, taunting me with his latest stolen goods: a pair of slobbery panties. It takes me a while to digest, to realize I'm not dreaming this up. Talk about unlucky. Of all the injuries a day before a Euro backpacking trip. We could have probably made do with a broken arm, or literally anything but a foot or leg. "Oh god. I'm sorry, Bianca. That's beyond unlucky."

"I'm the one who's sorry. I know how important this trip is, with your mom and the whole soulmate thing." I'd called her immediately after Mei left, and she screamed in my ear and demanded to be a bridesmaid (preferably maid of honor, but she understood if I appointed Teller as my man of honor). "But you'll still go, right? Our plane tickets are nonrefundable."

I massage my temple, mind racing. *What am I going to do about the trip?*

"Also, if you meet The One, you'll have the room to yourself," she says suggestively when I don't respond.

"Bianca." Realistically, I'd forgo privacy in favor of moral support when meeting my soulmate. But I don't tell her that. I don't want her to feel worse than she already does.

"You've always said you wanted to do a solo trip. And you make friends wherever you go. I've heard it's super easy to meet other travelers in hostels." She's not wrong. Like Bianca, I've never had an issue striking up a conversation with strangers, and I do have an adventurous streak.

Still, the prospect of traveling solo as a young woman is a little jarring. Dad's influence is rubbing off on me after all.

"Maybe your dad would go with you," she suggests.

I emit a laugh. It's the only thing I can do in place of crying. "Can you imagine him hovering over my shoulder when I meet The One? He'd be the ultimate cockblock. No thank you."

"Oh, come on. Eric could use some sun. He's pastier than a malnourished Victorian child."

"Definitely not." It isn't that I don't want to travel with Dad, but after living at home all year, this trip was supposed to mark my transition into adulthood, into independence. It was supposed to be Bianca and me, no curfew, no one breathing down our necks as we stumble to our hostels late at night after too much cheap wine. Then again, who else my age would have the money or time to impulsively drop everything and backpack around Italy with me for a month? "Maybe I could ask one of my aunts. Well, I guess not Ellen. She's too pregnant."

"What about Mei? She's always up for an adventure."

"So long as it's business class," I say with a snort. "I think her backpacking days are over. She also refuses to take time off from work. Last year they forced her to take two weeks of vacation, so she flew to a psychic convention in Vegas, redesigned her entire condo, and wrote twenty thousand words of a book about melding Eastern and Western psychic practices."

And that's when it comes to me.

I know just the person in need of a vacation.

$\sim$

"What is all this?" Teller asks, hands on hips over his barista apron.

He's taken aback by my presence, which is fair, because I stormed into the coffee shop without notice dressed in random yellow items of clothing I cobbled together: a yellow party hat with a floppy pom-pom, my childhood yellow life jacket that is way too tight around the chest, a yellow cape from my drama club days, and yellow leggings I bought for an eighties party on campus that make me look like Big Bird's deranged sister.

When a table of athleisure-clad women sipping iced coffees spin around to stare, I immediately regret making such a dramatic entrance.

I thought there was a possibility I might embarrass the shit out of him, but he doesn't seem to notice anyone else. His eyes are on me only. That's one of the things I've always liked about Teller. As different as we are, he's never once asked me to change or tone it down.

A surprise to us both, somewhere between selling tickets, preparing food and drink orders, stocking supplies, and cleaning that first summer, we just clicked. We worked most shifts together since Teller was always on the schedule. He worked as much as he could, always offering to take shifts for Paula, a single mom of twins who often needed time off.

We made the perfect team, making up for each other's shortcomings. Where he dreaded making small talk with customers, I'd shuffle impatiently, waiting for the end of the movie so I could ask them what they thought. And where I would have preferred to douse myself in boiling popcorn butter than clean, Teller found peace in the routine of mopping and stocking and organizing supplies.

Most of our downtime consisted of me forcing him to watch bits of rom-coms we were screening, scrolling through photos of pets for adoption, and playing card games Teller learned from his grandma: War, Crazy Eights, Slapjack, Go Fish, and Golf. He nearly always won.

One night he offered me a ride home from work, and then again the next night. And then every night for the rest of the summer. This tradition continued on even when school started. He'd pick me up on those dewy fall mornings and drop me off at the end of the day—until I started dating a guy named Tim Yates, a football bro. You know the type. Walks around with his chest puffed out, sits backward in chairs, and orders the XXX spicy wings just to prove a point. Anyway, he was weirdly paranoid that Teller wanted to hook up with me (he did not) and insisted on driving me instead. We broke up after a couple months, and of course, my routine with Teller resumed.

"Lo? What's with the . . . outfit?" he asks over the hiss and whirr of all the fancy coffee machinery. "You look like sunshine on legs."

"It's on brand with . . . your cheer-up kit! *Ta-da,*" I announce in my best game-show-host voice, setting a gigantic basket wrapped in yellow tulle on the counter. I hate seeing him all sad and mopey, so I had to go to extraordinary lengths to cheer him up.

He pretends to be chill as he wipes his hands on a cloth and tosses it over his shoulder. "A cheer-up kit? You really didn't have to do this," he says, though I don't miss the upward turn of his lips when he pulls out the first item—a box of Girl Scout Thin Mints, his absolute favorite because they make his mouth feel clean. "Where'd you get these? They're out of season."

I flash a coy smile. "I have my ways." By *ways*, I mean I badgered Jayde, our eight-year-old neighbor, for a box from her stash in exchange for a promise to bake her a funfetti cake when I get back from Italy.

Teller extracts the next gift, a pack of disinfectant wipes with a little note that reads *For a clean slate*. "Needed more of these for my car," he murmurs approvingly.

The next item is Quinton, a stuffed lemur he won for me in eleventh grade at the fall fair. I forced him to go; he doesn't trust the structural integrity of carnival rides. "You don't want to keep him?" he asks.

"You need him more than me," I say, motioning for him to pull out the next item. It's a pair of homemade coupons with offers to *Egg Sophie's apartment* and *Key her car* (valid until September 1st).

"Right," he says with a snort, moving on to a tiny flip calendar called Just Ponies.

"I have a feeling you'll love June's pony," I inform him.

He flips to June, where a blond pony gallops through a sunlit field, tutu flouncing in the breeze. A childlike grin spreads across Teller's face, lighting him up from the inside out. Not a lot makes Teller smile, and this right here is the first genuine smile I've seen from him in ages. Just seeing him happy gives me an instant high.

He rounds the counter to pull me into a hug, rocking me side to side. "Thank you, Lo. This means a lot. Really."

My cheek presses against the top of his chest, reminding me yet again of how ludicrously tall he is. "There's still more!"

I watch expectantly as he opens the rest of the items: a yellow smiley-face stress ball (to *bounce* back), a box of Paw Patrol Band-Aids (to mend your broken heart), a pack of matches (for a ceremonial burning of Sophie's things), and a candle with a homemade label that reads SMELLS LIKE THAT SHIT AIN'T YOUR PROBLEM ANYMORE in dainty script that amuses him.

I take in a sharp inhale when he reaches for the last item.

It feels like an eternity as I wait for him to pull it out. He even squints to ensure he's seeing it correctly. "What—what is this?"

A plane ticket.

"Surprise! You're coming to Italy with me," I announce.

He just blinks, eyes darting back to the ticket to reread it. I can't tell if he's happy or not. "Excuse me?"

"Bianca's foot shattered at Costco, so she can't come anymore. And you need to get your mind off Sophie. No more moping around and crying."

The decision to invite Teller was easy. He's the kind of person who spirals and gets into his head. He needs a change of scenery, stat.

"I have *not* been crying."

"There's nothing wrong with crying."

"I know there isn't. But I haven't been." It's probably true. I've actually never seen Teller cry. Not because he's one of those macho dudes, but because he's just not a touchy-feely person in general. It takes a lot to elevate him—mad, sad, happy. He's always been even-keeled, something I appreciate about him.

"You might as well have. You were listening to Coldplay until three in the morning. 'The Scientist,' when everyone knows 'Yellow' is their best."

He tilts his head in a warning, yet playful expression. "Hey, you're not allowed to use my Spotify account anymore if you're going to slander 'The Scientist.' And I'm always up until three."

Teller's been letting me use his account since I decided to take up marathon running. He even made me a motivational playlist and downloaded a couple podcasts he thought I'd like. Despite his best efforts, I couldn't run more than 2K without getting winded and collapsing on the side of the road in a heap of sweat and regret. But I've been mooching off his account ever since. "Fair. No more Coldplay slander so long as you agree to come with me."

He shakes his head and studies me, wary. "For a whole month? No way. I can't. I have . . . plans."

"You do not have plans. You just moved home unexpectedly. Yesterday."

"Actually, I was thinking of driving up to surprise Sophie. Maybe next week. Figured I'd give her some space and—"

I pretend to collapse face-first onto the counter. "Surprise her? You'd just show up at her door unannounced?"

He nods casually. "That's what I was thinking—"

"No. Absolutely not," I say point-blank. "Tel, that's just desperate and creepy."

The lines between his brows intensify. "I'm confused. When the PM knocks on every door in the neighborhood to find his assistant in *Love, Actually*, you said it was one of the most romantic gestures in all of cinema. But when I want to go see my girlfriend, it's desperate and creepy?"

Crap. Forcing Teller to watch all those rom-coms really messed with his head.

"First, she's your ex-girlfriend," I correct. "And second, most romantic gestures in movies don't actually translate to real life. Besides, your situation is different. *She* broke up with *you*. She needs space. If she wants to reconnect with you, she will."

He lets out a resigned sigh before wiping a mound of coffee grounds into the trash bin. "You're probably right."

"Since you no longer have plans . . . ," I start, flashing a hopeful smile.

"I told you. I don't do hostels. Or travel in general." He's not kidding. The farthest place he's ever traveled to is Niagara Falls.

"Hostels have a bad rap. Just think of them as small, budget-friendly hotels. And guess what? We didn't book ahead of time, so you can even vet them beforehand. Some even have private bathrooms if you pay a little extra." He gives me a look that says *What the hell?* I explain, "Bianca and I decided we didn't want to be beholden to a strict itinerary, since we weren't sure how long we'd want to stay in each place.

We planned to loosely follow my mom and Mei's trip, though. Minus the bookings."

"A vacation without any bookings," he says, lips pulled tight. "Sounds like the stuff of nightmares."

Damn. I'm really losing him here. Admittedly, I knew it would be a challenge to convince him. Maybe I was naive, but part of me thought he'd say yes purely because he'd want to spend a month with me. Though maybe I'm projecting my desire to spend that time with him.

Still, I shove all ego out the door and resort to begging, which looks like me draping my torso over the counter, arms outstretched, full-on pouting. Now I'm the desperate and creepy one. "We haven't seen each other in forever. We'll probably never have another opportunity to spend this kind of time together."

And I need your moral support when I meet my soulmate, I want to add. But I don't. It's not something I want to toss in casually, even though Teller knows about the family gift. I first told him after a late shift only about a month after we first met. And believe me, I didn't make that decision lightly. There was a high likelihood he'd write me off as a loon and never speak to me again. But if he was going to be my close friend, I couldn't hide that part of my family's identity, even if I didn't have the gift myself.

I led into the conversation in a very chill, casual way: by telling him my mom died.

The Cinema had done a screening of an old film about a mom dying and leaving her two children behind. It made me emotional, as most things with that subject matter do, so when it was over, I sat alone in the theater, stuffing my face with TWIZZLERS, trying not to cry.

"What's wrong?" Teller asked.

I jumped at the sound of his voice. I hadn't realized he was there. "Oh, um, the movie. Reminded me of my mom. She died."

"Shit. I'm sorry, Lo." His expression went solemn. "When did she pass?"

"When I was four. I don't really remember a lot about her, to be honest."

He didn't say anything, though he didn't need to. He just placed his hand on my shoulder, firm and reassuring.

"I've never told anyone that. Not having clear memories of her makes me feel like a terrible person. Of all people, I should remember her just by nature, shouldn't I? Like, if she suddenly came back to life, I don't know if I'd recognize her in a crowd if I didn't study her pictures. And everyone else in my family has all these memories of her and I don't."

"Lo, you were four years old," he reminded me, voice even and steady. "I hardly remember anything from that age, aside from my traumatic first day of school."

"I need to hear this story," I said, shoulders easing. I already felt so much lighter just talking to him. The more time I spent with Teller, the better he was getting at reading my emotions, almost interpreting them for me in plain language. I was never very good at making sense of all my big feelings.

"Another time."

I let out a shaky sigh. "It's weird. I mostly remember how she made me feel, that I was comfortable and happiest when I was with her, which makes me even more sad for the rest of my family, because they must miss her even more than I do."

"Grief is love persevering."

I blinked. "Wow, Tel. That's pretty . . . deep."

"It's a rom-com quote," he informed me, proud of himself for finally getting me after all the quotes I'd tricked him with.

I gave him a look, trying to rack my brain. "I haven't heard it before. From what?"

"*WandaVision*."

"*WandaVision* is not a rom-com. Nice try, though." I snorted, giving him a light elbow in the bicep.

He shrugged. "It was a good quote."

"I have this picture of her," I said, taking the photo out to show him.

He leaned in closer, head nearly touching mine as he followed my gaze over the photo. "I can see why you like this one. Your parents look . . . beyond . . . happy. Like they really belonged together."

It's true. They were just completely themselves, at home, no frills, having the best time because they have each other. "Because they did. Literally," I said.

He caught the seriousness in my tone. "What do you mean?"

"All right, I should backtrack. The women in my family are psychics. Every one of them. Except for me."

I figured he'd question me, give me a lecture about how psychics are frauds and take advantage of the emotionally vulnerable. But Teller didn't do anything of the sort. He just nodded as I enlightened him on the whole family history.

"After they started blending Eastern with Western practices, they developed this new gift." I explained the whole thing, just like my grandmother had explained it to me when I was around five. How it started with my great-grandmother. How every woman in our family has had The Vision since then and how every single one has come to fruition.

"So you're saying your aunt Ellen heard the same song over and over in her head as a kid, and then the moment that song came on at a club, she just happened to twirl into her fiancé?"

"Yes! I know it all sounds crazy, but I swear it's true."

He didn't argue. He just stayed quiet, like he was trying to work through the logic. I expected him to counter everything, bullet by bullet. But shockingly, all he said was, "No wonder you're such a hopeless romantic."

"It gives me hope that I'll find love like them one day. Do you think there's someone out there for me? Even if I can't foresee it like they can?"

"Absolutely, Lo."

I don't think he realized how much that meant to me.

The topic never came up again, even all these years later. I have a few theories as to why. First, I'm not entirely sure he believes in the whole psychic thing and probably doesn't have the heart to tell me. I also think he's avoided the topic because he knows how much it bothers me that I didn't inherit the family gift. How it's made me feel like a failure. It's also possible that he's forgotten the conversation altogether.

All to say, I don't dare tell him about The One. It feels like poor timing to announce I'm about to meet the love of my life—in Italy, no less—when he's just been dumped, kicked out of his apartment, forced to move home for the summer, and is now listening to Coldplay on a loop. I'll have to tell him eventually, but that can wait.

"Just think about it. A whole month together, exploring, eating Italian food, making friends with locals. And the legal drinking age is eighteen. We can actually go to bars. And clubs!" I say, not that the latter will win him over. He's not a huge drinker.

He bobs his head back and squeezes his eyes shut like it's all too much. "I just don't know. I'd have to take time off and things are pretty busy here and—"

I cut him off before he can come up with yet another excuse. "You literally told me last night that you had to beg your mom to give you shifts. You'd be doing her a favor by getting out of her hair and off the payroll. Come on, Tel. Be fun and spontaneous."

"Who says I'm not fun and spontaneous? This morning I put hot sauce on my eggs."

"You're . . ." I gaze at the exposed industrial ceiling, searching for the most delicate way to say it without crushing his ego. "You're a creature of habit. Don't you want to prove to Sophie you're not boring?"

The question slices the air like a knife. I can tell by the tick of his mouth that I've gotten to him.

"Hypothetically, if I decided I'd go, hypothetically, would we be sharing a room?"

I've thought about this a lot. Sure, it might be a little weird knowing Teller is naked in the shower, but how is sharing with Teller any different from sharing with Bianca? "Why? Would you rather stay in your own room?"

"No, not at all. I just thought you might get annoyed with me being up super late every night." What he really means is that he will surely get annoyed with me getting up at the ass crack of dawn every morning. I've always been an early riser, paranoid about missing out on the day. It's my chronic FOMO. Teller is the opposite, up until at least two in the morning each night, unable to fall asleep due to his anxiety.

"That's fine by me, so long as you're not listening to Coldplay all night. Besides, it's the only way we can afford it. And why wouldn't we share? Do you think it's weird or something?"

"Sorry. I was just clarifying. Did I make it weird?"

"Kind of. But it would be way less weird if you stopped being so cagey and just said yes."

He lowers his shoulders. "Fine. I'll think about it."

An *I'll think about it* from Teller is as close as I'll get to a *yes*. He's just too stubborn to outright say so.

"Great. Flight leaves tomorrow at 7:30 a.m."

5

Departure to Venice

"I still don't understand why we had to be here so early," I manage, dragging my feet into the airport lobby like a zombie. I may be a morning person, but by *morning*, I mean when the sun is actually up. It's still pitch black.

You could probably hear the footsteps of a single ant in here. The airport is deserted aside from me, Teller, and a few airport employees. Then again, we've arrived four hours early. Teller insists on being absurdly punctual for everything.

"You have to be at least three hours early for international flights," he tells me for the hundredth time as he speed-walks ahead. I doubt he even went to bed at all.

I'm struggling to keep up with his giraffe strides. Admittedly, I did not pack light. Dad nearly threw his back out putting my rucksack in the trunk. I'm not sure how I'll cart that thing around all month, but an array of cute options are worth back pain when you're meeting The One.

"You don't have to be *this* early. It's just one of those fake rules that don't really mean anything. Like expiration dates on yogurt."

He spins around, overcome with thinly veiled revulsion. "You eat expired yogurt?"

I don't respond as we reach the check-in kiosks.

When he lifts his T-shirt to retrieve his passport from the money belt fastened to his torso, I'm shocked. Not to be a creep, but I'm incapable of looking anywhere else.

Teller.

Owens.

Has.

Abs.

ABS. Six of them, to be exact.

Let's be clear. He's always been the infuriating kind of lean where abs just naturally poke through without a crunch or Cinema-popcorn deprivation. A monster, really. But this is different. These sculpted abdominals aren't there by happenstance. They are clearly hard earned.

It's only when he catches me staring that I wrench my eyes away. Vision blurred, I stub my toe on my rucksack as I charge to the kiosk on the left, loudly humming the Elton John song that was playing in the car on the way here. *What the hell is wrong with me?*

"Passport, passport, where are you?" I mumble, rooting around in the massive Kate Spade tote that Mei gifted me (Black Friday blowout deal). Bianca calls it my "bag of tricks" because it holds just about everything, from an umbrella to an extra pair of shoes. My shoulder will pay for its significant weight down the road, but given my tendency to forget things, it's nice to carry everything in one place.

"Don't tell me you lost your passport already," Teller says with a groan. He'd already triple-checked I had it before leaving my house.

"I think I feel it!" I say excitedly, finally locating it in the deepest of depths, next to a half-eaten protein bar.

"It's not too late to wear the money belt," he says. This morning he showed up with an extra money belt for me (his dad's, apparently). To prevent pickpockets from accessing my valuables, he claimed. And to humiliate me into oblivion. It was a kind gesture, but I can't meet my soulmate wearing a money belt. And I certainly can't be wearing it when he goes to cop a feel.

"Never," I say, distracted as I check in on the touch screen.

"You should reconsider. You're a prime target for a thief," he warns, bending over to retrieve his ticket and luggage tag from the machine. "Overly friendly, a bit aloof."

"I'm not aloof. And it's just not sexy. I don't make the rules."

"Safety is sexy. Look, it's discreet!" He tugs at the hem of his T-shirt defensively.

I point at the noticeable bulge, only allowing my eyes to linger for a half second, lest I accidently see a sliver of abs again. *Why can't I stop thinking about them?* "It's really not. And you sound like you're in an adult-diaper commercial."

"With our advanced technology and discreet design, you'll feel protected and secure, all day, every day," he says in his best commercial voice before we both dissolve into a fit of laughter.

Despite Teller's doom-and-gloom warnings about how long it takes to go through TSA, we're able to check our bags, get through security, and find our gate all in less than forty minutes. A TSA agent even praised Teller for his organization and attention to detail (liquids in clear bags, etc.), which I suspect he'll boast about for years to come. We're so early that there's an entirely different flight waiting to board at our gate.

"See? Told you we didn't have to come so early," I brag.

He rolls his eyes and plunks down in an open seat, strategically closest to where we'll line up. "You'd have been up in two hours anyways. And it's not typical to get through security that fast. You have to reserve time for potential delays."

"Based on all the times you've traveled?"

"Based on my research."

There's no point in arguing, so I plop down next to him and take my phone out. "Airport selfie. Smile!" I say, pressing my cheek to his. I hold my passport and ticket to the camera.

"I'll tag you so you can repost it. Sophie still follows you, right?"

"I think so," he says, pulling his phone out to double-check.

"Does she know you're going to Italy with me?"

"No, but for the record, I don't want you to think I'm only coming to show Sophie I have an adventurous side," he says, holding my gaze. "I'm going because I know how much this trip means to you."

Warmth floods my insides, like I've just guzzled warm tea. When Teller says something, he means it.

"Thanks, Tel. But if it just so happens to make Sophie second-guess dumping you, that's an added bonus."

Teller loosens up over the next few hours once all the stressful parts of flying are behind us. We spend our time doing our usual—people watching and eating candy. Apparently Vacation Teller is okay with sweets at six in the morning. He even fetches us breakfast sandwiches and snacks because he doesn't trust plane food.

All is going smoothly. Until it's not.

First, the flight is delayed twenty minutes due to high winds. Then thirty. Then almost two hours by the time we're actually allowed to board.

The plane is large, with seats in twos on either side, a wider row of three ribboning down the middle. Teller is less than impressed with our seats, which are in the middle. It doesn't help that our arms are pressed against each other's. Curse this airline for designing such tiny seats. I give Teller the aisle so he doesn't have a panic attack.

While the rest of the passengers take their seats, Teller goes to town wiping his tray with a wet wipe. Once he's satisfied, he extends a fresh wipe to me between pinched fingers. "Here. Airplane trays have three times more bacteria than the toilet flush button," he rattles off like an encyclopedia.

"Thanks," I say, taking the wipe. I note his knee is bouncing up and down too, a natural reflex when he's feeling anxious. "You okay? You're not scared of flying, are you?"

"No. Planes are safer than cars, statistically speaking. It's just . . . Sophie posted a story last night. With a guy . . ." His voice trails.

"Really? Let me see!"

He turns his screen toward me. It's a video clip of her arm, presumably, cheersing a foamy beer with someone across a small table.

"Is it a guy? It's hard to tell from the clip." I rewatch it a couple times, assuming there's more.

"Look at the arm." He leans in close, and his cheek grazes mine ever so slightly. He scrutinizes the screen like an FBI agent combing every pixel for evidence. "It's hairy. Definitely a dude."

"It does look that way," I admit. "But don't jump to conclusions. What if it's like, her dad? Or brother? Or just some random friend?"

"Her dad lives in Panama. And she doesn't have platonic one-on-one guy friends." I already knew the latter bit. It's the reason she never quite understood or trusted Teller's friendship with me.

"Remember back in tenth grade when Tim Yates broke up with me and then made out with Danika Pressley that same night?"

He relaxes against the headrest and smirks. "That was the first night you drank."

Teller's being kind. Here's the story: I decided chugging two strong drinks as fast as possible was a surefire way to get over Tim. This resulted in a dramatic public confrontation where I proceeded to topple into a beautifully decorated Christmas tree.

"Anyway, remember when he tried to get me back?"

Teller nods stiffly. "Yup."

"He only wanted me back because I went dark over Christmas break. I stopped texting him, stopped posting on social media. And he saw me with you on New Year's and got jealous."

"Ah yes. When he threatened to rearrange my face. Sweet memories."

I'd felt so vindicated, but I didn't go back to him after that.

"Exactly. The point is, maybe you need to use this trip as an opportunity to—"

"Make Sophie jealous? I don't know."

I level him with a look. "Okay, maybe not jealous. But make her miss you a little! Don't text her or like any of her posts." I can tell he's unsatisfied, so I add, "And if you decide to work the jealousy angle, we can find you a hot Italian girl. You'll take a bunch of mysterious photos with her, and I guarantee Sophie will text you."

I couldn't actually guarantee it. I didn't know Sophie all that well, despite her dating my best friend for the past three years.

The first time we met was at the bus station when she visited him for the weekend. He'd planned some activities for us, like mini golf and a game night. I didn't mind the idea of third-wheeling. After listening to Teller sing her praises for weeks, I couldn't wait to meet her and become the best friends I thought we were destined to be.

She was exactly what I'd pictured—the perfect girl for Teller. She'd dressed her dainty frame in a minimalist capsule wardrobe filled with white, navy, subtle stripes, and a shit-ton of neutrals to match her clean fingernails and glossy, pin-straight hair. She was my polar opposite. A straight-A student and president of multiple clubs, but pleasant and just self-deprecating enough not to hate. She didn't make penis jokes at the wrong times, nor did she scare strangers by asking to pet their dogs. She didn't embarrass Teller with a tendency to break into song or dramatically quote films. She lived life by color-coded schedule, always early for everything. Basically, she was Teller's dream girl.

She was sweet to me from that first awkward hug, remarking how it felt like we already knew each other, how she appreciated me keeping Teller in line (though it was really the opposite), and that she couldn't wait to see me beat Teller at mini golf. She loved my "unique" style, said she could never pull off such bold floral prints and vintage pieces.

We made enthusiastic small talk for at least fifteen minutes in the parking lot before Teller insisted we get on the road before rush-hour traffic. My first instinct was to return to the passenger seat. My seat. The seat I'd spent hours in, next to Teller. But when we stepped toward the door, I realized for the first time that it wasn't *my* seat. If someone had dibs, it was the girlfriend.

And so began a war of apologies and insisting the other take the front seat, despite both of us clearly wanting it. A battle of niceties, which I learned was her thing. She always apologized, even if she wasn't at fault, like if I unintentionally cut her off midsentence. Anyway, she won the car-seat battle. For the rest of the weekend, and every other time she visited, I was in the back seat.

Despite how "fine" things were between us, I never got the sense that she truly wanted to be friends. That she truly wanted to know me. There was an invisible barrier I couldn't seem to break down. Over time, it felt as though everything I did or said was too much, too loud for her (fair). Let's be real, I'm a lot to handle sometimes, but I worried that with Sophie's influence, Teller would finally realize he didn't want to be my friend. In reality, he probably didn't talk or think about me all that much when he was with her.

He doesn't seem sure about my plan to make her jealous. "I don't know. It seems a little juvenile, don't you think?"

"True. But you have to promise you'll actually enjoy this trip. Put the phone down and leave your baggage here in the US. I won't tolerate pouting."

"You're right. Officially putting the phone away," he says, tucking it into his pocket.

"Good. Just think, in seven hours, we'll be in Italy. The most beautiful country on the planet. You won't even have time to think about Sophie."

6

We are not in Italy in seven hours.

For the next hour, we freeze our butts off on the tarmac under the blasting AC. Teller is getting anxious about the tight quarters and lack of cleanliness in the bathroom. Not that I blame him. It's not comfortable to sit for so long with your thigh pushed against someone else's, even if said thigh happens to belong to your best friend. Just when I think he's going to lose it and demand to get off the plane, the wheels start moving and we're in flight. Bless.

I wish I could say things got better from there. That we fell asleep over the Atlantic. That we woke up refreshed and ready to embrace all Italy had to offer. But things got worse. Much worse.

For the hour we're actually in flight, the turbulence is awful. The plane dips and jostles from side to side so often, we don't have time for our stomachs to recover. It gets so bad, people request barf bags from the flight attendants, who are eventually ordered to take their seats too.

I'm the type of person who loves roller coasters, but even I can't hold in my gasps. I white-knuckle the armrest, teeth clenched. My insides feel like scrambled eggs.

"Hey, we're going to be okay," Teller assures me, taking my hand and giving it a squeeze.

I shake my head. "I—I don't believe you."

"Look at me," he instructs, shifting closer.

I focus on his steady gaze. The little flecks of hunter green in his eyes. The rings of bronze surrounding the pupils. It's an instant source of comfort. If Teller, of all people, is calm, I can be too. At least, I think.

"Take a big inhale," he says, waiting for me to do so. "Count to seven, and slowly let it out for seven."

I repeat his instructions several times as he drags the smooth pads of his fingers over the soft part of my forearm, leaving a tingly feeling in their wake. By the final exhale, I'm far less tense. There's still a stubborn knot in my gut, but I'm no longer gripping the armrest, bracing for impact. My knee is no longer bouncing up and down. "Where'd you learn that?"

"One of my mindfulness podcasts," he says. "I use it almost every day—"

He's interrupted by a ding, followed by a voice over the loudspeaker. "Ladies and gentlemen, this is your captain speaking. I regret to inform you that due to severe weather conditions on our flight path, we have to divert to the nearest airport."

Angry, nervous chatter erupts as a flight attendant goes on about prioritizing safety, fastening seat belts securely, and putting trays in an upright position as we prepare for the descent.

Teller rubs his temple, trying to make sense of it all. "Is it just me, or is this flight cursed?"

"Definitely cursed. But we'll get another one tonight once the weather clears," I say confidently.

Unfortunately, the weather does not improve.

"There are no more flights to Venice tonight," Miranda, one of the airport staff, informs us impatiently when we deboard at a midsize airport in Nowhere, America. I don't fully blame her. She has to deal with hundreds of cranky customers in this humungous line, which appears to be growing exponentially by the minute.

"What about Rome?" Teller asks.

A bored blink. "Nope."

"Florence?"

"Nope."

"Are there any flights at all to Italy? Or Europe in general?" he asks, eyes alight with something that looks a lot like desperation.

Miranda shakes her head. "No flights out of country until tomorrow morning. Everything is grounded until the storm passes," she says to the massive line of people behind us, who all grumble simultaneously. "My advice is that you find somewhere to stay overnight."

We accept the new tickets for early the next morning and haul our bags to a wooden bench to figure out next steps.

Upon a brief Google search, we realize our options are slim with all the flights that are canceled. We call at least ten hotels in the area, none of which have any vacancies. One receptionist even barks a single-syllable laugh and hangs up.

The only place with a vacancy is a motel on the outskirts of town.

A sixty-dollar Uber ride later, we're standing in front of the Shady Pines Inn.

"Could they not have come up with a better name?" I ask, taking in what was seemingly once a vibrant, neon sign that now reads H DY ES NN and flickers intermittently, casting an eerie glow over the potholed parking lot. The beige paint on the siding is chipped and faded. There's even a unit on the end with a rickety slab of wood nailed across the window, as though someone was trying to keep some dark entity in—or out.

Teller gulps and kicks at the gravel underneath his foot. "I'm sorry, but is this a joke? We can't stay here. It's straight from a horror movie."

"Well, we paid to Uber all the way here," I remind him, starting toward the lobby.

Teller begrudgingly follows close at my heels as we haul our rucksacks inside. Its entrance is bookended with rusty lawn chairs haphazardly turned toward the road. The lobby is a tiny, dimly lit, colorless room with a large walnut desk. At the desk is an elderly lady in glasses adorned with little pink rhinestones, a crocheted vest pulled over her ample chest.

"Hello, you're the fellow who called ahead? Mr. Owens?" Her oddly cheery demeanor only adds to the creepiness.

"Unfortunately," Teller mutters, though I don't think she hears him over the clacking of her keyboard as she checks us into a room with two double beds.

The room is as expected from what we've seen of the place. There are two beds with mattresses that dip in the center after years of wear. Their floral-patterned comforters have almost certainly been here since the motel's opening. Same goes for the heavy drapery, which are maroon on one side and sun-faded pink on the inside. A faint, musty scent of cigarette smoke hangs thick in the air.

And now it sinks in: I'll be sharing a room with Teller. For the entire trip. Something about this reality makes my stomach flip. It's not that I'm uncomfortable. Teller is probably the person I'm most comfortable with on Earth, aside from Dad and my aunts. But there's something intimate about sharing the same tiny space, the same toilet, with someone for a month.

It's the same as sharing with Bianca, I tell myself again. Only . . . Teller is a guy. A guy with newly formed abs and muscly arms.

"Is this blood?" Teller asks, pointing to some suspiciously dark-red drips next to the dresser on the frayed carpet. "Oh god. I think it's blood. Someone was for sure murdered here. Your dad would have a field day."

"Don't come in the bathroom," I warn, assessing the discolored tiles and moldy grout.

He ignores my warning, poking his head in, immediately zeroing in on the cracked soap dish, sporting a used bar of soap. "That's a pube," he says, nearly gagging.

I examine the bar of soap closer, turning my head sideways, like the angle will make a difference. "We can't know for sure. It could be a wiry beard hair."

"Nope. Most definitely a pube. Lo, I don't know if I can do this. Any hostel has to be better than this."

I give him a motivational slap on the back, trying to stay positive for his sake. "Exactly. It can only get better from here. Besides, we're just here for the night."

That doesn't comfort him in the slightest. Before I can unzip my bag, he's on his hands and knees, mattresses turned over, searching for bedbugs. Given the bathroom tap is emitting rusty water, I head outside in search of clean drinking water.

The one thing this place has going for it is a well-stocked vending machine.

"They have Raisinets!" I say when I return, two bottles of water and a bunch of snacks in hand.

Teller is parked on the edge of the bed, his butt taking up as little real estate as possible without falling off. He's wearing two hooded sweatshirts, a pair of plaid pajama bottoms, and thick socks. He refuses to sleep under the covers. "Seriously?" He inspects the box of Raisinets. "Just checking to make sure they're not expired," he says before peeling it open.

We make at least five more trips to the vending machine, spending way too much of our travel money on weird snacks like cheese-flavored Bugles, blueberry Pop-Tarts (my choice), and two rock-hard oatmeal-raisin cookies (obviously Teller's choice) that nearly break my teeth.

The rest of the day goes by shockingly fast, sitting among a pile of snack wrappers, playing all our old card games. When I get tired of losing, we flick back and forth between all forty cable channels. Eventually, we settle on an infomercial station that's advertising "Putt on the Potty," which is exactly what it sounds like—a tiny golf putter and ball with felt that hugs the toilet, allowing you to practice putting while pooping.

"Why are you snickering?" Teller asks, eyeing me suspiciously. He's still in all his layers, propped on my pillows at the head of the bed, while I'm draped at the foot.

I roll onto my back to hide my phone. "Nothing."

"You're up to something." The glint in his eye is mischievous. Then he pounces over me on all fours like a panther, arms on either side of my temples, caging me in. At the sudden movement, the worn mattress springs let out a deafening squeal, like it's protesting our weight.

Our eyes lock, and something shifts between us. I wonder if he feels it too.

"Tel, I think you just broke the bed," I whisper, avoiding sudden movement.

Three seconds.

Five seconds.

Seven seconds.

At the tenth, we both descend into a fit of snorts, and Teller rolls onto his back next to me, chest heaving.

When I finally catch my breath, I toss him my phone to reveal the Putt on the Potty website.

"I was ordering you the Putt on the Potty for your birthday," I say.

"Thanks," he manages, wiping a tear from laughing so hard. "You always know exactly what I need."

Ping.

His eyes flick to my screen. "Ack!" He tosses my phone back, blinking like my screen burned his retinas.

"What?" I lurch forward, only to find yet another dick pic from Mark B. This one is somehow even less flattering than the last. "Shoot. Sorry," I say, quickly swiping it away.

"Can I ask who it belongs to?" he asks, half-amused, half-disconcerted.

"Mark B. A guy I was seeing." I say it quickly in hopes that he'll just move on. I don't want to talk about Mark B., of all people.

"I'd ask if he was nice, but I can probably guess he isn't." *Is he nice?* That's always Teller's first question when I tell him about a date or someone of interest.

"Why wouldn't he be nice? Because he sent a dick pic?" He nods. "You're telling me you've never sent a dick pic?"

I expect him to make a show of disgust and say no, but he doesn't. Not exactly. "I've never sent a dick pic . . . unsolicited."

"So you have sent one!" I shriek, ignoring the goose bumps erupting everywhere as my mind goes *there*. Like really goes there. In a flash, I'm besieged with images of Teller—abs prominent, entirely nude. *Get your mind out of the gutter, Lo.*

"I was in a long-distance relationship for two years, okay?" he says, snapping me out of my deranged fantasy. From the neck up, he's the color of Santa's suit, and I can only assume I am too.

I tug at my collar, suddenly feeling sweaty. "Hey, no judgment over here. Just wondering why you'd assume he wasn't nice."

"First, you said you *were* seeing each other. Past tense. Unless you're still hooking up, sending that's a little uncalled for. And second, the picture was taken in a car. That's a serious road hazard."

Only Teller would think about the safety of taking a dick pic.

I examine the photo again and spot the bottom of the steering wheel. He's definitely driving. Sweet Christ. I don't even want to know. "Okay, it's weird. But in Mark B.'s defense, he's actually a nice guy, if you can look past his tendency to send spontaneous dick pics."

"So you're not, um, requesting these dick pics?"

"No. It's my own fault, really. He thinks I like them because I've been responding with the taco emoji. Or the sweat droplets."

"The taco emoji?"

"I'm just trying to boost his confidence," I manage through a hiccup. "And I feel kinda bad about how I ended things." I go on to explain the whole fleeing-through-the-basement-window debacle.

Teller lets out a fit of laughter before asking, "Why did you end it?"

"I mean, we were never official or anything. We just didn't *like* each other enough. I never thought about him when we weren't together. Every time we did hang out, I had this weird feeling. Like it wasn't where I was supposed to be. And there weren't any butterflies or any of that giddy stuff like in movies," I explain, all too aware how naive that sounds.

"That's fair. Though that kind of love is overrated, I think."

"Did you ever have that kind of love with Sophie?" I dare to ask.

A beat of silence. "In the beginning. And at the end. But not in between," he admits. "Things were really stable in the thick of our relationship, but they were never over the top, you know? But I'm also not that kind of person, and neither is she."

"Do you think it can be? Over the top the whole time?" I ask hopefully.

His gaze lifts to mine. "Yeah, I do."

"I want that kind of love."

"That's the kind of love you deserve."

Thank you, I say with my eyes. He has the uncanny ability to know exactly what I need to hear.

We may be in the shittiest of motels, eating food abomination after abomination, and watching ridiculous infomercials, when we should be in Venice eating pasta and meeting my soulmate. But I feel just as happy.

"I missed this," I say over the mechanical hum of the ice machine in the hallway.

He swings his gaze back to me. "Missed what?"

"You. Spending time with you. We haven't seen each other since you ditched me at Christmas," I tease, rolling to face him.

We had plans one night to watch *National Lampoon's Christmas Vacation*—me, him, and Sophie—but Teller canceled last minute because Sophie was feeling sick.

It was hard going from seeing each other almost every day and texting all the time, exchanging adorable animal videos—like a sloth crossing a road—to the odd text every few months. Teller's texts were really all or nothing. Either I'd receive a whole day of full-paragraph answers or radio silence.

"Sorry about that, by the way." He really means it. I can tell by the edge in his voice. The way he tilts his gaze downward, guiltily. A subdued blue glow from the television dances over his face, illuminating the soft arch of his brows, almost creating a halo effect. "I really wanted to see you at Christmas, but things were so busy and—"

"Honestly, don't worry about it. It's fine. I just really missed you this year." I consider telling him about all the times I started to text him. All the times I actually typed the message, only to change my mind and delete it once I realized my last one had gone unanswered. But I don't want to sound pathetic.

He looks hurt. "You never visited me either, Lo."

"You never invited me," I counter.

"You've never struck me as the kind of person who needs to be invited. I assumed if you wanted to come, you'd come."

He's not wrong. There were many times I wanted to pack up my car and drive to him. Times where I felt lonely, lost, overwhelmed by the demands of my classes. But between the months of silence, unanswered texts, and, well, Sophie, I never got the sense that there was an open-door invite.

"Let's promise we'll see each other at least twice next year. Definitely once at Christmas," he says.

"I'll hold you to it." The prospect of not seeing Teller again until Christmas is depressing. I've already mourned not being together every single day, but it's still crushing, knowing it's simply not a reality of adult life, unless we buy houses side by side. I've joking-but-not-so-jokingly brought it up one too many times, and Teller has never responded with more than a teasing snort. Yet another reminder to treasure the next month.

"I've been meaning to ask, how did you find classes last semester?" he asks, dropping a metaphorical brick on my chest.

"Oof" is all I can summon. I'd hoped to avoid this discussion as long as possible. "Honestly, no better than fall semester."

He prods me in the thigh with his toes. "Hey, the good news is, you made it through the first year. Everyone always says all those intro courses are boring, no matter what your major is. You'll take more specialized classes and electives next year."

"I don't know if I like it enough to stick it out." I truly thought I'd like forensics, like my parents. I was decent at bio and chem and enjoy watching true-crime documentaries with Dad. But that passive interest hasn't translated to my coursework. Unlike Dad or my peers, I'm not passionate enough about it to make it my life.

"You could always switch majors if you really hate it," he suggests.

"That's my problem. I took all types of intro electives, like English and social sciences, and I still don't love anything. I've never had *a thing*, you know?"

"Sure you have. You're passionate about life," he says, like it's as useful a field as medicine or education.

I roll my eyes. "Come on, Tel. Life?"

"I've never met someone who goes through life with the kind of optimism that you have. You just let yourself enjoy things. Crappy situations don't faze you. I mean, you could be"—he gestures around vaguely—"sleeping in a murder motel and still have a smile on your face."

He's not wrong. I've aways tried to live optimistically, talk to as many people as I can, as much as I can. I've always understood life is fragile, even at a young age. I guess Mom dying made me that way.

"I'm not gonna lie, I hate this place. But if I let myself think about it too much, I'll shrivel up and cry," I admit. *And knowing I'm going to meet the love of my life softens the blow a little.* I'm tempted to say this to him, but refrain. It still doesn't feel like the right time to tell him.

"Exactly my point. I've always wished I could be like you," he says affectionately, running his finger over a loose thread in the blanket. "If I can find something I love, you can too."

That surprises me. Teller has always been so put together, so sure of himself and how he moves through the world. He's never struck me as wanting to be like anyone but himself, let alone me. "Really? You mean you don't enjoy being a grumpy old man?"

He flashes a rueful smile. "I mean, I don't wake up every morning trying to be negative. It just kind of happens."

"Speaking of grumpy old men, what's with the sleep mask and earplugs?" My attention snags on the crisp black sleep mask and unopened packet of fluorescent-orange earplugs neatly stacked on the side table between our beds.

"What do you mean? I need them to fall asleep, otherwise I'll be up all night."

"Doing what?"

"Lying there, staring into the abyss, stressing about everything and anything."

"Oh, Teller."

"You're lucky I didn't bring my portable fan," he informs me, shifting over to his bed. "I sleep with white noise too. Tonight, I think we'll listen to ocean sounds. We can pretend we're in a five-star hotel overlooking the Mediterranean."

"Hey, we will be. This time tomorrow," I remind him, snapping a quick photo of him bundled up on top of the musty covers in all his layers.

He notices my sneak photo, but doesn't say anything. "Well, not a five-star hotel."

"True. But nothing can be worse than this."

7

Teller is standing at the foot of the bed, hair all tousled and water-kissed from his shower, abs displayed in all their glory. Fresh droplets cling to each smooth contour, making the ridges of his stomach appear almost shiny as he stuffs his belongings haphazardly into his rucksack.

I should be packing too, but I'm tense, mesmerized by the twist and pull of the muscles in his back and biceps. What is this feeling? Am I . . . turned on?

No.

I am not having sexy thoughts about Teller Owens. My best friend. Basically, my brother. The same Teller who used to unclog toilets with me at The Cinema. The same Teller who has been madly in love with Sophie for the past three years.

I only snap out of it when he skewers me with yet another sharp look, the second in the last minute and a half.

Here's the deal: he's rightfully annoyed with me because we're Very Late. I assured him numerous times last night that I'd set my alarm to catch our flight, but made the rookie mistake of hitting *PM* instead of *AM*. We ended up sleeping in an extra half hour.

Thankfully, we make it on time. The moment we're in the air, Teller slaps his earphones in and closes his eyes. I don't push it. He needs some time to decompress, which is fine, because I fall asleep, definitely *not* having any more illicit thoughts about my best friend.

I jolt awake when the wheels touch ground in Venice. Maybe it's the shudder-inducing sound of rubber skidding against the asphalt, or maybe it's the prospect of meeting The One. Who can say?

A shooting pain radiates down my neck and into my right shoulder. When I open my eyes, the source becomes clear. My head is cocked to the right at an odd angle, nuzzled into something warm, yet firm. It's a shoulder. A shoulder belonging to Teller, who hates unnecessary human touch.

I jerk my head back to my personal bubble and panic-pat the side of my mouth for drool. He flashes me a reassuring expression that says *It's really no big deal.*

Just when I think our bad travel luck has ended, I'm proven wrong. Upon our arrival, we wait at the luggage carousel for a solid forty minutes until it becomes clear our baggage hasn't arrived with us. The airline gives us fifty-euro vouchers for our trouble, which don't go far at the overpriced souvenir shop.

"For one of the most fashion-forward countries in the world, I expected more," Teller whispers, tugging at his black T-shirt that reads Sorry, I can't. I have plans in Italy.

"What are you talking about? I'm a vision in this tracksuit." I managed to find an outfit with a massive yellow lemon across the chest that reads When life hands you lemons, make limoncello.

If anyone wondered if we were tourists, they sure know it now.

Despite a rocky start, the feeling of being on Venetian soil is special. As we make our way out of the airport, my shoulders drop, my jaw relaxes. All the tension from the past few days just falls away as I take in the Italian signage, the romantic hum of passersby, the sweet, saucy aromas emanating from the airport restaurants.

There's something about this place—I can feel it. It's a strange familiarity, like sinking into a chair custom designed to fit every groove and curve of your body. Like being in exactly the place I need to be. I'm going to meet the love of my life in Venice, I just know it.

I think about how Mom must have felt after having her vision. Did she look for The One around every corner like I am? Was she just as excited? Eager? Anxious? Did she *know* the moment her and Dad laid eyes on each other?

I'd be lying if I said I hadn't thought of every possible movie-worthy scenario for the meet-cute. Maybe he'll whiz by on his red Vespa, silky windswept hair flowing from his helmet, and do a double take. Perhaps he'll be a charming waiter with rolled-up white sleeves (showcasing rippling forearms) who doles out extra meatballs to children and senior citizens. Or maybe I'll pull a Cinderella, lose a shoe to the cobblestone, and he'll dutifully pursue me, risking life and limb in a treacherously busy intersection to return it.

I may or may not have gone so far as researching luxury wedding venues in Tuscany where we'll inevitably return for our future nuptials. Despite sharing in my excitement, Bianca is concerned I'm getting "way too ahead of myself." Maybe she's right. But when it comes to love, it's just what I do. I can't help it.

"How do you still look good and rested after a nine-hour flight?" Teller asks as we make our way to a stone pier to catch a water taxi. I'm taken aback for a moment. Did he say I looked good, unshowered and in this hideous tracksuit?

"I had a good nap," I say, taking a long, purposeful inhale of the salty air, mesmerized by the dark water lapping against the side of the worn wooden mooring poles. I have half a mind to twirl around, arms outstretched, but I refrain.

As we motor toward the heart of Venice, it becomes clear the city is more than just the main canal you see on TV. It's made up entirely of channels, both wide and narrow, all connected by stone bridges, some more ornate than others. The buildings are tall, ancient, and enchantingly decayed. All appear to be slanted or uneven, which only adds to the charm. There's something about Venice that's magical, like I'm walking into my own dream.

The hostel Teller preapproved is located across from a tiny cathedral. It's a small three-story building painted clementine orange with green shutters adorning high arched windows. Under each sits a rectangular flower box with assorted wildflowers.

"See? Nice for a hostel, isn't it?" I ask. Next to the building appears to be a small restaurant with a patio. Bright-blue umbrellas fan out over each table, adding a pop of color. At one sits a posh-looking couple enjoying a romantic seafood dinner. The other side is a postcard-perfect gelato shop with a canary-striped awning. Teller and I pause in awe of the gelato. It has artful swirls and is sprinkled with cookies, nuts, berries, and even Parisian macarons.

I can tell he's impressed, though he won't admit it.

~

"I forgot how . . . small a single mattress is," Teller says. He scratches his head and turns it sideways, as though calculating how we'll both fit on there tonight.

We didn't book a reservation in advance, so I suppose this is our fault.

Admittedly, it looks quite dire. Scientifically speaking, it's barely wide enough to fit a kid comfortably. There's no way we won't be on top of each other. My nerves whir and hum from head to toe just thinking about it.

To add insult to injury, we're sharing a room with four strangers, which Teller is not keen on (because they could do weird shit at night, like watch us sleep, or steal our stuff). But I'm not letting this hiccup ruin the day. Besides, as I remind Teller, we have no belongings to steal.

It takes some serious trial and error to fall asleep, positioning ourselves in the least intrusive way. We settle turned butt to butt. It's strange, sleeping with my backside pressed into his, being lulled to sleep by the warmth of his body, the rise and fall of his breath. Unfortunately, it's near impossible to stay asleep over the creak of mattresses, the sound of zippers opening and closing, and the jingle of keys, which is why I'm lying here texting Bianca.

Bianca: OMG those Venice pics. 😭😭😭 So sad I'm not there. Ugh.

Lo: wish you were here too!! if it makes you feel better, at least you're not sharing a SINGLE bed with a very tall adult male.

Bianca: ????

I snap a quick picture, though my flash is on and it disturbs Teller. I hold my breath, worried I've woken him up as he flips over, facing me. He's still asleep, breath steady, sending goose bumps skating across the back of my neck.

Lo: there were no available doubles.

Bianca: So you and Teller are sharing a single bed??? That's weird.

Lo: it's not. would me and u sharing a bed be weird? No.

Bianca: That's different.

Lo: how?

Bianca: Because. It just is.

Lo: it really isn't, i swear!!

Should it be weird? It really isn't. In fact, it's peaceful, until the hard tune of Cardi B rings through the air. I squint through the darkness, trying to find the source. Finally, Veronica, the friendly hippie girl in the opposite bunk, sits up, the screen of her phone lighting up the room. "Hey, Mills!" she squeals into the phone. At Veronica's shrill, Teller startles, nearly rolling right off the top bunk when he realizes he's spooning me.

"Shit. Sorry, I—I thought you were—" He doesn't have to finish the sentence for me to know he was going to say Sophie's name.

"It's fine," I whisper. "I'm just glad you got some sleep."

"Barely. Maybe twenty minutes?"

We listen to Veronica's conversation for a couple more minutes before Teller lets out a loud sigh.

Her phone is so loud, you can basically hear whoever is on the other side. As she slowly puts her socks on, she tells "Mills" all about her adventure in Pisa. I'm praying she'll go outside to take the call, but instead she stands right outside the bedroom, door ajar. Her voice is almost drowned out by the sound of the guy in the bunk below us gorging on chips, bag crunching with each movement.

"I'm sorry, again. I really messed up," I say into the darkness. I know he's hating life even if he's trying to pretend like he's not.

He doesn't respond. He just turns on his back and stares at the ceiling, which is so low, we can't fully sit up without hitting our heads. I lean over to check if he's wearing his earplugs to drown out the many noises.

He's not. He's just mad. I can tell by the way he's breathing. Long, slow breaths, like he taught me on the plane yesterday. He's trying to calm himself down.

"I know you wanted this whole trip to be impromptu and spontaneous, but it's not working for me," he finally utters.

It's completely fair. Planning day by day sounds whimsical and romantic in theory, but really, it's just a lot of stressing over logistics. It would be nice to know where we're sleeping or which train to board.

I feel terrible and generally disappointed in myself. I should have planned better, anticipated what Teller would need to make this enjoyable for him.

"I totally understand if you want to go home—"

He rolls toward me. "I'm not ditching you in Italy, Lo. But you do need to promise me one thing."

"What?"

"I get to plan the rest of the logistics. We need some level of structure," he says.

I turn into the side of his chest, grateful, and maybe a little bit optimistic that this trip will be what I'd hoped. Maybe it'll bridge that gap that's been growing between us since last year.

So I don't hesitate to say, "Deal."

8

I can't be certain, but I think Teller regrets agreeing to stay. He's been in bed, thumbing through his phone for the past half hour after getting a ball of hair stuck between his toes in the shower and nearly passing out.

I need to salvage this, and quick. Once we're dressed, I drag Teller to the courtyard for breakfast. It's a charming common area for the guests to mingle, time-worn walls trailing with ivy and potted plants cascading from the balconies. Among the few sets of wrought iron tables and chairs are five people, happily chatting.

First to introduce themselves are Ernest and Posie Crosby from the UK. They're a salt-and-pepper-haired couple in matching khaki bucket hats and vests with an obscene number of pockets. We learn that they're retired schoolteachers. Years ago, they started a tradition of taking a vacation every summer based on a destination they pull out of a hat, which is frankly adorable. They've continued on into retirement, although they joke they're running out of destinations they can afford on pensions. I'd wrongfully assumed most backpackers would be young, but they're both energetic and celebrating their thirtieth wedding anniversary.

"Actually, babe, it's our thirty-first," Posie corrects, giving Ernest a swift swat on the chest.

Jenny Kumar and Riley James from Pittsburgh join our conversation. They're twentysomething-year-old best friends celebrating Riley's college graduation. Jenny looks like your stereotypical backpacker in worn hiking boots, wrists stacked with woven bracelets—badges of honor from her extensive travels. Riley appears a little more artsy and eclectic in a linen dress with a beaded belt.

I can't help but notice how Teller's eye keeps wandering in Riley's direction. One look at her tall, slender frame and elegant features and it's clear Riley is totally Teller's type. She's casually beautiful in an understated, quietly confident way, with clear, makeup-less skin, fiery auburn waves, and kind eyes a warm shade of hazel—the type that probably changes color based on the weather.

"Are you two newlyweds or something?" Lionel Jones, an unfairly handsome guy from Atlanta asks, gesturing toward us. He's here on a solo trip.

Teller swings me a sideways look, and we simultaneously burst into laughter. "No, not at all. We're best friends. Just friends," I say loudly to make the point. "We met back in high school working at a movie theater. I've always wanted to visit Italy. My mom came here with my aunt when they were the same age. I was planning to come with my friend Bianca, but she shattered her foot, so I begged Teller to come with me. He just came off a breakup and—"

Teller clears his throat. "Anyway, it's nice to meet you all," he says quickly, before I can divulge all our deepest secrets.

It's true what they say about making friends at hostels. I'm obsessed with everyone already (including Ernest and Posie), and I already don't want to go our separate ways. Jenny and Riley are even nice enough to let me borrow their clothes so I don't have to walk around in my lemon tracksuit.

We spend the day wandering around the canal. We end up at a seafood restaurant for lunch that's got spectacular views but below-average food. Still, we drink, laugh, and wander some more. By late afternoon, we've gone to at least four different pubs and swapped travel itineraries. Coincidentally, Jenny and Riley are also heading to Rome in a few days and share the name of their hostel. Teller carefully records all this information in a color-coded Google Calendar. He's taking the planning duties seriously.

When we return to the courtyard for a break, I notice Teller's eye wander to Riley again. She's stretched on the chaise, reading *Eat, Pray, Love.*

I give Teller a swift elbow in the ribs. "Hey, you should go talk to Riley."

He eyes me like I've suggested he cannonball into the canal. "Why?"

"I saw you checking her out. She's the perfect rebound."

He glances wistfully at her again, like a freshman gawking at their upperclassman crush. "She would never go for me."

"Tel, you don't give yourself enough credit. You have abs now." I poke him in the stomach to prove my point. It's so hard, I might as well have poked metal.

He quirks his brow. "When did you see my abs?"

On at least four occasions since this trip started. But who's counting? "Every time you lift your shirt to take something out of your money belt." His cheeks turn a dark shade of crimson. "Don't be ashamed. You worked hard for them. They deserve to be seen and fawned over by the world."

Teller both doesn't know how to take a compliment and isn't used to them. So he just ignores it entirely. "It doesn't change the fact that I don't know how to talk to women."

"You're talking to me right now."

"Okay, but you're not—" He stops himself.

"A woman? Wow. Thanks." I'm half teasing, but I can't help but feel a twinge in my chest.

"That's not what I meant. What I was going to say is, I'm comfortable with you because I know you. I don't do well striking up conversations with strangers."

"I was a stranger when we first met."

"And how did my first impression go over?" he asks, a brief smile playing across his lips.

I snort, recalling how uptight he was. "But we survived, terrible first impressions aside. It's really not that hard. Practice with me." I extend my hand theatrically and try to make my voice soft and dainty like Riley's. "Hi, I'm Riley. What's your name again?"

He looks horrified by my improv but goes along with it. "Teller."

"That's a unique name."

"I'm named after the OB that delivered me," he explains. "My mom was in labor for fifty hours before having an emergency C-section. So when the nurse asked what my name was, she said the first name she could think of in her delirium. Dr. Teller." He follows that up with awkward eye contact and total silence. Smooth, Tel. Before I can call him out, he waves a dismissive hand. "Okay, no more. This is too weird."

I roll my eyes. "It's only weird if you make it weird. Just don't bring up your birth story. Nothing about germs. Talk about the present. Something about travel. Italy. Ask what she's most excited about seeing. There's endless possibilities. You'll be vibing in no time," I say enthusiastically, tamping down the tiniest budding kernel that feels suspiciously like jealousy. But it can't be. Jealousy. If anything, I want Teller to have this moment with Riley. He needs a distraction from Sophie.

He tugs at the collar of his shirt, panning around at his surroundings. "Okay. Fine. But if I humiliate myself, you owe me dinner."

"Deal."

Reluctantly, he makes his way over to Riley. Over the chatter of passersby, he says, "Hot out here, huh?" At least he's trying. I'm proud of him—until he adds, "I'm basically dripping sweat."

Oh, sweet summer child, Teller.

It's not like I'm some expert flirt. But I know that talking about sweating isn't exactly a great conversation starter. He knows it, too, because he starts sweating even more.

"Me too! I seriously need a shower," Riley says, surprisingly not grossed out. She's smiling, and Teller's shoulders relax.

It's strange, seeing Teller flirt. Successfully. On some level, I knew he had game. He was in a long-term relationship. But after so many years of him only having eyes for Sophie, charming a total stranger in front of me is foreign territory. Suddenly feeling like a creep for eavesdropping, I distract myself by kicking back with Lionel. He offers me half his croissant, and suddenly I'm divulging my life story, excluding the whole soulmate thing. Instead, I give him a sanitized version about how I'm on the hunt for rom-com-worthy love. He hangs on my every word.

"I've already met the love of my life," he tells me, mouth softening in a slight upturn, his dark eyes lighting up at the mere thought of him. "His name is Paul. We met in the most romantic way. Definitely rom-com material."

"Do tell!"

"We were both at CVS. I was buying a jumbo bottle of Pepto-Bismol, and he was looking for Magnums," he says, and we both descend into laughter.

"He was supposed to come on this trip with me, but he ditched to spend the summer in New York doing a fancy publishing internship. Would have been nice to have him with me, you know, in case anyone gives me any trouble."

My brow shoots up. "Trouble?"

"In case you didn't notice, I'm Black. Traveling alone in a foreign country can be, well, you know." He pauses and swallows. "I don't always know how I'm going to be perceived when I go places."

I dip my chin, empathizing with him. "Ugh, I'm sorry you have to deal with that."

He shrugs. "So far, everyone seems friendly here. But you never know. Ignorance can happen anywhere. Like, I once went to Germany, and the bellhop at my hotel kept calling me Will because he somehow decided I looked like Will Smith."

"With all due respect to Will Smith, you look nothing alike. You are way hotter," I point out.

He clutches his chest. "Oh my god. Thank you for saying that."

"But that's horrible. This isn't as bad, but one time I tagged along with my dad on a work trip to the Netherlands, and our taxi driver asked me, *Where are you really from?* when I said I was American."

Lionel shakes his head. "See? This is what I'm saying. I always have to second-guess if someone is being rude because they're just an asshat or because of another reason." He tosses his head back in a sigh. "It would have been nice to have Paul here, at least."

"I almost came alone too. My friend broke her foot. But luckily, I forced him to come with me," I say, turning toward Teller. He was still swept up in conversation with Riley.

"He's hot. In a hottest-guy-in-the-chess-club kinda way. You sure he's not your soulmate?"

"He's my best friend. And I think he might be flirting?" I can only bear witness to the interaction for a couple more moments before it starts to feel a little weird.

Lionel agrees they're indeed flirting, and suggests we give Teller and Riley some private time. We sneak some complimentary biscotti and lemon-infused water from the fancy hotel next door and sip it under the awning. It's shaded, thank gosh. The Italian sun is no joke, even by late afternoon. I have major boob sweat.

Fatigue aside, I take a good long look at everyone who passes by, wondering whether they're my person.

Once we've cooled off, Lionel wanders across the street to take selfies on the idyllic cobblestone bridge. "Do you mind taking my pic?"

"Sure, no problem." I leave the comfort of my shaded area to take his photo, even lying on the hot ground to get a good shot.

"As my vacation wifey, I feel compelled to warn you: if you get my double chin, I'll consider it a violation of trust," he warns, checking every couple pictures to ensure the angle is optimal.

Keen to return to shade, I do a swift backward shuffle to the middle of the street to capture some quick full-body shots. Just when I'm about to take the last picture, there's a noisy rumble, followed by the rattle of metal clanking against concrete. Before I can identify the source, a deep voice bellows, "Watch out!"

I snap my neck to the left. And that's when I see it. A runaway trolley filled with luggage, hurtling down the cobblestone slope straight toward me.

9

This is it. This is how it ends.

Goodbye, sweet world. It's been a decent run. There's nothing to do but accept it, and maybe laugh at my cause of death: crushed like a pancake by a trolley of luggage. Funny how my death will be more remarkable than my actual life.

Let me set the scene. I'm frozen like a gangly deer on a busy highway, eyes squeezed shut, bracing myself to become roadkill. Because who wants to bear witness to their own brutal flattening? I hope it's quick and painless, at least.

Then, without notice, a statuesque blur darts in and shoves me backward, flat on my ass.

From here on, everything happens in slo-mo. The ripple and ridge of a muscled back visible under a moisture-wicking T-shirt that's strained to the max. It's truly a religious experience, catching the pulse and pull of each muscle as the figure stops the trolley with sheer brute force, rooting it in place. I've never seen such a specimen in real life.

And that's when he turns around and changes life as I know it.

If you look up *Lo Zhao-Jensen's type*, this guy's face, and let's be honest, whole body, would be it. Sure, Mark B. also has a killer physique, but this guy has the full package. In fact, his face should be under federal protection, forever preserved behind temperature-controlled glass for future generations to worship.

He's a rugged kind of handsome that sets him apart, with a jawline so angular, even under all that scruff, it could surely cut glass. As could his tanned cheekbones, dusted with light freckles from the sun. I'm positive his entire essence was etched by the gods. His slightly bulbous nose, pillowy lips, and a small scar above his thick right brow are the only qualities that make him look faintly approachable.

"Are you okay?" His deep baritone voice tickles my insides like a feather duster. As he leans closer, I'm overcome by a familiar scent. It's sweet, with deep, nutty notes of vanilla. Familiar. Too familiar. Exactly like in my vision.

I blink, mouth hanging wide open. This is the dude who saved my life. Marvel superhero–style. "I—uh—I—"

"Are you hurt?" he asks, running a hand through wavy, sun-bleached hair that's long enough to pull into a man bun.

I shake my head. My tailbone is throbbing from the impact and my elbow is bloody. But breathing in his earthy, chocolate-espresso scent proves an excellent painkiller.

He grins, nearly blinding me with his pearly whites. "Think you can stand?"

"I'll try."

By now, there are about ten people crowded around us. I think I spot Ernest and Posie, but their faces blur entirely when my rescuer reaches to help me up. His hand is nearly twice the size of my super sweaty palm, and the contact nearly turns all the bones in my body to Jell-O.

"I'm Caleb," he informs me as he pulls me to my own two feet.

Caleb.

"Pleasure to meet you, Caleb," I say in a strange movie accent.

"Do you have a name?" he asks, the corner of his lips teasing a smile.

There's something about his face that strikes a familiar chord, deep down in my gut. It's just like the feeling I had when we landed in Venice, like I've seen him before. But I haven't. The sensation is so overpowering, I barely register his question. "Uh, I think so," I answer, still with the weird accent.

"Are you staying here? At the Royal?" he asks when I fail to tell him my name.

I squeeze my eyes into a squint, making a concerted effort to force away the accent. *Be normal, Lo.* "Oh god no. I'm not fancy enough for that. I'm next door. At Doge's Delight. For the next two days."

"Me too!" he says with a charming wink. "Anyway, I gotta go check in. But looks like I'll be seeing you around, *girl with no name.*"

He flashes one last smile over his shoulder and my body is no longer my own. I want to bottle his image so I can remember it for all of eternity.

Before I can muster a response, Teller comes rushing out of the hostel. "Lo! Are you okay?"

"Better than okay," I say with full confidence. I just met The One.

10

Not to sound cocky, but I don't get nervous around guys.

I'm comfortable making the first move, striking up conversation, or smiling at a cute stranger. But there's something about Caleb that makes me blush like a schoolgirl. He isn't just a random person. He's my soulmate, a guy who came out of nowhere and literally saved my life, which is why walking up to him and making small talk is frankly terrifying. It feels bigger. High stakes. Like my entire future rests on it. The Soulmate Effect.

When he smiles at me in the hostel courtyard, my first instinct is to hide my face in Teller's hoodie. And when I spot him alone at breakfast the next morning, I'm rendered mute. My heart patters when he spots me with my Greek yogurt. I'm also alone. Teller likes to sleep in. Unlike me, Caleb is wholly at ease, munching on a decadent chocolate croissant, long legs outstretched under the table, one ropey arm slung over the back of the chair beside him. He's a Disney prince in the flesh, even gently dropping crumbs for a tiny bird hopping around his table. When he flashes me a megawatt smile, I nearly topple out of my chair.

Maybe it's the sun, but my entire body spikes with heat. I force myself to maintain eye contact like a functioning human, finally mumbling something along the lines of "Hihowareyou?" at 2x speed. The moment the words come out of my mouth, two tiny birds start squawking, fighting over a crumb between our tables.

Caleb's lips curve up as he snickers, theatrically placing a hand around the shell of his ear. "Sorry, I didn't catch that?"

"I said—" Before I can complete the sentence, the birds go at it again. "Sorry, the birds are—"

Squawk, squawk.

It's as though nature is trying to spare me the embarrassment. I can't help but laugh at myself, but mostly because Caleb is laughing, too, beautiful smile flashing.

He starts to pull his chair closer, and then abruptly stops. I wonder what I've done wrong until the overwhelming scent of coconut sunscreen floods my nostrils. Teller's arm reaches over my shoulder and swipes my yogurt. "Lo, you're lactose intolerant. You don't want to be sick or gassy on our first day of the tour," Teller warns, plunking down into the open seat across from me.

RIP me.

Of course, the pesky little birds choose now to be silent.

"Tel," I say through a wince, flashing him a silent *please stop talking* look.

My warning tone doesn't register. He continues on, oblivious, "I know you hate when I bring it up, but remember when you threw up in my car—" And this is yet another reason we are *just friends.* Only platonic friends talk about each other's bodily functions so freely.

"I have Lactaid," I say through clenched teeth, nearly crushing a full water bottle with my fist. I fix my stare at the water dripping on the table, unable to muster the strength to look at Caleb. Teller busts out his map of Venice and highlights our route for today's walking tour. I nod along, pretending to listen. Inside, I'm praying for another runaway trolley to finish me off once and for all.

~

"I found him," I croak, hiding under the blankets on the bunk bed. We're heading out for our walking tour soon, but I needed a quick pep talk from my aunts. It's only four in the morning back home, so naturally, Mei didn't pick up. Thankfully, Ellen did. Maisey has been waking up at "cruel hours" the past few days.

"Already? You've only been there for—" Ellen shouts over a high-pitched shriek in the background. "Maisey! What did I tell you about eating the remote? You're gonna break your teeth," she screeches.

I hold in a laugh when Maisey lets out a howl, presumably devastated that Ellen has taken the remote away.

"Sorry! That child needs an exorcism. She doesn't get it from me," Ellen whispers. "Anyway, tell me about him!"

I tell her all about Caleb, describing his muscles in vivid detail, followed by the story of how he saved my life with the trolley. It all sounds very cinematic when I say it out loud. "It's kind of wild how ridiculously good looking he is. Like, he is so far out of my league, it's hilarious."

"Why are you so shocked? Did you think your soulmate was gonna be a troll?"

"I mean, no. But I didn't expect someone who looks like an A-list movie star."

"How old is he?"

"My age . . . I think. I don't know. I haven't had much of a chance to chat with him yet, to be honest. After it all happened, I was too shocked to even tell him my name. And then this morning I tried talking to him, but these birds kept interrupting. And then Teller came out and started lecturing me about eating yogurt because I'm lactose intolerant. Kill me now."

A witchy cackle erupts. "That's embarrassing. But you can't let that get in the way of destiny. Besides, if he's your future person, he better get used to bodily functions. Farting and all."

She keeps laughing while I will myself to sink into the mattress and disappear. "Do you think the universe is trying to tell me this isn't going to work out?"

"Sometimes the universe likes to mess with us. It can't just give us exactly what we want, when we want it."

"Why not?" I whine.

"Because what's the fun in that? Life would be pretty boring if we got whatever we wanted, when we wanted it, right?"

"I can't say I agree. Serve it to me on a platter. I'm exhausted already."

"You're exhausted already? Good luck adulting, hon." Ellen laughs. "But honestly, kid? Don't sweat it. It's not like you'll end up like Cousin Lin or anything—" She slaps her hand over her mouth.

I can't help but laugh. I was planning to broach the subject strategically, but her big mouth has a mind of its own. "Okay, so what's the deal with Cousin Lin? Why was Mei so weird about her the other morning?"

"I'm not sure what you're talking about," she says robotically. Ellen is a terrible liar.

"Oh, come on. You can't keep me in the dark. Was Lin like, cursed or something?"

"Basically," she says, caving immediately.

My stomach free-falls. "Wait, what? She was actually cursed?"

"No, no! Cursed isn't really the right word. It's more of a . . . consequence." That doesn't sound any less forbidding or terrifying.

I straighten my spine. "A consequence? Of what?"

"Well, any Zhao woman who doesn't end up with their soulmate ends up alone, miserable, and subject to a lifetime of bad luck," she informs me, far too casually.

A cough spews out of me. "Alone and miserable? Why am I only finding out about this now?"

"Because it's so rare. And Mei didn't want to scare you—which is ridiculous, in my opinion. Because you won't end up like that. Forever alone and whatnot." Her tone is still way too relaxed for my liking.

Goose bumps erupt on my arms. "So wait, what happened to Lin?"

"She despised the man she was supposed to be with, Glen. He was a real loser. Not a nice guy, according to your grandmother. So she broke things off, decided she'd rather be alone than be with him. And that's when the bad luck began."

"What kind of bad luck are we talking about? Getting pooped on by a bird? Getting caught in the rain? A drawn-out, painful death?"

"Well, the day after she broke things off, she got hit by a bus while riding her bike."

I gasp. "A bus?! Was she okay?"

"She broke a bunch of bones, but she survived. Then, a couple years later, her house flooded and she lost everything. A few years after that, she tried to start a restaurant, but it failed and she was left in financial ruin. Had to move in with us, actually, for a few years. I remember her sleeping in the guest room when I was around eight before she could afford her own place. To top it all off, she never found love again. We invited her for dinner all the time, but she'd refuse. Your grandmother always said she was too proud."

I cringe. A series of images flashes through my mind. Eating dinner alone. Watching movies alone. Traveling to foreign countries all by my lonesome. Just like Dad, when I'm not around. "That's the most depressing thing I've ever heard."

She nods. "But don't worry, you won't end up like them."

"Who's them? I thought we were just talking about Cousin Lin? Did this happen to someone else?"

"Apparently, your First Great-Aunt Shu. The details are fuzzy. She lived across the country, so no one was all that close with her."

"What happened?"

"Similar story. Died alone, broke and eternally lonely. But don't worry, Lo," she adds, her tone turning optimistic a little too quickly. "It's only happened twice in our whole family history."

"Is that supposed to reassure me?" Up until a few days ago, I was the only woman in the family who hadn't inherited the gift. I'm no stranger to being the exception.

"Things will pick up with Caleb; you'll see. What's the plan for today?" she asks, promptly ignoring my question.

"Um, we're doing a walking tour around Venice," I explain. "Then we're going on those gondola rides through the canal tonight."

She cradles her right cheek. "Sounds like the perfect opportunity for romance."

~

I'm still weary from Teller's comments for the majority of the morning and, frankly, a little shook by my conversation with Ellen. How did I not know about the consequences of not ending up with my soulmate? I can't help but feel a little offended that my aunts would keep something like this from me. That up until a few days ago, they thought I'd be another cautionary tale.

Despite Ellen's optimism, I'm not out of the woods yet. I actually need to talk to Caleb to seal the deal. By the time we've completed our glassblowing demonstration and the tour of Saint Mark's Basilica, most of the humiliation and shock has faded.

Maybe it's a by-product of doing embarrassing things on the regular. It's also easy to forget your problems when you're in one of the most beautiful cities in the world on a tour with all your newest hostel friends—including your soulmate (Posie invited him)—exactly where your mom was thirty years before. And when you're looking at Venetian Gothic architecture dating back to the 1400s.

Our tour guide, Gia, is a tiny, spiky-haired woman. She's a force to be reckoned with, navigating crowds like a total boss.

"If I were a flavor, I'd be espresso cream because I like to keep things high energy," she told our group. She's not lying. She practically vibrates as she speaks, moving her hands in all manner of directions. It's proving infectious; we're all bright-eyed and hanging on every word about how her great-grandfather, a former opera singer, started their tour company out of pure passion for sharing their culture with the world.

We take a quick break in the shady square, mostly for Ernest's and Posie's sakes. They're understandably exhausted and spritzing each other with water bottles. According to Jenny's Fitbit, we've walked fifteen thousand steps today.

As Gia goes on about Venice's 300 bridges that connect all 116 islands, I spy Caleb leaning against an ornate column, smiling and tapping his foot to a street performer playing the accordion.

Now's your chance to talk to him. You can do this, Lo. The only thing standing in the way is my own insecurity.

"Lo," I say, surprised that my legs have carried my body this far.

He tears his eyes from Accordion Guy and looks at me. I can't help but stare at the dusting of freckles clustered over the bridge of his nose. "Sorry, what?"

"Lo. It's my name. Short for Loren," I tell him, mentally patting myself on the back for uttering a sentence to him in my normal voice. *Must stay cool and avoid saying something terribly inappropriate.*

His lips curve into a smirk, which instantly puts me at ease. "Look at that, girl with no name does have a name. Nice to officially meet you, Lo. I'm Caleb."

"Oh, I know." I cringe. That sounded super creepy. "Because you told me yesterday. When you saved my life," I add.

He waves his hand like he's pushing my words away. "Ah, it was nothing."

"You say that like you go around saving people from being flattened regularly."

His eyes skim the gaggle of tourists weaving around us. "That was a first. Though, wait. I did actually save a woman from falling off a ski lift in Mont-Tremblant. Caught her by the collar."

The image of him saving someone with his brute strength makes me weak in the knees. I shake one sandaled foot out to get the blood circulating. "See? You've saved two lives. You're basically a superhero."

"Eh, not quite. I kind of threw my back out a little with the trolley," he admits, doing a stiff stretch side to side.

"Oh shit. I'm so sorry—"

"Hey, it's okay. You were too beautiful not to save." He flashes me a megawatt smile. "Damn. That was cheesy, wasn't it?"

"The cheesiest," I say. I can't help but giggle over the accordion's cheerful tune.

"Is it too late to take it back?"

"Unfortunately. But I'll take the compliment," I say bashfully. I'm air punching on the inside. Caleb thinks I'm beautiful.

Caleb.

Thinks.

I'm.

Beautiful.

I log this moment. The heat of the beating sun. The vibrant melody of the accordion. The synchronized clapping from the audience. This fizzy feeling in my chest, like a balloon expanding at a breakneck pace. "I owe you, though," I say coolly, leaning against the stone pillar. I'm finally starting to feel more like myself.

He runs a hand over his square jaw, pretending to be in deep thought. "Well, if you insist. I'll take payment in the form of food."

"You're a foodie, huh?"

"Sweets, in particular. I'd do unsettling things for a good panna cotta."

"I've never had it."

His eyes widen like dinner plates. "Oh, sweetheart. You haven't lived until you've had panna cotta. I discovered it when I did Florence last week. Niccolo's panna cotta. You have to go." *When I did Florence.* Teller would die.

"We're going to Florence after Rome, actually. What's so special about it?"

"So most panna cotta is all about rich, velvety creaminess. But Niccolo's has this caramelized layer on top with a berry compote. It's the perfect blend of tart and sweet. Like pure heaven in your mouth."

"Wow, you're really hyping this up." I can't help but smile at how animated he is over a dessert. I probably can't eat it without becoming violently ill. I don't mention that part, though.

"Absolutely. I mean, it's one of those small things that make the experience. Even if you don't speak the same language, food is still universal. It's tradition, history, custom in itself. And best of all, it brings people together."

"I was just saying to my aunt before I came here that I was most excited to try the food."

"Hey, that's my type of travel. That's why I keep coming back to Italy. That and I'm Italian," he says proudly.

"How many times have you been here?"

"Twice with my family. And then I started my travels here a year ago and couldn't wait to come back."

"A year ago?"

"Oh yeah. I haven't been home for a year."

"You said you're from Ottawa, right?" I ask, though I definitely know the answer.

He nods. "Technically. But I like to think the world is my home now." His face lights up even brighter as he tells me about the places he's been. Australia and New Zealand, and parts of Asia. He's also done seemingly everything, from swimming with sharks in the Pacific to meditating with monks in Tibet.

Two things dawn on me as he describes how delicious scorpion on a stick is in Vietnam: First, that he seems so much older than me. And second, my life has been so sheltered compared to his. "I'm starting to think I haven't truly lived until now. I haven't traveled anywhere," I admit.

"What's stopping you?"

I think about that. "My dad was an army brat growing up. He moved all over the place as a kid and hated it, so travel just wasn't something we did. Just a bit in-country. And there's also money. Things are a little tighter since I started college."

"It's not cheap to travel, even when you live frugally. It's definitely a privilege I don't take for granted," he admits. "But I make it work, mostly by picking up odd jobs here and there. When I was in Australia, I taught surfing. Worked on a sheep farm for a while in New Zealand too."

I let out an embarrassingly loud shriek. "That's my literal dream. I love sheep." I recall a girl at the animal shelter talking about working at a sheep farm in New Zealand. She told me and another volunteer all about the rolling green hills, the ever-present mist, and how they fed baby lambs bottles at night.

"They're cute, but they're a nuisance." He holds up his finger, which seems to be missing a tiny chunk along the side. "One named Tilly got me."

"Jeez, that looks painful."

"Oh yeah. She was a cutie so I forgave her, just like I'll forgive you for messing up my back." He shoots me a disarming wink. "But aside from working, I keep my expenses low. I only have with me what I really need. Turns out, it's easy to part with a lot of shit once you carry it on your back for months at a time. I actually ditched half of what I brought with me initially."

"Wow, I can't imagine throwing my things away."

"It's just material stuff," he says with a shrug. "There's something really freeing about shedding the deadweight, traveling with only the essentials, and trusting yourself to get from point A to point B. I also don't have any bills, no phone or anything."

I cough. "Wait, you don't even have a phone?" Who is this unicorn?

"Ditched my phone after my first month of travel. If I need to get in touch with family or friends, most hostels have a computer you can use."

When I cracked my phone screen, I had to go without it for an entire week while Dad's tech friend repaired it. And the whole time, I found my hands reaching for it constantly like an addict. Relief surged through me when I finally held it again. But Caleb looks so relaxed, so untethered by the shackles of modern society, but not in a pretentious way.

"I just can't imagine not having it. For safety, even."

"I get it. It's a privilege to not feel like I need it. I mean, I'd never let my sister go on a trip like this without a phone. Sorry—I hope that doesn't sound sexist or anything."

"No! I mean, male privilege is just a reality," I say. "But what do you do if you need directions? Or information about something?"

Caleb shrugs. "The old-fashioned way. Ask people for directions. And paper maps and brochures. It's been the best decision of my life, honestly. It's wild how much more I notice when I'm not glued to my phone."

God, this guy is so cool. He could probably stand in the middle of Saint Mark's Square singing "Baby Shark" and still look undeniably cool.

"So how long are you traveling before you head home?"

He leans back against the column next to me, eyes trained ahead as the street performer packs up his accordion. "Not sure. I'm supposed to go home at the end of the summer for school. I deferred my history program for a year. So if I don't go back, I'd have to reapply. But honestly, I don't know if I even want to go to college." *Wait. Are we the same person?*

"I'm considering deferring too—well, taking a leave, actually, or dropping out entirely," I confess. It feels freakin' amazing to finally say that to someone who understands.

"Really?"

"I've really tried to love it. I've taken so many different courses but just don't like anything enough to pay so much money. It's not that I want to close the door on college, but I want to have a better idea of what I want to study before I spend that much coin."

"That makes total sense. It feels like such a waste of the best time of our lives, you know? I bet I've learned a hell of a lot more in my year traveling than I'd ever learn in some dim lecture hall. Abiding by traditional markers of success just seems like a recipe for unhappiness, you know? I mean, having that dream job and money only makes you happy for so long. Once you have your basic needs and a little extra to enjoy life, happiness is probably pretty stagnant." I nod in vigorous agreement. "So does that mean you're sticking around Europe for a while?" he asks.

"Just a month," I say. "Going to Rome from here, then Florence. And then who knows. I wanted to leave things flexible . . . well, as flexible as Teller will tolerate."

He smirks, nodding toward Teller, who's squinting down at his phone. "He seems like a guy who abides by a schedule."

"Oh yeah. But I need that. Otherwise, I wouldn't know what I'm doing or where I'm going day to day. He's got a whole itinerary planned for us in Rome."

His eyes light up. "A full schedule, eh? Well, I'm happy to show you guys around Rome if you want, give you a more authentic experience. Show you some places off the beaten path. I'm no expert by any means, but—"

"Yes!" I practically scream. "You're more than welcome to join us, if you don't already have plans." I have an immediate pang of guilt. I probably should have checked with Teller first. But I'm sure he won't mind, seeing as Jenny and Riley already basically invited themselves to Rome with us.

Caleb smiles, flashing his perfect teeth. "I don't have a schedule for exactly this reason, so I can go with the flow. And trust me, one week in Rome and you will fall in love."

I think you're probably right.

"Anyway, we better get back to the group." He tilts his chin in their direction. "It was cool chatting with you. Really cool. I just said *cool* like, five times, didn't I?" he says, cheeks flushed in the most endearing way.

"Three," I correct.

"You're weirdly easy to talk to."

Of course I am. We're soulmates, after all. No big deal.

I want to tell him. But I refrain. This is going so well. The last thing I want is to prematurely scare the crap out of him with the psychic business. "So are you."

A beat goes by and we're just standing there, smiling at each other. It feels like a movie scene, a slo-mo moment when the light hits just right. The moment you just *know* this person is going to be in your life in a big way.

"You excited for tonight?" he asks.

I try to recall our group's itinerary for the evening, but my brain is basically mush at this point. "What's tonight again?"

"The most romantic activity in all of Italy. Gondola rides."

11

Caleb is right. There's nothing more romantic than a gondola ride at sunset in Venice.

Everything about it screams romance. The main canal is cast in warm, orange sunlight, the calm water reflecting it like fireflies. Handcrafted wooden gondolas are stationed in neat rows, all handled by young, fit Italian men in classic red-and-white-striped shirts.

I can picture it now—the moment Caleb and I fall in love. It will be like the movies as we float under the majestic Rialto Bridge.

As though fate knew I needed a win, our rucksacks were waiting at the hostel when we returned from the walking tour. Teller nearly teared up using his own toothbrush and wearing his slippers for the first time in days. And while I'm grateful to have my floral shift dress with dramatic ruffle sleeves for tonight (Bianca says it elongates my legs), I think about what Caleb said about being happier without material things. Making do with less. I can't help but feel silly for packing so much.

Our group crowds along the dock, waiting to board the gondolas, which appear to seat two at a time. Caleb is chatting with Posie. He's dressed in a snug Henley that accentuates his muscles. I'm sure he could give these fit gondola drivers a run for their money.

He waves me over. "Wow, you look incredible."

"You told me to expect romance," I say, nodding toward the empty boat to our right. "Are we taking this boat?"

"I would absolutely love to. It's just—" He nervously runs a hand over the back of his neck, and my heart nearly falls out of my body. He's about to tell me I've got it all wrong. To get lost because he's not interested, or that he's got a girlfriend, or he's betrothed.

I squeeze my eyes shut, bracing for the worst.

"I already told another beautiful lady I'd go with her. Posie," he whispers, flashing her a pearly smile as she approaches. "Ernest isn't here because of his hip. I guess he overdid it today. She was saying how much she was looking forward to the gondola, and I don't want her to have to ride alone. I hope that's okay. Can we do a rain check?"

He says it so adorably, I can't possibly be disappointed. In fact, I think my ovaries have exploded. There's nothing more attractive than a man who's kind and thoughtful to senior citizens. "Of course. No worries at all."

He gives me a quick smile before taking Posie's arm and helping her into the wobbly boat. It's quite frankly the cutest thing I've ever seen. There's a velvet upholstered love seat facing the water and then a smaller bench with a side view.

I find Teller seated on a bench on the dock, staring at the water like it's raw sewage. He's still rigid, jaw clenched, white-knuckling the bench so tight, the veins protrude in his forearms, and his face is the grayish shade of oatmeal.

"I thought you'd be riding the gondola with Riley," I say, plopping down next to him. He spent most of the walking tour with her today, and from the looks of it, there was some heavy flirting.

"She asked me to. But I hate water. You know that." I feel like a dimwit. He's always hated water. I found that out soon after we first met. He was staying home all weekend while his family went out to a family friend's cottage on the lake.

"Ah yes. Water—your sworn enemy."

"Who knows what lurks beneath," he says, vaguely gesturing to the canal.

"Probably lots of teeny-tiny fish. And bits of trash from tourists, from the looks of it."

His eyes bulge and he sits up a little straighter. "Okay, but this is the Adriatic Sea, which is connected to the literal ocean, of which eighty percent is unexplored. We can't even begin to imagine what lives down there."

"You're really going to pass up a once-in-a-lifetime Venetian opportunity for the minuscule chance you'll fall overboard?"

He shrugs. "I haven't decided yet."

I can't help but crack a smile. "Say you did fall overboard, which you won't—"

"I might."

"Highly unlikely."

"I could. Do you see the bags under these guys' eyes? They're way too exhausted to be any use in an emergency situation."

He's not wrong. Beyond the muscles and good looks, some of the drivers are a tad gaunt and dead-eyed. According to Gia, they're livelier earlier in the day, which makes sense. Driving a gondola all day looks labor intensive.

"Worst case, you go into the water," I start. "What's going to get you? You said yourself the scary, unknown creatures live at the very bottom of the ocean. I doubt these canals are that deep."

Teller leans forward and casts an uneasy glance at the water. "They look pretty deep to me."

"Excuse me, sir," I call to one of the drivers, suddenly feeling gutsy. "How deep is the canal?"

"This one? About fifteen feet. You two coming?"

I barely hold back a laugh. "Come on. You heard the man. It's only fifteen feet deep. You could probably touch bottom and float back to the top in seconds."

He lets out a tortured sigh and cautiously follows me to the boat. He parks himself on the seat, stiff as ever.

~

Our gondola driver, Alfie, is a great tour guide, which marginally helps defuse my disappointment. I can see Caleb and Posie just ahead.

"The Rialto Bridge was built in the sixteenth century. For hundreds of years, it was the only way to cross the canal," he explains, voice soft and melodic. He looks to be in his midtwenties, if I had to guess. "It connects the San Polo and San Marco districts of Venice."

"How long have you been a gondolier?" Teller asks Alfie.

"Since I was fourteen. My father was a gondolier, as was my grandfather," he says proudly while expertly navigating through a tight turn.

"What a legacy," I say. A pang of deficiency shoots through me. Unlike me, Alfie is upholding his family's tradition.

"You could say it is in my blood. Though in the past few years, droughts have been causing the smaller canals to dry up."

"Really? From global warming?" Teller asks.

Alfie nods with a pained expression. "We have been having some, how you say, extreme weather. Flooding, then droughts. It is bad for us locals because we do not have many roads for commuting. We rely on the canals for transportation."

"That is terrible. I can understand why you're worried about it. I mean, the canals are what make Venice *Venice*," I say.

Alfie talks a little bit about some environmental initiatives he's part of. He then winds us through some of the smaller channels, pointing out the colorful houses of Burano Island and the Santa Maria della Salute Basilica. Teller snaps shots of each site like a stereotypical tourist.

He also peppers Alfie with a bajillion questions. Curious Teller is a favorite. It's nice to see him relax and enjoy himself, and not alone in his room pining over Sophie.

The gondola floats atop the water with such grace, you can't even hear anything but the gentle slap of the water against the side of the vessel mixed with quintessential Italian music.

"Now we're coming up to the Bridge of Sighs, which connected Doge's Palace to a prison in the sixteenth century," Alfie explains. The bridge's shadows dance across the water as we approach. "This structure is very special. According to legend, a couple that kisses under this bridge will enjoy eternal love."

He looks at us expectantly, as though we're a couple or something.

An audible groan escapes me as we pass underneath, lamenting the missed opportunity with Caleb. It would have been a beautiful memory to share with generations to come.

There's a lull as Alfie chats with a passing gondolier. "Where'd your sunshine go?" Teller asks.

I look up at him.

He shrugs. "Usually you're off the walls, radiating with excitement over these things. You seem a little . . . subdued."

I hesitate, unsure if I want to open that can of worms with him. "It's just, I kind of hoped I'd get to ride the gondola with someone else. No offense," I add. "I love you, you're just not—"

"Caleb?"

"Shh!" I shoot him a warning glare, paranoid everyone in our group heard. Voices carry on the water, after all.

"No one is around," he assures me, nodding toward the closest gondola twenty feet ahead.

Still, I lower my voice to just above a whisper. "How did you know?" I ask quietly. But of course he knows. He can read me like a book.

"You've been kind of obsessing over him since you met," he says matter-of-factly.

I wince and shield my face in my hands. "Am I that obvious?"

"When you like something, you really like it. You get all giddy and talk super fast. I could tell pretty much right away after the whole trolley thing. And when you were talking to him today, you were nervous . . . and you're never nervous."

I go on a long ramble about my chat with him today and how straight-up awesome he is. "And did you know he doesn't even have a cell phone?"

"You've mentioned it once or twice," Teller teases. "Seems like a really cool guy, though."

I wince. "Is it okay? Me potentially being with someone on this trip?"

"It's not like you need my permission."

"I know that logically, but I still feel like I'm breaking some sort of cardinal best-friend rule."

He smirks. "Ah, that's why you're pushing Riley, so I'm not a sad-sack third wheel?"

"You're so dramatic. But no. I actually just want you to have a rebound. That's all. Nothing to do with me."

"I appreciate you looking out for me. And as long as you're not hooking up in the bed next to me, I have no issue with you doing your thang," he says.

I let out a cackle. "Please never say *doing your thang* ever again."

He squeezes his eyes shut and face-palms. "I know, I know. It sounded wrong the moment I said it."

We quietly snicker so as not to ruin the ambience.

He goes still as Alfie turns down a narrow waterway and under a smaller bridge. "But I have to ask, why Caleb? He doesn't seem like your type."

I'm not sure whether to be offended or not. "What do you mean?"

He smirks. "I didn't want to say it, but, you know, Cindy-ish. Upper-middle-class dude taking a gap year funded by his parents to *experience the world beyond the gates in all its raw, poor glory.*"

I snort, feigning offense. "What? Caleb is not like Cindy. I mean, sure, he lives the backpacker life, but he's not having photo shoots with Ugandan orphans so everyone knows what a virtuous person he is."

"You already creeped his social media, didn't you?"

"He doesn't have socials. Well, I mean, he technically does. But he doesn't use them because he doesn't have a phone."

"Proves my point even more. Not your type."

I raise my brow. "Okay, then what's my type?"

"Back in high school you went for these caveman football-captain dudes with no brains—"

I give him a swift kick in the shin. "Hey, Tim Yates has brains. So does Mark B. There are different ways you can be smart. Like Caleb, he knows all these historic facts—" I pause when Teller starts chuckling.

"Jeez, he must have made an impression on you."

"You could say that. I mean, it's kind of a long story," I say carefully, trying to figure out the most natural way to ease into the whole soulmate conversation.

Teller sits back. "We have time."

I suck in a long breath and finally come out with it. "Remember that time I told you the women in my family can foresee their soulmates?"

I can't help but feel a twinge of surprise when he casually nods, as though I've merely reminded him diabetes runs in the family—not some wild psychic power.

"Well, I had a vision."

He sits forward, eyes wide. "Wait. You had an actual vision? When?"

"The other night, right before you picked me up from that frat party."

"But I thought you didn't have—" he starts, brows pinched.

"I thought so too. I mean, I don't have any other psychic abilities that I know of. It was just this one vision." I explain the vision as we continue through a labyrinth of waterways, passing an old brick building that was allegedly Marco Polo's house. "I told my aunts that night, and they said it was pretty much identical to the one my mom had about my dad. They interpreted it to mean I was going to meet The One in Venice."

"Caleb," he says.

"Exactly."

He leans back and stares at the canal ahead, taking it all in. "Wow. No wonder you've been so gung ho about this trip. How come you didn't tell me?" He sounds a little wounded, understandably so.

"I wanted to that night. But you were so sad about Sophie, it seemed like the wrong time. And I guess I was scared you wouldn't believe in the whole soulmate thing."

"Well, you're both comfortable being shoeless in public places. If that doesn't scream soulmates, I don't know what does," he says, deadpan. Last night, when Caleb entered the courtyard barefoot, Teller and I immediately locked eyes and snorted.

"Anyway, that's not all. My aunt Ellen told me there's also a related curse. Anyone in the family who doesn't end up with their soulmate is eternally lonely and miserable."

His eyes widen even more. "Eternally?"

"You bet. Promising, huh?"

"But what's wrong with being alone?" Teller asks. "Some people are perfectly happy without a partner."

I shrug. "I'm sure they are. But not in my family. Ellen told me a pretty alarming story about my cousin, twice removed. She decided not to be with her soulmate and got hit by a bus; then her house flooded."

"Jeez," Teller croaks.

"Seriously, though. You think I'm a loser weirdo, don't you?"

His laugh echoes over the slap of the water against Alfie's ore. "I don't think you're a loser weirdo." He runs a hand over his chin, seemingly choosing his words carefully. "It's not that I don't believe you or your family and the whole psychic-curse thing. But as far as soulmates . . . statistically speaking, it seems a little wild, don't you think? And scary. Like, the idea that there's only one other person out there for you, among all eight billion?"

"That's exactly what's so romantic about it. Of all eight billion people in the world, we're fated for one."

"Okay, so what if the one person you're meant to be with lives half-way around the world in a remote village with no technology? What if socioeconomic barriers prevent them from ever meeting you?"

"We'd find a way to meet," I say confidently.

He narrows his gaze, uncertain. "Even if they never leave their village? What if you don't even speak the same language?"

I squeeze my eyes shut. "I don't see how this is even relevant. If there were that many barriers to meeting or connecting, that person wouldn't be my soulmate."

"But you would agree that, generally, most people who fall in love typically live in the same geographic location, share the same language, class, probably age." His points are valid, and I'm absolutely unequipped to respond with any sort of authority.

"I guess so."

"So doesn't it make more sense that it's just totally random? That people choose others based on those factors and not some predetermined cosmic force?"

"No." I shake my head stubbornly, making a mental note to ask my aunts for their opinion.

"Okay then. What if your soulmate is like, a hundred years older than you and dies tragically before you even get to meet? Does that mean you're shit out of luck for another soulmate?"

I scratch my neck like someone's surprised me with a math test. "I—I don't really know the logistics."

He can tell I'm getting flustered. "It's okay, Lo."

"But you don't believe me."

"That's not true. I'm just trying to make sense of it. You know I need to logic everything. For the record, I believe you saw what you saw."

"Really? You're not just trying to make me feel better?"

He levels me with a knowing look. "No. And even if I didn't believe it, it wouldn't matter."

"That's true."

"So, Canadian Boy is your soulmate. You're sure on that?"

"I'm sure."

"All right." He gazes up at an old cathedral. "Then I'll do whatever I can to help your vision come to fruition, Lo, even if it has to be a Leafs fan."

I'm grateful for his support, if only for a flash before giving him a quick kick in the shin. "Way to ruin the moment, Owens."

He smirks and tosses an arm around my shoulders, pulling me into his side. "Seriously, though. I can picture it. You guys getting married, moving to an off-grid hut somewhere tropical and remote with no cell service, living off the land with your little barefoot kids."

Honestly, that sounds pretty perfect. Alfie steers us around the corner and back into the main canal. My breath hitches as I take it all in. The illumination of the buildings, the burnt oranges and yellows playing off the glassy surface of the water like fire. The melodic serenade of other gondoliers singing in the distance.

Regardless of all the headache we went through to get here, even Teller can't deny that this is pure magic.

"Hey, Tel?"

"Yeah?"

"Now we can say we *did* Venice."

A bubble of laughter escapes his throat—mixing with mine.

12

Rome

"No one can say we didn't *do* Rome." Teller waits for me as we take our final steps up the rocky incline atop Palatine Hill.

"We did the shit out of Rome," I manage through a thick wheeze, drawing a smile from him as he passes me his ginormous water bottle. It's unfair how out of shape I am compared to him.

"I've been to Rome three times and it still takes my breath away," Caleb says, admiring the scattered remnants of what were once towering columns of the Roman Forum, one of the many ancient ruins sprinkled throughout the city.

I can see why. Venice was enchanting and serene, but Rome is alive. Regardless of whether it's seven in the morning or three in the morning when we stumble back to the hostel, its narrow streets are always bustling with people. Everything is grand and ornate, even run-of-the-mill apartment buildings with their rustic terra-cotta planters weaving greenery around wrought iron railings.

We've covered a lot of ground in just three days, touring all the attractions on Mom and Mei's original itinerary, like the Vatican, the Spanish Steps, the Pantheon, Piazza Navona, and the Galleria Borghese.

It would have been fun with just Teller and me, chuckling like fifth graders over marble statues with huge packages. But it's all the more enjoyable with our group. We travel together like a well-oiled machine.

Teller and Jenny are the planners, Caleb balances their type A–ness with his laid-back we'll-get-there-when-we-get-there attitude, often convincing us to avoid a typical tour in favor of a more authentic experience. Lionel provides comic relief, while Riley and I are the social butterflies who make sure everyone is having fun. And to be straight up, Teller and I are way too naive to do this whole backpacking thing alone. We're lucky to have experts like Jenny and Caleb to guide us.

"Who would have thought us little nerds would both have dates in Rome?" I say to Teller, belly-flopping on the bed, shoes on, buzzing with nervous energy at the prospect of being alone with Caleb for the first time. While we've gotten to know each other over shared cups of gelato, exploring shops, and wandering random little alleyways, it's always been in a group context—until tonight.

"Mine isn't a date," Teller says, ironing his T-shirt and a pair of jeans to perfection.

When we found out our hostel had a private room with two double beds and our very own bathroom, Teller did a celebratory dance. It's certainly no Ritz, or even Best Western, but it's clean—at least, his side of the room is. Mine looks like a cyclone tore through, then doubled back for more carnage. Clothes, sandals, souvenirs, and makeup are strewn everywhere.

"She asked you for dinner and a romantic walk along the Tiber. That's a date," I point out, rolling out of bed to pick out my outfit. I decide on a blue gingham mini dress with a square neckline.

"It's a casual walk that just so happens to be in a stereotypically romantic setting," he argues. Despite his denial, I can tell by his vigorous ironing that he's excited.

"Are you going to finally tell her you don't share food?" I tease, dipping into the bathroom to put my dress on. Every time we stop to eat, Riley asks Teller for a bite of his food. He's too polite to admit he does *not*, under any circumstances, share food.

"That was one thing about Sophie. She never asked to share food." This is the first time in a while he's brought her up.

"Speaking of Sophie, I got a quick shot of you walking with Riley at the Colosseum in my Stories. Sophie 'liked' it." Sophie's been viewing all my Italy Stories and liking all my posts. No comments, though.

I assumed that would cheer him up, but when I emerge from the bathroom, he's frowning at his ironing. Ugh. He definitely still misses her.

Must switch gears before he spirals. "Any advice for me tonight?"

He shrugs, inspecting his jeans. "Uh, be yourself?" he suggests.

I park myself on the floor in front of the mirror with my makeup bag. "Real helpful, Tel. Shouldn't this be the part where you coach me on how to act? What to say? Where you tell me I should tone down my quirky style?"

"I like the way you dress, aside from those elephant-print pants you bought the other day," he says.

I toss a foundation-blender sponge at him. "Those pants are adorable!" Frankly, they're not really my style. But I've seen so many backpacker girls wearing them, I felt compelled to get a pair too.

"And what do you mean by 'coach'? In what world do you think I'm qualified to give relationship advice? In case you forgot, my people skills are in the toilet."

"Teller, you were with Sophie for three years. Clearly you have game," I point out, dabbing shimmery eyeshadow on my lids.

He flops back on his bed and props himself up on his side, watching me. "You overestimate me."

"You're super romantic," I remind him. "Remember that time you borrowed my starry night projector and set up a whole makeshift bed and movie for Sophie in your living room? Or when I helped you arrange that elaborate scavenger hunt all over the neighborhood?"

He bites the inside of his cheek and sighs, like the memory has taken a year off his life. "Can I tell you a secret?"

"Always."

"I hated doing all that. They were so stressful. I was always trying to think of something big to top the last one. It was impossible to genuinely surprise her. Actually, on Valentine's Day last year, we got into a fight and she told me she hated all the huge gestures. She thought they were hokey and desperate."

"But she loved them," I say, recalling the first birthday I helped Teller plan. I'd been there for the surprise, releasing the balloons and hitting Play on their "song" (Ed Sheeran, which surprised me since Teller once told me he didn't trust his face). The whole reveal was quite cinematic, with Sophie crying and dramatically leaping into Teller's arms.

"She acted like she did because she felt like she had to," he says.

"I don't get it. What girl wouldn't want a huge gesture like that?"

"That's the thing. It's proof of how little I actually knew about her."

"Okay, but that's kind of bullshit. You were together for three years. She should have been honest with you," I say, gripping my makeup brush, angry on Teller's behalf.

He shakes his head. "She was right, though. I knew she wasn't the kind of girl who watched rom-coms. She wasn't mushy or interested in talking about her feelings. So why did I expect her to be comfortable with all these public, grand gestures? It never made sense, and I was too self-absorbed to even notice or care."

I know I won't change Teller's mind on this anytime soon. When he's stuck in a vortex of self-loathing, it's nearly impossible to pull him out. So I pivot. "Okay, well, my point still stands. You have game, even if you don't think so."

"Coming from the girl who could make friends with a rock. But thanks, Lo."

I check my full reflection in the mirror, and my findings are grim. I seriously need to brush my hair. Blot my forehead. Maybe change my entire outfit. "Do you think I need to be more—"

He cuts me a serious look and sits up. "This isn't a nineties rom-com. You look great. You don't have to change a thing."

"Even my tendency to bring up my dead mom?" I ask. I'd told Caleb about my mom out of the blue while we were walking through the Borghese.

He tilts his head. "Okay, yeah. It might have been preferable to ease him in there. But you've never really been the type to beat around the bush. If he really is the one, he should probably get to know the real you, not a sanitized version."

"He *is* the one," I say, finger-combing a tangle at the back of my head. I ignore the zip down my spine when our eyes meet in the mirror and look away. *What is going on with me?* I really need to get some air.

Teller stands, brushing the wrinkles from his shorts. "Okay. Any idea what time you'll be back?"

"We'll see where the night takes us," I chirp, motoring around to grab my earrings from my suitcase.

He blinks. "Oh, okay."

It's only after I see Teller's face that I realize how that sounded. I didn't mean to insinuate anything sexual happening tonight—not that I'd be against it. But backtracking and explaining would probably just make it sound worse. The room suddenly feels smaller. Too small, like the four walls are closing in, inch by inch. With only the hiss of the cooling iron to quell the silence, Teller busies himself on his phone while I hurriedly put in my earrings. I do a quick check in the mirror. My dress isn't horribly wrinkled or tucked in my underwear, and my eyeliner isn't too aggressive. Check.

I'm grateful for the distraction. This is the first time on our trip that sharing a room feels awkward. Despite the fact that Teller and I talk about pretty much everything, there's one line we've never crossed. We don't talk about sex. Sure, we've waded close to the fire, talking about dick pics and sexual things in general, but never specifically about one another doing the deed.

I growl into the mirror, unsure whether I'm more frustrated by the unnecessary images of Teller flashing through my mind or my hair. It refuses to cooperate, as per usual.

"You okay?"

I blink away the images. "I hate my hair. I never should have cut it," I whine, trying in vain to press down a piece that keeps flopping the wrong way.

"Why? It looks . . ." He falters.

"Like an inverted triangle? I'm all too aware."

He doesn't deny it. "Um, maybe you should put it up?"

"I tried. It's too short and I'm not good at fancy styles."

"Maybe I can help."

I level him with a look. "Do you secretly know how to do hair?"

"Well, no. But I'm sure I can learn. There has to be something online. An instructional video or something."

There are. Millions. I do a quick search for the account Dad used to do my hair when I was little and find a cute french braid that folds into a bun. I pass him the phone. "It looks easy enough," he says.

I gather some bobby pins and hair ties and sit with my back facing him on his bed.

"Um, you'll have to come a bit closer," he says.

I shimmy until my back hits his leg. "Good?" I ask, ignoring the warmth tumbling down my spine.

"Yup."

I close my eyes as his fingers comb through my hair, a bit unsure.

"If I pull your hair or something, just tell me," he says, his breath tickling my ear.

The air shifts and my entire body goes hot at his fingers brushing against my neck. All this thinking about sex has gotten me feeling tingly. What would it be like if I just turned around and kissed him? Nope. Thinking about Teller like this is dangerous and highly inappropriate.

Not that it means anything. These thoughts. They're born out of natural curiosity, right? I can snap back to real life and push them aside like a pesky little celebrity crush and go on about my day.

"Oh, I will. And anyway, I'll be careful with Caleb. Always am," I assure, working down a swallow. "And you too."

"I'm not planning on having sex with Riley," he says, sweeping my hair back and separating it into three sections. *Tug, pull, tug, pull.*

"Why not? You deserve some wild vacation-rebound sex." I cringe. I sound like Bianca. There's a part of me that secretly hopes hooking up with Riley will help him get over Sophie sooner.

"Wild vacation-rebound sex?" he repeats.

"Sorry, I don't mean to pressure you. I know you're not into that kind of thing."

A beat passes. "You don't know that."

"I—I don't?"

The pull loosens as he finishes tying a bun. I turn around slowly to find his lips pressed together, like he's holding in a wicked smile. "All right, all done."

My whole body flares with heat at the thought of Teller having hot rebound sex. In fact, I actually fan myself and spin around, groping for a hair tie I tossed somewhere on the bed. Clearly I'm the one who needs some vacation sex.

"You good?" he asks.

"Yeah!" I squeak, toting my hand mirror to the bathroom. Shockingly, the braid actually looks half-decent. It's not as tight as I'd like, but it's a hell of a lot better than the inverted triangle. "You missed your calling," I yell, lingering in the bathroom. If I look directly at him, I might spontaneously combust.

"You okay in there?"

"Yeah! Just, uh, looking for my purse."

"It's out here."

I manage to avoid eye contact as I shuffle out, then pretend to riffle around in my purse.

There's a tap against the sliding glass door of our room. It barely registers until I hear it again. It's too rhythmic to be a fluke. "What was that?" I ask.

"It sounded like a . . . rock?" The mattress squeaks under his weight as he stands to inspect. "Lo, you're gonna want to see this," Teller says, peeking through the sheer drapery.

13

I always thought throwing rocks at a girl's window only happens in movies. But there's Caleb, looking straight out of a fevered daydream, hair windswept and tousled. He's in a plain white T-shirt that has no business hugging his torso like it does. As if that isn't enough, he's leaning casually against a shiny red Vespa, shiny black helmet tucked under his arm.

He pats the seat of the Vespa, and I swear his eyes sparkle. "You up for an adventure?"

~

Teller comes down to see me off, and to pepper Caleb with questions:

Do you own this bike?

Do you have a license to drive it?

Caleb assures him the bike was rented legitimately and that he knows how to drive it safely. He even pulls out an extra helmet for me from the storage compartment under the seat.

"I'll have her back by midnight," he promises once I'm secured on the back of the Vespa.

I wrap my arms around his hard stomach, and with a gentle roar of the engine, we're off into the glittery night.

We zip through the narrow streets, weaving through the late-night traffic and down hidden alleys and squares. Occasionally, he points out things, like a gorgeous Gothic cathedral and street art. He gives tidbits about some of the sights, although I can't fully hear him over the hum of the engine. That's okay. We're pulsing in sync with the city's energy.

I try to log this memory. The smell of oregano wafting from the tiny trattorias. The reflection of lights on the Tiber as we cross over the bridge. Caleb's hair blowing in the breeze from under his helmet, tickling my nose.

We stop in a square that boasts ruins just below the street level, history seamlessly blending with modern day.

"This is Largo di Torre Argentina, the site of Julius Caesar's assassination in 44 BC," Caleb explains while pulling his helmet off. He may look like a hippie-surfer dude, but he has this uncanny ability to read something once and retain it. He gets off the bike first, then turns to help me. "Now, this place, you might think it's just another set of ruins, but it's special."

"Special?" I ask as he leads me up a small staircase. It's well preserved compared to some of the other ruins we've seen.

"Look closer and listen." He closes his eyes, and we're silent for a moment.

Somewhere over the hum of traffic, I hear it. Soft meows. "It sounds like . . . cats?" I open my eyes and Caleb points to movement in the darkness.

Sure enough, there's an adorably fluffy ginger cat hanging out atop one of the walls, watching us. As my eyes adjust in the darkness, it becomes clear there are dozens of cats hanging out among the ruins.

"Oh my god!" I say, bending down to pet a particularly curious little guy. "Why are there so many cats here?"

"The ruins were excavated in the early 1900s, and a bunch of feral cats moved in. A group of ladies started taking care of them and established a sanctuary. The shelter is over there," he says, pointing to a far corner of the site.

"There's one right there!" I say, pointing to a tiny gray cat walking toward us. I stroke its back, and it immediately starts purring and rubbing its bony body along my legs. "They're so freakin' cute." I'm suddenly very aware of my high-pitched cat-baby voice. I rub the ear of another curious little ginger cat that seems to have only one eye. "And misunderstood."

Caleb bends down to let another calico sniff his hand, but it's skittish and runs away. "How so?"

"Well, everyone talks about the bond with dogs, right? Don't get me wrong—dogs will always be number one in my eyes. I have two. They're blindly loyal. They live to please their human. But cats deserve credit too. They don't care about pleasing anyone else. You really have to earn their love. It might take some effort, but once they trust you, you're in. It's a huge deal."

We hang there for at least fifteen minutes, making a game out of spotting new cats and coaxing them to come greet us. I take selfies with every one, basking in the softness of their fur against my skin.

"Thanks for bringing me here. It was really sweet. And thoughtful," I say, cheeks aching from smiling so much.

"Hey, I still have one more place I want to show you."

He drives us a ways from the bustle to an area with fewer lights, fewer people. It's quiet, more intimate. He parks on a side street and leads me up a hill toward a massive stone gate, its dramatic silhouette casting shadows on the cobblestone.

From there, we stroll through the garden pathways and make our way to a terrace.

"Best view in Rome," he says, gesturing to the panoramic view of the Colosseum and the Roman Forum.

We saw it earlier today, but it's an entirely different experience at night. It's almost majestic against the black sky, arches dramatically backlit in rich gold.

"You mentioned you were going to major in history?" I say.

"Yeah. I love history. But I've never been a good student."

"Really? That surprises me. It seems like you know everything. Dates, facts . . ." And I mean it. Every time someone asks him a question, he can pretty much answer it.

"I don't learn well through books and research," he says. "I learned most of what I know from actual travel, from talking to people and listening."

"Is there anywhere you haven't traveled?"

"Tons of places. All of South America, and the US."

"Where in the States do you want to go?"

"I want to see New York City for sure, and the entire West Coast. And your hometown, of course," he adds with a wink.

My heart thumps at the thought. "God, it would be so depressing showing you around. I mean, it's nice. It's home. But compared to this . . . and the food. It would be embarrassing."

"First, you can find beauty anywhere. And I wouldn't be going there for the food." At that, my heart soars. It's confirmation all this isn't in my head.

"Have you always been this way?" I ask, unable to pull my gaze from the freckles on his nose, sun kissed from hours spent exploring the world.

He gives me a goofy smile. "What way?"

"Free spirited, curious, easygoing—"

"Keep it coming," he says with a smirk, clearly flattered. "But no, I was actually the opposite. I was kind of an outcast growing up."

"You? An outcast? I don't see it."

"Oh yeah. I was obsessed with nature. Always running around in the woods at our cottage, making random animal traps and bows and arrows. Trying to pretend I was a *Swiss Family Robinson* kid."

"Okay, but at what point did you become this super fit surfer type who meditates daily?"

He wrinkles his nose. "Literally last year when I left home."

"Only last year?"

"I had a bit of an epiphany while watching the news with my parents. All I kept seeing was conflict, mostly over religion or ideology. I just thought . . . so many things in the world would be solved if we understood each other better, really lived in each other's shoes. And then I realized I'm a huge hypocrite who doesn't know anything about the world and lives in a bubble. If I really wanted to make any change and avoid the rat race, I should get off my ass and walk the walk. So I did."

"I love that you're so passionate about travel. It's contagious."

"I can't picture doing anything else," he says. "Like a desk job? Forget it. It seems like everyone—my siblings, for example—is living this corporate bore of a life. My sister is super materialistic. She's always buying the newest bags and shit just to compete with friends or to take a picture for social media. And sure, getting something new makes her happy for five minutes. But it's fleeting. At the end of the day, I think she's pretty miserable."

I think about Aunt Mei and how hard she's worked to achieve her position. Sure, she's got money, but she doesn't like to spend it unless she's getting a deal. Between all the late nights and weekends spent in the office, I'm not sure she's any happier than she was at the beginning of her career.

He continues, "I actually think I'd die if I couldn't be out in the world, living and experiencing. Without adventure."

"Are your parents supportive?"

He frowns and I immediately feel bad for asking. "Eh, they aren't thrilled. But luckily my older brother is the one they put all the pressure on. He's supposed to take over the lodge my family owns in cottage country—as the responsible one."

"You're not responsible?" I ask.

He shrugs. "Depends on who you ask. Let's put it this way. While my brother is in grad school, I'm backpacking around Europe and living in random hostels."

"I get feeling like you don't live up to expectations."

"Anyway, sorry for the tangent. You barely know me and I just dumped all that family stuff on you," he says, a soft grin playing over his chiseled face.

"No. Thank you for sharing," I say. If only I had even 10 percent of his passion for . . . anything. I imagine my life with Caleb. How much bigger it would be, not just living in a boring city with my dad and pets.

"Well, I promised Teller I'd get you home by midnight," he reminds me earnestly.

"Ah yes. My curfew," I joke.

"I've been meaning to ask, what's the deal with you and him?"

It's not the first time someone's inquired about us. People in high school used to think Teller and I were dating because we were together all the time. Even Bianca teases me about Teller being my boyfriend. "Me and Tel?"

"You two are just friends?"

"We've been best friends since tenth grade. Totally platonic," I assure.

His brow pinches, skeptical. "Really? You haven't even kissed or anything?"

"Oh god no!" I make a sour face as though he's suggested I share a romantic kiss with my dad or something. "No kissing. Or anything else."

"Interesting."

"Why? Does it seem like there's something between us?" I ask, face aflame and suddenly paranoid as an image of Teller's abs rockets through my mind.

He shrugs. "Nah, I mean, he just seems . . . suspicious of me. He was also grilling me about my intentions with you when we were touring the Vatican."

I face-palm. I had no idea. "He's just overprotective. I'm basically like his sister," I explain, though he's never referred to me that way.

"So you've never even talked about it?"

"No. We've always been with other people. And we're just friends, anyway." Even during that first summer we were both single, I was too busy trying to make him like me as a coworker and friend. Besides, he's always just been . . . Teller. "Actually, Teller and his long-time girlfriend broke up. That's why I invited him on this trip. To help him get his mojo back." Caleb gives me a look, and I can't tell if he believes me or not. "Anyway, we should probably get back. We have a busy day tomorrow," I remind him. Teller booked us a day trip to Viterbo, a medieval town outside Rome.

"Ah yes. The itinerary," Caleb says. I get the sense he's been less than thrilled about all the scheduled tours.

"I'm sorry if it's been a bit much for you. I know you're not huge on plans and stuff—"

"It's not the way I like to travel. But can I tell you a secret?"

"Of course."

"I'm putting up with the itinerary because I want to spend more time with you."

A quick shiver surges through me. "Really?"

He watches expectantly. "I like you," he says. "Is it too soon to say that? It's probably too soon—"

If you only knew. "It's not," I murmur. "I feel the same way."

"Your hair is . . ." He tries to fix it, but I can already tell it's too far gone. My bangs are all tangled from the wind.

I pat it down, embarrassed. "How bad is it?"

"Oh, terrible. You'll need all the help you can get."

I hold back a snort, body seizing under his adorable gaze. I wish I could read his mind. "Oh yeah?"

"Yup." He leans forward to smooth stray hairs away from my face, gently placing them behind my ear. I shiver at his touch and he smiles, eyes fixed on me. He slowly closes the gap between us, tilting my chin up to bring his lips to mine. They're soft, yet firm, demanding in a way that strikes me like a match. One spark and my body whirs, forever altered in the best way.

I think about fate and how much had to line up for me to be here, right now. Teller coming home after his breakup, Bianca injuring her foot, Teller choosing the hostel in Venice, next to the hotel with the runaway trolley.

My fingers curl into his thick hair as he pulls me closer. My back is pressed into the cool grass. I burrow my face into his neck, memorizing the feeling of his pulse thrumming against my skin, all that nervous energy coursing through me. I inhale his espresso scent one last time, freezing that moment in my mind.

He kisses me again and again, and I'm overcome with a bubbling from deep within. It feels like I could float up and away. I don't ever want to come back down. I imagine this is how Mom felt when she met Dad. How all the women in my family felt when they just knew they'd met their soulmates. It's nothing short of magic.

I squeeze him tighter, delighting in the weight of him, as though holding on to him will prolong the moment. We find a rhythm, him leading the way, me following in sync. He brands me with each kiss, each caress.

I could do this forever. In fact, I have no idea how I've gone so long without him.

He finally stops to take a breath, resting his nose against mine. "All right. We better go before we get too carried away."

I run my hand over his T-shirt, tempted to pull him back to me. The separation feels unnatural. "That wouldn't be the worst."

"Same time tomorrow night?" he asks, almost teasing, eyes sparkling.

It's the easiest yes of my life.

14

"So, tell me about these late-night rendezvous," Dad says pointedly on FaceTime.

"You heard?" Damn, news travels fast.

I just got back twenty minutes ago. It's the third night Caleb has taken me on an adventure. Each night, we've wandered and gotten lost, winding up in a completely different part of Rome than we expected.

These adventures are Caleb's compromise for following Teller and Jenny's strict itineraries during the day. And I have to say, there's something thrilling about not having a destination. About discovering hidden gems, going with the flow, and embracing the unknown.

Tonight resulted in taking the wrong subway and getting stranded at the station for over an hour. But Caleb took it all with a smile, despite how hungry and tired we both were. By the time we found ourselves in Testaccio at a huge late-night food market, it felt like we were destined to wind up there. After trying our weights' worth of street foods that required me to pop multiple Lactaids, like panzerottis, suppli, zeppole, and meat skewers, we wandered into a karaoke bar and passionately (and terribly) performed a duet to "Shallow" by Lady Gaga and Bradley Cooper. We got a standing ovation.

With each night, I fall harder and harder for Caleb. He's so present when we're together. Maybe it's that he's not distracted by his phone. He doesn't have the urge to constantly check his texts or notifications. His thumb isn't itching to scroll mindlessly through his feed. He looks at me like I'm the only object in his field of vision. Listens to me like I'm the only sound for miles.

Being around him makes me want so much more out of life than I thought possible. With him, I'm not stressing over obligations or money. I don't have Dad or Teller making sure every decision is measured and thought through. Caleb lives his life without fear or stress about what tomorrow might bring. He takes risks and is always searching for ways to push himself. He even signed up for a one-hundred-kilometer bike ride in Spain. I wish I could bottle Caleb's spontaneity and sense of adventure and douse myself with it every day. I've never had a guy make me feel so alive.

"Aunt Mei told me. I also heard you've been going out on a motorcycle." I can tell he isn't pleased about this detail.

"I did. And it's a Vespa. Everyone drives them here."

"Remember Mr. Talbot across the street?"

"How could I forget?" Whenever we so much as see a motorcycle, Dad reminds me of Mr. Talbot, the nice man in our old neighborhood who got clipped while driving his Harley. "It doesn't take much to knock you right off," Dad used to warn.

"Are you at least wearing a helmet?"

"Of course. And don't worry. Caleb is super safe."

He goes a little quiet. "How are things going with him, anyway?"

I'm giddy at the question. Caleb feels like a first crush, when you're wild for each other and can't stand the thought of being apart for a single second.

"Do you think he's The One?" Dad asks.

"Absolutely. It all adds up, according to my vision." I recount that it was sweltering hot when he rescued me, just like the heat I felt in the vision. "And then there was the scent. I smelled espresso, and he smells exactly like that. Besides, Aunt Mei and Aunt Ellen said the vision meant I'd meet him here. And I did. It was the perfect meet-cute," I point out.

"I guess I just don't know what's so romantic about almost getting killed."

"He did save my life," I remind him. "Which is probably the most romantic thing someone could do."

Dad goes on to ask a series of questions—like how old is he, how do I know he's not a criminal who will sell me into a trafficking ring, what do I know about his family—most of which I can't really answer.

"You know when you just connect with someone? He's incredible. We've talked about pretty much everything, like current events and religion. He's so open-minded. I mean, he has opinions, but no hills he's willing to die on, aside from poutine being the world's greatest food."

Dad laughs. "Gravy and cheese, huh? Sounds sociopathic."

"Maybe. But honestly, I don't think I've ever had so much in common with someone." I've always longed to find that, someone who loved all the same things as me, just like Mom and Dad. I suck in a deep breath, finally building up the courage to ask, "Did Mom know you were The One when she first saw you? She had the vision before meeting you, right?"

"She did."

It's nice knowing I share my romantic tendencies with my mom, but I still can't help but wish she was here. I can't help but long to talk to her about love. Ask her advice about the vision. About how she navigated things with Dad after they met.

He doesn't elaborate, not that I expected him to. I feel guilty for making him uncomfortable, so I switch gears. "So what are you up to these days?" I ask instead, hoping he isn't too lonely without me.

Overbearing as Dad is, this is the first time we've talked since we arrived in Rome. I've texted him updates and sent photos. I assumed he'd nerd out about the Roman architecture, but his responses have been uncharacteristically sparse, so much so, I even texted my aunts to check in on him. Mei thought maybe this was a breakthrough—that he's finally loosening the leash. But then he brought up human trafficking and that theory went out the window.

"I'm fantastic," he says, oddly chipper. I expect him to tell me about the latest true-crime series he's binging, but instead, he says, "I'm actually about to go play pickleball."

"Pickleball?" I repeat, unable to mask my shock. Dad has never played a sport or done anything remotely athletic for as long as I can remember. I can't imagine his lanky self on a court. "Since when do you play pickleball?"

"I just started the other night. Excellent cardio."

"Who are you playing with?" I ask.

There's a longer-than-normal pause before he says, "Just a friend." His response strikes me as odd. His only two friends, Jones and Arjun, aren't athletic either. "All right, hon, it must be nearly midnight over there. I'll let you go."

I barely have time to say goodbye before he's hung up.

15

Florence

I wake up to a sharp nudge in the shoulder. "Lo, you're drooling on me," Teller whispers in my ear.

My eyes fling open. We're still on the train to Florence.

I rub my lids, still exhausted from a late night of wandering Rome with Caleb. I fell asleep five minutes after we left, only waking up intermittently to the sound of Caleb's voice. He's a row ahead, pointing out small villages of historical significance, the Tuscan vineyards, olive groves, and quintessential rolling hills.

Mortified, I wipe the side of my mouth. "Shit. Sorry. I fell asleep on you again, didn't I?"

"You can sleep on me all you want, so long as you keep your drool to yourself," Teller teases, passing me my water bottle.

"I'm so tired," I say through a yawn, gratefully taking the water. "Long night."

I've told Teller all about my rendezvous with Caleb, but I've never told him we made out in the garden, or in the middle of a random sidewalk, or a little bit in Caleb's room the second night. Even though Caleb and I have started holding hands when we're out and about, revealing more to Teller feels too . . . personal, which is strange, because up until now, I've always been open with him about my relationships.

"What time did you get back?" Teller asks.

"Around midnight. I went to the roof and FaceTimed my dad first."

He raises a brow. "How's he doing? I bet he misses you."

"Nah, he's living his best life. Playing pickleball, apparently."

"I like pickleball."

"Isn't it for people north of fifty?"

"Am I not basically a fifty-year-old on the inside?" he asks, unironically reaching under his shirt to tug his money belt down.

"Valid point."

"Who's he playing pickleball with?" Teller asks.

Good question. "I actually don't know."

"Maybe he's seeing someone."

I snort. "Doubtful."

"Has he ever dated? Since your mom?"

"No. Never."

Dad has been single since Mom passed, even though my aunts have encouraged him to date. Every time the topic comes up, he gets solemn and tells us about someone who went on an online date and wound up chopped up and buried in someone's potted plants. Aunt Ellen once told me it's his coping mechanism, that Mom still has his heart. Maybe she always will.

Romantic as the sentiment is, it reminds me of Cousin Lin. Just thinking about the reality of eternal loneliness is heartbreaking. One day, I'll eventually move out and Dad will be all alone, eating dinner at our dining table every night. Maybe he'll start eating on the couch in front of the TV. Just him—and Brandon and Brian.

"It makes sense that he wouldn't date," Teller continues. "He was raising a daughter all on his own. I'm sure dating and having friends was the last thing on his mind for a long time. It's probably hard to get out of that mindset even though you're nineteen, especially since you're still at home."

He's not wrong. Dad has always done his best to be involved. He showed up to every extracurricular, every school event. He dropped me off at school and supervised my homework after dinner, trying his best to keep me on track when I'd inevitably get distracted. For anything he didn't know how to handle, he'd call in my aunts for support. Lucky for him, I was a pretty independent teenager, but I always knew he was there if I needed him.

That's something Teller and I bonded over—our dads being our primary caregivers. Teller's mom is very much alive, but she pours her everything into the coffee shop, working early mornings and into the evenings when they couldn't afford more employees. His dad held down the fort at home, cooking meals, refereeing, and chauffeuring the boys around. He wasn't resentful either. Every time I saw him, his forearms covered in suds from washing the dishes, he seemed happy.

"It was kind of weird, though. Our conversation."

"How so?"

"Well, he got really awkward when we talked about my mom and Caleb."

"Understandable. His daughter did fly halfway across the world searching for her soulmate. He could be anyone. A murderer." Teller glares at the back of Caleb's head suspiciously, and I roll my eyes. "Just kidding. Anyway, sounds like it was a weird conversation. Maybe talking about your mom makes him sad. And he doesn't want you to see him sad."

"That's possible. But it felt like something bigger, something specific. I can't help but feel jealous. It's like . . . he's hoarding all these memories with her. My whole life he's been like this. Most of what I know about my mom comes from my aunts."

"Have you ever told him it upsets you?"

"No."

"How come?"

A heaviness gathers in my throat just thinking about it. "I feel guilty, I guess. I don't want to upset him. I think most people assume I'm not really impacted because I was so young. I've always kind of had to pretend I'm not sad about it." One time, a teacher said to me point-blank, "You're lucky it happened when you were too young to understand." Apparently, Mom's family felt the same, assuming I didn't know what was going on, putting on fake smiles, pretending like everything was okay. Their logic was, the happier they appear, the easier it'll be for me. They couldn't have been more wrong.

Teller shakes his head. "Sure, it's harder on them in the sense that they have years' worth of memories with her. But in my opinion, the sadder thing is that you were robbed of time with her, and your own memories."

His words strike me in the gut. No one has ever framed it that way before, or validated my feelings. "That's why being here, in Italy, means so much. It feels like I'm building a memory with her, in a weird way. It's how I felt when I used to watch all those rom-coms . . . I don't know why, but they made me feel connected to her."

"It makes sense. They reminded you of your parents and all your family stories."

I nod. "That's exactly it. Thanks, by the way."

"For what?"

"Understanding me. I'm not an easy person to understand."

He shakes his head, eyes catching mine. "I disagree. I think I understand you pretty easily."

He does and I'm so grateful. I can't help but smile. "That's why you're my best friend. Forever."

~

Call me crazy, but there's just something about weaving through a dense crowd—a chaotic flurry of strangers who find themselves in the same place at the same time, all sharing the same itch to explore and discover.

We've been in Florence for three days, exploring cathedrals, museums, and galleries until our feet are swollen and blistered. But today is particularly exciting because Caleb, Teller, Riley, and I are going on our first double date.

It was my idea. I proposed it so Teller could get to know Caleb a bit better, and for me to spend more time with Riley, without Jenny. She tends to overshadow Riley in group situations.

"I think you and Caleb will really hit it off," I told Teller, sounding more confident than I felt.

"You think? He's different than me. And not just in looks."

"*We're* pretty opposite."

"Touché."

Frankly, they're vastly different. But if they're going to be such integral parts of my life, I can't imagine them not getting along. That's why laying the foundation for their friendship is crucial.

Still, I'm taken aback by a pinch at the sight of Teller's hand, resting low on Riley's back as they walk ahead of us. Maybe it's the heat. Definitely the heat.

Luckily, our first double-date activity is a cooking class indoors.

We enter a nondescript building a couple streets away from the hustle and bustle. Inside, it's lined with long stainless-steel tables arranged in a big square. Chef Guidice is exactly what I'd pictured. A classic white chef's coat stretches around his stout frame. He has a bighearted smile that immediately makes you feel at home. His dark eyes light up as he greets us and tells us about his background. It all started with his family's trattoria.

The four of us listen intently as Chef Guidice demonstrates how to make fiori di zucca fritti (fried zucchini flowers stuffed with cheese), guinea fowl cooked with grapes, and then dessert—a tiramisu. We watch closely, copying the way he whisks the velvety mascarpone and delicately arranges the ladyfingers in the dish. When he pours the espresso, it reminds me yet again of the scent in my vision.

When our class is over, we wander around the medieval quarter, listening to the street artists play cheerful piano tunes. Lemon granitas in hand to quench our thirst, we duck in and out of random shops to take breaks from the beating sun. We try on every hat, admire every watercolor postcard and cheap trinket and fridge magnet of the Leaning Tower of Pisa.

Every inch of the cobblestone is packed with tourists in wide-brimmed hats, eyes alight, armed with maps and cameras, licking messy drips of gelato off their forearms. I can't help but think this is what life is about.

Perhaps the best part is witnessing Caleb in his element. He finds joy in the little things, like stopping to listen to the buskers, the vendors selling goats'-milk soap and mini jars of homemade pesto from Cinque Terre, even the pesky pigeons that dive-bomb us as we attempt to eat street meat. Caleb takes everything in like it's the first time, despite having been to Florence three times already. It occurs to me that this is what makes him so likable—his genuine passion for discovery, finding something new and exciting everywhere he goes.

The restaurant is a cute little place with rustic wooden tables and red-leather booths. The walls are adorned with art depicting vine-yards and black-and-white photographs of celebrities who have visited through the years.

Despite being together all afternoon, we haven't had much opportunity to talk—or maybe I've just been too caught up with Caleb. While Teller and Caleb have stilted conversation about the Roman empire, I get to know Riley a bit better. She's an aspiring schoolteacher from the Midwest, and she recounts a bunch of funny stories about student-teaching third grade. She likes horseback riding and painting in her spare time, has a particular interest in Formula 1, and also loves Coldplay, which is just further proof that she's potentially Teller's perfect match.

"Did you know Riley is a Coldplay fan too?" I ask Teller.

His eyes light up. "Seriously? Everyone hates on them. Including Lo."

"What?" Riley looks offended.

"I actually really like Coldplay," I correct. "There's just a time and a place for their super depressing songs."

The waitress comes around and we put in our orders. I watch as Riley leans in toward Teller, double-checking the menu to make sure they're ordering the right pasta dishes. *Teller must be an amazing boy-friend.* He always thinks of others before himself. Always does every-thing he can to make sure his person is happy and comfortable.

"I hope it's good," Riley says.

"It's a bit of a tourist trap, but it's not bad," Caleb says over the soft melody of the Italian music.

"I'm loving this place." I'm delighted by the open kitchen, where chefs are deftly tossing raw noodles in the air, spinning them into the perfect thickness and shape.

"You love everything," Caleb says.

Conversation is pretty casual after our food arrives. Riley tells us about how she and Teller toured the Palace and spent some time at a nearby park. I watch as Riley drums her nails on Teller's shoulder as he talks. He isn't usually a fan of unnecessary touch, but he doesn't seem to mind this. In fact, he looks quite relaxed with her. I don't recall him being so calm with Sophie. But perhaps the most annoying part is the goofy smile plastered across his face whenever he looks at Riley. Something about it bugs me, like the tiniest, itchiest mosquito bite. It's not enough to ruin your day, but it's always there. Simmering. Itching. In fact, the only time he's not smiling at her is when she steals a piece of prosciutto off his plate. I cough, unable to contain myself.

It's strange, Teller and I being here with our significant others. It's always been just the two of us, minus the few times Sophie was around. And it strikes me that as we enter our twenties and have more serious relationships, it'll never really be just us again. I doubt we'll be hanging out alone and going on trips together when we're married and have families of our own. I'm not entirely sure I'm ready to say goodbye to the old Teller and Lo. The idea turns my stomach, and I have to set my fork down.

At one point, Riley asks Caleb about all of his travels. Riley gets excited when he mentions Asia. Apparently, she spent a summer teach-ing English in Korea. This sparks a ten-minute convo about street food while Teller drinks glass after glass of water, and I just sit there picking at my pasta.

"So you two." Riley gestures toward Teller and me. "How long have you known each other?"

Teller's eyes meet mine, like he's expecting me to respond first. But I don't. "Um . . . since the summer going into tenth grade. We met working at a movie theater. She was only wearing one flip-flop," he explains, midsip.

"Why only one flip-flop?" Caleb asks. He leans back in the booth, legs outstretched.

"Long story," Teller and I say simultaneously. We both look at each other, only to realize Riley and Caleb are still waiting to hear more.

"Anyway," I say before clearing my throat. "We went to the same high school and I haven't stopped bugging him since, even though he decided to be a jerk and move away for school."

"What are you in school for again?" Caleb asks him.

"Data science."

Caleb leans in to give him a high five, which Teller accepts, albeit confused. "Props. I could never work a nine-to-five office job. I think I'd jump off a cliff. No offense. We need people like you keeping the rest of the world afloat." I know Caleb is trying to be complimentary, but I'm not sure it's coming across given the tightness in Teller's lips.

I can't actually tell whether Teller likes Caleb or not. Teller holds his cards close to his chest. Even if he dislikes someone, he's pretty discreet about it. I can usually tell he's annoyed if he gets really quiet or avoids them, but with Caleb, he's not showing any aforementioned signs. Then again, I can barely tell if he likes me most days.

"I don't see it as boring, actually," he says.

"Nothing exhilarates Teller more than a spreadsheet," I say, shooting him a reassuring smile.

"And you guys have been able to stay in close touch even though you're at different schools?" Riley asks.

"Only because she won't leave me alone." Teller gives me a playful smile. I know he's kidding, but that stings a little.

Actually, it stings a lot. Only, it's not just a metaphorical sting. It's the literal feeling of pin prickles on my back.

And that's when it registers. I'm somewhere else—mentally, that is. I'm in a lush green field. The tall grass sways in the wind, revealing clusters of daisies and a kaleidoscope of wildflowers.

It's just like when I was mid–make out with Mark B. in the frat-house basement. Technically, I'm still sitting next to Caleb, but instead of looking at my plate, or Teller and Riley across the table, this crystal-clear image of a field has hacked my brain.

A deep, familiar laugh rings out beside me over the hum of cicadas. I'm not alone. It's Teller, walking next to me. We're talking, laughing, though I can't discern what we're saying. It's comfortable, familiar, this gentle back-and-forth, the little knowing looks that fill the space. The way we don't need to say anything at all to understand. The way we know each other better than anyone else.

As we continue through the field, Teller's pace quickens. He's walking so fast. I can't keep up. I shout, "Slow down!" and he stops, turning around to face me. Only now, there's something different about him. There's something different in his eyes, and it's more than general annoyance. It's cold, distant. Disdain?

We stand, staring at each other in heavy silence. It doesn't feel the same, me and him. Seconds ago, I could tell him everything. But now there's only tension, an invisible barrier between us. That's when I notice the wildflowers and daisies have transitioned to dense, thorny bushes, their sharp edges scratching and digging into my skin with every minuscule movement.

"Teller?" I scream, trying to reach for him, only to realize the ground is spreading between us, pulling us farther and farther apart.

I try to step, but the ground is uneven and shifty, like it's about to give way. And it does.

I'm standing in total blackness. Teller is still there, only he's not. He's a blur of images and snapshots. He's happy, strolling through campus, hand in hand with someone who looks like Sophie. He's driving his Corolla, arm out the window, singing to the radio. He's in a suit on his wedding day. He's playing in a sunlit yard with children.

I'm just an observer, watching helplessly as he lives his life entirely without me. There's a heaviness in my chest that feels like loss, weighing me down. I couldn't get to him if I tried.

And then it's black again. He's gone and I'm alone. I can barely breathe. I think I'm going to lose him.

"Lo?" someone shouts. Something warm nudges me in the shoulder, snapping me back. It's Caleb, waving his hand in front of my face.

Teller and Riley are watching me, perplexed. A surge of relief washes over me. Teller isn't gone. He's very much here . . . at least, right now.

"You good?" Teller asks.

"I—uh, yeah. Sorry. I just zoned out," I say, brushing it off. He doesn't seem convinced, eyes lingering over me for an extended beat as I replay it all in my mind. Was that another vision? It certainly felt like it did the first time, only this one was much more vivid. My aunts used to tell me about their visions all the time. They were random, symbolic, mostly to do with other people—and they were always right.

The rest of the double date goes as well as it can. There's a short debate over whether cereal should be considered soup, and then the waiter comes with the bill. I think Riley can tell I'm a little off, because she asks to see pictures of Brandon and Brian. She seems genuinely interested, and frankly, I'm grateful for the distraction.

Everyone else decides to have a nightcap at another restaurant nearby, but I opt to hightail it back to the hostel. I need to call Aunt Mei. She picks up immediately.

I describe everything in detail, from the field to the images of Teller at the end. She asks clarifying questions, like whether I was in my body or watching as a third party, because apparently these things matter.

"Do you think it was actually a vision?" I ask, holding my breath. After so many years wishing for this ability, I now find myself wishing the opposite. Could it have just been a silly figment of my imagination?

"You said it was clear, vivid, right? That it randomly struck you and pulled you out of the moment?"

"Yeah."

"Then it sounds like a vision, based on what you've described," she responds.

I take a shaky breath. "What does it mean?"

"It could mean a few different things, but the most obvious interpretation would be that there might be distance between you and Teller in the future."

"Distance," I repeat. "I felt like a total bystander in his life. Like I wasn't part of it at all. Like we didn't even know each other."

"That would make sense. You haven't seen him much since he moved away, right?" Mei confirms.

"Technically, no. We've texted . . . here and there." Well, I've texted. I've always wondered whether Teller and I would still be friends had it not been for me constantly reaching out. In those rare times he actually did text me back, it's usually because I texted first. I'm convinced we wouldn't have talked all year if I hadn't initiated. Same with when we first met. If I hadn't forced him to talk to me, would we have just been casual coworkers? Would we have just gone our separate ways at school? Will things go back to the way they were when he returns to college and gets back together with Sophie? Likely.

I'd intended for this trip to bring us back to the way things used to be. But maybe it's really marking the end of an era. Though maybe that era is already long gone.

"Does this mean I'm losing him?" I finally ask.

There's a long pause. "Friends come in and out of our lives for a reason."

I can't help but laugh, because if I don't, I might cry. "That sounds like one of those motivational quotes. About footprints in sand and shit."

"I'm sorry. I know it's not what you want to hear," she says quietly.

"But it can change, right? I can change it?" I ask hopefully.

"It's possible. Things aren't set in stone. But it's also important to let things take their natural course."

"But it's not natural. Me and Teller not being friends," I argue.

"It's one of those crappy parts of life. Not everyone we love is meant to stay. You and I both know that."

16

It never occurred to me that maybe Teller and I weren't meant to be best friends forever. The possibility of an expiration date on our friendship makes me want to crawl into a corner and cry. He was the first person to really listen to me, understand me, make me feel worthy. I can't live in a reality where he's not in my life.

That's why, for our second-to-last day in Florence, I attach myself to his hip. It's the better alternative to moping around and going over every possible scenario that could lead to our demise. Besides, as Aunt Mei said, premonitions and visions aren't necessarily locked in stone. I can change the course of our friendship. And I will.

Based on Teller's probing looks, he can tell something is off with me. But I don't tell him about my vision, and I don't plan to. Because Teller is Teller. He's the type of person who tenses up for the entirety of a scary movie because he knows the jumps are coming. If I tell him there's a possibility our friendship might end, he won't be able to think about anything else.

Instead, I choose to live in the now, soaking up every moment with him. We spend all afternoon weaving through a sea of colorful vendors selling fresh produce, intricate jewelry, ceramics, and textiles. I'm pressured by a particularly aggressive vendor into trying an array of soft-cheese samples that taste like feet. Teller finds a nice belt and attempts to haggle. The vendor is uncharacteristically stubborn about the price, and Teller caves and purchases it. The sucker.

Riley and Caleb join to wander around the Basilica of Santa Croce. On the way, the four of us stop to listen to a musician playing "What a Wonderful World" on the piano. I watch, admiring how his fingers dance over the weathered keys like it's second nature.

"Dance with me," Caleb says, eyes twinkling.

His hand gently tugs mine, and the crowd seems to part as he spins me effortlessly. I feel like Olivia Newton-John in *Grease*, gracefully twirling, dress catching the breeze, billowing up with a perfectly timed gust of wind blowing through the market. In all reality, I probably look like an injured ostrich, but nothing could spoil this moment. Not even Teller watching me from the sidelines with an expression I can't quite figure out. Then again, everything is a blur of colors. I can't stop laughing as Caleb twirls me faster and faster until—

A jolt, followed by a clatter, stops us. When I look down, I see that the clasp of my purse has come undone after snagging on Caleb's belt.

"Crap," I mutter. When I go to yank my strap free, the bag tips and its entire contents spill out. Caleb and I watch, frozen, as my belongings scatter across the pavement, rolling every which way.

Before I can bend down to collect everything, Teller is already on his hands and knees. I've got to hand it to him—he's fast, snatching my lip gloss and mints before a tourist in a floppy hat stomps on them with her chunky sandals.

"Thanks, Tel," I say, grateful as he passes me the little bottle of hand sanitizer he gave me at the airport.

After the shock wears off, Caleb and Riley jump in to help, searching around for anything we may have missed. I hadn't realized how much junk I'd accumulated in here. Cards, money, random receipts, a bottle of Tylenol, and random items like bobby pins and a nail file.

After everything is picked up, we head to the Basilica and walk around before meeting up with the rest of the group. On the way out, I spot a young couple relaxing on a picnic blanket. She's nestled between his outstretched legs, back resting against his chest like she belongs there. He plants a tiny kiss on her temple. For him, she's the view. It's exactly the kind of love I've wanted all my life. The kind I hope to find. The kind Mom and Dad had. My fingers tingle with the urge to look at the photo of them in my bag, to remind myself. Only, when I check my purse pocket, it's not there.

"It's not here," I mutter, my ears ringing as I frantically comb through my bag, praying it accidently got stuck between ID cards or lodged in a crevice. But the more I search, the more reality sets in. There's no sign of the picture.

Did it fall out when my bag spilled in the square? The Basilica? Or worse, did it fall out somewhere in between and I didn't notice?

It feels like the wind has been knocked out of me, like there's a weight sitting on my chest, constricting every breath.

I can't lose it. I can't lose her. I have to go back.

"Guys, wait. I—I have to go back to the square!" I shout, panicked when everyone starts walking ahead.

"Why?" Caleb asks, eyes widening as he takes in my demeanor.

"My picture. It's gone" is all that comes out. I don't know how to explain without everyone thinking I'm ridiculous. I'm starting to hyperventilate. The tears sting my cheeks as I frantically root through my purse, praying it'll appear.

I've lost a lot of things over the years: money, family jewelry from my aunts, even my passport. But this photo is the one item I've managed to keep close. The fact that I've willy-nilly dropped it, on a random street in a foreign country, fills me with an overwhelming sadness and self-loathing I can't quite describe. It feels like a gaping hole in my heart. Like I've lost her.

"What picture?" Riley asks.

Teller sees I have no bandwidth to explain. "It's a picture of her mom. Where did you last see the photo?" he asks.

"I don't remember . . . maybe when we checked into the hostel? I think I had it when I got my key card. But my bag spilled before we got to the Basilica and—I don't know—"

"Could you print a new one?" Caleb asks. It's a perfectly legitimate question. I could. It's a copy of the original picture, after all. But this photo has been with me since I was twelve. I've treasured it, taken it everywhere, and I especially want Mom with me in Italy.

Before I'm forced to explain that no, I can't simply replace it, Teller places his hand on my shoulder. "Lo, I'll go back with you. We're going to find it."

I don't know why, but when our eyes meet, I believe him. Against all odds, I actually think we'll find it.

"We can wait," Caleb offers.

"No, we'll catch up with you guys back at the hostel. Don't worry about me," I call over my shoulder.

Teller and I take off running back to the square, though it's more like a slow jog for Teller, given his stride is at least twice mine. Pure adrenaline and desperation keep me going through the sweaty blur of traffic and tourists.

All I can think about is that photo.

It takes a good twenty minutes to get back to where my bag spilled. In typical Teller fashion, he starts a methodical search. Meanwhile, I'm a total mess, scanning the ground aimlessly among thousands of feet. Twenty minutes of knee-scraping crawling on the hot, jagged cobblestone turns up nothing but a bunch of torn receipts and trash. The moment I'm vertical again, my vision starts to tunnel.

Before I even realize I'm dizzy, Teller's arm is around my waist. He leads me to the edge of a trickling fountain and sits me down, digging out his water bottle from his backpack. "Here. You need to drink some water."

"It's okay, I don't want to get my germs all over it."

He gives me a look that says *come on* and extends it toward me. "You need it more than I do."

"Thank you," I say, taking it from his hands. The bottom of the water bottle is cold and refreshing against my hot thighs. I chug the whole thing in record time, only stopping when reality hits me again. "It's gone, isn't it?"

"We're going to find it, Lo," he says with conviction.

"How can you be so sure? We've looked everywhere. It's probably miles from here, stuck in a gutter or on the bottom of someone's shoe," I say, lip trembling.

Normal Teller would nod and say, "Probably." Normal, logical Teller would pronounce the statistical chances of finding it again basically zilch. But instead, he looks me dead in the eye and says, "We'll search all of Florence if we need to, okay?"

Usually, I'm the annoyingly optimistic one. But if he, of all people, thinks we'll find it, I can't help but feel hopeful.

We widen the search, retracing our steps from the site of the accident to the Basilica. We continue in circles, long past sunset, until both our eyes are strained and our feet are blistered, and all hope is lost.

"It's gone," I say with a sinking in my chest. It's gone forever and it's all my fault.

I expect him to ramble about how I shouldn't blame myself. That it's just a photo, that my dad has a digital copy, that I can print a new one. But he doesn't. Instead, he pulls me into his side and says, "I'm so, so sorry."

It feels good, hearing that simple acknowledgment of my pain without all the attempts to look on the bright side. I'm grateful that he allows me to sit in my sadness, more than he'll ever know.

I rest my head on his shoulder and close my eyes, embracing the stillness for what feels like forever, until he finally says, "You know, losing the picture doesn't mean you're any less connected to your mom."

"It doesn't feel that way," I say. I'll never be able to look at the photo again without the guilt of knowing I lost the original. I'll never be able to run my fingers along its worn edges, remembering all the times it's brought me comfort.

"Maybe you don't have the picture, but you forgot the most important part."

"What's that?"

"The picture isn't the legacy. Finding your soulmate is."

I internalize those words for a few moments. He's right. Sure, the picture is a huge loss. But what connects me to Mom goes beyond that. It's exactly what Teller says. I'll carry on her legacy by falling in love. That's the real gift she passed to me, and I'm well on my way.

That kernel of optimism gives me enough strength to stand. "Thank you for searching so long, even though you knew we probably wouldn't find it."

He shrugs, pulling himself up. "It was one of the rare times you weren't sure, so I figured one of us had to be." I'm struck by Teller's wisdom and kindness. He went against his natural inclinations—for me.

"You're a good friend, Tel."

He smiles, and damn. That smile. It nearly knocks me sideways. "Is now a bad time to say I was right about the money belt?"

I laugh, trying to hold on to this moment, cement it in my mind. There's no way I'm letting him go.

17

Teller isn't in our hostel room.

We'd planned to watch a movie tonight after being on the go since the beginning of the trip. After my vision on our double date, I've been desperate for some quality friend time, just us. But when I return from a walk with Caleb, box of cannoli in hand, our room is dark and the bottom bunk (his bunk) is empty, bed made tight.

He's never been flaky with plans—ever. I turn my bedside lamp on and scroll through my phone for a few minutes to kill time.

After twenty long minutes and two cannoli, I break and throw him a text.

Lo: hey! back at the room.

Lo: when do you think you'll be back?

Lo: that sounded like I'm rushing you.

Lo: i'm not. PROMISE.

Lo: just curious if you still want to watch a movie?

While I wait for a response, I pace around the room. Maybe he got lost?

Teller: Shit. I'm so sorry. I lost track of time. Rain check? Don't wait up.

I stare at my phone. Does he mean don't wait up out of politeness? Or don't wait up as in *I'm getting laid and I'll be out until all hours of the morning*? Not that he owes me any details.

Despite teasing him about hooking up with Riley all week, there's a part of me that didn't think he actually would.

Desperate to calm my nerves, I slip into bed and try to fall asleep. Whenever I close my eyes, my mind runs amuck, replaying my night with Caleb and then picturing Teller with Riley. I need a distraction, stat. So I try calling my aunts.

It's almost midnight, which means it's evening back home.

"Lo, I was just thinking about you," Mei says, whir of the treadmill in the background. A steeply inclined walk, followed by yoga and a peruse of the latest grocery store–sale flyers is her post-dinner routine. According to her, quiet evenings are when she feels most connected to the spirit world, so she likes to take advantage.

"It's like you're psychic or something," I tease. It happens often enough—that she's thinking about me right before I call her.

"I read a woman's palm yesterday at an estate sale." That's the norm. She likes doing readings for people at random. Sometimes people recoil, assuming she's a very well-dressed crazy person. Or they won't let her leave, convinced she can talk to the dead (she cannot). Apparently, Mei determined there was something amiss with this lady's health. She slipped her her business card, and the woman contacted her later that night. Turns out, she had appendicitis and ended up in the hospital.

"That's wild. Is she going to be okay?"

"I think so. I'm going to visit her in the hospital after work to do a full reading. Anyway." She pauses, shutting her eyes for a brief moment. "Things are going well with Caleb." She says it like a statement, not a question, because she just *knows*. She may not be able to read my mind, but the woman is intuitive as hell. An "intuitive empath." That's what she and Ellen call it—the ability to connect with a living person's energy and emotions.

I confirm, recounting my dates and conversations with Caleb in vivid detail, how we're both basically dogs masquerading as humans, how I want to travel the world with him, and how much fun we have together, all while the treadmill whirs in the background. The more I say out loud, the giddier I feel.

"He sounds like the blueprint for your perfect guy," she says, not even a tad out of breath.

"Honestly, I think he is. Everything just feels right and easy. Almost too good to be true. Is that how it's supposed to feel?"

"When Layla and I reconnected again, it felt more than easy. It was like coming home after a long, harrowing journey. A wild sense of belonging I've never felt before. Suddenly, it was like every dull, empty bit of me was full, alive. Not that I didn't have to put in effort, but when it's your soulmate, it doesn't feel like work, you know?"

Mei already knew Layla from summer camp when she had The Vision. She saw an anonymous figure standing at the edge of a dock at sunset. Despite reconnecting with Layla as camp counselors the following summer, she didn't put two and two together. Not even after a secret footsie under a blanket by the crackling campfire, followed by a starlit rendezvous on the dock. See, Mei hadn't realized that her soulmate may be a woman, that she might like both men and women.

After a few years of self-discovery, Mei finally reconnected with Layla. They happened to be reaching for the same pair of leopard-print loafers in the bowels of a thrift shop. Layla let Mei have the shoes, and Mei let Layla have her heart.

Finally, I understood what my family members had told me all these years. That feeling of total harmony deep within your soul. It's like I've always known Caleb.

"Have you told him yet?" Aunt Ellen asks. She's just joined the call.

"Told Caleb he's my soulmate? No. Isn't it a little too soon?" I ask.

"No—" Ellen starts.

"Way too soon!" Mei cuts in.

There have been many little moments where I wanted to tell him. But it's only been two weeks since we've met. Tomorrow also happens to be our last day in Florence, and our last day as a big group. We'll be parting ways for our own adventures. Jenny and Riley are headed to Cinque Terre, Lionel is going home, and Caleb is coming with Teller and me to Tuscany and then Amalfi for the last leg of the trip.

"I told Uncle Hank I'd had a vision about him ten minutes after we first met," Ellen says smugly.

"Yes, and scared the bejesus out of him in the process. He avoided eye contact with you for weeks," Mei reminds her.

Ellen lets out a witchy cackle. "He was convinced I could read his mind and hypnotize him or something. To this day, he still doesn't know for sure. Sometimes I still say things to mess with him. The poor sucker."

"This is exactly why I'm scared to tell Caleb," I say. Based on our conversations, I know he believes in spirituality, karma, energy, and the like. But you never know how people are going to react to the whole psychic thing. Knowing psychics exist in theory is one thing, but being told, *Hey, by the way, I'm your one true love* is a different story.

"I say wait until things get more serious," Mei suggests, leaning so close to the camera, I can see straight up her nostrils.

"How much more serious can things get in two more weeks? I feel like I have to tell him before I come home," I point out. It's wild how fast the days are flying by. We're at the halfway point of the trip. It feels like yesterday Teller and I took that first water taxi into Venice.

Mei disagrees. "If he's really your soulmate, you have your whole life to tell him."

∿

I close my eyes for what feels like a few minutes before the sound of the door wakes me up. Teller. He's back.

"How was your night?" I ask, peering down from the top bunk and flicking the light on.

Teller squints, eyes adjusting to the light. He paces around the room in search of something to clean or arrange. "It was good. Listen, I'm really sorry. I completely forgot we were supposed to watch a movie. I got my days mixed up. I thought it was tomorrow, but then when you texted, I realized tomorrow is the cruise. It's my bad—"

"No worries at all. I'd rather you be hooking up with Riley," I say, even though I'm not sure that's entirely true.

"We didn't hook up," he says, almost offended. "After we toured Palazzo degli Uffizi, we walked around and got some gelato and talked." They didn't hook up. I'm not sure why that's so relieving. "How about your night?"

I casually lift a shoulder. "It was chill. We got cannoli. Feel free to have some. They're on the bedside table. Oh, and I talked to my aunts for a while."

"Oh yeah? How are they?"

"Same old. They think I should wait to tell Caleb about the soulmate thing."

He studies me for a beat before climbing the ladder to sit next to me. "Do you want to wait?"

"No. You know me and my big mouth. I feel like I need to tell him before we go home. Preferably earlier, so we can figure out what we're doing . . . you know, relationship wise. It's killing me to keep it in. And it feels dishonest, like I'm lying to him, even though I'm not," I ramble, adding, "I'm scared it'll freak him out."

"Telling him you're a psychic? Nah," he teases, dangling his long legs over the edge.

"A terrible psychic at that," I add reflexively, despite Mei's excitement over my second vision. There is a bright side, she said. Based on the vivid detail, she hypothesized that I might have stronger powers than I thought.

"Just because you only had one vision doesn't mean you're terrible," he says. Heat flushes my neck. I'm tempted to tell him what I foresaw on our double date, but I stop myself. What good would it do? If anything, it would speed up the inevitable. "Maybe you really do have your family's abilities and you just don't know it."

"Maybe."

"Do a palm reading on me," Teller says. "Just for fun," he adds when he sees the mortified look on my face.

"Okay, but I'm going to be crap at it," I warn.

"Well, I'm going to be judging. Harshly. Comparing you to the hundreds of other palm readings I've gotten," he says sarcastically.

I examine his palm, running my finger over it, trying to summon all the bits of knowledge I've gathered over the years from my aunts.

"All right, so your life line is unnaturally shallow," I say, watching Teller's brows pinch as he scrutinizes his hand. For the record, I'm just messing with him.

"What does that mean?"

"It tends to indicate you may get sick more easily, probably because you use an excess of disinfectant—"

He gives me a soft slap on the wrist. "Okay, seriously, though. Am I going to die young? Will it be painful?"

I shake my head. "No. You actually have a really long and deep life line. It doesn't necessarily represent a long life, but it means you're healthy."

"I'll take that."

I move my finger upward to the wisdom line, which extends from the edge of his thumb and index finger. "Your wisdom and life lines kind of overlap, which means you're introverted and detail-oriented. I remember my aunts used to say that too much overlap means you're a worrywart."

He smirks. "All true. Go on."

I run my finger over the line right under his pinkie, extending across the palm and ending right below the middle finger. "Your love line kind of curves down, which tells me you're stubborn but willing to sacrifice for love."

He nods. "True again."

"There are some circular creases around your health line, which also indicate nose and throat problems."

"I do have horrible allergies, so that checks."

"Sure does."

"See? You're more talented than you think."

I shake my head. "No. It's the same as when I was a kid. I can memorize all the rules, but I don't have that . . . natural intuition my aunts use in tandem. They use the palm reading as added proof of what they already know."

"Still, you were pretty accurate with me. If I could leave you a five-star Google review, I would."

"Because I know everything about you already," I say. "Bias."

"Don't stress, Lo. If he's truly your soulmate, he'll be thrilled." He stretches out on the bed, yawning.

"Oh, come on, it's too early to sleep." It's really not, but after missing out on our movie night, I feel a bit cheated out of time with him.

He quirks his brow. "What do you propose we do instead?"

I shrug. "Let's do something fun, like . . . get tattoos!" I've always wanted a tattoo, though I have no idea of what.

"Absolutely not."

"Come on. We could get friendship tattoos."

"I will never get a tattoo. Do you know how easily you can contract hep C from unsterilized needles?"

"Oh, Teller. Highly unlikely."

His eyes shift, like he's searching for an excuse. "Besides, there's nothing I like enough to put on my body permanently."

"Excuse you. Is my friendship not important enough to commemorate?"

"I didn't say that—"

"We could each get one half of a smiley face on our baby toes so it only looks like a full face when we put them together." I swing my feet up, brandishing my toes in his direction. He's naturally revolted and bats them away.

"You know I hate bare feet."

"My feet are gorgeous. I bet they'd be in high demand on those foot-fetish sites," I shoot back.

He giggles and it's adorable. "Maybe that's your calling. Selling your worn socks and stuff."

I snort. "Look, I'm not above it. And okay, back to the issue at hand. Can I interest you in a tattoo of a duck in sunglasses? Chinese characters? A barbed-wire armband? Or a tramp stamp of an eagle?"

He bites back a laugh, not bothering to dignify me with a response.

18

onfessions of love look so easy in the movies.

They're generally impromptu, spur of the moment, because that's just more cinematic and entertaining. What you don't see is the hours of turmoil and deliberation in the lead-up.

We're in an ideal setting—the Bardini Gardens, surrounded by a vibrant collection of azaleas and roses and several ornate fountains, with a panoramic view overlooking the Duomo, the Palazzo Vecchio, and the river. Caleb even brought wine and fettuccine alfredo from his favorite restaurant. I can't eat the fettuccine without getting a serious stomachache. But when in Rome (or, Florence).

Maybe it's the fast onset of my stomach cramps, but I'm internally melting down. Caleb is talking about how he eventually wants to go vegan, but I can barely pay attention. I've been practicing over and over in my head, just waiting for the moment to magically present itself. Spoiler alert: it doesn't. See, I'm not confessing love like a normal human. There is no *How to Confess That Your Someone's Soulmate for Dummies* guidebook.

For reasons beyond me, I choose the moment he takes a heaping mouthful of pasta. "I have a confession to make. I've been . . . keeping something from you."

Caleb forces down a swallow and straightens his posture, eyes fixed on me.

Why did I have to sound so cryptic and sinister? I mean, it's not like I'm telling him I'm a fugitive, or masterminded a pyramid scheme, or that I've killed someone. I'm merely telling him he's my one true love—my twin flame, if you will. No big deal or anything.

"Oh no," Caleb says, tone uneasy. "Do you secretly have eleven toes or something?"

If only. I can't help but laugh, grateful for the comedic relief. "Maybe. Would that be a deal-breaker?"

"No," he says genuinely, but not before peeking at my bare feet. "I would still like you and your extra toe just as much."

"Really?" I whisper, heart kicking into overdrive.

"Of course. Isn't that obvious?"

"It is," I say. Based on how often he takes my hand and kisses my knuckles, or wraps his arms around my waist from behind, he's made his feelings pretty clear. But it still feels like a fever dream, too good to be true. Sometimes, I'm scared to go to sleep at night in case I wake up at home, in my bed, in my normal, boring life. "It's just—I'm scared that I'm not enough for you. You're this super cool guy who's traveled everywhere, who's done everything. And I've never even left the country until now," I say, easing into deeper conversation. I can't just segue from toes to soulmates seamlessly.

"You haven't traveled as much as me. But the point is that you want to, right?"

I nod, ripping out a blade of grass to shred.

"What matters is you want to get out there. You want adventure. You're always in a good mood. Always happy, down for anything."

"It's funny, I've always seen that as a weakness."

"What do you mean?"

"I'm a bit . . . flighty. I like a lot of things, but I have no real passions. I don't know what I want to do with my life."

"You're passionate about animals. What about being an animal doctor?"

I sigh. "I wanted to be a vet when I was really young. But I also don't want to put animals down. I don't think I'd be able to handle that side of it."

"There must be something you could do with animals."

I stare at the torn blade of grass and contemplate. "In an ideal world, I'd love to buy a huge ranch and open an animal rescue for disabled pets."

"Why can't you?"

"It's expensive. And I don't exactly have the money to run something like that. They rely on donations and they're always super underfunded."

He shrugs like it's no big deal. "You of all people could rally donations."

"Yeah. Maybe." I smile wistfully. It's nice to know he doesn't think I'm a total loser.

"I can see it. You, dedicating your life to wounded and unwanted animals."

"You think I'm a weirdo, don't you?"

"No, sweetheart. I think it's adorable."

Sweetheart. My heart flutters.

Only days ago, Caleb was nothing more than an idea. I was terrified to talk to him at first. And now he's here, right in front of me. And I'm casually running my fingers across his forearm. I open my mouth, poised to finally bring up *the* topic, but Caleb has other plans.

He leans in, hovering over my lips for a beat before exhaling just as I inhale. It's embarrassing how loud my heart is jackhammering as he glides his hand up my arm, over my shoulder, and down my back. He finally rests his mouth over mine, and I fall back onto the cool grass, dizzy.

As our tongues meld together in an intricate dance, I can't help but compare Caleb and Teller. Caleb is broader and more barrel-chested to Teller's lankiness. His hugs are more commanding, gruffer than Teller's measured touch. Not that I should, or have any reason to compare the two. *Why am I thinking about Teller at all right now?* But I can't help but wonder what he's doing on his last day with Riley.

Caleb's hands lock around my wrists as he rolls over me. His fingertips trace down my dress, over the soft part of my knee. I nearly unravel. We kiss like this for I don't even know how long, until my updo has fully fallen out and our mouths are red.

And while I'm tempted to do a whole lot more, this is as far as I want to go physically. Something about having sex before he knows the truth feels . . . wrong. I also want to contain this—whatever this is between us—capture it exactly as it is. Besides, we have our whole lives ahead of us to have sex.

"Is it just me, or does it feel like we've known each other longer than just two weeks?" he asks.

"It's not just you," I say. "I feel the same way."

"It's wild. I feel like I was meant to meet you or something."

"Do you believe in that kind of thing?" I sit up straight. This is it. This is my time to tell him the truth. "Like . . . soulmates?" A flush creeps across my cheeks and I squeeze my eyes shut, bracing for his reaction.

"Totally. I believe in soulmates. Why?"

Strangely, this response doesn't make me feel any less terrified. But I come out with it anyway. I tell him everything. About my family history, about my vision, all the way until almost getting crushed by the trolley.

He sits glass-eyed, in silence for a few beats before letting out a low whistle. "Wow. That's—"

I cover my face with my hands, suddenly regretting telling him so soon. "I know. It sounds ridiculous when I say it out loud—"

"No," he says, eyes darting to everything but me. The loose thread in the blanket. A rock in the bottom of his sandal.

"But?"

He's silent, still as a marble statue for far too long. I'm about to bolt before he finally meets my eyes. "I like you, Lo. A lot. And I believe you.

I absolutely can see us together. But I guess I—" He bites his lip. "I just I don't know if I'm . . . ready for something like that. I feel like I'm still in the exploratory phase of my life, you know? I don't know that I want anything serious romantically. At least right now. Actually, I'm not sure I really believe in monogamy . . . if that makes sense."

My cheeks are burning, flush with a mixture of shame and embarrassment. I can barely hear the rest of his ramble. Something about how he does have feelings for me and he wishes he were ready for that type of commitment. About rigid societal expectations of relationships and how he values autonomy and freedom, and how monogamy isn't natural for humans.

I feel like I've just been judo-kicked in the gut. I'm desperate to crawl inside myself, to hide away for all eternity, but my limbs feel too heavy to move, to do anything but float face down in this sad, pathetic pool of rejection.

He tries to change the subject and act like everything is normal as we pack up. I can tell he's flustered. He can't stop rambling about how the garden dates back to the thirteenth century, was owned by the Mozzi family, and on and on. The longer he talks about prominent Italian families, the more panicked I get that I've blown it entirely.

Mei was right. It was too early to tell him.

When we get back to the hostel, we pause outside my door. "I don't suppose it's possible to forget about everything I said today?" I ask.

He flashes one of his dazzling Caleb smiles, which makes me feel marginally better. "About your eleven toes? Impossible."

"Seriously," I say.

"It's fine, Lo. We can talk more tonight on the cruise, okay?"

I nod, and he gives me a stiff hug before heading to his room.

Despite his assurance, I text Mei and Ellen an SOS, followed by a multiparagraph rundown of what happened.

Ellen: I'm sorry, hon!! I bet he'll come around soon enough.

Mei: Remember, just because someone is your soulmate, doesn't mean they're automatically yours. It doesn't always come easy and it isn't always instantaneous. You might need to give him some space.

Ellen: Yeah lots of space!

I always assumed I'd meet my soulmate and *bam*, we'd be inseparable from then on. But maybe this is a long game. Maybe it'll take months, even years, for Caleb to be ready.

Frustrating as it is, I'm only nineteen. I have time . . . even if that time has to be spent in a holding pattern. Why am I rushing things?

With this new perspective, I pad over to Caleb's room. I need to smooth things over, make it clear I'm not looking to marry him ASAP, or even be exclusive in any way. That I'm happy to give him time and space. As much as he needs.

Just as I'm about to knock, the door swings open.

It's not Caleb. It's a maid.

"Um, is Caleb here?" I ask, looking over her shoulder at the empty bed.

She shakes her head. "No one in this room," she says in a heavy Italian accent.

She closes the door and I just stand in the hallway, trying to put two and two together. I know for a fact this is Caleb's room. I've spent hours in here and watched him go in literally an hour ago. So if he's not here, where is he?

I head to the lobby and check with the front desk. The clerk cheerily informs me that Caleb checked out half an hour ago.

My chest hitches. There's a squeezing sensation in my ribs as it all sinks in. Caleb is gone. He left.

Without even telling me.

I'm officially the only Zhao woman in history to scare off her soulmate.

19

How have I messed things up in such a huge way? One moment, Caleb and I are making out, confessing how much we like each other, and the next, he's fleeing the city. This is not the *space* I had in mind.

I spend the next hour sobbing in bed while Teller holds me.

"What happened?" he asks when I pause to blow my nose.

I wave my wad of wrinkly Kleenex and tell him everything.

"I never should have said anything so early. Why did I expect a nineteen-year-old dude to take that news well?" I bury my face in my pillow to hide the onslaught of tears.

He's silent for a few moments, then wraps his arms around me. "You didn't do anything wrong. You were right to tell him. He deserved to know. And why wouldn't you put yourself out there? He gave every signal that he was interested in you. How were you to know he's scared of commitment and doesn't believe in monogamy?"

I sigh, blowing my nose yet again. I may or may not have snotted on Teller's shoulder. "I should have known, though. That's who he is. He lives his life like that, not committing to anything or anyone."

"There. What you just said. That's proof that it isn't personal. It's not about you. He just isn't in a place to commit right now. But that doesn't mean he isn't your soulmate. Maybe you're destined to meet again?"

I want to believe that. I know that's what my aunts think. But it's hard to conceive of him coming around after *that*.

"Tel, the man literally fled the city because of me. There's no way I have another chance with him. And I can't even contact him because he doesn't have a cell phone."

"He has social media. He showed me a picture of something on his Instagram. You can contact him. He just won't get it right away," Teller assures me. "But for now, screw him. He's an asshole for leaving you like this."

My world may be crumbling, but I can't help but laugh. Teller rarely swears, let alone passionately like that. "Yeah. Screw him."

He watches me expectantly, like he's waiting for me to break down and cry again. His instincts are correct. Everything in me wants to curl up in a ball and remain motionless for the foreseeable future, but then I remember where I am—in Italy with my best friend. I can't let Caleb ruin this.

I sniff back my incoming tears and steel my spine. "Promise me we won't talk about Caleb for the rest of the night?"

"Caleb who?" he asks without a beat, glancing down to check the time on his phone. "Shit. It's almost seven. We're late for the cruise."

～

We officially miss the riverboat cruise.

When we finally arrive at the docks, red-faced, clothes plastered to our bodies with sweat, we're notified by an employee that it already left.

It's the least disappointing thing to happen to me all day, but I feel terrible for Teller. I assume I've ruined his last night with Riley, but he just looks at me and says, "You hungry?"

"Starving," I say. After all that running, I could use some food. "What do you want?"

"I was thinking pizza. We haven't had good Italian pizza yet, and I feel cheated."

"All right. Commence mission Find Good Pizza in Italy."

It only takes Teller a couple minutes to organize a list of the top-rated pizza spots in Florence. He explains his methodology of cross-referencing multiple "best of" lists, and we decide to head to the first one on his list. "This place is famous for their mushroom pizza. And it's only a ten-minute walk."

As soon as we arrive, it's evident we've made a grave error. This restaurant is fancy. Like, the customers are dressed in suits and the hostess looks like a supermodel-from-Milan type of fancy. When we approach, me in a denim dress and Teller in khaki shorts and a T-shirt, she looks like she's sucked a lemon.

"Do you have a reservation?" she asks, like our mere presence is an inconvenience.

"No, but we were hoping you had room for two?" I ask, tossing in a weak smile.

She shakes her head. "Our tables book months in advance."

"Jeez. She really filled me with the warm and fuzzies. How about you?" Teller asks as we walk away.

I smirk. "Fancy restaurant, rude staff. It's a rule."

The next hour and a half is a whirlwind. We run from one restaurant to another, literally. The second restaurant is completely booked, the third is closed; then we finally get seated at the fourth, only to realize that it's extremely out of budget.

I'm not sure why we've decided it's some sort of race. We're not on any time crunch or schedule. Perhaps that's why it's so fun. It's like we're on a pizza treasure hunt. It's also the perfect distraction from Caleb.

"Guess it was a bad idea to try going out for dinner on a Saturday without reservations," Teller says after another failure at the fifth restaurant. The sun has now drifted low in the sky. We're leaning against a brick building, ready to give up, when I spot a deli across the street with a sun-faded photo of a meatball sub in the window.

It's certainly not fine dining. The inside has cracked tile and scuffed walls, though the cheese, cured meats, and breads behind the display look fresh. The shelves are lined with local olive oil, balsamic vinegar, some dried pastas, and Tuscan condiments. Teller points to the chalk-board above the counter listing the day's specials, including flatbread pizza, which he promptly orders.

We sit on the curb and devour our flatbread. The crust is light, fluffy, melt-in-your-mouth, with generous dollops of pesto and fresh mozza-rella (for Teller). They even have a lactose-free cheese option for me.

"This is actually the best pizza I've ever had in my entire life," I say, sinking my teeth into a juicy sun-kissed tomato.

"Same. This sauce is incredible. And the crust is the perfect balance of crispy and soft."

"And it wasn't even on your list," I tease through a bite.

"I'm not sure why. The ambience is pretty top notch," he says, watching a restaurant worker haul a huge garbage bag into a dumpster.

"I'm still sorry I had a life crisis and made you miss the cruise. It probably would have been really romantic. You could have done the Titanic pose with Riley."

He draws his brows tight. "You wouldn't catch me near the railing like that."

"I should have known."

He's quiet for a minute as he watches the traffic go by. "Also, I'm not actually sure there's anything between Riley and me."

"Are you just saying that because she stole food off your plate like Nicola Rumford?" Nicola Rumford was the first girl Teller ever told me about, pre-Sophie. He was interested in her . . . until she made a habit of vulture-ing his food before he was done with it.

"No, though that was a serious concern."

"Okay, so if it's not her eating off your plate, why don't you think there's potential? You guys seemed pretty cozy on our double date the other day. She kept touching your shoulder."

He shrugs, thumbing his ear. "I dunno. She and Jenny are going their separate ways tomorrow, and it feels like the right time to end things. I'm not ready for any sort of commitment, anyways."

"You still miss Sophie, huh?"

A heavy pause. "I've been thinking about it lately, and I don't know if I miss her or being in a relationship more." This throws me for a loop. "I miss having someone to have inside jokes with. To look at when someone says something dumb, weird things like that. And Sophie and I weren't really doing that toward the end. We were just fighting all the time."

"Really? But you guys seemed so in sync."

"We were . . . but things started to fall apart when we moved in together. Being long distance made things exciting. And then when we were around each other all day, every day, going to the same classes, extracurriculars, and parties—it was different."

"Maybe you just had to get used to living together."

"It was more than that. She was right, I think. We stopped enjoying each other's company. It was like we ran out of things to talk about. And I don't mean silence every now and then, because you know I don't mind silence. It was all the time, days on end, where we didn't have any meaningful conversation apart from what we were having for dinner."

"Why did you stay with her all year, then?" I soften my expression for fear I'm coming across judgy.

"I wanted it to work. I got used to the security of *having* someone."

"I get that."

"You haven't dated anyone seriously this year, have you? Aside from dick-pic guy?"

I tilt my head, feeling a little pathetic. "Not really. I've always felt weird about getting into relationships. I guess I've been holding out for The One, and I knew I hadn't met him yet. It felt like wasting my time, and theirs. And it would be dishonest of me to not tell them they aren't my soulmate, knowing it isn't going anywhere long term."

That's why this potential delay with Caleb feels so pointless. Sure, I could date around like I always have. But putting a face to my soulmate makes the family gift all the more real. How can I focus on someone else with Caleb in the back of my mind? It's like my life is in limbo until he comes around.

"I agree with you on that one. That would be a hard pill to swallow," he says. A beat goes by where I think he's going to say something else but instead tosses his pizza container in the trash.

After our curbside dinner, we wander along a bustling street filled with small bars and trattorias, my sandals clacking over the cobblestone until we come across a bar called Tuscan Tipples. Its blinking lights and multicolor mosaic tile caught my eye. There are vintage posters and an antique bicycle hanging from the ceiling. It's not overly crowded, which I know Teller appreciates. The vibe is chill and relaxed, with a Mumford & Sons song playing over the sound system.

We take a seat at the bar and face each other, knees touching while an impossibly tall bartender takes our drink orders. He also hands us a food menu, which is one of those sticky plastic menus Teller hates, but he's a good sport about it. We pass on the food and order our first round of drinks. Teller gets an Aperol spritz, and I get a glass of red, as well as two shots of limoncello for us. Before we know it, we're on drink number six.

20

"We'll always have Florence," I say over the chatter of a group doing trivia behind us, although I can't be certain, given they're speaking Italian.

"That's from a movie!" Teller shouts, proud of himself for catching on. His eyes drift upward, searching his brain for the title.

"Technically, the line is *Paris*, not *Florence*. And it's from *Casablanca*."

"Never seen it. But it sounded cinematic."

"Seriously, though. I'm glad we're here, despite it all," I say, blowing my bangs out of my eyes.

"It may have plastic menus, but it's better than those fancy places I tried to take us to," Teller says.

I laugh, enjoying the freedom of speaking loud without feeling like people are watching and judging. "That hostess at the first restaurant wanted us skinned alive. But I'm glad the night turned out this way. Even if I got snot on your shirt."

Teller's eyes are trained on the rainbow lights reflecting on the glass behind the bar. He gives me an earnest shrug. "What are best friends for if not to wipe your snot on?"

I cough a little, throat drier than the Sahara. I hadn't expected him to say that. "I'm still your best friend?"

"Why wouldn't you be? Am I not yours?"

"No, you are. I just figured I wasn't yours anymore. That you'd met other friends at college and replaced me."

He throws me a funny look. "Me? Make friends? Ha!"

"You did make new friends. The B-school fam?" I remind him. He and Sophie made a group of friends in their business program that they called the "B-school fam," according to Sophie's social media captions. I was secretly jealous of their group Halloween costumes, Friendsgiving, and Super Bowl parties.

"Correction, I inherited those friends through Sophie. I was just along for her ride, as usual. That's why I was so . . . weirded out when you wanted to be friends with me. My whole life, I've never been a person anyone wanted to be friends with." He hangs his head.

"That's not true," I start.

"It is. Even with my siblings—when we were younger, my brothers were inseparable. Always playing together, doing sports. Everywhere we went, they'd pair up. I still remember going to Disney, where almost every ride is for two, like most of the roller coasters. They'd always go together. Then there was me. The odd one out. And I know it's dumb. Obviously, there's gonna be one left over with three kids. But it was *all* the time."

My heart splinters. I always got the sense he didn't fit in with his siblings. Whenever I went to his house, there was barely a moment where his brothers weren't roughhousing and being generally loud. All things Teller hates. His parents and both brothers are all quintessential extroverts. I can't imagine feeling like an outsider in your own family. "Like I said, you're the best Owens brother, even if you don't believe me."

He places his hand over mine and gives it a solid squeeze. "Thanks, Lo."

I think back to the night we "officially" became best friends. It was nearing the end of summer, and I could feel autumn creeping its way in.

"We only have two more weeks working together," Teller said, breaking the silence on the drive home from work. It had been a

particularly eventful shift. The handicapped stall in the women's bathroom had clogged again and flooded. It took hours to clean.

I pressed my fingers into the edge of my seat, as if holding on to the
last bit of summer disappearing behind the trees lining the road. "Ugh.
Don't remind me. I hate fall."

He wrinkled his nose. "I'm offended. Halloween is not hateable."

"My sincerest apologies," I said with a snort. "Why do you love
Halloween so much?"

"It's just fun. It's the one night of the year you can be someone else."

"Do you want to be someone else?"

A pause. "Doesn't everyone?"

That made me sad. "I wouldn't want you to be anyone else."

"Thanks, Lo," he said. "I didn't always love Halloween, actually.
It was always a pissing contest with my brothers. Always a huge battle
to get the most candy. Lots of stealing and fighting over the best ones,
a lot of Kit Kat robbery. Anyway, in third grade, my dad helped me
make this Transformers costume out of boxes from the garage. It was
so cool, because if I crouched down, the boxes would actually fold and
transform."

"That is really awesome," I said, closing my eyes to picture nine-
year-old Teller.

"The kids at school thought I was like, the second coming of Christ
or something. Suddenly, they all wanted to be my friend. Not that I
usually love attention, but it was nice. Just for that day."

"I love that. Okay, I'll forgive Halloween. Even if fall sucks."

"Don't girls love fall? Isn't that a thing? Pumpkin spice lattes, cozy
sweaters, changing leaves and all that?"

I shook my head vehemently. "I'm the Scrooge of fall. I mean, why
would I want to celebrate death and decay? It's morbid, if you ask me."
I loved my summer routine. Soaking up the sun in my backyard before
a Cinema shift. The guarantee of seeing Teller almost every afternoon
and evening. And it was all coming to an end. The Cinema didn't need
both of us during the school year since business was pretty dead. Teller

would work at his mom's coffee shop, but I would pick up some shifts here and there.

"The Cinema isn't gonna be the same without you," I said.

"You'll be perfectly fine without me. I trained you well." He pauses, before adding, "I'm glad you started working there, for what it's worth."

"Really?" I asked, flattered. This was the closest to a compliment he'd ever given me.

"Yeah," he said. "Who else would help me unclog the toilets?"

I pelted him in the chest with a Raisinet. "Seriously, though. I'll miss you."

He raised a brow. "Really? Haven't I annoyed you enough?"

I shrugged. "No more than I annoy you. Anyway, you'll be my only friend at school."

"You'll make tons of friends and forget all about me," he said. I couldn't tell if this was disappointing or a total relief to him.

"Of course I won't." The idea seemed absurd. I'd spent more time with him than anyone else all summer, including Dad and my aunts. On the two days a week we didn't work together (Sundays and Mondays, The Cinema was closed), I missed hanging out with him. I wasn't sure whether things were going to change once school started. At least at The Cinema, we were forced to spend time together. But if we were going to stay friends at school, we'd have to actually make the effort.

I was also scared for Teller to know me outside of work. At The Cinema, I was just me. I didn't have to be the weird, quirky girl with a dead mom like I was at my old school.

When I confessed I thought he'd ditch me, he gave me a sideways look and said, "Lo, I'm in the computer science club at school. I don't exactly have a lineup of friends." He was being dramatic. He wasn't the massive loser he thought he was. Sure, he wasn't at all the parties or the center of attention in the cafeteria, but he was generally well liked. He had a small group of friends—guys and girls—who were on the nerdier side but weren't totally on the fringes of the social landscape. Still, Teller never really felt like he belonged anywhere.

"Well, good. Because I wasn't going to let you go anyways. You're my best friend."

The moment that statement slipped past my lips, I held my breath, desperate to take it back. Teller was *my* best friend, sure. I'd told him more about me than I'd told anyone else. Different as he was, he was a good listener. He listened when I told him what it was like not to have a mom. He didn't look at me with pity. He just acknowledged my feelings.

Most of all, I didn't have to do anything to impress him. But what if I wasn't his?

Instead of looking at me like the weirdo I was, he just grinned with eyes trained on the road ahead.

"Am I *your* best friend?" I ventured.

A moment of silence went by before he finally answered, "Yes. Why?"

I reined in my smile. Best to play it cool. "Well, I wasn't sure. But thank goodness. It would have been embarrassing if you'd said no."

He just smirked. "Why are you so shocked?"

"I figured I annoy the crap out of you."

"Oh, you definitely annoy me," he said with a laugh. "But you're the only person I can be around for long periods of time without wanting to submerge myself in the nearest body of water."

"That is the highest compliment."

He studied my face for a beat. "As your *best* friend, I should probably tell you . . ." His voice trailed as he pointed to my mouth with a wry smile.

I slapped my hand over my mouth, mortified. "What? Do I have something in my teeth?"

"A bit of raisin. Right in the front."

Yup, we were officially best friends.

He looks at me now like he knows I'm thinking about the past.

"Why are you always so surprised when I say you're my best friend?" he asks.

I shrug. "Maybe because we're so different? I don't know. And you said on our double date that I *made* you be my friend."

"I mean, you kind of did. It's not an insult. It's just how I am. The friends I have are the ones that have made the effort. I don't mean it like my friendship is so exclusive or anything. I guess I just assume no one is that interested in me, so I don't really go out of my way to try."

"People are interested in you," I assure him. "Why would you think otherwise?"

"Because I'm going to be a data analyst," he says straight up. I remember when he told me he wanted to major in data science. I gave him a hard time at first. Who wakes up one day and decides their dream job is crunching numbers? But the more I thought about it, the more I realized it was the perfect job for him. Numbers and statistics are predictable, logical.

"Caleb didn't mean that offensively," I say, realizing I've uttered the name we weren't going to mention tonight. A fresh wave of sadness washes over me. In all our running around, I've managed to avoid thinking about him most of the night. I will myself to stay in this moment with Teller. But I need to make my point. "He was just trying to say it wasn't something he could picture himself doing."

He shakes his head. "That's exactly it. Numbers and data are boring to most people, especially Mr. I'm Not Like a Regular Tourist I'm a Traveler—shit. Sorry. I know we aren't talking about him."

I can't help the giggle that escapes me. "I'm not a tourist, I'm a traveler," I say in my best deep Caleb voice. I don't make a habit of talking badly about people I care about, but a little shit talking feels justified. "You hated him, didn't you?"

"Not at all. We're just different people." I observe Teller for a few beats. "Okay, every time he said, 'Let's do something authentic,' I almost expired. Like, what does that even mean? Let me do this touristy Colosseum tour without you reminding us how you've already seen it five times."

186

We devolve into laughter and vow to do the most quintessentially touristy stuff for the rest of the trip.

Roasting Caleb feels kind of good, strangely cathartic. "Remember the time he talked about volunteering with starving orphans in Chad? We get it, you're virtuous."

Teller snorts. "Or when he stared into the eyes of a lion in Kenya . . . which, to be fair, is pretty freakin' cool. No wonder he thinks I'm a boring number cruncher."

"That's exactly why you're not boring, though. Most people like to travel. But you find excitement in things not a lot of people do, even though you hate most things," I add with a little sauce.

"I do not hate most things."

I swing him a look. "You hated me when we first met."

"I did not! I admired you."

I do a double take. "Admired me?" I certainly never got that impression.

"You were . . . fearless. About the world, about everything."

"That's completely untrue," I argue, righting myself on the stool, knee brushing against his.

His eyes catch mine. "I know now that you aren't completely fearless, but I thought you were. You let your dogs lick your mouth."

I nearly topple off the stool laughing. "Touché," I say.

"By the way, I like that you like so many things," he says before taking a sip of his drink. "The world excites you."

"That's kind of my problem, though. I like everything, but I don't love anything enough to stick with it."

"Have you tried tackling it the opposite way? Thinking about what you dislike instead?"

I consider that, dragging my fingers through the condensation under my glass.

"There isn't much I dislike."

"Oh, come on. Even an irrational hatred?"

"Oh! I have an irrational hatred of butterflies."

"That's not irrational. Butterflies are terrifying. An irrational hatred is something like . . . how I hate this song." "Happy" by Pharrell Williams is piping through the speakers.

"You hate 'Happy'? That's just dark. This song is literally joy personified." I clap the surface of the sticky bar to the beat, just to get a rise out of him.

Teller buries his head in his hands. "I hate it with a passion."

"What else do you hate irrationally?" I shift closer, like a reporter waiting for their subject to reveal something juicy.

"Claymation. It makes my blood boil."

"Claymation? Oh my god. What did poor little Claymation Rudolph ever do to you?"

"It's so creepy, with the wide mouths, bug eyes, and weird expressions. The movement. It's awful."

I can't stop giggling—and neither can he. Hanging with Teller like this feels like second nature. Like old times. It's so natural, there's no way we won't be doing this in ten, twenty, thirty years' time.

It's even more fun to witness Tipsy Teller in action. There are a few telltale signs Tipsy Teller is here. First, he starts exhibiting unusual behavior. He doesn't second-guess everything he does or use his sleeve to open door handles. And tonight, Tipsy Teller is weirdly giddy, swaying on his stool and humming to the music while clumsily sipping his drink through a rainbow-striped straw. He's also social, chatting it up with the bartender, asking about his family and children, waving at customers as they walk in. He even buys a beefy dude covered in tattoos (including his face) a fruity drink with an umbrella because he "looked lonely."

Beefy Tattooed Guy's name is Kai. He takes the free drink as an invitation to sidle up next to us, umbrella tucked fashionably behind his ear. He *loves* the umbrella.

Over the next half hour, he twirls his umbrella, orders us each another drink (with umbrella, please), and tells us all about his baby back in Scotland (a pit bull named Norman). We bond immediately over our pets, taking turns showing each other photos. This evolves into him trying to entice me to buy a fake Louis Vuitton tote that apparently matches my eyes. When he's not being a devoted dog dad or hawking fake luxury handbags, he works in the paint department at Homebase, the Scottish equivalent of Home Depot.

Teller asks Kai all about his tattoos, the explanations for which vary considerably. Some mean absolutely nothing, like the dragon emblazoned on his chest when he was fourteen and feeling himself, while he gets a little teary talking about others (the deflated balloon with a party hat on his calf). By the time he's ready to leave, he wants to get the umbrella tattooed on his left index finger.

"Kai. What a stand-up guy. I want to be him when I grow up," Teller says before he's even out of earshot.

"Aside from being a criminal, yes."

"Eh, it's what's inside that counts." He waves his hand in the air, swooping it around to fold me into his side.

That's another thing about Tipsy Teller. He's, dare I say, affectionate. And carefree. And silly. He wouldn't stop poking me and laughing in the Uber back to the hostel.

I watch as the silver glow of the moon dances off his face, giving his skin an almost iridescent effect.

"Excuse me!" he shouts suddenly to the driver. "Can you let us out here?"

"We're not even close to the hostel," I say as he practically flings himself out of the car. Jeez, he must be really wasted. It isn't until I look out the window that I see the neon-pink sign.

A tattoo shop.

I swing him a wild look. "Are you kidding?"

By the time I get out of the car, he's already walked in. It's like he's been taken over by Kai's essence.

An hour later, we emerge with new ink.

I got a dime-size outline of a crescent moon to symbolize him, and he got a sun to symbolize me. All Teller's idea.

"The sun to my moon," he'd said, which would have been more adorable if he hadn't slurred it, hand over his eyes so he didn't have to see the needle.

Neither of us thought it hurt that badly, probably because the tattoos are tiny, barely noticeable on the inner part of our index fingers. He'll regret this tomorrow morning. I'm sure of it. But right now, I couldn't be happier.

"We're in the most magical place on Earth, and I still have the most fun with you in a dingy tattoo parlor," I gush.

"Let's just hope we don't have hep C," he slurs into the shell of my ear, nestling his head on my shoulder.

As we look out the window and count the number of fountains we pass, I can't help but smile down at my tattoo. It feels like a middle finger to the vision. Proof our friendship is too strong to crumble.

21

Tuscany

W hat the fu—"

That's what I wake up to the next morning.

Teller woke up to a sore finger and a lot of regrets. "Why did you let me do this?"

"Nothing could have stopped you, Tel. You were a man on a mission," I say, recalling him confidently telling the tattoo artist what he wanted without so much as a blink. "And now you have a nice reminder of me on your finger, forever," I remind him.

That seems to placate him, slightly. Though he still stares at the tattoo like it's a bug the entire train ride to Tuscany.

"According to my GPS, the hostel looks like it's pretty close to the train station," I say as we haul our rucksacks from the luggage area of the train.

"Well, actually, I booked us another place," Teller says, passing me my rucksack.

I roll my eyes. "Why? I thought this one was up to your standards. Did you go down the rabbit hole reading one-star reviews again?"

He shakes his head. "Nah. I just found a better place."

He's weirdly chill about this "better place" the entire long taxi ride there. Unlike the original booking, which was close to town, this one is deep in the rolling hills of the Chianti countryside.

It isn't until we pull up to the gates that I understand where we are. I recognize the name on the wrought iron sign immediately.

Villa Campagna.

Where Mom and Mei stayed. And it's just as stunning as Mei described, surrounded by a landscape of lush green rolling hills dotted with rows of grapevines as far as the eye can see. The building is covered with leafy greenery stretching all the way to the terra-cotta-tiled roof.

"Holy shit, Tel," I manage over my gasp. "How did you know?"

He shrugs. "You mentioned it. The night I came back to town." I recall talking about it briefly in passing. I can't believe he actually remembered.

"We aren't staying here, are we?"

He nods. "We are."

"But how? This place is like, hundreds of dollars a night. We can't afford it—"

"Consider it all your birthday and Christmas presents for the next ten years combined. And before you say anything, the booking is nonrefundable. After you lost the photo, I figured you might want to feel closer to your mom," he adds, eyes softening.

I can barely pick my jaw up off the ground. "I—I literally don't know what to say." It's by far the most thoughtful thing anyone has ever done for me.

I'm still wrecked over Caleb, but being here, exactly where Mom stood so many years ago, is sure to dull the pain.

We traverse the grounds, passing workers tending to the vines, harvesting grapes. The owner's name is Roc. He's young, in his thirties if I had to guess. Based on his band tee and corduroys, he strikes me as more of an IPA-and-kombucha guy than a wine connoisseur, but Roc definitely knows what's up. He takes us on a tour of the underground wine cellar before we even check into our rooms, explaining the diverse varieties of grapes they grow in great detail.

The inn is warm, decorated with art and dark-wood antique furnishings that remind me of pieces at the estate sales Aunt Mei used to drag me to as a kid. I can see why she and Mom loved this place so much.

Eager to rest before dinner, Teller unlocks our door, stopping so abruptly, I nearly crash into his rucksack. "Um . . . I think they messed up the reservation."

"What?" I peek over his shoulder.

The room is cute and minimalist, with cool tile floor and a quilted bedspread. Behind heavy wooden shutters is a sun-drenched balcony boasting a sprawling view of an olive grove. A queen-size bed adorned with at least seven throw pillows takes up most of the middle of the room. And that's when it hits me. There's only one bed.

My skin tingles at the thought of sharing a bed again. But unlike that single bunk bed in Venice, the prospect of sharing this bed feels . . . different somehow.

"Uh, I'll go check at the front desk," I say, backing away slowly.

Roc confirms this was not a mix-up. "My sincere apologies. I assumed you were a couple. We don't actually have any more rooms with two beds available. But there might be a pullout couch in the basement. Let me check if we still have it—"

Teller gives me an uneasy look that screams *so much for splurging.*

I shake my head, making the best of the situation. "It's fine, really."

"Is it?" Teller asks.

"Why not? It's a big bed. No big deal. Honestly, I'd sleep in a sleeping bag on the lawn if it means we get to stay here." It really isn't an issue, especially when we've already shared a twin.

Teller runs a hand over the back of his neck, surveying the room. "Right. It's totally fine."

It really is. Fine. At least, I think so.

∼

"Welcome to Tuscany, everyone, also known as the heart of Italy," Noreen, our adorable five-foot-nothing tour guide says once everyone has deboarded the bus. "Tuscany is mostly famous for its—"

She widens her eyes like a cartoon character and places her hand around her ear for emphasis, waiting for someone to fill in the blank. Gotta give props for the gusto.

Everyone is giving their best soulless, blank expressions, so I shout, "Wine!" which she seems to appreciate.

"Yes! Very good. The vineyards, the wine, the world-class olive oil. But Tuscany is also known for its delectable artisanal cheese, including Pecorino, made from sheep's milk. That's why we'll be spending the morning at one of my favorite places, Cascina Formaggio Toscana."

I can see why it's one of her favorite places. The villa is a stone farmhouse surrounded completely by olive groves. Noreen introduces us to an older gentleman in brown overalls named Louis, the owner of the farm. She translates his Italian into English as he leads us around the lush estate and through the pastures of sheep roaming and munching on grass. In between, they converse in Italian, and I'd wager Noreen has a massive crush on Louis based on how many times she touches his elbow.

"These are the true stars," Louis explains, pointing to the pasture. "Sardinian sheep. They provide us with the milk that's the heart of our cheesemaking process. If you're feeling frisky, you can see if they'll let you scratch behind their ears—they're quite the charmers."

Louis tells us about their generations-old techniques for cheesemaking, including milking the sheep and the intricacies of curd formation. We even get to watch the workers demonstrate how each cheese wheel is carefully curated and topped with Louis's secret blend of herbs and spices.

Clutching handfuls of cheese samples, we meander through the fields, where Louis discusses sustainable farming. We're trailed by a big black farm dog named Jeanie who begs for cheese slices—her favorite snack. I give her nearly all my samples so I don't get a stomachache, and so does Teller.

Then we head to an enclosure containing a herd of alpacas. There are about seven of varying sizes and colors, and all named after Shakespearean characters. To my delight, we're allowed to walk them on the pathways. I steer a brown one with massive teeth named Malvolio, and Teller walks a smaller white one with a mushroom cut named Horatio.

"I'm not sure we could have picked a better activity for you. You haven't stopped smiling since we got here," Teller says, giving Horatio a nice pat on the back.

"Playing with dogs, sheep, and alpacas? You'll have to drag me out kicking and screaming. Sorry, there are no ponies."

"Ah, that's okay. I have my pony calendar now." His lips tug in the slightest grin.

"Who needs *Playboy* when you have ponies?" I tease, attempting to tug Malvolio away from a patch of weeds. He won't budge, so we stop and let him graze.

Teller gives me a gentle elbow. "Have you ever thought about starting a hobby farm or something?"

I tell him about my conversation with Caleb, about getting a big piece of land for rescue animals. "It's just . . . it doesn't seem realistic, does it?"

Teller thinks as we resume walking. "Maybe not right now. But you could get a job at a local rescue, or the humane society."

"Maybe. I'd probably love it. Though I'd be tempted to adopt every dog."

"I could definitely see you ending up with like, twelve dogs."

I run my fingers through Malvolio's thick, woolly fur. "Forever alone with ten dogs and ten cats. That's my future."

Teller shrugs. "That sounds like your ultimate fantasy."

I laugh because otherwise I'll cry. "Maybe my true soulmate is a dog."

He swings me a look. "Well, if you're still alone and miserable at fifty, I'll marry you."

Blood rushes to my ears, singeing the tips. Did he really just say that? "Even if I have all those dogs and cats? You would not. You would die of allergies."

"Not if you get poodles and those naked cats. I'd name one of them Vlad," he says with a grin. He's far too relaxed for someone who's just declared they'd marry me.

"I feel like you'd be great with a sphynx. They're high maintenance like you. Did you know they need suntan lotion so they don't get burned?"

"I did not know that, and somehow that makes me like them even more. Even if I'd still be allergic to their saliva."

"Okay, deal. If we're both single at fifty, we'll move to the country and adopt poodles and sphynxes." I think about that for a moment, just Teller and me. It's strange and a little illicit, thinking about a future with anyone but Caleb. Still, it's reassuring, knowing that Teller has no intention of not being my friend. Most of the time, marriage pacts seem depressing, but given the alternative of being forever alone and ridden with bad luck, it's the best life plan I've had yet, even better than side-by-side houses.

"Deal."

"My aunts seem to think things will work out with him. Caleb, I mean. They keep saying if he's meant for me, we'll find our way back to each other." I explain that soulmates don't always come together easily, which he quietly absorbs. "It's worked out for everyone else in my family, except Cousin Lin and Great-Aunt Shu." If it doesn't, I don't even want to think about what that says about me.

"You won't end up like them, Lo," he assures me.

After our alpaca walk, we snake through rows of vibrant grapevines stretched out in perfectly straight lines. The sun is starting to set, and the leaves catch the sunlight, casting a mosaic of shadows.

"Thank you," I say over the buzz of a bee hanging out on a cluster of grapes.

"For what?"

"For being here, for supporting me."

"How are you doing?" he asks, studying my face closely.

I sigh. "I miss him, I'm not gonna lie. But you've really helped take my mind off things. Thanks for booking this place, by the way. It's really special. I feel more connected to my mom here, in Tuscany, than I ever have," I admit, taking in the rolling hills.

"It's the most worthwhile expense so far," Teller says, looking me in the eye. In the light, his eyes look the color of honey, speckled with flecks of forest green. "Seeing you sad is the worst thing in the world. If I can make you laugh by eating random pizza on a curb and making an ass of myself at the pub, I will." It hadn't occurred to me that he went out of his comfort zone just for me. "And if anything, I should be thanking you."

"For what?"

"Everything. Bringing me that cheer-up kit. Making me come on this trip. Adding some excitement to my life. I even got a tattoo because of you! But mostly, being my friend." My heart soars. It means everything to hear him say that, especially after this year, not knowing where I stood in the lineup of his life.

"Always."

After the tour is over, we head back to the villa. Our afternoon is spent under the shade of a pergola, getting to know the other guests. We're seated at a long rustic, wooden table with wine barrels repurposed as seats, where Roc provides never-ending samples of various reds, whites, and even rosé. We hit it off with a pair of bleached-blond middle-aged friends, Loraine and Nettie, who are taking full advantage of the samples, their giggling clear evidence.

"How long have you two been friends?" I ask.

"We were roommates freshman year of college," Loraine explains. "Me, Nettie, and Marta."

"Don't forget Becs," Nettie adds.

"Oh yeah. But she was barely there. I think we saw her three times total. She mostly stayed with her boyfriend."

"Anyway, when my parents first dropped me off, Loraine had gone for lunch or something, so I snooped through her things. She had a bunch of crocheted face cloths and this huge photo of Jesus in a gilded frame on her bed, so naturally I assumed she was some basket-weaving ultrareligious type."

Loraine slaps the table and snorts. "My mom gave it to me. And to be fair, I hadn't been to a party or even had a boyfriend at that point. Net corrupted me."

Nettie rolls her eyes. "The first night, we went to the campus bar, and she made out with two different guys. That basically describes her next four years."

"Honestly, they're such a blur," Loraine admits.

I can't help but smile, already jealous of their long-time friendship, exactly what I so desperately want for Teller and me. "It's nice you guys have stayed so close. Do you live in the same city?"

"No, actually. Loraine moved to SoCal, and I'm in upstate New York. But we make a point to see each other once a year."

I make a mental note to pitch that to Teller. We may have promised to see each other twice next year, but what about all the years after that?

We eat dinner with Nettie and Loraine, which is homemade truffle gnocchi paired with various wines. Even Teller is enjoying himself thoroughly. I didn't know he was such a fan of wine. By the end of the night, Tipsy Teller has reappeared. He's animated and wildly competitive, playing Trivial Pursuit against Loraine and Nettie. So far, they're crushing us, mostly because they're more familiar with the slightly more dated pop culture. And Teller is pretty useless in that category, aside from music.

"Okay, last question for the win. This one is music," Nettie says, covering the back of the card to prevent Teller from peeking (Sober Teller would never). "Which British band released an album titled *A Rush of Blood to the Head* in 2002?"

Teller slams the tabletop as though there's an invisible buzzer. "Coldplay!"

Hysterical, we jump up and down, clapping our hands together like maniacs. When Nettie confirms it's the correct answer, he closes his hands over mine and squeezes, holding them for a beat.

"It's his favorite band," I explain to a confused Loraine and Nettie, who smile and congratulate us, but not before challenging us to a rematch tomorrow.

"Thank god you have terrible taste in music," I say, utterly winded as Loraine and Nettie head off.

He tips his head back in a laugh. "Guess what we're listening to when we get back to the room?"

"Only one song. Choose wisely," I say, unable to hide my grin at his enthusiasm.

He places both index fingers over his temples, thinking long and hard. "'Viva La Vida.'" He nearly knocks over my glass with his elbow in excitement.

"You're very drunk."

"So are you."

I think he's right.

22

We're lying side by side in our bed, staring up at the rattan ceiling fan creaking with each turn. A total of one minute into "Speed of Sound" (Teller changed his mind about ten times before settling on this song), he says, "I've been thinking."

"About what?"

"Just thinking."

I turn to face him. He studies me for a few beats before tracing his finger over his sun tattoo.

"About what I said back in Venice. About not believing in soulmates. It's been bugging me ever since because I feel like I didn't explain myself properly."

"It's okay, Tel. You don't have to believe in them." And I mean that. It never offended me. It's a lot for people to understand. Especially someone like Teller, who bases his life in logic and fact. Even I sometimes doubt it.

"I know. I sounded like a dick, though. Here's the thing—I think I could believe in soulmates, but only if you can have more than one."

"It would be cool if there was more than one out there," I say.

"Yeah. And if you can find one of them, I'd say you're pretty lucky."

The idea is comforting, especially given what happened with Caleb. "I hope you're right."

He's pensive through "Clocks."

"What are you thinking about now?" I finally ask.

"How cardboard is made."

I can't help but snicker at the ceiling. "Cardboard? The mystery of cardboard is keeping you up at night?"

"Okay, when you put it that way, it sounds ridiculous. But seriously, like, how do they make it? I think about this often. Don't you?"

"I literally never think about that. Who thinks about that?"

"Me!" he shouts, and we both ugly-laugh, chin to chest, double chins galore, until we're crying and begging the other to stop.

Once our laughter finally dissipates, Teller suggests we go to the pool—which is shocking, given his aversion to public pools. Tipsy Teller is still here and well. Before he changes his mind, I jump out of bed. We eagerly throw on our bathing suits and stumble downstairs (with Coldplay blasting through his portable speaker, of course). Unfortunately, the sign on the gate reads "Chiuso" after 9:00 pm. It's 8:55.

"Damn. It closes in five minutes," Teller says, already turning back.

"That means five minutes to swim," I say with a wink, pulling the gate open. I dive right in, plunging into the deep end. The cool water envelops me, whooshing through my ears, drowning out the distant, warped sound of Coldplay.

I rise to the surface just in time to see him peel his towel away. Sharing sleeping quarters with him for the past few weeks, I've seen his abs too many times to justify a reaction. But against the moonlight and the illuminated pool, the ridges of his body make my breath hitch. He plunges into the deep end, long limbs piercing through the water elegantly. Mesmerizing.

He resurfaces, wiping away the water dripping into his eyes, and taps my shoulder. "Tag, you're it!" By the time I come to, he's already swimming away, kicking up copious amounts of water in his wake.

No one kicks us out of the pool at nine. We play water tag for what feels like forever until I can barely keep up. If this were last year, I would have been a semi-decent match for him. But after his year of kickboxing, I'm left in the proverbial dust. Drained, I reach for the side of the pool, only to fall short in my exhaustion. Teller notices and tugs me close, steadying me around the waist. "Gotcha," he says quietly, and I don't resist.

Warmth shoots through me like liquid as I sway against him. His hands gently trace up and down the sides of my abdomen, sending a tingling sensation through my body. I secure my arms around his shoulders, feeling every groove of his muscles as he moves. I can feel his heart pounding, nearly in sync with mine. Even though I'm a bit uneasy in the deep end, I feel safe in his arms.

And when his eyes catch mine, lashes flecked with water droplets, I forget where we are. It's like we're in our own bubble. Everything else drowns out, even the sounds. Something inside me desperately wants to be even closer to him, if that's possible. His eyes drift toward my lips. For a moment, it seems like he wants to kiss me. And I want him to—so badly, down to my bones. But with a swish of the water, the moment passes. He releases me and swims to the side of the pool, hoisting himself up.

"Since when did you become Michael Phelps?" I ask, pushing all those thoughts to the recesses of my mind. "I thought you were scared of water. You were practically trembling on the gondola in Venice."

"I don't mess with open bodies of water. Pools are different. At least I can see what's at the bottom." He wrings the water from his hair. "I am still afraid of it, though. That's why I took swimming lessons this year."

"Shut up. You did not!"

"Don't make fun," he warns. "But yes. I did, and it's not what you think. I had a friend who was a lifeguard teach me."

I raise a hand to proclaim innocence, although I can't help but smile at the image of him wading around in a kiddie pool with a bunch of drooling toddlers, inflatable water wings circling each arm. "I wasn't going to. I think that's really brave of you. Why didn't you tell me?"

He winces. "I was embarrassed, I guess. Figured I'd wow you with my skills first," he adds with a deliriously charming wink.

"I think it's brave of you to confront your fears head-on."

"What about you? What are you scared of?" he asks, breaking the silence.

Lots of things, but I start with the most obvious. "Disappointing my family. Not living up to the legacy."

"But you have. You've had the vision like everyone else."

"And look how that turned out," I say wryly, deflecting. Because I already know the big answer. The one that first came to mind when he asked. It's *losing him*. My second vision coming to fruition. That's what I'm most afraid of. But instead, all that comes out is "Somersaults."

His brow pinches, confused. "Somersaults? Like, seeing other people do a somersault or doing one yourself?"

"Doing one myself. Don't laugh," I say, splashing him a little.

He stifles his snickering. "I'm sorry. But how did I not know this about you? I have a feeling there's a story here."

"Oh, there is. When I was in first grade, all these girls were doing somersaults at recess. One of the girls, Renee, was the best. She would do like, ten in a row, all around the yard."

"Sounds like a show-off," Teller teases.

"She totally was. But get this. One day we were all watching and counting how many she could do in a row, and she ended up somersaulting right off the brick retaining wall and falling like, three feet. She had to get stitches all down her face, Frankenstein-style. There was blood everywhere."

"Holy shit. That's traumatizing. But my question is, why didn't anyone stop her from going over the wall?"

I laugh. "I mean, we were like, six years old."

"So you've been too scared to try one since?"

"I've always wanted to. I felt like the only kid who didn't know how. But the older I got, the more embarrassing it was not to know how. It's a heavy cross to bear, I know," I tease.

He shakes some water out of his ear. "You should try."

"Like, right now?" I ask, gesturing to the grassy area by the pool.

"Why not? There's space."

I stand on the stairs, shaking out my limbs as I get out of the pool. I bend over to touch my toes. "I don't know where to start. This doesn't feel natural."

He positions himself behind me and straightens my arms over my head. I freeze slightly at the span of his chest against my back. "Okay, so on the count of three, you're going to bring your arms down to the ground and tuck your head between your legs. Easy."

"If it's so easy, you do it."

Sober Teller would never do an impromptu somersault on a tiny patch of grass beside a pool. But Tipsy Teller is so down.

"Sure." He's uncharacteristically confident as he proceeds to do a very poor excuse for a somersault. It more closely resembles a cartwheel, legs flailing and crooked like a spider. "Why are you laughing? It was a perfect somersault."

It was not, but I don't want to burst his bubble, so I let him have it. "You're basically Simone Biles. But I still can't do it."

"You absolutely can. Look, I'll find a step-by-step guide."

He grabs his phone from the side of the pool and, after multiple typos, manages to bring up a YouTube tutorial on how to somersault.

We spend the next half hour attempting to follow the steps, each resulting in total disaster. I keep veering sideways, while Teller is a little too aggressive and continually topples into the gate. We both end up on the grass, cold and hooting with laughter until a light flicks on nearby, sending us racing back to the room in a fit of hysterics.

"What else are you scared of?" he asks once we're dry and warm, collapsed in a heap on the bed, Coldplay still playing. I can't help but notice how his shirt is slightly bunched, revealing his lower abs.

Ugh. There's that stomach dip again. I stare at the ceiling, hands folded over my middle, thoughts churning. "Losing people I love," I finally admit.

He reaches over, sliding a warm hand over mine. I suck in my breath and close my eyes, relaxing under his gentle squeeze. I can't lose him. I won't let it happen. I'll do whatever it takes.

"I love you, Lo," he mumbles, though it sounds more like, "IlubyouLuuh."

The words strike me in the heart. He's never told me he loves me. Bianca and I say *I love you* all the time, but Teller has never been that gushy kind of friend. "You really need some sleep, Tel. But I appreciate it."

He rolls over, peering at me through sleepy eyes. "Do you love me?"

My breath hitches, the rubber band between us pulling tight. "Of course I do."

"Because I really, really do."

I freeze, stomach curling into a tight knot as his eyes wander over me, awaiting a response. Does he mean what I think he means? No. There's absolutely no way. He's still in love with Sophie, and even if he wasn't, he's never once shown any sign that he feels anything more. I try assessing him through the darkness. He's rolled onto his side, breath growing heavier until he's fully asleep.

I lie awake for what feels like hours.

~

I wake up, warm and cozy, at some point in the night, only to realize I'm wrapped tight like a burrito—and it's not the sheets. Teller's warm chest is pressed against my back, arm slung around my stomach.

My body stiffens, acutely aware of every nerve ending in my body. Is that what we're doing now? Casually cuddling? Is this a normal thing friends do? I suspect not.

He tightens his arm around me. Judging by his slow, deep breaths, he's still sleeping—at least, I think so. I stay still, lest I surrender to the strong urge to turn around and kiss him. It's not lost on me that this is the second time I've had that urge tonight.

We lie like that for what feels like forever while I try to figure out what led us to this point. First, there are our broken hearts. Second, there were a lot of drinks tonight. I've always been a bit affectionate when under the influence. Let's blame it on the wine. Wine makes everyone cuddly, even Teller Owens.

Still, I think of Caleb and Sophie. And while neither of us are beholden to either of them, the thought is enough to bring me back. It doesn't feel wrong, but after being so sure about my future, it also doesn't feel right.

I tuck and roll out of his embrace and feel the absence of his warmth immediately. As I curl into a ball on the other side of the bed, I can't help but wish I'd stayed right next to him.

23

"Sorry if I was annoying last night. I was way too drunk," Teller groans, voice so hoarse and rough, you'd think he just came off a twelve-day bender. He pulls his sunglasses down to get a better look as our bus arrives at our destination.

"You were not. I'm sorry if I snored," I say weakly, avoiding eye contact. We're both suffering from terrible hangovers. I have no idea if he remembers anything from last night, let alone cuddling, holding my hand, or telling me he loves me. But aside from guzzling a liter of water and general silence all morning, he's not acting completely out of character.

"You hogged the blankets, though I got better sleep last night than I've had this whole trip," he says, stretching his arms over his head.

"Must be the one-thousand-thread-count sheets."

He agrees and starts comparing the firmness of our mattress to the hostels'. Back to the old Teller. But I don't really listen. I'm still thinking about being nestled in his arms. The thud of his heartbeat against my back quickening as I arched into him. Yup, maybe him not remembering is for the best.

I push aside those thoughts as we get off the bus for our first activity—a bike tour. I insisted we go despite Teller's urging that we skip it and sleep off our hangovers. Maybe it's my chronic fear of missing out, and the fact that we're in Italy, but the last thing I want to do is lie in bed all day, caught up in my shitstorm of emotions. I keep oscillating between wanting to kiss Teller and missing Caleb, neither of which are productive or actionable.

Unfortunately, I did not think realistically about pedaling a bike in the beating-hot sun for three hours while deathly hungover. We begin with what is supposedly a leisurely ride through winding roads lined with cypress trees and olive groves. It would be gorgeous if my head weren't pounding and my legs didn't feel like jelly. There's not even a hint of a breeze. After the first hill, I know I've made a grave error coming on this tour. Teller feels the same way, based on the look he gives me when we take a break.

Our first stop is a vineyard for a wine tasting, though Teller and I both opt for water. I can barely look at wine without my stomach turning. Later, we stop at a small trattoria to try bruschetta and breads dipped in various types of olive oil, all of which taste the same to me. But the carbs help soak up the remaining alcohol in our systems, and we both start to feel a bit better. After relaxing under the shaded terrace to sample pasta and risotto, we go back to the villa to freshen up for the night.

Loraine and Nettie invited us to a restaurant/bar with a huge court-yard where they play live music. It's magical, with fairy lights strung above us in a crisscross pattern. White lanterns dangle from the lights, casting a soft yellow glow. A mix of contemporary and classical Italian songs purr through the air.

Teller and I opt to remain sober, although that doesn't stop me from dancing with Loraine and Nettie. Teller is his normal, observant self, spectating from the comfort of the table and offering the odd thumbs-up. He reminds me of Dad perched on the sidelines at my science fairs as a kid.

At the risk of Teller growing bored, I sashay over to the table and extend my hand. "Come on. Dance with us!"

He shakes his head, pushing his chair back, out of my reach. "Oh no. I'm great right here."

Despite his protests, I pull him to his feet and bring him into the fold. He begrudgingly bobs his head to the beat, legs and torso stiff while he clumsily sways his long arms.

"Okay, you really need to loosen up a little," I say, shaking his arms. They feel like lead.

"I'm totally loose," he argues. He appears to be doing the Robot, though I don't think it's purposeful.

I collapse into his chest, laughing.

"What's wrong with my dancing?" he asks, a knowing smile flitting across his face. When his eyes lift to mine, I feel it right in my chest. That feeling from last night. I attempt to swallow, only to find my throat has gone dry. "Absolutely nothing," I manage.

Without notice, he grabs my hand, spinning me twice, twinkling lights melding into streaks of golden luminescence all around us. I spin him, too, or attempt to. Due to his height, he's forced to duck like he's doing the limbo, which amuses everyone on the crowded dance floor.

Three songs pass and I barely notice—because I'm having the time of my life. We're not in sync or in rhythm in any way. We're a bunch of misguided twirls, spinning off-balance, crushed toes, and mini collisions. But we don't stop laughing until a slow song interrupts the vibe. I pause for a beat, assuming he's had enough and wants to return to the safety of our table. Instead, he takes my hand and places it on his shoulder. His hands settle along my waist and we sway together, left, right, left, right.

My mind clutters with a rush of thoughts, tiny fractions of memories of us at The Cinema, wiping tears on his hoodie as we said goodbye in front of his packed Corolla before he left for college, the way he held me last night in the pool, of Sophie and Caleb. But despite it all, I know for sure that this feels good.

His eyes search mine and I stare back, dizzy from his proximity, breath catching in my chest. When he pulls me closer, I nestle my head on his shoulder and close my eyes, wishing I could stay in this moment forever. Something feels different. It's in the thickness of the air. In the lingering of a glance. I can't explain it, but I no longer think it's all in my head.

He smiles against my cheek and asks, "Do you remember prom?"

I snort. "I remember forcing you to dance all night. You hated your life. Kind of like right now."

"I did not, and don't currently, hate my life. Not even a little," he says.

I level him with a look. "You absolutely did. I had to force you to dance with me. You were sad Sophie wasn't there and kept slinking off to text her."

We hadn't gone together or anything. He was planning to skip it because Sophie was at a family event and they'd already attended her prom. He didn't see the point in going to two.

And technically, I had a date. Bryce Shipman. He was a grade below and exclusively wore black turtlenecks (drama kid, can't you tell?) but decided prom was a good time to wear a stark-white suit. He only asked me to go because juniors weren't allowed unless they had a senior date. He forgot my corsage at home and disappeared during couples' photos at the koi ponds in Woodsbury Park. We'd ridden in the limo with some kids from the drama club, but he didn't pay much attention to me most of the night. He spent most of his time getting high under the bleachers. Truthfully, I'd have rather gone alone.

Teller lowers his head in acknowledgment. "I know. I'm really sorry. That probably ruined your night, didn't it?"

"No. I still had the best time." That was the truth. Sure, I'd straight-up forced him to come. And sure, he spent most of the night slumped at the table, moping over Sophie's absence.

But that's not what I remember most. What sticks with me is Teller finding a half-crushed corsage with wrinkled petals on the ground and presenting it to me on one knee. I remember running back and forth to the DJ booth requesting "Get Low" over and over and scream-singing the lyrics. And I remember singing it the whole way as he walked me home. And I remember how it felt when he tossed me over his shoulder when my feet started to hurt in my heels.

"Really?"

"Because I got to spend most of it with you," I tell him.

He studies me for a few seconds. "I've always loved that about you." There it is again. The *L* word.

I swallow the lump in my throat and blink. "What?"

"Your optimism. Like, you can find the good in anything." He smiles at me affectionately. "And for the record, I wasn't upset that night because I missed Sophie."

"You weren't?"

His jaw pulses. "We'd actually gotten in a bit of a tiff before I left. She was jealous of you."

"Jealous? Of me? Because we were dancing?"

"Well, I guess that too. But more than that. She was jealous of you in general. My relationship with you."

All my interactions with Sophie flit through my mind, and suddenly, it all clicks into place.

It all makes sense.

I always figured she didn't like me. And sure, I thought it could be that she was uncomfortable with our friendship. But Teller assured me she wasn't. I tried to look for the evidence, but the signs that I was being paranoid were louder. She was sweet to me. She was one of the first people to like my stuff on social media. She'd always comment with the same three heart emojis, no words.

"She had no reason to be jealous," I say. *Or did she?*

"No." His voice drops, low and husky in a way I've never heard before. "No reason at all."

He holds my gaze for a beat, and the world tilts. Heat radiates from his chest, which is now firmly pressed against mine. His lips hover inches away and I can barely speak, let alone breathe. And for the third time, I can't help but think about how soft they look, about how they would feel against mine.

So, I do what I always do. I act on impulse.

24

Aunt Mei always says, "The first time is happenstance, the second is coincidence, but the third is a pattern. It's deliberate."

It feels deliberate, the way my lips brush against his, featherlight and tentative. Our breath melds, and it takes me a couple seconds to realize he isn't pulling away.

But he's also not actively kissing me back either.

Alarm bells sound in my head, and I pull back abruptly. "I'm so sorry," I blurt over the band's cover of "Everybody Wants to Rule the World." "I shouldn't have done that."

His lips twitch ever so slightly, but his expression remains unreadable. I expect his face to contort in that particular grimace; it usually appears when something grosses him out. But it doesn't. The pads of his fingers brush against my cheek, moving aside a strand of hair. With the precision of a surgeon, he gently tucks it behind my ear. His knuckles ghost the crests of my cheeks, eliciting a shiver.

I don't know who, but one of us closes the gap. Our lips touch and it's soft, undemanding, lighting me up like the tiniest pinpricks of static shock. Then we pull away and just look at each other for a moment. I silently count to three. Just after I hit two, his mouth meets mine. His kiss is achingly soft and slow, like he wants to take his time. There is no mistake: Teller Owens is kissing me back.

I wasn't prepared for what his kiss would feel like. I feel it in every part of my body, all the way to my toes. Our kissing becomes deeper, more urgent, like we're both desperate to release the tension that's been brewing all these years. He kisses me like I'm already his, like I've always been his. Like we always should have been doing this. And it's everything.

His tongue swirls against mine, filling me with a deep ache in the core of my stomach. His hands rake through my hair as I breathe in his fresh-cut-grass scent.

I've never had a better kiss. Ever.

"Wait a minute . . . I didn't think nice boys kissed like that," I say when he pulls away.

His brow flicks wickedly. *"Oh yes, they fucking do."*

I'm not sure if it's that he knows the quote from *Bridget Jones's Diary*, but I've never been so turned on. I tug him back toward me immediately.

We meld together, firmer this time. It takes me by surprise. I expected kissing Teller would be soft, slow, and steady, just like everything he does. But it's anything but.

In all the commotion, we've drifted into the corner of the courtyard, nearing the wall. He pins me against the brick and kisses me like we're star-crossed lovers reuniting after years of anguished separation. It's fast and intense, igniting me from the inside out. With each gasp and slide of our tongues, we make clear how much we've wanted this. He threads his fingers through my hair, and a low, sensual moan escapes him.

Since when is Teller Owens so unbelievably *hot*?

I inhale as he pulls me flush to his chest, absorbing the solid weight of him against me. His fingers trace the soft skin of my hips under my shirt. I rock against him.

When my hands drift to his waistband, his hand presses over mine.

I feel the heat from his mouth and I pull in a breath, waiting for his lips to touch mine again. But they don't. They hover, like a whisper, just close enough but not quite closing the gap. My heart pounds the longer our breath mingles.

I roam his face for any sign of discomfort, but he looks at ease. His eyes meet mine in a look I'm not sure I've ever seen. He's no longer the sweet Teller I know. He looks like someone who knows what he wants and is going to take it.

Abruptly, Nettie and Loraine peel around the corner to catch their ride back. I've never been so grateful for an interruption.

25

We head back to Villa Campagna with Loraine and Nettie. Despite being stone-cold sober, we're in hysterics as we make our way to our room. We're so exhausted from the day, and giddy from what happened on the dance floor, that everything makes us vibrate with laughter.

The shirtless dude outside the restaurant listening to heavy metal with no earphones? Hilarious.

Loraine and Nettie belting Britney Spears? Snorting uncontrollably.

The villa employee who was running at full tilt through the living room with a pile of toilet paper rolls? Gut-busting, stomach-clenching laughter. I'm pretty certain we sound like squealing rodents.

Teller almost tripping on the carpet and face-planting when he tries to race me down the hall? Dead. Goodbye, earthlings.

Once we're back in our room, just us two, the laughter dissolves into silence. I collapse into bed, makeup and clothes still on, but Teller spends longer than usual in the bathroom going through his usual nighttime routine.

What's taking so long? I can't help but wonder if he's avoiding me. If he regrets what happened back at the restaurant.

The anticipation of him coming to bed nearly ends me. I shift and turn, unable to settle, not knowing what's going to happen when he comes out. I should probably close my eyes and go to sleep. But my mind won't stop racing. Thinking about his lips on mine. How warm his chest felt against me. How I've never had a better kiss in my life. How those wild flutters in my stomach from earlier just won't quit.

I know it was a one-time thing, a random kiss. But after one hit, I'm craving it all over again. It's like I'm addicted to the sensation, his taste, his low moans.

Before I know it, I'm hovering outside the bathroom. I knock and the door swings open.

Our eyes meet in the mirror. He's finished brushing his teeth and is leaning on the sink like he's bracing himself. He's shirtless and his abs are on prominent display.

"You good?" I ask, mouth suddenly dry as my eyes greedily take it all in, unable to concentrate. I think I've gone into overdrive. His stomach is so chiseled. Does he have a six-pack or an eight-pack? I can't be sure.

My infatuation with his abs isn't lost on him. "Are you?" he retorts, smug as he spins around so his back is against the counter.

Energy flashes between us like a live wire. I approach confidently, running my finger down the hard ridges of his abs, exploring, moving up his shoulders and down his arm, all the way to his sun tattoo. Gooseflesh erupts in my wake. I pull in a breath and all feels calm. Like I've always known this was going to happen.

He swallows. "What are you doing?"

"Seducing you." It's only when I say it out loud that I freeze. Am I actually trying to hook up with Teller Owens? The one who drives me crazy with his planning and disinfecting? The person I feel most comfortable with in the entire world? All without an ounce of liquid courage?

"Shit," he hisses, lips hovering somewhere around my forehead. Something about his voice, the heady, fiery look in his eyes. He's suddenly transformed into Sexy Teller again. With a featherlight touch, his fingertips skate up my arms, landing on either side of my face. He tips his head down so his nose slides along the curve of my cheek.

"Or at least, I'm trying to," I say through the shiver running through me.

"It's working." He swallows hard, eyes sliding down every inch of me.

I could angle my head ever so slightly to line my mouth up with his. I'm dying to feel his soft lips on mine again, even for just a fraction of a second. By the hungry look in his eyes, I think he wants to kiss me too. The question is, is this a horrendous idea?

I rise onto my toes and test the waters, slow and steady. At the restaurant, the kiss happened so fast, so I want to savor this. *This is right,* his lips say, exploring, softly biting my lower lip. I drag my fingers through his thick hair and down the back of his neck. Then I work my way over his shoulders and down the planes of his back, pressing him to me and savoring every flex of his new muscles.

His hands move over my hips and in one swift movement, he's spun us around and propped me on the counter. We're a dizzy whirl of hands and fast kisses. Not the measured Teller I'm used to.

Suddenly, I feel constricted. There are far too many layers between us. I reach to the back of my dress, and he gets the hint, pulling me off the counter to help me take it off. With one swift flick, my bra is off too. Who knew Teller was so skilled in the bedroom?

"Wow." His eyes slide down my body, slow, like he's taking it all in. As they go lower, I catch the smallest upward curve of his lips.

"Why are you smiling?"

His eyes flick back to mine, and the blood rushes through me, pounding through my ears. "Because you're perfect. Even more perfect than I already thought," he whispers, lips catching mine again.

Teller knows I've always been a bit self-conscious about the roundness of my stomach and the stretch marks on my inner thighs. And now, I'm entirely exposed in the harsh light of the bathroom. He still makes me feel perfect.

Teller picks me up and carries me back to the bed. I pull him on top of me and we lie there, his hand over my hammering heart. His moan vibrates against my mouth, and I want to catalog this moment, the way he sounds and tastes as he pulls my knee over his hip.

He squeezes my thigh and pauses, placing his opposite hand beside my face to support himself. "Wait, I just want to check in."

"Okay?"

"Are you sure you want to do this?" he asks softly, gaze imploring. "Because I don't want you to regret it."

"Do you think you'll regret it?"

"No. Not at all. I just don't want you to. I care about you too much," he says with a gentle swipe of his thumb on my hip bone.

I can't help but smile. I'm grateful for the check-in. At the prospect of sex, most guys would waste no time getting straight to business. But Teller is still Teller, incredibly thoughtful, always thinking about others.

"I won't regret it. I mean, we're just two friends soberly consenting, right?"

He pulls back slightly, blinking through the darkness. "Right. It's totally normal. Friends have sex all the time. It doesn't have to mean anything."

"Just casual vacation sex," I say, even though this certainly doesn't feel casual.

"Things won't be weird after, right?"

"After we make each other come? No, not at all." We both laugh, his chest vibrating against mine. "Seriously, though. It won't be weird if we don't make it weird," I whisper, reaching to trace the waistband of his boxers.

We shed the remainder of his clothes quickly. Maybe it's me being awkward about the fact that he's entirely naked, but I can't help but laugh when he blindly tosses them into the darkness. Regular Teller would never.

Before he climbs back over me, he pauses. "Wait." He dives off the bed to grab his jeans from the floor, pulling a condom from his wallet. "Safety first." A glimpse of Regular Teller.

I laugh. "I didn't take you for someone who carries condoms around *just in case.*"

"Maybe there's a lot you don't know about me."

His voice is low and husky again. He climbs back over me, threading his hands through mine. A hush falls over us. There's only the sound of our hearts beating, the bursts of our breaths. My mind is quiet, peaceful, and it occurs to me how comfortable I am. How safe I feel with Teller. Sure, this is entirely foreign, but it still feels like us. Even when he's looking into my eyes, telling me how beautiful I am and how much he wants this. Even when we're skin to skin and he's touching me exactly how I want to be touched, as though he knows my body better than I do.

When we've finished and I'm cocooned in his arms, listening to the soft hum of his breath, I can't help but wish we'd done this sooner. And now that we have, I'm not sure things will ever be the same.

26

A strand of sunlight peeks through a crack in the blackout drapes, blasting me in the face. I wake with a jolt, covering myself with the sheets, hiding from the light like a vampire. Instinctively, I stretch my arm out, feeling for the solid mass of Teller's body. But his side of the bed is empty.

And that's when last night comes back to me. Dancing at the restaurant under the soft glow of the lanterns. Laughing so hard our stomachs hurt. The quickening of his warm breath against my neck. The feeling of his soft lips melding with mine. The coldness of the marble under my thighs when he hoisted me on the counter. And the weight of him over me, joining us together.

Teller and I had sex. Twice.

Incredible sex, if I may add.

By the time I succumb to reality and pull myself out of bed, there's still no sign of him. Not in the bathroom, not in the hallway. Could he have left? This early in the morning? It feels out of character, given his tendency to sleep in.

Flashes of my vision snap through my mind at rapid speed. No. He couldn't have. Frantic, I open the closet door, double-checking that his belongings are still there. They are, thank god. He wouldn't have left without them.

He must have gone to breakfast. Or maybe a morning walk? Run? Then again, Teller isn't huge on breakfast, or physical activity, before noon. The only other scenario I can come up with is that he's been kidnapped by the Italian Mob.

Before I alert the authorities, I realize I haven't checked the balcony. I spot his loafer, stretched against the guardrail.

Bingo.

He's been sitting outside the whole time. He lifts his eyes, but only for a fraction of a second, like my dogs when they get caught eating something they shouldn't. My suspicion is confirmed. He's avoiding me. Things are officially weird.

"Morning! I'm shocked to see you up before me." My tone is chipper, maybe a little too loud.

He pretends to suddenly see me, ears turning a deep shade of pink. "Oh, hey. Yeah, I got hungry. Didn't eat much yesterday. I grabbed breakfast for you at the buffet. The yogurt is lactose free," he mumbles, nodding toward the tray on the table.

"Thank you," I say, tepidly pulling up a chair. After last night, I'm famished. "You feeling okay this morning?"

He tips his head. "Yeah. Oh, by the way, it's gonna be hot out today. I got some waters from downstairs. Left one on your bedside table."

Are we really talking weather like retired Floridians? "Thanks," I say, feeling antsy and nervous. I don't know what to do with my hands, so I slide my phone out too.

We sit there for a few minutes, scrolling on our phones. Truth be told, I'm scrolling mindlessly, not taking anything in. I'm too busy battling invasive thoughts, like did we make a terrible mistake? Did I throw myself at him and now he's feeling uncomfortable? Did he really want to hook up, or was he just too nice to say no?

No. There's no way I could have misinterpreted last night. He wanted it as much as I did.

Or maybe it's worse than that. Maybe he wanted it but ended up hating it. Maybe I'm a terrible kisser, or just generally terrible in bed. It occurs to me that I might have made a massive mistake. In an effort to keep him close, I did the exact opposite. Maybe *this* is what marks the beginning of the end for us.

Before I spiral and start saying all of that aloud, I fire off a quick SOS to Bianca.

Bianca: It's 2:30am. What's up?

Lo: I SLEPT WITH TELLER

I'm never one to beat around the bush.

Bianca: ????

Bianca: 😲 😲 😲 😲 😲

She follows up the question marks with five GIFs of varying surprised reactions ranging from bug eyes to public fainting.

Sometimes, I like to leave her in suspense, so I take a beat, set my phone down, and eye Teller. "Who are you texting?" I ask casually, trying to ignore my flaming-hot ears.

He hesitates, working down a swallow. "Um . . . Sophie." He says it so nonchalantly, as though they haven't broken up, as though we didn't just spend an intimate night together, as though texting her is just part of his morning routine. Did I slip into an alternate dimension or something?

Either way, his response hits me straight in the gut. I can't help but imagine the texts. Is he telling her we hooked up? Profusely apologizing? Telling her it was a huge mistake? Likely. I'm tempted to ask him straight up, but that would make me seem overly invested. He'd think I have feelings for him. So instead, I scarf down my breakfast in silence, trying my best to act as normal as possible. It's cowardly, but I can't look at him without blushing. I can't look at his lips without remembering about how they felt against my skin.

Thankfully, a FaceTime from Bianca gives me an excuse to go back inside.

She's in the dark, blankets pulled to her neck, eyes wide, hand over her mouth. By the way the camera jolts around, I'm fairly certain she's kicking her feet.

I try to warn her not to move her broken foot too much, but she's got a one-track mind.

"You slept together?" she shouts.

"Yes," I mouth, locking myself in the bathroom.

"How was it?" she asks.

"Um . . . good." Understatement of the century.

She blinks, silently calling me out. "I need details."

So I break down and tell her everything.

She giggles and screeches through the whole thing. "Hell yes. You deserve this. But wait. What about Caleb?"

My eyes widen. "Shit. You're right. I didn't even think about Caleb at all. Is that horrible of me? I'm a terrible person, aren't I?"

It's strange how something can feel so right in the moment. While we were dancing and kissing, it was like we were in our own world. Nothing else mattered. Last night, I didn't have feelings for Caleb. Last night, Caleb wasn't the person I was supposed to be with. And, dare I even think, last night Caleb wasn't my soulmate.

She shakes her head. "No! You're not technically together, even if he is your soulmate. And let's not forget, he's the one who ditched you in Florence."

Before we hang up, Bianca tells me all about the time she slept with another guy while on a "break" from her then boyfriend and how it was justified. "Similar situation," she assures me, letting me off the hook.

She's right. Logically, I know I didn't cheat or anything. Caleb is technically out of the picture right now. But it still feels wrong. Like I've both betrayed my destiny and messed up my most valued friendship in the process.

I'm grateful when we meet up with Loraine, Nettie, and a couple other guests for today's activity—truffle hunting. Having other people around takes the pressure off. On the bus, we choose seats opposite each other on the aisle. It's a subtle shift, as we've always sat next to each other.

We stop at a rustic farmhouse and are greeted by a burly farmer named Antonio. He's gracious and welcoming, but speaks so softly, we can barely hear him. As it turns out, truffle hunting isn't as glamorous as it sounds. In reality, it's just digging around in the dirt with a basket and a rusty spade. The only consolation is the cool shade of the forest.

I spend most of my time petting Antonio's loyal truffle-hunting dog, Mimi, a Lagotto Romagnolo. Eventually, Antonio politely requests that I refrain from petting her. I'm distracting her from her job.

I catch Teller digging around in the dirt under the shade of a huge tree. We haven't said more than two words to each other since this morning, and it's starting to wear on me. I have to fix this. Now.

"We're okay, right?" I ask, unable to stand the silence any longer.

His gaze meets mine. "Yeah. Why wouldn't we be?" he says after a long pause.

"Well, we did have sex."

His eyes widen. "We did?"

I back up a step. How could he not remember? We were both entirely sober—at least I was. "Wait, you don't remem—"

Before I can finish, his face breaks into a wide, goofy smile. "I'm just kidding, Lo. I remember it. Trust me." *Trust me.*

There are so many ways I could interpret that statement. But at this point, I don't really trust myself to interpret anything about Teller.

"This doesn't change things between us, does it? Like, we can just forget it ever happened, right? Go back to being totally normal? Just us?" I'm technically asking him, but really, I'm asking myself. Can I forget when the night is emblazoned in my mind? Unlikely.

A beat. Two beats. "Yeah. I mean, if that's what you want, we can agree to never speak of it from here on out. It's just casual vacation sex, remember?"

"Right. Casual vacation sex." I try to say it confidently, even though it feels like anything but.

~

Thankfully, the best distraction comes at dinner.

At least we're back on speaking terms. It's taken a while to get there, but I force it through a series of inappropriate jokes and unnatural conversation, and things are much improved from this morning. Hopefully, by the time we go to Amalfi tomorrow, things will be back to normal.

Neither of us wants to return to our room, the scene of the crime. So we stay on the communal patio long after our dinner plates are empty. The conversation flows: about the food, the beauty of the villa, memories from the trip. But there's a weird energy hanging between us. Normally, Teller is one of the only people I can tolerate long stretches of silence with. But tonight, it's like he's desperate to fill any lull.

"Hey, did I show you Doris's Halloween costume from last year?" he asks, pulling his phone out to find a picture.

I smile politely, leaning in to look again. "You showed me that one a few weeks ago. The ladybug one your mom made?"

A flash of disappointment flits across his face, and I can tell he's racking his brain for something else to talk about.

"What do you think Doris is up to right now?" I ask.

"She's most likely holding court on my dad's lap."

I laugh, though I'm desperate, internally combing through various potential topics. When I come up short, I start tearing my napkin into shreds. This is it. This is the end of us. In my panic, I blurt, "Have you finally figured out how to express Doris's anal glands?" I am clearly not okay. Send the police.

Teller's eyes go round. He's horrified. Before he can respond, the villa owner's daughter approaches, as though she knew we needed saving. I assume she's checking if we want the bill, but instead, she leans into my ear and whispers, "There's someone at the front desk for you."

I look at Teller. "What?"

Based on his expression, he has no clue who it is either.

I think about all of our hostel friends. Only one person could possibly know we were staying here, since up until a few days ago, he was supposed to join us.

Caleb.

Teller must have told him about the surprise booking. I set my napkin on the table and follow her. He came back for me. Holy shit.

I pause before heading into the entryway, trying to collect my thoughts. I'm cautiously ecstatic, because this means Caleb has come back. I didn't entirely scare him off. But after last night, the timing couldn't be worse.

I round the corner, bracing myself to see Caleb's sun-kissed curls, his surfer charm on full display. Instead, there's a man in an all-khaki outfit, complete with a safari hat, towering over a dark-haired woman in a hot-pink tunic with matching hot-pink wedges.

Dad and Aunt Mei. What are they doing here?

27

I must be hallucinating.

It's only when Mei shuffles toward me, chunky wedges clunking against the tile floor, and flings her arms open that I know it's real. They're actually here.

Seconds into the hug, she shrinks back like I've burned her. A simple hug. That's all it takes for her to pick up on my negative energy. And while I haven't told her about Caleb leaving me in Florence, or about Teller, I get the feeling she'll figure it out. If she hasn't already. I deliberately avoid eye contact as she gives me a once-over.

"What are you guys doing here?" I ask before she can interrogate me.

"Had to make sure you didn't get any weird face tattoos or body piercings," Dad says.

I cough, shoving my hand in my pocket to hide my moon tattoo. That's a conversation for a different day.

"Three weeks was too long to go without seeing you," he says, oblivious to the weird vibes as he wraps me in a bear hug. I let myself sag into him as he rocks me back and forth, grateful for his solid, steady presence.

"I thought you never wanted to travel again," I say to Dad.

He shrugs. "Well, you know I've always wanted to see Pompeii. When you told me it was next on the itinerary, on the way to Amalfi, I couldn't resist."

"He's been having total FOMO," Mei explains, taking her sunglasses off to get a better look at the villa. "Personally, I came for the pasta. I've been thinking about it ever since your mom and I left this place. And you'll never believe the promo on travel points with my credit card. And being back here is just—" She pauses, eyes welling for a flash. "This place hasn't changed a bit."

Before she can get too teary, Dad's arm shoots up in a wave. "Teller!"

Behind me, Teller approaches sheepishly. We make brief, yet hesitant, eye contact before he turns on a smile. Dad is eager to hear all about Teller's first year at college, while Mei demands to know when he got so tall. And fit. She hasn't seen him since Lunar New Year three years ago.

After they check in, we take the evening to drive around Tuscany with no specific agenda. Mei likes to be in control of her transportation, so she and Dad rent a small hatchback. It's nice to go at our own pace for once. We stop at a few farms and vineyards that Mei has a "feeling" about. Neither Dad nor Mei are huge wine drinkers, so we don't spend long at any one place.

"I hope we didn't cramp your style," Mei says once we've settled in bed. I opt to stay in her room tonight, for obvious reasons. Frankly, Teller seemed relieved, and I don't blame him. Space is good. We need this.

"Not at all," I say, staring at the ceiling. Of course, I was initially disappointed it wasn't Caleb coming back for me. But it's hard to be sad when Dad and Mei flew halfway across the world to be with me. They're also proving an excellent buffer between Teller and me. "I really needed you here, actually."

I mean that. Teller and I may be back on speaking terms, but there's still limited eye contact. Long bouts of silence that don't feel natural. Teller is usually one of the people I'm most comfortable with, but being alone with him right now is almost unbearable. Besides, it's much easier to pretend you didn't hook up with your best friend when you're around other people.

"I know," Mei says simply. She just *knows* things, sometimes even before me. When I was twelve, she kept me home from school one day because she had a "bad feeling." Turns out, a couple girls at school had started an "I Hate Lo" club based on some lie that I'd held hands with one of their boyfriends at a birthday party that weekend (I did not). And while Mei wasn't able to protect me from finding out about it, she saved me the humiliation of seeing their "I Hate Lo" friendship bracelets, which soon came off when they found out it was Becca Ryan, not me, who'd held said boyfriend's hand. There is truly no one crueler than a middle school girl.

I let out a shaky sigh. "Yeah. I officially scared Caleb off for good."

She gives me one of those looks, as if to say, *You're being dramatic.* "What happened?"

I tell her that I'd come clean about my vision, revealed the whole soulmate thing. Then how he checked out of the hostel without even saying goodbye, without leaving any contact information.

Why did I even have these visions in the first place? Things were better when I was just Ordinary Lo. Sure, it sucked that I was the one big fat failure in the family, but at least I'd gotten used to that reality. By nineteen, everyone had stopped expecting things from me.

"When I first told Layla, she laughed her ass off and asked if I was on drugs," Mei tells me to make me feel better. It doesn't work.

"But she didn't flee the city. She came around, obviously," I point out.

"They always do, because they're meant to," she says simply. "It's fate, after all."

~

We're ready to go before the sun comes up. It's a full day's drive to Amalfi, including our stop in Pompeii. Despite Mei's multiple bathroom breaks, we make it to Pompeii by late afternoon.

Everything is totally and completely normal with Teller. I mean, if you overlook the fact that he can't make eye contact without his entire face turning red. Or the fact that when he speaks, all I can hear is the noise he made when he—

"Guys! Hurry up!" Dad shouts, practically running to the entrance of Pompeii like a child at Disneyland.

Teller quietly hands me a water bottle. Before I can finish uttering, "Thank you," he picks up the pace, long legs carrying him toward the awe-inspiring city.

"Did it hurt?" Dad asks.

I squint up at him. "Did what hurt?"

He tilts his chin toward my finger. "Your tattoo." Dad never misses a beat. His expression stays neutral, so I can't tell if he's mad about it.

Still, my cheeks redden. "A little bit, but it wasn't as bad as I thought it would be. It's small, though. Are you mad?"

A pause. "It's not my body. And I'm just glad you got something discreet."

"Well, I was thinking of getting a full back tattoo of Brandon and Brian."

This makes him laugh.

"Speaking of, how are my boys doing?" I ask Dad as we journey through the ruins. Mei and Teller follow close behind. I don't know what I was expecting, but it certainly wasn't a fully preserved city, with grand villas and ancient streets dating back two thousand years.

"Brandon is the same as ever. Brian is gassier than usual. Probably because the scoundrel got into that box of Nature Valley granola bars in the pantry. Ate eleven."

"Eleven? Well, at least this time it wasn't my birth control pills." I snort, recalling the time he ate a whole pack and the vet had to induce vomiting. Brian has always had an obsession with eating things, including items that are absolutely not edible, like pens and Dad's glasses.

"Yup. Came home the other day and the wrappers were all over the floor. When I dropped them off with Ellen, I warned her not to leave anything out. But apparently, he's already done a number on her shoes."

"Oh, Brian." I sigh. "And things with you? How are you doing? I hope you aren't too bored by yourself."

Dad looks a little startled by the question, stare fixed on a group of tourists weaving through the square. "Not at all. I'm keeping busy, actually."

His response doesn't surprise me. He never admits to feeling lonely. "Oh yeah? Working on a big case?"

He nods. "You could say that."

"And keeping busy with pickleball?" I tease as we enter the thermal baths.

"Hey, don't knock it 'til you try it."

"I'm still confused as to how this new hobby started. I've never seen you play a sport in my life."

He doesn't answer. Instead, he snaps shots of the mosaics with intricate mythological battles. Strange. It's only once we make our way to the plaster casts that he responds, "Actually, I wanted to talk to you about that."

I quirk my brow, eyeing Teller up ahead. "About pickleball?"

"In a manner of speaking. But first, I wanted to ask how things are going with Caleb."

"I scared him off by telling him about my vision and now he's gone forever," I say, hanging my head. Dad has always been wary of the whole soulmate thing. But I can't help but feel like I'm disappointing the entire family, yet again.

Dad frowns. "Ah, I guess that could scare off the best of them, huh?"

"Afraid so. How did you react when Mom told you about her vision? Did you think she was crazy too?"

He's quiet for a couple moments. "It certainly threw me for a loop. But it didn't scare me off."

I sigh, resting my weight on a stone bench outside the amphitheater. "Ugh. I can't believe I messed up my one and only shot at love."

"You didn't, Lo. Don't get too hung up on what you think you saw."

This takes me by surprise. Sure, Dad is logical like Teller. But he's never outwardly expressed disbelief in the family gifts. "What I think I saw? Do you not believe I had a vision?"

He winces. "No. That's not necessarily what I meant."

"Then why are you skeptical?"

A weak smile flits across his face that I can't help but interpret as pity. "I'm your father. It's my job to be skeptical about every man you date, isn't it?"

"For everyone else, yes. But not when he's The One. Mom had this same vision about you. And you two were the epitome of soulmates."

"You don't understand everything, Lo."

I clench my jaw. Here he goes again, treating me like a child, insinuating that I'm not mature enough to comprehend things, especially about my mother. About my family. I narrow my gaze. "You're right. I don't understand everything. Because you refuse to tell me anything about Mom."

"That's not true at all."

Is he for real? A surge of annoyance shoots through me, and I think back to my talk with Teller on the train to Florence—about being more honest with Dad. "Come on. Every time I bring her up, you get all weird. I know it's been hard for you, but it's hard for me too. I've tried to be good about not asking too many details, but given the situation with Caleb, the least you can do is throw me a few breadcrumbs."

He shakes his head and turns away, like he's searching for a quick exit. "Honey, trust me. If there was anything important for you to know, I would tell you."

"I'll settle for anything, important or not."

"Lo, just drop it. Please." This isn't his casual avoidance. There's agitation in his eyes, and I don't know if it's him being protective or simply the fact that he hates talking about Mom.

I don't want to make him uncomfortable or ruin Pompeii for us, so I just drop it. And we're back to the same place, lingering in the silence of Mom's absence.

28

Positano, Amalfi Coast

Lucky for Dad, I'm easily distracted. When you're in a place as beautiful as the Amalfi Coast, the last thing you want is to rehash a fight you're never going to win. So I leave it alone . . . for now.

Not that I have much of a choice. Dad is treating us to an adorable little Airbnb. It's orange with green shutters, nestled into the cliffs of Positano. The inside is cozy, decorated in soothing shades of blue and white. There are only two bedrooms—one for Mei and me, one for Dad. Teller seems perfectly happy to take the pullout couch in the living room, probably because it's a million times better than the hostels we've grown accustomed to. But the real crown jewel is the lull of the waves crashing over the pebbly beach below. They're audible from everywhere in the house.

After we unpack, Dad takes a work call and Teller takes a nap. Keen to explore, Mei and I set out on foot, meandering through the narrow, winding streets and alleyways dappled in sunlight.

There's something about Positano that feels simple, timeless. Sure, it's crowded like the other cities we've visited, but the people here are relaxed. No one is elbowing each other on the sidewalks or speeding ahead of slower walkers. Everyone meanders in bathing suits and knit wraps, padding around the worn cobblestone in flip-flops. Unhurried. These are my people. This is my vibe.

It seems it's Mei's vibe, too, considering she's already stopped at two art galleries, one pottery shop, and four local artisan stands along the way. She's purchased a whole new "Amalfi aesthetic" wardrobe, including a linen dress embroidered with lemons, funky sea-themed jewelry, and a straw fedora with a blue-striped ribbon (all on sale, of course).

"You and Mom didn't come to Amalfi, right?" I ask Mei. We've stopped at a cute little café overlooking the glimmering water.

She pauses for a moment to sip her cappuccino. "We both wanted to come here, but it was way too expensive. Too bougie, even back then. She would have loved it here, though. Her butt would have been glued to those loungers at the beach the entire week. The ocean was her happy place. She wanted to travel everywhere, but especially places near water." There's a hint of sadness in her voice.

Yet another thing I didn't know about my mom. "Really?" I ask through a mouthful of cannoli.

"Except she had this fear of whales."

I crinkle my brow. "Whales? Do you mean sharks?"

"Nope. Whales. Like, *Free Willy*," she says, eyes partially obscured by the brim of her new hat.

"Why?"

"I have no idea. Maybe it was their size? But once, we were on a family trip in Cape Cod, and we saw some breaching in a cove and she cried. Ellen and I made fun of her for days," she says, eyes brimming with nostalgia. "She would have loved knowing you're traveling, seeing the world."

"You think?"

"When we were little, she had this atlas where she color-coded all the countries based on how much she wanted to go. She always had a system for everything."

"Sometimes I don't know who I take after. I grew up in a family of total nerds," I say teasingly.

Mei smirks. "You're like Ellen, I think. A free spirit."

I give a half-hearted chuckle. "Speaking of family, Dad's been acting weird."

"You'll have to be more specific. Your dad is always weird."

"When we were in Pompeii, I brought up Mom and asked about when they first met. He totally shut down."

She's quiet for a moment, shifting in her seat to cross her legs. "I'm sorry, Lo. What did you want to know about her? Maybe I can help fill in the gaps."

"I asked about her vision. If she knew he was The One when they met."

She tilts her head in thought. "From what I remember her saying, she did. She thought he was cute but a bit of a dweeb, which wasn't her normal type. We actually didn't get to meet your dad for almost six months after they met."

That surprises me. "Six months? That seems like a long time."

"They had to sneak around for a little while because they worked together. That, and I think they were just in a love bubble. Didn't want anything to disturb it. And when she finally introduced us, she was so . . . scared, for some reason. Maybe because he was The One? Maybe because he was so different from the rest of us? I don't know. I think she just wanted us to love him as much as she did, especially Nai Nai," she says.

"Understandable. The women in our family are pretty scary. Did he fit in?"

"He was like a scared deer at first. But eventually, he got used to us. She liked to joke that Nai Nai loved him more than her."

I smile. Nai Nai always treated Dad like her biological son. After Mom passed, there wasn't a week where she didn't stop by to bring us food, way more than we could eat. She didn't approve of me living off Dad's specials, a.k.a. frozen McCain's curly fries and chicken fingers. I still remember the heaps of saucy food crammed into clear containers with rainbow-colored lids. The steam always singed my fingers when I eagerly lifted the lids to smell it. Dad always washed the Tupperware, and she'd refill it with another feast. When Nai Nai passed, Ellen took it upon herself to continue the tradition, despite being a notoriously terrible cook. It took Dad months to work up the courage to tell her we didn't need her to cook for us. The transition back to bland, frozen food was a tough one.

"Anyway, your dad isn't the most open guy," Mei says. "It still hurts him, even though he doesn't show it. He loved her more than anything. When she passed so suddenly, it broke him, and he hasn't been the same since. I wish you could have seen them together when you were old enough to really remember."

Same, Mei. Same.

This right here is exactly why I don't love talking to Mei or Ellen about Mom. On one hand, it's comforting to hear about her. It feels good to talk about her like she was a real person. But it's a double-edged sword. They have so many memories with her that I simply don't have. And as ridiculous as it seems, I'm bitter, almost angry, about the time I was robbed of. About not getting to know for myself that she hated peanut butter, or that she made up a whole dance routine to the song "Push It!" by Salt-N-Pepa.

We're quiet for a few moments, with only the Italian radio from inside the café and chatter of patrons to quell the silence. Quiet is rare around Mei. It strikes me that she seems a little sad. Maybe being back to Italy without Mom is difficult. I guess I'm not the only one struggling with memories of her.

I plunk my elbows on the table, biting the inside of my mouth. "What if I'm like Cousin Lin? Destined for a lifetime of loneliness and shit luck?"

Mei frowns suspiciously. "Ellen told you?"

"Don't get mad. I made her. She had no choice," I explain.

She sighs. "Well, you're not going to end up alone. Things will work out with Caleb." I should probably feel some sort of relief. Mei is rarely wrong when it comes to these things. But at the memory of the horror on Caleb's face, it's hard to imagine how things will work out.

"But what if they don't?"

"They will. Again, this only happened to two people. In every other case, things have worked out, even if there were some hiccups."

"Hiccups?" I confirm, feeling even worse about myself.

She tilts her head in thought. "Well, there was Second Great-Aunt Chun. She fell in love with another man after she was already married to Fourth Great-Uncle."

I nearly choke on my half of the macaron we decided to split. "Wait, Uncle Wen? Excuse me? Why didn't I know about this?" Apparently, there's a lot I don't know about my family.

"It's not really a secret. You've never asked."

"Who was this other man?" I whisper, unsure I actually want to know. Nai Nai had always told me stories about them when I was young. Supposedly, Great-Aunt Chun and Great-Uncle Wen were married for seventy-five years, the longest of any couple in the family. They even died only two days apart, unable to bear life without each other.

"Bart. He was the neighbor. Totally cliché. They'd had an affair. Everyone in the family was horrified. Anyway, she was convinced she loved him more than Wen, her soulmate. And so she left Wen to be with Bart. Three years later, she was diagnosed with Alzheimer's. And guess what? Bart left her."

"Left her? Really? That's awful."

"Yup. And guess who came back to take care of her? Wen."

"Wow. That's wild." The thought of frail Chun and doting Wen made me sad.

"Yup. In her lucid moments, she was completely devoted to Wen after that. She felt awful that she'd made such a huge mistake, went against the vision. And so she corrected her mistake."

"So technically, the vision did work out. Chun ended up with her soulmate regardless," I say, unsure if this makes me feel hopeful or even more pathetic.

"Are things okay with Teller?" Mei asks, interrupting my reflection.

Her abruptness takes me aback, and I turn my gaze to avoid eye contact. "What do you mean? Why wouldn't things be okay with us?"

Teller and I had been pretty conversational in the car, at least enough to cover up any weird vibes.

She gives me a puzzled look. "I didn't mean between you two. I meant how are things going with him since his breakup."

"Ohhh." I toss my head back, momentarily relieved. "He's doing well. I think he still misses Sophie, though," I add with a grumble, thinking about his text to her after we hooked up.

Mei dares me to make eye contact. Her gaze is penetrating, and I swear she's reading my mind. A small smile curves her lips, like she's just made a miraculous discovery.

"Something happened between you two—sexually," she says matter-of-factly.

Shit. Nothing gets past Mei.

"No! Ew!" I practically yelp, scooting back in my chair. "We're just friends, obviously." But she keeps staring at me with that knowing look, and I break in record time. God, I'm weak. "It's really annoying and unfair that you're psychic, you know. Makes it hard to lie."

"Sweetie, I don't need to be psychic to know something happened between you two. I can tell by the way you look at each other."

"Is it that obvious?"

"You could cut the tension with a teaspoon. But you've always had a bit of a crush on him, haven't you? That's why you were so freaked out about your vision?" she asks.

"What? A crush on Teller? No. Never. Absolutely not," I say, almost as a reflex. I check over my shoulder to make sure he's not standing right behind me or something.

"Be honest, Lo," she says softly.

"No," I say, without as much confidence as I'm used to. Through the years, people have asked me if there was something between Teller and me. I've always answered, "No," without a beat. Without an ounce of hesitation. Until now. Still, I hold firm until Mei's penetrating gaze breaks me.

Teller has always been off-limits to me, whether he's with someone else or not, because he's . . . just Teller. He's my Teller. He's the guy who makes sure I drink my daily recommended intake of water and bans me from eating lactose so I don't get constipated. The guy I tell about my ridiculous ideas, share all my wacky pet names with.

"There can't be anything between us," I say.

Mei leans forward. "Why not?"

Where do I even begin? "We're total opposites. We'd never work in that way."

I think about how cold and distant we've been the past few days. It doesn't feel like *us* in the slightest. Then again, we just slept together. It's bound to take some time for things to normalize. When we're back home, in our normal environment where we're just us—the same us that met at The Cinema—surely this weird, pesky tension will disappear for good. Right?

"Besides, we aren't supposed to be together," I add, blinking away clips of the vision—of our fractured friendship. "He's going back to Sophie the moment we get home, and I'm destined to be alone forever because I messed things up with Caleb."

"Not true. Maybe it was just the universe's way of telling you you're not ready for Caleb yet."

"Why wouldn't I be ready? I was totally ready. He was the one who wasn't ready for me."

"That might be true. But you have to be honest with yourself, Lo. Remember, we can't be fully ready for forever until we've fully closed the chapter on the past. You have to let go of what's holding you back."

"Like what? There's nothing holding me back."

Her lips curl in a sly smile. "What about the possibility that your heart belongs to someone else?"

29

"Can you believe Mei accused me of having feelings for Teller?" I rake my brush through my hair a little too hard. Bianca and I have been FaceTiming for the past half hour while she waits in the doctor's office to get her new foot cast.

"Um . . ." Bianca pauses, face freezing.

"You still there?" I can't tell if it's the Wi-Fi.

Apparently not. "Yeah. Sorry. I just . . . the entire time I've known you, you haven't shut up about Teller. Like, you will use any opportunity you can to bring him up."

I scrunch my face into the camera, lowering the volume in case Teller overhears through the door. It's a small place. "Not true."

She rolls her eyes so hard, I'm afraid they'll disappear into her skull. "Basically, any time we pass a bathroom, you bring up unclogging the toilets at The Cinema. Any time a depressing song comes on, you talk about how Teller would like it. And don't even get me started on movies—"

"I don't have feelings for Teller, okay?" I say.

It is ridiculous, after all. Teller and I are just friends.

Just.

Friends.

"I mean, sure, there was chemistry when we hooked up. And sure, I haven't been able to stop thinking about it. But the other night was the result of almost a month of forced proximity. Being on vacation. And they always say it's easy to get emotionally attached after sex, especially to someone I'm scared of losing."

Bianca opens her mouth to say something, but I can't stop rambling. "Also, lest we forget, I haven't hooked up with someone since Mark B., forever ago. Maybe that's all it was, me craving to be touched, desired in that way. I desperately wanted that with Caleb, and when he left, I needed to channel that energy elsewhere. Teller just happened to be available."

Bianca slow-nods. "Right. Absolutely no feelings to be had over here." I can tell she still doesn't believe me. Not that it really matters. I don't have to prove anything.

"Anyway, we need to get to the real matter at hand."

"And what's that?"

"Things are still weird since we hooked up."

She shrugs. "Maybe you've been going about this the wrong way. I mean, you've been avoiding each other."

"He's been avoiding me," I correct.

"You're currently hiding in your aunt's room," she points out. "Too much distance has probably made things way worse. There are too many opportunities to fill in the blanks, make assumptions."

"B? You're a freakin' genius," I say, blowing her a kiss before signing off.

She's absolutely right. If I know Teller like I think I do, space only makes him spiral into a negative vortex. Maybe what we really need is a reminder of how things used to be. A reminder that we can be us again.

~

"You sure you don't want to stay in with your dad and Mei tonight? You were on the go all afternoon," Teller says, walking a step behind as I lead the charge into town.

"Tel, we're in Positano. We're not staying in and playing dominos like old people," I say, charging toward our destination.

Teller peers into the brightly lit courtyard. It's lined with white canvases on wooden easels. "Painting?" He throws a skeptical look in my direction, but I pull him along.

Keeping on trend with our vow back in Florence to do touristy things, I found us a last-minute painting class on Airbnb Experiences. Random? Absolutely. Neither of us are particularly artistic, but I figured a night of creative expression, surrounded by other tourists, ought to loosen us up.

Our teacher, Robert (pronounced *Ro-bear*), is very serious in a jaunty beret and paint-splattered apron. He tells us to channel our "inner Picasso" by painting each other.

"Let the colors speak to you!" Robert says, dramatically waving an imaginary paintbrush.

Truth be told, if I'd known we were painting each other, I probably wouldn't have booked this particular class. Sitting across from Teller and examining each other's faces is making me itch and sweat.

I do not have feelings for Teller.

Still, I'm making good headway on my portrait. I've settled on my favorite Teller expression. It's his half smile. The one he does when he's genuinely content. Like when we fell into a rhythm stacking cups at The Cinema. Or when Coldplay came on the radio. The expression is always fleeting, lasting no longer than a few moments. Because Teller is Teller. He's always thinking ahead, calculating cost benefits, logic-ing his way through life.

Our eyes meet at the same time. He seems to be studying me, but looks away like I've spooked him. "How's the painting going?"

He swallows. "Um . . ."

Before he can finish, I stand up and peer over at his canvas. It's entirely blank. "You haven't even started? Am I that ugly that you can't even paint me?" I tease.

"The opposite, actually." He hesitates, clean brush at his side. "I'm trying to plan it all in my head first." He approaches painting like he approaches life, with caution. I shouldn't be surprised.

"Let the colors speak to you," I say in my best Robert voice. Robert shoots me a look, and I wish I could melt into the floor.

Teller smirks.

"It doesn't have to be good, Tel. No expectations. Look at mine. I think I really captured your essence here." I turn my canvas toward him and he smiles.

"Wow, I look like . . . Shrek, but with irresistibly sexy hair."

I snort. "You do have some nice flow." Credit is due where credit is due.

He tilts his head to look at me from another angle, and I reach over and dab a thick glob of blue onto his canvas. He quickly dabs my hand. I fire back with red to the forearm. Eventually, our entire arms are covered. Even my nose.

A well-dressed woman sitting behind us lets out a loud sigh and glowers, shaking her head like we're children goofing off in church. Robert notices and makes his way toward us. I work down a swallow, certain he's going to kick us out. "Art has no boundaries!" he declares, which sends Teller into a fit of giggles.

Finally, Teller puts brush to canvas. Turns out, he's not half-bad. Instead of attempting a realistic painting, he does a rough sketch in black paint using a skinnier brush. It's messy, like . . .

"Like sunshine," he says, eyeing it with pride.

By the time the class is over, the paint has hardened on our arms, so we head to the beach to wash it off.

"Thanks for dragging me out tonight," he says while letting the cold waves crash over his arms.

"The night isn't over. I'm hungry," I say as we shiver our way off the beach, soaked shoes in hands. I never thought I'd see Teller walk barefoot in public. I store a mental image to remember this moment. How far we've come from the day we met.

"Same. But I'm not really in the mood for Italian. Is that an asshole thing to say?"

I let out a sigh of relief. I'd been wondering the same. Am I a massive brat for being in the country with the best food, only to secretly crave McDonald's? Most certainly. "I've been thinking that for the past week, actually. I might throw up if we eat pasta again."

Thus begins are search for non-Italian food. Unfortunately, Positano is not exactly a global-food mecca. The one sushi bar we found on Google closed an hour ago. And we realize that we can't walk into a restaurant covered in bits of paint and shoeless.

So we make our way back to the Airbnb.

I open the fridge and my findings are bleak. There's a dusty container of tomatoes, a forgotten jar of capers in the far corner, and some fresh mozzarella and cured meat from the market that Mei picked up. "I think we can probably make something out of what's here, though it will be . . . Italian adjacent."

Teller doesn't look bothered as he washes the remaining flecks of paint off his hands. "I'll eat anything at this point."

We start slicing the meat and crushing the tomatoes, only to realize that without a paste, it's just a watery, chunky mess. Still, it's too late to abort. We've already invested too much. So we toss the tomatoes in the pan, adding the cheese, slices of cured meat, and capers.

Teller tilts his head, stepping back to get a better look like an art curator. "This looks disgusting."

"It's not all about presentation," I say, hoisting myself atop the counter with a bowl, ready to tuck in. "This is going to be epic. I know it."

Teller's assumption is confirmed. It's absolutely awful. And yet, we act like it's the best thing in the world, muttering every variation of *"Mmmm"* and *"Wow"* after every bite. And giggling.

"The savory hints of . . . these thick tomato chunks really offset the saltiness from the sliced meat," Teller says in a thick British accent, doing his best Food Network–judge impression.

"You can really taste the depth of flavors here. Loving the subtle undertones of . . . um—"

"Desperation. You can really taste it throughout."

I lob my head back, laughing, only to bang it into the cupboard. Teller chokes on his bite of food. "Are you okay?"

I nod through a fit of laughter. I can't seem to stop.

To wash down the terrible excuse for a dinner, we attempt to make mug cakes in the microwave. They turn out deflated and burned, seeing as we don't have nearly enough of the ingredients. Still, we eat them (praising the shit out of them for good measure) while splayed on the couch, searching through the wide array of old DVDs under the TV.

"No way. I can't believe they have this," Teller says, brandishing a sun-faded copy of *Indiana Jones and the Raiders of the Lost Ark*. The Cinema did a whole Indiana Jones marathon a few weeks after I started working there. Teller and I watched every single one, completely out of order.

We slip the disc into the dusty DVD player and smile through the cheesy dialogue and overly serious expressions.

"Not gonna lie, Harrison Ford was pretty sexy," I say, feet resting in Teller's lap. "The satchel is really working for me."

He swings me a look. "Okay, it may look cool, but it's a prime target for thieves. The strap could snag on a branch in the jungle. He'd have been better off carrying his valuables in a sensible money bag."

I snort and give him a soft kick. "He can't fit his notebook and ammo in a money bag. And in an emergency, he certainly isn't going to lift his whole shirt to dig it out like a dweeb."

There's nothing quite like witnessing Teller laugh. The crinkle of his eyes. The way he shoots his head back in a roar. It's joy personified.

"This is fun," he says, and I couldn't agree more. For the first time since Tuscany, it feels like us again. The old us.

It reminds me of being back at The Cinema. Just the two of us, best friends, driving home with grape Slurpees, rehashing bizarre customer encounters, quoting iconic movie lines. It gives me hope that if we can get through these next few days, any lingering weirdness will be but a distant memory. A strange blip in the timeline of our lifelong friendship.

"I never told you about the day I applied to The Cinema," I say, tracing my finger over my tattoo. I'd avoided telling him that first summer, mostly so he wouldn't think I was sappier than he already did. Until now, there wasn't a time that seemed right.

He eyes me with curiosity. "No, you haven't."

I take a deep breath, picturing my fifteen-year-old self. "I was feeling really lost. I'd just moved away from the house I grew up in to a whole new neighborhood. I was disappointing my aunts and just . . . overall upset that I didn't have this connection to my mom that I wanted so badly. My dad was working all the time, and I figured since I didn't have any friends, maybe I should get a job. So I printed off a bunch of résumés one morning and walked around the neighborhood, handing them out at random fast-food places. I'm pretty sure I actually dropped one off at your mom's coffee shop. Anyway, I saw that The Cinema was advertising *The Wedding Singer*."

"That movie with Adam Sandler?"

"Yup. That was my mom's favorite movie. I only know because my aunts told me. She used to watch it over and over because she had a massive crush on Adam Sandler."

Teller crinkles his eyes. "Wow. That's a choice."

"Right? But if you look at my dad, it makes sense. She liked them a little dorky."

He tips his head. "Okay, good point. Before you keep going, I feel like I should tell you: I actually remember putting those letters on the board. Halfway through *Wedding*, it started hailing. Hard. Like, golf-ball size. I had to stop and wait for it to finish."

That revelation hits me in the chest. "Okay, so this was the morning after. I remember some of the cars nearby were damaged from the hail. Anyway, I looked in the window to check the showtimes. But then I saw the HELP WANTED sign, so I left a résumé with Cindy."

"So you literally saw a sign."

Literally. One that Teller had put up himself. "I know it sounds dumb, but I guess I've always thought it was my mom who led me to you. Like she knew I needed a friend. A good friend."

"No. It doesn't sound dumb at all," he says, eyes a little glossy. I can tell he's genuinely touched. "The only thing that gets me is that your mom would choose me, of all people? Why not someone way cooler?"

"I didn't need cool. I needed . . ." I pause, voice faltering. "I needed you. You made me realize how much I loved talking to people. That letting people in was worthwhile."

"Honestly, same, Lo. Most people just think of me as another Owens brother. The one no one remembers the name of."

"Like I said, you will always be the superior Owens brother to me." Our eyes snag and hold for a beat. Teller doesn't say anything, but he doesn't have to. I see the gratitude in his soft gaze. I know that means a lot to him.

"Well, I need to brush my teeth. I can still taste the capers," he says, gently shifting my legs off him.

"Yeah. It's getting late. We should probably go to bed." I stand and try to hide my mild disappointment with a stretch. He follows me down the hall toward my bedroom, which is right across the hall from the bathroom.

He leans in and whispers, "I can hear Mei snoring from here. No wonder you can't sleep." I'm standing so close, his breath tickles my ear, and my body tingles.

Shit. Maybe things won't be going back to normal.

"Right? It's so loud," I say, skin getting hot. God, I wish he would touch me again.

He runs his hand over the back of his neck, contemplative. "You're welcome to stay on the pullout if you want to." He squeezes his eyes shut when he realizes how that sounds. "Not in that way. I mean, unless—I just meant so you can get a good sleep. That's all."

My stomach barrel-rolls and I study him, trying to discern what he meant by that. Did he just invite me to stay in the same bed as him?

Or is he simply extending the offer as a courtesy? It's impossible to say. His breathing isn't all heavy and labored like the other night, but it's also not entirely casual.

We linger in the hallway, just inches from each other. The frayed thread between us pulls tighter than before, in dire risk of breaking. If I really wanted to, I could close that distance. Why can't I stop thinking about kissing him again? My heart hammers in my chest and I wonder if he feels it too. A million thoughts race through my mind. The way his hand felt squeezing mine. The weight of him over me as we joined together.

No.

We're supposed to be going back to being friends. Being us. We can't let this become a habit. If it does, I'm not sure I'll ever be able to break it. And it may be the thing that breaks us.

"It's okay, I'll survive," I whisper, already regretting the decision.

He just nods, like I knew he would. Teller would never push.

"Okay, see you tomorrow." His gaze flicks down to my lips and he reaches for my finger, pulling me toward him. But he doesn't pull me in for a kiss. Instead, he wraps his arms around me and holds me with just the right amount of pressure. Somehow, this feels even more illicit than a kiss, with our bodies pressed together. I bury my face in his neck and inhale that clean, gentle Teller smell. In his arms, my insides bubble with a feeling I can only describe as happiness in the purest sense.

"Good night, Lo," he says into my hair, voice low and husky.

I want nothing more than to pop onto my toes and kiss him, and I think he wants me to.

I blink up at him as our breaths meld, waiting a second for things to feel awkward again. For the alarms to go off inside me, reminding me how fragile our friendship is. A jolt to warn me what will happen if we dare cross that boundary again.

But it feels startlingly safe and steady. So safe, I feel at home. Even when we're thousands of miles away.

But as his face moves closer to mine, I panic. What the hell are we doing? After last time, we'd been stilted, awkward, avoided eye contact. And while now things feel normal, we've only slapped a Band-Aid on a fresh wound. Crossing the line again will only deepen the scarring. At what point will the damage be irreversible?

"Um, well, good night!"

He steps back, seemingly amused. "Good night, Lo."

In an effort to retreat as fast as possible, I somehow manage to stumble over my own foot.

"You almost fell," he says with a soft chuckle, stabilizing me by the arm.

I'm falling, that's for sure. Only it's not for my soulmate.

30

This is bad. How have I let myself catch feelings—real feelings—for Teller?

It's not that lightning bolt of infatuation I felt with Caleb. No. It's more like a song that's been playing in the background, waiting for me to slow down and listen hard enough to learn the lyrics. It's a simmer of affection that's been churning under the surface all along, only now it's finally bubbled over.

I think back to our Cinema days, all the stolen glances while cleaning. How I'd marvel over his profile from the passenger seat of his car, how his jaw would flex and tense when he was deep in thought. I think about the flutters in my stomach whenever his name pops up on my phone. How my fingers fly over the keyboard whenever I text him, how there's always so much I want to say but never enough time.

I don't know if I realized how lost I felt this year without him. Inviting him on this trip wasn't purely for moral support when meeting The One, or to help distract him from Sophie. Truthfully, the idea of being near him again made me happier than I could admit.

Still, none of it sits right. Do I think Teller wants to hook up with me? Absolutely. Do I think he's in love with me? No. He's still in love with Sophie. I've spent almost our entire friendship witnessing Teller Owens in love. He gives his all. And Sophie was his everything. He can't just move on in one month.

And even if Sophie or Caleb weren't a factor, we're so different; it's almost laughable. Half the time, I'm convinced he can only put up with me in short bursts. These differences may work for our friendship. But romantically? I'm not so sure.

Then there's the glaring fact: Teller simply isn't my soulmate. Regardless of my feelings, he's not meant to be mine and I'm not meant to be his. So even if our feelings are mutual, how would we live with the fact that it's only temporary? That there is someone better for him out there, and for me, and we're just delaying the inevitable. Our friendship has meant so much to me over the years, but it's like a tightrope. Any misstep could tip the balance.

It's better this way because I have a soulmate. Caleb. That's the thing about being a Zhao woman. Everyone you might like or even love is temporary until The One comes along. And Teller isn't someone I could ever classify as "temporary." Losing him would be absolutely devastating, which is why it's crucial we stay friends.

As good as it felt to be with him, it's not worth losing him. Nothing is.

That's why I've adopted a new strategy—Get Through the Next Few Days. What does that entail? Basically, avoid him as much as possible without ignoring him or making things worse. That means not getting too close, no prolonged eye contact, absolutely no alone time, and certainly no touching. Not even a hug. Italy is far too romantic for any potential slipups.

Luckily, the Amalfi Coast makes for an easy distraction.

The four of us spend the next morning weaving back and forth along the winding pathways, exploring the town center. While Dad and Mei check out a museum, Teller follows me dutifully as I dip in and out of various boutiques, riffling through racks of linens and vibrant resort wear. We explore the labyrinth of alleyways and endless staircases, most of which offer views of the Crayola buildings along the sea. We scour jewelry shops and souvenir shops lined with novelty T-shirts, refrigerator magnets, and tea towels. We even stumble into a ceramics studio, where we find pottery and decorative pieces made of colorful glass mosaics. Teller buys an intricately patterned plate for his mom.

On the way to meet up with Dad and Mei, we duck into one more store at the end of a narrow alley. Its whitewashed walls cascade with bougainvillea. There's an array of beachwear that's neither of our styles, but we pretend to look with interest so as not to offend the watchful store clerk.

She spies Teller eyeing a floor-length zebra-print muumuu and swoops in like a bat out of hell, her floral poncho swishing with every step. "I'll get you a dressing room for that," she declares.

Teller stiffens. "Oh, um, no thank you. I'm just browsing."

"I really think you ought to try it on. It's one of those polarizing pieces. Some people can pull it off, some people can't," she says.

"No, really—I—"

"You wouldn't want to get home and find it doesn't fit," she argues.

He shoots me a look that says *Please extract me from this situation,* so I sidle up next to him. "We'll both try one on," I say cheerfully, pointing to the bold orange-and-pink muumuu next to it.

"I hate you so much," Teller mouths as the clerk whisks them to the changing rooms.

I figured she was just having a bit of fun, but when Teller emerges in the zebra muumuu, the clerk quite literally gasps. "Oh my word. It was made for you," she says, dead serious.

She actually has a point. Teller looks good. Though I think it has less to do with the zebra muumuu and more to do with his adorably handsome face. Why did it take me so long to notice?

"Yeah, Tel. It was *made* for you," I say, twirling and posing like a pageant girl. I have to admit, the muumuu is comfortable as heck. I think I need it. Teller shoots me daggers, and I shimmy into the changing room to hide my silent fit of laughter.

"I can't believe I got pressured into buying an animal-print muumuu," Teller mutters as we exit the store. After minutes of the clerk listing all the ways it flatters his coloring, his eyes, his hair, his "sexy" figure, he got overwhelmed and caved.

"Oh, come on, we reached a new level in our friendship—friendship muumuus!" I say, far too enthusiastically. I really don't know how to act around him anymore.

"I'm not talking to you for the rest of the trip," he grumbles, eyeing his bag like it's filled with angry wasps.

We're just approaching the restaurant when I hear "Lo!"

My body zings at the sound. It's too familiar.

"Lo!" I hear again, so I spin around.

Rucksack on his back, sun-kissed curls blowing in the coastal breeze. Caleb is standing right in front of me.

~

"Caleb?" I manage.

He gives me a warm smile and scoops me into his arms. I'm taken aback. This is a far cry from his look of utter terror the last time we saw each other.

What is he doing here? And why is he acting like he didn't just vanish from Florence without notice?

"How . . . How are you here?"

He opens his mouth to say something, but a lanky redheaded guy in one of those low-cut, neon bro–tank tops interrupts. One look and I can see he and Caleb are friends. He has that same hippie-surfer vibe.

Either his friend doesn't register the tension between us or he's ignoring it.

"Nice to meet you, Lo," he says, extending his hand. "I've heard a lot about you. I'm Freddie." *Heard a lot about me? That I'm a crazy person?*

I peer at Caleb, who just smiles back at me nervously. "Nice to meet you too. And all good things, I hope."

"This is my friend—the one I backpacked with through Australia and New Zealand. We met up in Naples," Caleb explains, eyes flicking toward Teller in the periphery. I wave him over, and he and Caleb do one of those awkward bro hugs where they clap each other on the back. Teller gives him a harder-than-normal *thwack*, which delights me more than it should.

"Can we talk really quick?" Caleb asks, turning back to me.

I nod and follow him out of earshot. My legs are two strips of jelly. One gust of wind too many and I might topple over. I assumed that if I ever saw Caleb again, I'd be delighted, relieved that I wasn't wrong about him after all. His presence would affirm that he is The One. But now he's here, mere feet from me, wringing his hands and looking apologetic as hell. "Lo, I am so, so sorry. I have so much to explain."

I may be mad at him, but his apology face is adorable. So adorable, I have to look away for the sake of my dignity. "Yeah, you do."

He presses his palms together. "I knew when I left that it was a bitch move. I guess I was just—" He runs his hand through his curls. "I was just caught off guard by what you said, and I freaked out."

"It was. You didn't owe me anything, but you could have given me a heads-up that you were leaving. I was really hurt," I say.

"I get it. And I know it's probably too little, too late. And you're only here a couple more days, but I'd like to try to make it up to you, if you'll let me."

"It's—sorry, I'm just a little surprised," I say. I'm desperately trying to wrap my mind around what he's saying, but it's all hard to process in the middle of a bustling street with tourists milling about. And Teller only a few feet away.

The universe is really gunning for me. Right then, Mei and Dad happen upon us. Mei wastes no time introducing herself as my favorite aunt. Dad is polite and all smiles, but his handshake is firm.

"I know it's a lot to spring on you, and I don't expect an answer right now. But do you think you'd meet up with me later to talk?" he asks, swallowing nervously. It's jarring to see him like this. He's always so confident, and I seem to be making him nervous.

I manage a nod. "Yeah, I'd like that."

He checks his watch and looks over his shoulder at his friend. "Shit. Freddie and I are going ocean kayaking. Here, I'll give you his number." He reaches for my phone and adds Freddie to my contacts. "I'll text you through him, okay?"

I take my phone back and send a text that says Lo's number. "Okay. See you later."

Caleb shoots me a hopeful smile over his shoulder that hits me right in the heart. I sag against a nearby building, trying to process what just happened.

"You didn't know he was going to be here, huh?" Mei asks.

"No. He knew my itinerary, though. He came here for me. But what are the chances of running into each other on the street, of all the thousands of people in Positano right now? Do you think it's fate?"

Mei's chuckle echoes in the salty air. "If that's not fate, I don't know what is."

31

When the next morning comes, I'm still shook.

The four of us are on the balcony for breakfast, although Mei is talking to a neighbor about restaurant recommendations, Dad is buried in his phone, and I've been texting Bianca, updating her on this whole mess (she is Team Caleb, of course).

"Excuse me, I have to take a call," Dad says abruptly, heading inside.

I shoot him a curious look. "With who?"

"Uh . . . it's a work call," he says quickly, avoiding eye contact. "It's an emergency."

Teller gives me a look that says *That was weird.*

I raise my brows as if to say *See, I told you he's acting off.* Dad works long hours. He always has. But I can't remember a time he had an urgent call. Something is fishy, but I don't have the energy to investigate. There are more pressing matters at hand.

I let out a strained sigh, though I don't realize how loud it is until Teller asks, "Did Caleb reach out yet?"

"Nope." My stomach does a barrel roll and I'm sensing it's not out of excitement. It's anticipation, I think. I need to know why he left.

Teller nudges me in the shin under the table. "Why do you sound so blah about it? I figured you'd be over the moon. It's that big grand gesture you always hoped for, isn't it?" When I give a half-hearted shrug, he continues, "I mean, he came all the way to the Amalfi Coast for you. I'd say it even tops the airport grand gesture in *Love, Actually.* Or the boom box serenade in *Say Anything*. Though nothing beats the M&M *Sorry* pizza in *The Princess Diaries*."

I think back to all those hours we've spent in the back row of the theater watching old movies, feet resting on the backs of the seats in the row ahead. Me sobbing into my popcorn, Teller rolling his eyes at the cheesiest parts. It instantly brings me back to myself. "I love that you're an encyclopedia of grand gestures now."

"Guess I've become an expert over the years," Teller says.

"I've lost count of how many elaborate gestures we brainstormed."

"Sometimes I think it's because of you that I won Sophie over."

I shake my head. "No way. You were the best boyfriend, Tel. Most you came up with all by yourself. Like when you drove up and surprised her with a hot-air balloon ride for your one-year anniversary."

"Still. You were instrumental in the planning."

"I'll happily take credit," I say.

We're quiet again. Teller's gaze is searching but gentle, if a little awkward after everything that's happened. I think we both feel it. Still, he's giving me the space to speak if I want to.

"Caleb coming here was really romantic," I finally agree. When I hear myself say it, I realize there's no emotion behind it. It's like I'm saying a scientific fact. Teller is completely right—Caleb showing up in the most beautiful place on Earth is probably the grand gesture of all grand gestures. Add the whole fate-and-soulmate thing in and it's a true love story for the books. A story for future generations to swoon over. "I should be over the moon, gushing and giddy like I was when we first arrived in Venice. So why aren't I?"

"Maybe you're still mad at him?" It's a fair deduction. I was angry when he first left, and I should still be mad. I have every right to be. But when I was with him today, that emotion didn't quite feel right. What I feel toward him isn't anger or frustration—it's something heavier.

Guilt. Not just about what happened with Teller in Tuscany, but about the feelings I have for him now. The feelings that just won't go away no matter how hard I try to push them aside.

But I can't admit any of this to Teller, so I just nod. "Yeah, I think I'm still probably a bit salty over the whole thing."

Teller leans forward. "Understandable. But he did make the effort. That has to count for something."

"It does. But what if he leaves again? What if he's still not ready?"
Or worse, what if I'm not ready?

"I think you should at least hear him out. I don't think he'd have come for you if he wasn't ready," he assures me. His confidence burns a little. As grateful as I am for his support, it feels a little cheap, Teller so easily passing me off to someone else after what happened between us.

"Yeah. It's fate, right?" I say, trying to convince myself more than him. After all, I can't argue with fate. Fate is forever. These misplaced feelings for Teller are fleeting.

He gulps. "Yeah. Fate."

Ding.

My phone lights up.

Caleb: Can u talk?

"Speaking of fate. Caleb just texted. He wants to meet up now."

Teller sits up and smooths his hair out. "Right now?"

I nod. "Right now."

"All right, well, I won't hold you back. Your future awaits." He reaches for my hand, and as he pulls me up, I search his face. For something. Sadness? Jealousy? Anything. But there's nothing there.

I ignore the dense forest of his lash line. The way I want to curl into him like he's a pile of fresh, warm laundry. I ignore it all. As complicated as my feelings are for Teller, this is fate pointing me in the right direction. Teller was never supposed to be mine.

32

Caleb and I meet up at the Path of the Gods, a rugged pathway that connects Positano to smaller villages, offering panoramic views of the coast and the little villages and their quintessential pastel-colored buildings. The path is beautiful, filled with wildflowers and lush greenery. It takes a solid three hours to complete, giving us plenty of time to talk.

We ease in, spending the first half of the hike catching up. He tells me all about his adventures with Freddie in Naples, and I recount our time in Tuscany—or at least, a sanitized version.

"All right, so let's be serious for five minutes," he says, flashing me that sunny smile. It reminds me why I liked him so much to begin with. He parks himself on a flat rock, patting the space next to him.

"My record is four, but let's try," I say with a sly smile. I relish the feeling of the coastal air on my face, a welcome reprieve from the blazing sun.

"All right, I'll make it quick. I owe you an apology. I'm sorrier than you'll ever know," he says over the echo of a group of hikers ahead.

"You don't. You already apologized," I remind him. I don't feel at liberty to be mad, considering what happened with Teller. I'm the one who's committed the ultimate betrayal. I'll have to tell him eventually, if I don't screw this up yet again.

"I know. But I don't think one sorry is enough. I mean, I ditched you in Florence right after you told me all of this stuff about your family, your mom. All that history. I just straight-up left without telling you, like a complete coward. If I were you, I'd never talk to me again."

I get the feeling he needs to get this off his chest, so I let him.

He hangs his head, letting his feet drag in the dirt. "Like I said yesterday, I got scared."

"I did drop a pretty big bomb on you. The whole soulmate thing is a touch terrifying to the average person," I say over the rustle of the lemon tree above us.

"Maybe. But I'm grateful you did. You forced me to stop and think about how I'm living my life. I always thought while I'm young and traveling, I had to be alone. I couldn't be tied down. But when I was on the train to Naples, I realized that it would be nice to have someone by my side. And truthfully, the time I spent with you was some of the best I've had."

I let it all sink in, studying the uneven path, kicking a small rock between my feet. He's taken full accountability for what he's done, no excuses. He's also admitted that his feelings for me aren't just casual. In fact, they're pretty freakin' big. Still, I'm hesitant.

"I have to ask, though, are you still scared? Monogamy isn't really something that's negotiable for me."

"I won't lie—I am, a little bit," he admits. "I've never actually been in love. I've never even had a relationship longer than two months."

"Me either, actually."

"Maybe we can learn together?" He gives me an earnest look that nearly knocks me off my feet. It's the same jolt I got when our eyes locked for the first time.

"I—I'd like to, but I'm leaving. In a few days," I say before I get too carried away.

He leans into me and plants soft kisses on my shoulder. "I think you should stay. Please? I've never had a connection like this with anyone. It feels big for me too. Even if you never told me we were supposed to be together, I'd still feel like there was something different about us. Something bigger."

"I wish I could stay." I can't help but think this is how it should have been the first time around, when I first told him he was The One. Things could have been so different if he hadn't left. Teller and I never would have—

"Seriously, I mean, you said yourself you were thinking of deferring. You could stay a couple extra weeks and travel around with me. Stay as long as you want."

The prospect sounds amazing in theory. But I've only budgeted enough for one month. "I don't know. I mean, I don't know if I can afford it."

"I travel extremely cheap, as you know," he says. "Plus, we'd be splitting a room."

I've fixed in my mind that this is just a monthlong adventure. That I'd inevitably go home, back to reality. It never occurred to me that I could stay. At least, I think I could.

"I'll have to think about that. My dad might have a heart attack," I say. Then again, he doesn't have to agree. I am an adult. I don't need his permission to stay.

Caleb goes quiet. "Ah, think your dad will hate my guts?"

"Absolutely not. He's just . . . overprotective. He doesn't want us rushing into anything."

"That's understandable. I wouldn't want my daughter rushing into a relationship with a strange guy she met abroad."

"Well, when you put it that way," I say with a laugh.

As we head back to Positano, I stop to take in the view. The blue sea stretches beneath the dramatic cliffs and hillsides. I'm not sure I'm ready to leave this.

33

After our hike, Caleb and I hang out at the beach, sprawled out on wrinkled, sandy towels, only getting up for the necessities (gelato). The sun hangs lazily in the sky, casting everything in the perfect peachy hue. Caleb reads a tattered old paperback he found in a Little Free Library in London, while I pretend to read a thriller.

I think about what I'd be going home to. It's a blank slate. I feel a glaring pressure to fill it with something I'm passionate about. Something worth deferring college for. I'd have to find a more permanent job. Bianca will be back home, a couple hours away, for the rest of summer, and who knows if we'll even hang out next year if I'm no longer a student. And then I'd have to deal with the disappointment of how things played out with Teller, not to mention him leaving and probably getting back together with Sophie.

Caleb and I haven't had adequate time yet to figure out where we go from here. Staying for a few extra weeks probably isn't a terrible idea. We need to figure things out between us. He is my soulmate, after all.

As the sun goes down, he runs into the water with his clothes still on and I follow. It's exhilarating, impulsive, a surge of childlike joy. I want to remember this moment forever. The sprinkle of colored houses stacked along the rocky cliffside, glowing and sun-tinted. The glimmer on the surface of the water when the sun hits it just right. The shock of the cold water enveloping my body. This is how Caleb makes me feel—free.

And yet, when he pulls me to him and kisses me, I don't feel that same electric spark. When we first kissed in Rome, it felt like I could lose myself in him entirely. It's still nice, but it's like I'm going through the motions. Because I'm supposed to. Because this is what's destined to happen.

Is that why there's a dullness when we touch? Is that why I don't catalog the way the pads of his fingers feel against my cheek, or the taste of his mouth as he slides his tongue against mine? Because it feels predetermined? There's a disconnect, like we're kissing and touching through a barrier, dulling the experience.

When he pulls back and smiles at me, my mind surges with intrusive thoughts. Teller's face. Teller's lips. Teller's eyes. I'm overthinking this. I'm too in my head after everything. Too in my head to give Caleb my full attention.

We part ways shortly after getting out of the water but not before I invite him on the catamaran excursion tomorrow that Mei booked. When I get back to the Airbnb, Mei is still awake, on her phone, propped up by pillows against the headboard. I quickly change out of my wet clothes and into my muumuu.

"Nice night?" she asks, scrutinizing my new outfit. She doesn't say anything, though I can tell by the crease between her brows she thinks it's hideous. She'd be horrified that I paid full price.

"Yeah," I say, though I don't know if I sound convincing.

She raises her brow. "You're not happy. What's wrong?"

She's right. I should be happier than ever. Why don't I feel happy? It's like a funhouse. Everything is technically where it should be but a little off. Ajar. Crooked.

"Well, I hate school. I'm thinking of deferring," I say, finally feeling brave enough to admit it.

"That's why your life line is splintered!" Her eyes go wide like she's cracked a puzzle.

My shoulders drop in shame. "I really tried all year to give it a chance. But I just can't do it anymore. It didn't feel right, being there.

Even while applying for colleges, everyone else made getting accepted their whole world. I never really cared because I never felt like it was what I was supposed to be doing. But I felt this obligation."

"See? You're more intuitive than you thought. I'm proud of you for following your gut. For having the courage to go against the grain and not just blindly doing what you think you're supposed to. Not many people your age can do that."

"It's not like it's gotten me anywhere. I have no idea what I'm doing with my life—" I pause, sucking in a deep breath. "Do you think Mom would have been disappointed?" According to my aunts, my mom was the nerd of the sisters. She loved school.

Mei doesn't hesitate to shake her head. "Not at all. Hon, you're only nineteen years old. You have a lot of time to figure life out. Look at Aunt Ellen. She went to teachers college at thirty-two. It's never too late to find your passion. Your mom would have supported that."

"You know who won't be as supportive . . ."

"I'll handle your dad when the time comes," she vows. "What else is going on?" she asks, still sensing I'm a total mess.

"Things with Caleb feel weird now. It's hard to explain. I like him. A lot. He's literally the blueprint of my perfect guy. His personality, his looks, all eleven out of ten," I add. "We have everything in common. Same interests, same views on most things. I always feel on top of the world when I'm with him. Like, I'm inspired to do more, see more, experience everything. He makes me want to live my best life. And he has feelings for me too. Big feelings."

"But now?"

"I'm scared I don't like him as much as I should." Heavy from the weight of it all, I rest my head on her lap.

She runs her fingers through my hair. "You've only known each other a few weeks. A soulmate doesn't mean instant fireworks. Sometimes it takes a while to develop a connection."

"Fair. But when we first met, I thought we had that electric connection. Now it feels like it's faded. I don't know where that feeling went."

"You know what, we need to call Ellen."

We ring Ellen and luckily, she picks up. "You better not send me one more picture of your delicious food. Do you know how cruel that is? I'm a very pregnant woman!"

"Hi, Aunt Ellen," I say.

"Oh, hey, Lo." She perks up knowing I'm here too. Mei prods me to explain everything to Ellen.

"Do you think you could love Caleb?" she asks.

"I mean, I don't really know. Is that bad? Shouldn't I automatically love my soulmate?"

"Ellen, this reminds me of Hank," Mei says. Hank is Ellen's husband. "Remember how hard it was to pin him down?"

Ellen laughs. "I knew he was The One when we met. But he wasn't interested in marriage or children. It took me, what . . . three years to make him fall in love with me?"

"It did? So it wasn't instant?"

"Nope. Not at all. Fate doesn't have a sell-by date," Ellen says.

Mei agrees. "Just because we know someone might be our soulmate doesn't mean we don't have to work at it."

"We have to build that connection from the ground up, just like everyone else. But the work doesn't feel like work when it's the right person."

Maybe they're right. Maybe I just need to give things more time with Caleb. Maybe those extra few weeks are crucial.

I think about how long it took Teller and I to build a friendship. We certainly didn't like each other instantly. Our connection took time to build. Maybe that's what I need with Caleb. Time.

"Oh, speaking of. Caleb asked me to stay a few extra weeks." I say *a few extra weeks* casually, but it feels anything but casual. Because those *few extra weeks* really symbolize something else—a massive decision. A decision that is going to affect the trajectory of my entire life. The decision to honor the vision and, therefore, fate.

"I think you absolutely should. You need extra time to get to know each other," Ellen says, like it's no big deal.

"But you're due next month! Who else is gonna sanitize all your bottles and pump parts?" I protest. We'd already agreed that when the baby is born, I'd go over and help out with chores and cooking, just like I did when Maisey was born two years ago.

Ellen rubs her belly. "As much as I'd love your help, you can't leave Italy just because of me. Baby will be here to meet you whenever you decide to come back."

Mei nods in agreement.

"Do you think Mom would have wanted me to stay?" I ask.

"Your mom would have absolutely loved Caleb," Mei says, unable to contain her smile.

"Really?"

"She was obsessed with travel too. I imagine they could have talked for hours and hours about it. He would have charmed the socks off her in two seconds flat."

It's bittersweet, knowing Mom would have loved my soulmate but also dealing with the reality that I'll never know for sure. I'll never get to experience that—Caleb meeting my mom for the first time, giving her flowers, trying to make her laugh.

Ellen clears her throat. "In the end, it doesn't matter what your mom would have wanted. It's about fate."

I take a deep exhale, exhausted from the mental gymnastics. It feels like life is extending its hand and pulling me through another doorway, onto a path that just *makes sense*.

Why would I pass up the opportunity to travel and explore? Why would I pass up happiness with the person I'm destined to be with? And for what? Going home to my directionless, Teller-less life?

Mei places an assuring hand on my shoulder. "This is where you're supposed to be, Lo."

34

I'm restless and twitchy. The sheets are pulled unnaturally tight, binding me like an ancient mummy. Damp and claustrophobic, I manage to free my arms and stare up at the plaster ceiling, replaying the night.

Caleb joined us for dinner this evening. While Dad was initially hesitant about my soulmate, there's no one Caleb can't charm. All he had to do was feign ignorance about Marvel and he had Dad eating from the palm of his hand. Dad would never say it, but I know this is going to make the news easier to swallow.

I can't stop thinking about my decision to stay. If this is really fate, then why do I feel such a deep ache? A sadness for the life I'm leaving behind? I'd been so excited about meeting The One that I never registered the reality—that my life would completely change from here on. I'd potentially have to uproot entirely, leaving Dad, my aunts, Brandon and Brian.

I toss and twist, pretzeling myself into every position—to no avail. It doesn't help that Mei is snoring and mumbling about ETFs and TFSAs in her sleep. When I finally accept that I'm not falling asleep anytime soon, I pull on a cardigan and tiptoe past the living room, out the front door.

The plan was to take a short walk to stretch my muscles and tire myself out. But instead, I pad down the steep stone staircase to the beach, the glittering lights a beacon along the jagged cliffs. The salty breeze wafting in from the sea has cooled the air. It's quiet without the tourists and traffic. There's only the flutter of leaves, the distant chirp of crickets, and the gentle lull of the frothy waves lapping against the pebbly shore. I sit, squishing the cool sand between my feet, and take in the briny aroma of the sea.

A figure catches my eye in my periphery. There's someone sitting in the sand to my right, partially hidden behind a folded-up beach lounger. The dark, mussed-up hair is a dead giveaway. It's Teller, sitting with his legs pulled to his chest, gazing out at the vast sea stretching before us.

"Couldn't sleep either?" I call out.

I expect him to jump, but he doesn't appear surprised by my presence. "Nah. What's keeping you up?" he asks, moving from behind the lounger to sit next to me.

Oh, just everything. No big deal. "Aunt Mei was talking in her sleep," I say. "A lot of finance jargon. Sounded like a nightmare, if you ask me."

"At least I never brought up equity and audits while we were rooming together," he says with an impish smile. The moonlight plays over his features, casting a subtle glow over his profile. My gaze locks on his full lips, absorbing every word.

"I used to dream about you staying in town for college and us getting an apartment together," I admit.

"Really?"

"Back before you decided you were leaving. When it was all kind of up in the air. I wanted to get one of those cute places with stained glass windows near the west edge of campus, one of the walk-ups. I remember driving by when we were in high school and seeing college kids hanging out on their balconies, feet resting over the railing. I thought they were so cool, so free."

Teller smirks. "Little did you know, college is almost worse. The cooking, cleaning, never-ending schoolwork. And the student debt."

"Right? I foolishly thought it would be just like working at The Cinema, but better because we'd get to goof off all the time, drive to campus together, grab fast food on the way home. Make blanket forts in the living room for study dates. Throw candy at each other while we work. It would have been fun, in an alternate universe."

He smiles one of those smiles that doesn't quite reach his eyes.

"Though you'd probably get sick of me pretty quick," I say, the cool pebbles settling between my toes.

"What? No way."

"You would," I argue. "I'd probably leave toast crumbs on the counter. I'd probably be too lazy to put a new garbage bag in the trash bin. And I've never been good at unloading the dishwasher. Ask my dad. I'd be kind of a gross roommate, really."

"Why do you always do that?"

I blink. "Do what?"

"Talk about yourself like that. You're always putting yourself down. And I know you're half joking, but sometimes I think you actually believe it."

I consider that. "Sorry, I don't even notice I'm doing it anymore." I used to be the most confident kid in the room. But I've just felt lost. Untethered.

Maybe that's why I've always gone for the Calebs, Tims, and Mark B.'s of the world—the alpha types that seem out of reach. It felt nice to be validated by someone like that. I thought maybe some of that confidence would rub off on me. If they're so sure of themselves, that must mean they're sure of *me*.

"I guess it feels . . . safer to point out my insecurities before someone else has the chance to."

"There is absolutely nothing you should be insecure about," he says, eyes latching on mine.

Well, shit. Why does he always have to disarm me like that?

I pull my gaze away abruptly, terrified he'll see right through me. "So you're talking to Sophie again?"

He pauses, a little thrown off. "Uh, yeah. Here and there. She actually asked me to talk when I get back." I think back to the look of devastation on his face the night he picked me up from the frat party, the night he told me about their breakup. This has to mean everything to him. This is what he so desperately wanted, another chance.

"Do you think she wants to get back together?" I dare to ask.

He bites his lip. "When we broke up, she said there was nothing left to say. That cutting ties would be the easiest thing to do. So wanting to talk is a development."

I search his face for any sign of hope, but he keeps his expression neutral, probably to avoid disappointment. I should be happy that things may work out between them. For him. It would be selfish not to since I'm staying here with Caleb.

Still, my stomach curdles. It feels inevitable that Teller will get back together with Sophie. This whole trip will be a distant memory, just like our friendship, fading into the rearview. Because how could it ever be the same now that real feelings are involved?

I slide my feet up, bringing my knees to my chest for warmth. "If you guys get back together, our friendship would be over, wouldn't it?"

He shakes his head, confused. "No. Why would that mean our friendship would be over?"

"Because. We hooked up. Twice." When I say it, my mind is inundated with flashbacks. Him hovering over me in the darkness. The safety of his weight. My fingers running down his back, feeling every ridge of muscle along the way. In my heart of hearts, the hooking-up factor isn't the reason for the demise of our relationship. Until recently, I was sure we could push past it. But now, it's become clearer: it's the feelings, the more-than-friend feelings, that are the real killer.

He shifts his gaze to the water.

Also, Teller would never, in good conscience, keep this secret from her. And I couldn't blame her for being uncomfortable with our friendship after what happened on this trip. Therefore, our friendship will inevitably end. And I have to be okay with that. I want Teller to be happy.

He resettles, wrapping his arms around his knees. "I'll tell her it didn't mean anything."

My gut twists. I can't tell if that's a statement of fact or a lie. *Did it mean anything?* my gaze asks.

He raises a brow. *Did it mean anything to you?*

This is the one time I wish we didn't have the ability to communicate silently. We should talk this through, for real. But like the coward I am, I offer us a way out. "Even if you tell her it didn't mean anything, she'll never believe it."

He rakes his fingers through the sand silently. "She'll have to."

I note the tense. *She'll have to.* The pit in my stomach expands, and I know what I have to do. I have to let him go. Because if I truly care about him, I won't stand in the way of his happiness.

"It's hard to believe it's our second-to-last day," Teller says, breaking the long stretch of silence. "You ready for normal life?"

I hesitate. "I don't know if I'm going back. Not Thursday, at least."

"Wait, what? Really? You're staying here with Caleb?"

"Yeah. I'm considering it. Just for a few weeks. Maybe a month? I honestly don't know."

"And when you go back for school, what will he do?"

I turn my gaze down. "Well, about that . . . I'm actually not going back. I'm going to defer a semester. Maybe even a year."

He straightens his spine. "Really?"

"I know you think it's stupid. But I was honestly about to do it before Caleb, before the vision. I've just felt so out of place. I hate all my classes. I—" I pause, overwhelmed, unable to continue through increasingly shallow breathing.

He places his hands on my shoulders. "It's okay, Lo. You don't have to explain yourself. Just breathe, like we did on the plane."

I take a few moments, practicing Teller's technique. *Count to seven, and slowly let it out for seven.*

My breathing gradually goes back to a steady rhythm. "Sorry."

"Don't apologize."

"No, really, though. I should have told you earlier."

"Why didn't you?" he asks.

"Because I was embarrassed. I didn't tell anyone. Not even my dad. I thought you would think it was a rash decision and try to change my mind. Everyone's said that if I stick with it, I'll find something I love. And I really tried, but there's just something about college . . . about the lectures and the studying, the labs, and all the freakin' theory. I'd rather be *doing* something, you know?"

"I get where you're coming from," he says evenly. "You were iffy about it even when we were applying in high school. Maybe it does make sense to take the year and figure things out."

I'm taken aback. "I thought you'd argue with me. Tell me it's the worst idea you've ever heard."

"It gives me anxiety, for sure. Not the deferral, but you staying here."

I huff. "You're telling me. This is the guy who left me in Florence. How do I know he won't do it again? Leave me in some random city? And this time, you won't be there." I realize that's a huge reason I'm so uneasy—the prospect of Caleb leaving me again.

"I don't think he'll do it again, Lo. And if he does, you come home. Call me and I'll pick you up from the airport."

"Thanks, Tel. I just hope this is the right choice."

"If there's any reason to travel around in a foreign country, it's to be with the love of your life." I can tell he's being genuine. I don't know why I'm surprised that everyone is on board with me staying (well, we'll see about Dad). All signs point to this being the right choice. Maybe I'm just looking for excuses to buck against the course charted for me.

"Fate," I finally say.

His mouth curves up in the smallest smile. "Exactly. Fate, or something like it."

"But if it's really fate, why doesn't it feel easy?"

"Nobody said it was easy," he says, bumping his shoulder into mine.

I roll my eyes at him. "You did not just quote Coldplay lyrics to me."

"I absolutely did. Coldplay is basically required listening for an existential crisis."

He's not wrong. It weirdly suits my mood. I start singing, entirely out of tune.

He smiles and we sing in unison, humming the *"Ooohhhh ohh ohh oh ohhhhhh"* part until our voices grow hoarse. Eventually, we run out of breath and fall back in the sand in a fit of giggles, staring up at the glittering sky.

Teller taps my pinkie with his. "Well, we should probably head back," he whispers.

I latch my pinkie around his, both our eyes glancing down at our tattoos. "Can we stay? Just five more minutes?"

We stay for ten.

I soak it all in, every second. The sound of the water lapping against the sand. The distant squawk of birds. The buzz of traffic. The grainy sand in my hair, my neck, down the back of my shirt. The way he looks at me with that quintessential Teller half grin I tried so hard to capture in our painting class.

I want to remember it. Savor it. Because after he goes home, things won't ever be the same.

35

Being on a catamaran with your soulmate and your best friend you hooked up with and also might be in love with is awkward. There's no way around it.

Maybe it's the fact that it's a gorgeous day—not a cloud in the vast sky—or maybe it's the delicious seafood the crew is serving (not pasta), but Teller has fully embraced Caleb. Not that he was ever a jerk to him, but they gravitated toward other people when we were traveling in a bigger group. Today, they're fishing, playing cards, and bonding over their shared love of eighties synth music.

If I know Teller, this is his way of showing me he accepts Caleb. He's making an effort to really get to know him. I didn't know how much I needed his approval until now. Caleb's even teaching him how to snorkel. I expect Teller to decline and explain his fear of open water, but he enthusiastically slaps on a pair of goggles, shirks the life jacket I offer, and follows Caleb down the ladder. I watch from the safety of the trampoline net, ready to dive in should Teller require assistance, though he seems to be holding his own. The two of them don't seem to need me at all, in fact.

There's a gentle, warm breeze on the spacious deck. We huddle, basking in the sound of the waves slapping against the hull. Mei and Dad chat with our captain, who goes by Frosty and is keen on doling out homemade limoncello shots. Every so often, they clamber to get photos in front of the mansions that speckle the rugged shoreline, as well as the odd mountain goat.

By midafternoon, Frosty docks at Marina Grande, where we take a few hours to stroll around the island of Capri. The piazzetta feels fancy, with its posh boutiques; it's a contrast to the beachwear shops of Positano. After a jaunt in the Gardens of Augustus, Dad, Mei, and Teller opt for a quick tour of the Church of San Michele. Caleb and I head back to the boat for more swimming. Caleb tries to teach me the proper technique for a butterfly stroke, but I'm in my head, psyching myself up to tell him I'm going to stay. Logically, I know he asked me to, but after the whole leaving-me-in-Florence situation, he still makes me nervous.

I finally blurt out, "I'm staying." I hold my breath to gauge his reaction.

The sunshine sparkles over the crystal-clear water, making his eyes appear a vibrant shade of turquoise. "What? That's amazing," he says enthusiastically. "And your dad is okay with it?"

"I haven't told him yet. I'm going to. Later today." Truth be told, I've been hard-core avoiding the discussion. I already know how it's going to go.

"What will we do?" I ask Caleb.

His eyes light up. "I've always wanted to go up north. To the Dolomites. Though we don't even have to stay in Italy. We could go anywhere we want." It's a wild feeling, having the whole world at our fingertips—well, on a very strict budget.

"I still can't believe we ran into each other," I say, spinning around to take in the view. We're surrounded by megayachts and beautiful boats and everything just feels perfect.

"Yeah, I guess we have Teller to thank for that."

My arms freeze. "Teller?" I ask, midcough. *What does Teller have to do with this?*

His lips part. "Teller reached out a few days ago and told me you guys were heading to Positano. He told me where you'd be staying. He was pretty straight up—said I was an asshole for leaving you in Florence and that I owed you an explanation. That I'd be a total tool for passing up an opportunity to be with someone like you. He was completely right."

I clutch the ladder hanging off the side of the boat, trying to stay afloat. "Wait. Teller reached out to you? Are you serious?"

He eyes me, the lines between his brows creased with confusion. "You didn't know that?"

"I thought . . ." I think back to that day, coming out of the store with our ugly-ass muumuus, hearing Caleb's voice call my name over the breeze. "I thought we just randomly ran into each other."

He snaps his head back. "No, definitely not. Have you seen the crowds? I'm shocked I found you as is. He emailed me when you guys were in Tuscany. I just happened to be using a friend's laptop to Zoom with my mom when I got his message."

"What day was this?"

"He sent it Sunday morning."

Sunday morning. The morning after we'd hooked up. I think back to how distracted he was when I found him on the balcony.

My world tilts and everything blurs, a mixture of confusion and embarrassment swirling around me in a thick fog. I hoist myself onto the boat and park myself with a squish on the padded bench, water dripping everywhere. It feels like someone's just told me the Earth is, in fact, not actually round. I thought running into Caleb was confirmation that my vision was correct. That we're supposed to be together.

It wasn't fate, Caleb finding me again. Not really.

It was Teller.

~

I barely speak for the rest of the day—not that anyone really notices. Everyone is sapped from the sun, content to sit back and enjoy the views as we boat back to the marina. I'm still angry when my feet hit the dock in Positano. Caleb is oblivious to my mood. Still, we say a brief goodbye, agreeing to meet up tomorrow after Dad, Mei, and Teller head to the airport.

As we journey back to the Airbnb, I laser focus on the dark mop of hair on the back of Teller's head, as though trying to read his mind. Why would he message Caleb after telling me Caleb is an asshole? And why would he do it the morning after we hooked up? Was it that bad? I need answers.

"Hey, can I talk to you for a second?" I say, charging up the stairs to catch up with him.

"Sure, what's up?" he asks, pausing so we fall back behind Dad and Mei.

"Why didn't you tell me you reached out to Caleb?" I ask, not bothering to beat around the bush.

He turns his gaze up the steep staircase and blows the air out of his cheeks. "Because I knew you wouldn't want me to."

"No shit! I was letting things take their natural course. This whole time I was walking around talking about fate. Thinking he found me here because the universe willed it. But it was you." Just thinking about it makes me want to crawl into a hole. "How could you not tell me something like that?"

He lowers his head, grabbing the ends of the towel wrapped around his neck. "Crap. I'm sorry, Lo. I thought I was doing the right thing. I mean, didn't I? You're back together. You're staying. It's still kind of fate." I think back to what he said on the beach: *Fate, or something like it.*

I press my fingers to my temples to ward off the impending headache. "I guess I'm just confused. What was your motive? Did you feel sorry for me or something after we hooked up?"

"Are you kidding me? Why would I feel bad for you after we hooked up?" he asks, like he's offended I'd even question it.

"I don't know. Maybe you thought it was terrible and wanted to distract me?"

He lets out a huff, pausing to let someone pass by on the stairs.

"No. It's just the opposite, actually." He watches me for a moment. "*I* was the one that needed the distraction."

I spin around to face him on the step below me. "But . . . the next morning you were so distant. I woke up and you were on the balcony texting Sophie."

He squeezes his eyes shut and rakes both hands through his hair. "Shit. I wasn't. I mean, I have texted her a bit, but I wasn't texting her that morning. She was the last person I wanted to talk to that morning."

"Then why did you lie?"

"Because when you came onto the balcony, I was messaging Caleb. I thought you saw it over my shoulder so I panicked."

"But why did you message Caleb in the first place?"

He sucks in a breath. "Because I'm in love with you, Lo. Okay?"

36

I'm leaning on the side of a stone retaining wall, trying to catch my breath.

"Excuse me?"

He sucks in another breath, seemingly in shock that he's said it. He's not the only one.

"Did you mean what you just said?" I implore.

"Yes," he says, coming to a full stop in front of me. His eyes are red, although I don't know if it's from emotion or the salty water. "Why do you think I got you inked on my body?"

"Okay, but I pressured you into it. And you were wasted," I point out.

"I've never wanted a tattoo before, that's true. Because there was nothing I could imagine wanting on my body forever. Except you."

A crowd of tourists armed with cameras and beach bags whirl up the steps past us, and I cover my eyes to block it all out.

"Are you okay?" Teller asks.

I shake my head. "I just don't understand. In all these years, you've never shown any interest in me."

"Are you kidding me? I was always interested in you. That whole first summer we worked together, I liked you," he continues, sensing my skepticism. "I thought it was pretty obvious. I drove you everywhere."

I can't help but scoff. "I'm supposed to know you secretly liked me because you drove me places?"

"Well, no. I . . . I didn't know how to tell you, so I just tried to hang out with you as much as I could. And then when you started dating Tim, I assumed you weren't interested. And by the time you guys broke up . . ."

"You'd met Sophie," I whisper, the realization sinking in. "Did you still have feelings for me when you were with her?" I hold my breath, almost scared to know.

He's quiet for a few long moments. "I did truly love Sophie. When I met her, I stopped thinking about you like that for a while, pushed the feelings away, I guess. But deep down, I think they've always kind of been there. I cared about you more than a friend should, and Sophie knew that. It drove her crazy how much I talked about you. How much I missed you last year."

"But you didn't talk to me all year," I remind him, still unsure this whole conversation isn't just a fever dream. "I missed you all the damn time. There were so many things that reminded me of you and made me wish you were there. So I'd text you, but you'd barely respond. I have so many unanswered texts from you on my phone."

"Because I couldn't do that to Sophie. Every time I talked to you, it was like opening a wound. I'd think about you constantly. I thought not talking to you at all would make things easier—out of sight, out of mind."

"Is that the real reason you broke up?" The guilt hits me, as though someone's dropped a sack of bricks on my chest.

He shakes his head. "Yes and no. She was legitimately bored. But I think the bigger issue was that she didn't have all of me. I guess she never did, which is why I felt so guilty. That's why I was trying so hard to get her back. I thought I could get over you once and for all and fully invest in her. I wanted to—so badly."

I hang my head in my hands. "God, Tel. This is . . . Why now? Why haven't you said anything before now? Things could have been so different."

"Because, Lo!" His expression almost looks pained. "You scare the living shit out of me. You're loud, spontaneous, and you say the most random things at the most inappropriate times. You're a living nightmare. And also, a living dream. My whole life I've thought with my head, and you . . . you make me think with my heart."

Each word comes at me like puzzle pieces that I haven't quite figured out how to put together. He continues when I don't respond.

"And if you want to get technical, I never had time to tell you. I'd just gotten home and out of a relationship and we flew to Italy almost immediately. And *bam*, you tell me you have a soulmate. There was never a right time to confess my feelings, certainly not in a way to do them justice. And I knew I could never compete with your damn soulmate."

"You could," I choke out. "What if we—"

"Don't say it." The words die on my lips, but he knows what I was going to say. *What if we try?*

"Why not? If you're so in love with me, why couldn't you fight for me? You could have told me how you felt, asked me to choose you."

He scoffs. "Because you never saw me that way."

"But—" I stop, unable to defend myself.

"You liked guys like Tim Yates, Lo. Why would I ever think I had a chance?"

"But after we hooked up . . ." My voice trails.

His gaze narrows. "Would you really choose me over your soulmate?" I think about that. How could I?

"I—"

"If you could say with a hundred percent certainty that you'd choose me, I would be with you in a heartbeat." He pauses, watching me. "But if I know you, you can't say that. There would always be part of you that wonders about him. Maybe even regrets not seeing it through. I know how important your family is. How important that vision is to you. I can't let you walk away from that."

I suck in a breath. "Why do you have to be so selfless?"

"It's not totally selfless," he confesses. "I don't want to be your second choice. I've been invisible my entire life. The backup. The brother only played with when everyone else is busy. I *can't* be your second choice."

"So that's why you messaged Caleb?"

He nods before meeting my gaze again. "I needed you to choose me because you wanted to. Not because he was gone and I was just . . . there. I thought I could block my feelings while you figured things out with Caleb, but turns out, I can't."

I sigh, dragging my hands down my cheeks. "This is such a mess."

He dips his chin forward. "It's really not. This is how things were supposed to be," he says vehemently, kneeling in front of me on the steps so we're finally level. "Look, all I want is for you to be happy. And if the person you're supposed to be with, who makes you happiest, is Caleb, then I have to be okay with that."

My stomach cramps as I realize it could have been different. *Could have been.*

We're quiet for a couple beats. "This changes things between us, doesn't it?" he asks.

My eyes find his and he swallows. I think he knows the answer already. "Yeah. It does."

37

It's just Dad and me on the patio.

I fold myself into the slatted teak chair, only partially listening as Dad rehashes tomorrow's travel details. Something about getting there early enough to drop the rental car off.

"I have to talk to you about something," I blurt, unable to hold it in. *Many things*, if we're being honest.

He resettles and turns toward me. "I was going to say the same."

I grip the armrest, bracing myself. Mei must have told him. That's why he's so pale. I'm not scared that he'll freak out or have some strong reaction. Dad is even, kind of like Teller. He rarely gets elevated about anything. But he makes this certain expression when he's disappointed. And that's what I'm terrified of. Disappointing him.

"Did Mei say something? About me deferring to stay with Caleb?" I ask, just as he says, "Wait, did Mei tell you about Scheana?"

It's a face-off. "Scheana? Who is Scheana?" I ask over and over while he goes rigid, repeating, "You deferred?"

The onslaught comes next: "What are you thinking?" "What about our decision to stick it out for one more year?" "What are you planning to do instead?" "You can't stay in a foreign country with someone you barely know!"

I don't respond. All I want to know is "Who the heck is Scheana?" This one got through to him.

"Is she your girlfriend or something?" I say flippantly, not really expecting that to be a possibility.

I note the way he's fidgeting with his water bottle before he responds. "Yes."

My stomach free-falls. Dad has a girlfriend? What in sweet hell?

His shoulders hitch. "I never expected it to happen—neither of us did."

I turn away, though only partially. I need answers. "Who is she?"

"I met her a couple months ago. She's new at work." Maybe it's because he also met Mom at work, but that stings.

"Why didn't you tell me about her?" I ask, unable to hide my irritation.

"Because there was nothing to say at first. We started off just friends. She invited me to play pickleball and I didn't realize it was a date." Normally, I'd laugh at something like that, but right now all I feel is anger and resentment. "I didn't want to say anything until I knew it was serious. And then when it got serious, you were on your trip and I wanted to tell you in person."

I let out a snort. "Is that why you came all the way here? To tell me you have a girlfriend?"

His lips twist in offense. "No. I came to see you because I was concerned. And apparently, I had a right to be."

"You *don't* need to be concerned. I'm perfectly fine," I say, unable to cap the bitterness.

"You went backpacking, met some guy, and dropped out without even discussing it with me. Does that sound like someone who's fine?"

"Dad, I deferred. I didn't drop out. And I wanted to do it before I left a month ago. I didn't tell you because I knew you'd react like this. Like you always have when I do something that's not in line with your specific plan for me." He rolls his eyes and I toss my arms in the air. "I never wanted to go to college in the first place. I told you it wasn't for me—that I'd rather do something hands-on. Something with animals. And you couldn't accept that. You just wanted me to be exactly like you, to follow in your footsteps. Be super smart and academic, do everything cookie cutter and conventional like you and Mom did."

"And what's so wrong with that? You always loved true crime. And science, you were so good at it. You're capable of so much more if you'd just apply yourself."

Frustration builds in my throat. "See? This is exactly the problem. You don't even listen. If you did, you'd know it has nothing to do with not applying myself and everything to do with the fact that I've never liked forensics!" I pause momentarily, only to catch my breath. "And you don't have a leg to stand on, being mad at me for not telling you when you've been hiding a whole new relationship."

"I understand why you'd feel hurt—"

"Do you really, though?" Based on how this whole conversation is going, I'd wager he's still clueless.

"I've done extensive reading about how difficult it is for children of deceased parents when their living parent starts dating again."

I shake my head, startled by how off the mark he is.

"I've tried for years to avoid this. To make sure you were happy and content. I never wanted to bring anyone else into our lives until you were older. But you have to understand that it's healthy for me to finally move on. To have a companion—"

"Dad, you have no idea why I'm actually upset, do you?"

"Then tell me."

"I don't want to talk about this now. Please leave me alone."

"I hoped you'd be happy for me."

"It's hard to be happy for you when you're content to forget Mom." The words leave a sting in my mouth as soon as they come out, like venom.

He winces.

"I'm sorry," I say immediately. I'm officially an asshole. All these years, I've worried about what would happen if I left home. The idea of Dad being all by himself was crushing. And now, he's found a companion, someone to keep him company, someone to eat dinner with when

I'm not there. I should be thrilled, not acting like a complete brat. "I don't know why I said all that. Of course I want you to be happy. I was just . . . surprised."

He breaks, too, his expression a mixture of sadness and shame. "I'm sorry too. I do avoid talking about Mom. But I hope you know it's not because I want to forget about her. It's the opposite. It's because I miss her so much that it's painful to talk about her."

Tears cascade over my lash lines before I have the chance to stop them. "I'm sorry, Dad. I get it."

He pulls me into his chest. "But you're right. It's selfish of me to avoid talking about her. I just assumed it would make you sad too. I didn't want you to grow up being constantly reminded of her absence."

I pull back, wiping my tear-logged bangs away from my forehead. "I mean, I was anyways. Every time I'd go to a friend's house, or whenever girls talked about shopping with their moms on the weekend or their moms helped them pick out a dress for semiformal. She died when I was so young. I have such a hard time remembering. Talking about her is the only proof I have that she was real."

He nods. "I'm sorry, Lo. I promise to work on that. But believe me when I tell you, not talking about her has nothing to do with trying to forget her."

"I know that. I really do want you to be happy. You deserve to find happiness after Mom." And I mean it. My reaction was less about him moving on and more about being upset by my own situation.

He smiles and I think he's holding back tears. "Thank you. And I hope you know I never meant to hide it from you. We only met a few months before you left for Italy, and I just wanted to make sure it was right before I told you."

"Is it right?"

He smiles. "Yeah. It feels right."

"Good." I smile, and it feels like a weight has been lifted off my shoulders. Knowing that Dad has someone who makes him genuinely happy makes me feel good. I lean forward. "Just promise not to like, make out in front of me and stuff."

Dad puts his hand over his heart. "Solemnly swear. Though you'd have to actually be at home to make that promise." His eyes well. I know me not coming home is killing him.

I hang my head. "I know I'm a huge disappointment."

He sets a firm hand on my knee and looks me square in the eye. "You've never disappointed me. Not a day in your life. I was always so proud of you, entering those science competitions, even if you didn't win."

I sigh. "That's the thing. I only did them because I wanted you to be proud of me. I never liked them. And then when I mentioned possibly taking forensics, you were so happy and I just couldn't tell you the truth. And I thought, I don't hate it. Maybe I could stick it out."

"I get it. I probably wouldn't have been supportive if you had told me you were thinking of deferring. You know, your mom had a rough year in her first year. She almost dropped out."

"Really?"

He nods. "She went home every weekend, homesick. But she stuck it out and I mistakenly thought that was what you had to do, without realizing feeling lost in school and being homesick were totally different things."

"I'm sorry, Dad. I've really tried."

He nods. "It's okay. You tried, and that's all I can ask for. I'd rather you be happy, doing something you love, than see you miserable. And if it's going to take a while to figure out what's going to make you happy, so be it. It's just . . . Ever since your mother—" He stops himself, swallowing hard.

"Ever since Mom what?"

"Nothing."

He can see I'm upset, so he continues reluctantly, "I was just going to say, ever since your mom died, I've been terrified to lose you."

It's a big confession, probably the most vulnerable he's been with me. I've always known this was part of why he was so protective. My aunts always told me so. But this is the first time he's vocalized it instead of logic-ing all the reasons why things aren't safe or smart.

I squeeze his hand. "You won't lose me, Dad. I do plan on coming home. It'll just be a few weeks. Maybe another month."

"Okay. But you're welcome to come back earlier. If you need to."

"So you're saying you won't turn my room into a Marvel shrine?"

He laughs. "I may clear some shelf space."

"So, tell me about Scheana."

We sit for a solid two hours as he tells me all about his girlfriend. She's a fellow scientist and a massive nerd for anything comic-book related. In her spare time, she writes romance novels and loves to knit. She'll be good for Dad, I think.

And if my uptight-scientist dad is starting a whole new chapter, maybe I need to stop being so scared to start my own.

38

For the past four years, I've had one constant in my life: Teller Owens is my best friend. We may not have talked regularly last year, but I was comforted knowing that if I really needed him, he would be there.

Now something has shifted between us. Despite our attempts to act like everything is normal as they rush around packing up the Airbnb, I can tell by the look in his eyes, in that prolonged hug. I can tell by the way he folds me in tight, like it's the last time things will ever be like this. How can they be? Maybe the vision was correct. How can we go back to just being friends after confessing we're in love with each other? After acknowledging that we can't be together?

"Hey, before I go, I want to give you a parting gift," he says, releasing his grip around me, fully aware Dad and Mei are watching from the car.

I suck in one last breath of that fresh-cut-grass scent and finally let go. "Yeah?"

He whips out his money belt from behind his back, and a laugh rockets out of me. "For your travels. And look, there's even a secret pocket inside. Look."

I follow his lead, cracking the tiny, hidden pocket open. My finger brushes up against something. It's card stock.

Gently, I tug it out, knees nearly buckling at the sight of it. It's not *the* photo. It's one I haven't seen before. It looks to have been taken at Nai Nai's, based on the mustard-colored wall. Mom is holding me on the couch, smiling down at me with a love so intense, I feel it through the photo. I'm swaddled tight in a pale-pink blanket like a burrito, no older than a month. Dad is sitting next to her, mouth open like he's talking, one arm wrapped protectively around Mom's shoulder. They both look intensely sleep deprived, hair a mess, eyes dark and heavy, shirts untucked. It's everything I love about the original photo: it's not posed. It's entirely candid, a snapshot of a mere second. And in that moment, we're so incredibly happy.

"I know it's not *the* photo," Teller says. "But when your aunt Ellen sent a copy of the original, she sent a bunch of others too. And I saw this one and I just . . . thought you might like it."

My heart threatens to burst. It's absolutely perfect. Why does he have to be so thoughtful? "Thank you, Tel. This means everything," I say, rocking the money belt and photo close to my chest. Before we left for this trip, I'd have burned it at the stake if I could. And now, it's my most prized possession.

Our eyes catch and a long beat passes. It feels like we're in the center of a snow globe, just waiting for someone to shake it. Neither of us are ready to say goodbye. Instead, I burrow my head into his neck and wrap my arms around his torso, holding on for dear life. Because he's truly the best friend I've ever had.

"I would have liked doing laundry and taxes together," I whisper.

"Me too," he says, adding, "And yes, I know that was from *Everything Everywhere All at Once*."

I can only laugh. Otherwise, I might cry. "I'm sorry."

He pulls back to look me dead in the eye. "Don't be. I want you to be happy. That's all I've ever wanted," he says, pressing a kiss to the side of my head. Then he turns away and heads toward the car.

I wrap my arms around myself, watching them reverse out of the driveway. Dad gives me an embarrassingly aggressive wave through the window, like he used to when he left for work in the mornings. I barely hold it together as I wave back. As their car gets smaller and smaller, I let the tears flow. I'm still crying when I meet up with Caleb. He takes my rucksack and sets it on the ground beside us, pulling me into his arms.

"You miss your fam," he says, drawing a sympathetic circle on my lower back.

I nod, although it's only a partial truth. I'm crying because I know I've just lost my best friend.

I mope the rest of the day as we whip around on Caleb's rental Vespa. I'm thankful for the setup. He can't hear my silence or see my frown on the scooter. I decide to allow myself one day to wallow in my feelings. Just one day. Any longer and I fear I won't be able to snap out of it.

From tomorrow on, I vow to relish the privilege of being untethered, with no plan, no obligations. I vow to fully embrace Caleb, and fate, or something like that.

39

I've always had the ability to compartmentalize. To push my worries away and pretend they don't exist—temporarily.

I dive headfirst into the hectic blur that is Cinque Terre, a picturesque coastal region north of the Amalfi Coast. Caleb and I make a strict vow to do everything on foot, which means waking up with the sun to hike the rocky pathways between villages. We talk about everything from religion to our stances on social issues. He's interested in hearing more about my family, our history, and what it was like growing up without my mom. It's on our morning hike between Manarola and Riomaggiore that I learn why he's so scared of commitment and monogamy—his parents' marriage traumatized him.

"They're both downright miserable, and have been ever since I can remember," he tells me.

My stomach clenches at his lack of emotion, like it's a normal fact of life. "Do they fight a lot?"

He smirks. "I wish they would fight. At least then I'd know they care. But they're so indifferent in their misery, just going through the motions, barely talking, occasionally whisper-bickering. They try to spend as little time as possible together. My mom lives at the cottage and my dad spends all his time golfing with friends."

"Why don't they divorce?"

"Nah. They're both traditional to a fault. Once they signed on the dotted line, it was a commitment, come hell or high water. That's why commitment is such a big deal to me. I never want to trap myself in something like that," he explains. Then he stops in his tracks and his eyes meet mine. "I swear I'm not doing that with you. I'm really trying. I just wanted you to understand why I'm all messed up."

I can't fault him for that. If anything, it makes me sad for him. If I grew up in his family, I'd probably feel the same way about love.

Aching and delirious from hiking and hours of chatting, we wander into the bustling villages. We find a food cart and gorge on deep-fried seafood cones overflowing with crispy calamari so scorching, it burns our tongues. From there, we make our way to the beach and indulge in a pool's worth of lemon granitas. We cheers to everything—getting a good spot on the beach, the hiking boots I found on sale (Mei would be proud), that the rain held off for the day.

Most afternoons we grab fresh ingredients from the market and return to the cramped hostel kitchen. Usually, we make heaping bowls of pasta, fuel to do it all again the next day. Then we dance it all off at the pubs as the sun dips, stumbling back to the hostel to make out until we fall asleep.

We're so busy, I barely get the chance to look at my phone, except for the few days Ellen is in the hospital giving birth to my new cousin, Rosie. Perhaps I'm avoiding it too. The one time I did find myself on Instagram, I saw Sophie's post, a shot of her, Teller, and Doris. I don't know why it affected me so much. It was inevitable that they'd get back together; I knew that. But after what happened between us, what we confessed to each other, seeing the cold hard proof stung. It was enough to turn off my phone entirely. If it weren't for safety, I'd sell it like Caleb.

From then on, I make another vow not to think about home, the past, or anything that might remind me of Teller. Instead, I put all my energy into Caleb. I embrace every opportunity to get to know him—what makes him happy (complete and total freedom, new experiences), what drives him crazy (constraints, rules, schedules of any kind), and everything in between. I let him set the pace, decide what's too expensive or not worth our time. Not in a "you're the boss" kind of way, but because I genuinely agree with his opinions and trust his decisions. Probably because we're essentially the same person.

We're both morning people. We both have a laissez-faire approach to travel. We want to see everything, but we'd rather stumble upon it than make any concrete plan or checklist. In fact, we haven't even discussed our plans. Will I go home in a few weeks? Will Caleb? I'm scared to ask for fear of bursting our carefree bubble.

My favorite thing to do is watch Caleb in a group setting, making friends with all the people we meet in our hostel. We become another tight-knit gang, just like in Venice. Teller isn't a group kind of guy. I always have a better time with him one-on-one. But Caleb thrives in a group. He's a master at remembering little details people said the night before, and at telling stories with just the right amount of detail and emphasis to pull you in. It's magic to witness, people hanging on his every word, gravitating toward him whenever he enters a room.

Like everyone else, I want to absorb myself in his orbit, embrace all his Caleb-ness. So much so, that I adopt a Caleb-like mentality of saying yes to everything. Trying raw seafood? Sure. Zip-lining? Let's do it. Diving off a random cliff? Sure thing. We are soulmates, after all.

We're on a rocky peak looking over Riomaggiore where I clutch the new photo of me and my parents, my heart panging with longing on her behalf, wishing she could have seen this in person. For the first time, I have the overwhelming sense that she might be proud of me for following in her footsteps, for going all the places she never had the chance to visit.

And most importantly, for carrying on her legacy. For being brave enough to set out on this wild-goose chase to find The One.

I think about what Mei said, about how Mom would have loved Caleb. I play out a scenario in my mind, of her convincing apprehensive Dad to give him a chance.

"Come on, Eric. He's a real nice guy," Pretend Mom says, only to be met with a stubborn shrug. "Your daughter is in love with this boy. You owe it to her to give him a chance."

Your daughter is in love with this boy. The scenario is entirely a figment of my imagination, even her voice. But it feels so intensely real, like it's her speaking to me, even though I know that's not possible. Somehow, I just know she would have approved. She would have wanted this for me.

Your daughter is in love with this boy.

And then it hits me like a burst of sunshine: *I think I love Caleb.* The realization creeps over me, settling over me like the most obvious thing in the world. This is it. It has to be. The feeling I've been chasing this whole time.

Of course I was going to fall for Caleb, the person I'm destined to be with. The thing is, I wasn't sure I'd have this with anyone except Teller. But there's something about Caleb that's relieved me of all that guilt I carried. Somehow, he's made me feel brand new.

But I don't want to tell Caleb how I feel yet. After what happened in Florence, part of me is scared to come on too strong. It feels safer to marinate in it for a little while longer. But I do throw myself headfirst into our adventures, and hiking seems to be our thing.

"You wanna do more hiking?" Caleb asks, draped in a red apron. We're cramped over the tiny counter in the hostel kitchen, learning how to make pesto on YouTube in lieu of a legitimate class we couldn't afford.

"Yes! All the hikes!" I shout with boundless enthusiasm, or maybe it's the bottle of wine we've nearly finished.

He fixes his luminous smile on me and takes my hand across the counter. "All right, let's go to the Dolomites."

The next day, we take a series of trains north to the Italian Alps, bordering Switzerland and Austria. The north is like a different country entirely. It's filled with Alpine-like villages with sleek chalet-style buildings and steep roofs to shed snow in the harsh winters. The backdrop of the Alps is just stunning.

I continue with my *yes* mentality.

Staying in a rustic outdoor yurt? Let's do it.

Doing a nearly vertical sixteen-kilometer hike in the mountains? Why not?

Stay another month? Abso-freakin-lutely.

40

Caleb decides not to return for school in the fall and officially drops out with zero regrets, though it does result in a nasty argument with his parents over the phone. But even his parents can't dampen our spirits. We make the Dolomites our home base from which to launch our travels around Europe. We both manage to get jobs. Caleb serves at a little restaurant in town that specializes in Tyrolean dumplings, and I find work at a farm.

One day when Caleb and I are out for a bike ride, a huge hound wearing a bowtie starts chasing us. It follows us up a hill, where we meet Martine and Dax, hobby farmers who take in and rehabilitate abused or neglected animals with the aim of putting them up for adoption. I spend the entire day there, in heaven with the animals. And by the time I leave, they offer me a part-time job.

I help with whatever they need, refilling water bowls, washing blankets, playing with the dogs, and assisting with clerical work.

Martine tells me I have a special way with the dogs, and it occurs to me that maybe this is what I want to do. *Maybe this is my path.* Work with dogs. Maybe become a trainer, own a kennel, and open up a rescue eventually. It's not that I hadn't considered it, but it never seemed like a viable path. More like a pipe dream. Until now. Caleb thinks it's an excellent idea, although we don't discuss that it's not a career conducive to traveling for long periods of time. That seems like a problem for future us.

For the next six months, we use our days off to travel around Switzerland, Germany, and Austria. We challenge ourselves to the most extreme hikes. Winter arrives early in the north, so Caleb wants to hit as many trails as possible before the snow comes.

I develop killer calves and muscle tone in places I didn't even realize I could. It's only when we're hiking the Tofana di Mezzo with some hostel friends (our fourth hike in two weeks) that my body decides it's done. I take a misstep on a loose rock, and a sharp twinge of pain shoots through my knee. I shift awkwardly before I can utter a sound, and my legs give way.

"Shit. Are you okay?" Caleb asks, clutching my arm to help me up.

"No, I can't stand," I manage through a wince. The pain is intense, like a lightning bolt radiating up my leg.

Caleb carries me on his back to the hostel. But by the time we get ice on my knee, it's already massively swollen. The next day, I'm still unable to put weight on it, which sucks since we'd planned another big hike. To be honest, after all our adventuring, I could use a little quiet time. I suggest we watch a movie at the hostel. Hovering over my iPad in our crappy, creaky hostel bed with my leg propped up isn't exactly an ideal night in. But it feels like a luxury after being on the go for so long.

We select a heist film, one where they drive flashy cars all over Europe that Caleb seemed intrigued by. Only twenty minutes in and he's bored. He's tapping his knee, fidgeting. Usually, he's in a good mood. But he seems down and irritated.

I can't help but imagine watching this with Teller. We would have already dissected how unrealistic the car stunts are, or bickered about who would drive (me, obviously) and who would shoot (also me) in the event of a high-speed chase.

"Sorry," Caleb says when I ask what's wrong. "I haven't watched TV in ages. My attention span is shot."

"Usually people try to detox from screen time, not nature," I tease.

He doesn't smile. "It just really sucks your knee isn't going to be better for the hike tomorrow," he says, pouting like a child being told they can't go outside for recess.

"I know. I really wanted to go on that hike." It's a lie. Even if I could, I don't really want to go. I'm burned out and just need to sit still for a bit. But now doesn't feel like the time to admit that.

Caleb is quiet for a few minutes, trying to watch the movie. But he finally gets so antsy, he has to stand. "Wanna go play some Frisbee or something?"

"I can't run with my knee," I remind him.

"Shit. True. How about just a walk around?"

"There are stairs and cobblestone literally everywhere," I point out, frustrated by his inability to comprehend my handicap. I know he doesn't intend it, but he's making me feel bad for being injured. Like I'm putting him out, holding him back from life or something.

He lets out a sigh and turns a wistful gaze toward the window. "Can we at least go sit by the lake or something?"

It's December, so the weather is frigid. The last thing I feel like doing is bundling up in my snow gear.

It makes me think back to Cinque Terre. Sure, we did some relaxing on the beach, but it was always after an exhausting day. And it was never long before Caleb ran into the water, desperate to move. At first, Caleb's "always on the go" persona was exhilarating. But lately, it's exhausting.

"You could still go, you know," I finally say. "On the hike tomorrow."

He perks up and leans forward, shifting his weight on his elbow. "And leave you?"

"I'm fine," I assure stiffly. "Bianca wants to have a FaceTime date anyway. And I could probably use the rest." Now, I know it's unfair of me, but I kind of expect him to protest. Not because I want him to stay, but because it just doesn't feel like the right thing to do. Leave your injured kind-of-girlfriend behind to go hiking.

But he doesn't. "You really wouldn't mind?"

I shift my gaze to my lap. "Nope," I say, because I don't have a choice.

~

While he's hiking, I spend the afternoon in bed, resting and commiserating with Bianca about my injury. She's finally healed and back on her feet, but she knows how it feels to be sidelined. After we're done comparing wounds, she gushes about how I'm living the dream and how jealous she is that I'm not coming back to school.

"Where's Caleb?" she asks, sipping a cup of hot chocolate in front of her parents' fireplace. I count four fluffy-looking stockings hanging behind her.

"On a hike."

"Oh. And he just went without you?"

"Yeah. But I told him to. I don't need him here with me at all times," I say quickly, realizing what my real beef is. I'm not actually annoyed that he went on the hike. He's allowed to do things without me. What irks me is his shift in attitude since I injured myself. He's less patient, seemingly annoyed and inconvenienced by me.

"I'd have killed Chris if he left me here to rot all by my lonesome." Turns out, he's not her flavor of the week. They've been serious since I left for Italy. To his credit, he's been wonderful. He brought her food and helped with errands while her foot was healing over the summer. And they've been loyal to each other ever since.

"Do you think it's selfish of him?" I dare to ask. I gnaw on the inside of my mouth, ridden with guilt for speaking about Caleb like that.

She tilts her head. "Kind of. But we can't all be perfect, can we? I mean, he's great in every other way. At least he's straight up and honest with you about his feelings, unlike someone else."

She's referring to Teller, of course. When I told her about how Teller confessed he was secretly in love with me this whole time, she upgraded her one-way ticket on the Caleb train. Bianca likes a straight shooter.

"Speaking of, I meant to text you this earlier, but I thought you'd rather hear it over the phone. I saw Teller. He is way taller and hotter in person. I think he has one of those faces that look better in motion—"

She stops when my mouth falls open. I haven't allowed myself to think about him for more than a few fleeting moments in months. It's also a defense mechanism, because him no longer being in my life is too painful to think about. Admittedly, avoiding that reality has been easier than expected, probably because I'm across the world, distracted. I know being back at home will be another story. And I plan on putting that off as long as possible. "My Teller?"

"Is there another Teller?" Bianca asks.

"Technically, the doctor he's named after," I point out, not that Bianca knows that whole story. "But that's beside the point. Where did you see him?"

"At his mom's coffee shop. He's home for Christmas break, I guess. Super random, huh?"

Not entirely random. It makes sense he'd take a few shifts if he were home for Christmas. But last year, he spent Christmas with Sophie. Does that mean they bro . . . ? No. I'm overthinking it. They're probably doing Christmas at Teller's this year. Not that I should care.

Apparently, Bianca's a mind reader, because she says, "Actually, I haven't seen Sophie post anything about Teller in a while. Maybe they broke up." That's news to me. I unfollowed Sophie months ago to avoid the temptation to snoop. Bianca did not get that memo, apparently.

"Did he recognize you?" I ask. Technically, they've never met, aside from a FaceTime chat last fall.

"Yup. Well, only after I asked if he was *the* Teller. He asked how you were doing and I told you were thriving, never been better."

I cringe. Bianca can be a bit heavy-handed. "How did he seem?"

"Normal? I don't really have a baseline, though. He seemed happy to know you were doing well." She pauses for a beat to study my reaction. "Please don't be sad about it. I knew I shouldn't have brought it up."

"No, no!" I argue. "I'm not sad. I'm perfectly fine," I say, forcing a smile with all my might.

"Don't smile like that. You look like the Crypt Keeper."

I right my face. "Sorry."

"Anyway, like I said, I know you and Teller have history. It's hard to ignore that. But here's the deal—you two had the opportunity to get together for four years. You were both single when you first met. But nothing happened. That's not by accident. Timing never worked out, and there's a reason for that."

I blow the air out of my cheeks, mentally exhausted all over again. "I know."

"And! Let's not forget, he hid his feelings from you for years and dated some other chick at the same time. That's some serious coward behavior. You don't need that in your life."

"I don't need that in my life," I repeat, mostly to appease her.

There's a knot in my gut when we hang up. A knot that I'd uncoiled when he left. And now it's back. It lingers the next day, and the day after that, as Caleb goes out and adventures while I hang back and rest my knee. Every day he returns eager to tell me about the people he met, the sights he saw, the food he ate, how he can't wait until I'm healed and ready to go again.

Thrilled as I am for him, I have two realizations: 1) That I don't care if I ever go on another hike again. Don't get me wrong, the odd hike is fun, but I don't see this becoming my identity like Caleb's or some of the hard-core people we've met with ice picks and spikes on their boots. 2) That I feel a little resentful about being left alone for days on end. Because now that Teller is back on my mind, I'm desperate to busy myself again.

After about a week, Caleb can tell I'm testy, so he suggests we go out for dinner, a luxury since he's not big on spending money at restaurants. The place boasts a gorgeous panoramic view of the sky, a blend of vibrant oranges and deep purples over the mountaintops.

Just as Caleb helps me into my chair, someone shouts, "Caleb!" from behind. I assume it's someone from the hostel, but when I turn around, I realize it's Ernest and Posie, the older couple from Venice. Two tables away from us.

"Oh my goodness! And Lola," Posie says, jumping up to greet us. I don't bother to remind her my name is just Lo.

They invite us to sit with them near the huge stone fireplace, and we fill each other in on the last many months of travel. After Venice, they also went to Tuscany for a few weeks before heading home. But now they're back for a little winter excursion to try snowboarding (of all things) before Christmas.

"I knew there was something between you two," Posie says when Caleb excuses himself to the bathroom. "You really seem to like each other." She's not wrong. I can picture my life with him, or some version of it. We'd always be on some wild adventure, exploring parts of the world we've only ever dreamed of visiting. Working odd jobs to make sure we had enough money to cover our expenses. We wouldn't have much, but I would be happy.

"Thank you. And you and Ernest are adorable."

She smiles at Ernest, who's examining the cocktail menu over his wire-framed glasses. "We've had a lot of adventures together, I'll tell you."

"What are your favorites? You guys must have traveled a lot."

She nods. "We've been to some absolutely magnificent places. But my favorite memories with him are at home, in our squat little flat."

"At home?" It strikes me as odd, considering how much they've prioritized travel in their lives.

"It's easy to have fun with someone on all these elaborate adventures. But the real challenge is finding someone to enjoy the mundane.

Someone who makes you look forward to the blurry gray of everyday life. That takes someone special. That's what's real."

I think about Caleb and these past few months. All these grand escapades, moments straight from the movies—all he has to do is hold his hand out and we'll be off into the glittery night on some beautiful adventure. When I'm not injured, that is. And yet, my best memories are with Teller when everything was entirely ordinary, or at their worst. Laughing our asses off in the creaky, broken beds at the Shady Pines Inn. Starved and eating deli pizza on the side of the road in Florence. Watching movie marathons and cleaning toilets at The Cinema. It feels like ages ago.

"What do you want to do tomorrow?" Caleb asks as he piggybacks me back to the hostel. He's in a particularly good mood after dinner. Social Caleb loved seeing Posie and Ernest, who he's invited to our place later tonight to play cards.

I inhale, bracing myself. "I think I need to go home." It comes out before I've fully registered it.

I think I need space.

It's scary, the prospect of leaving. Of not knowing what that means for Caleb and me. But I can't ignore that, for the first time, going home feels more right than staying.

"Home? For the holidays?" Originally, I'd been intent on going home to spend the holidays with Dad. But given the flight costs and our jobs, we decided we wouldn't go home for Christmas. Instead, we'd head home for the summer. Dad had planned a Caribbean cruise with Scheana, anyway, so it made more sense to stay.

I nod toward my knee. "My knee makes it pretty difficult to do anything. And if I'm going to be stuck in a room, I'd rather not be paying for it. I may as well be home for Christmas, at least."

"Isn't your dad going on some cruise?"

"Yeah. But he's not leaving until Christmas Eve. And my aunts will be home. I'll spend it with them."

"Understandable. I wouldn't want to be in Italy with a knee injury either." He doesn't argue or try to convince me to stay. In fact, I think it's a relief. I can see it in his face.

Our gazes hold for a beat, and I think we're both finding some clarity. It's not just about my knee. My injury represents something a lot bigger. We both know it. I've always wanted epic love. But I'm starting to think I've had it all wrong. Maybe epic love isn't dashing off to faraway places and passionately kissing amid postcard-worthy views. How could it be, when you're living a life that isn't your own? I think about what Posie said, how it's easy to be in love on vacation. You're pretending, in a way.

But what about when you're at home, on any given Tuesday? When you're in matching sweats, rock-paper-scissoring who unloads the dishwasher for the fifth time that week. When you're both so exhausted that you barely have the energy to throw chicken nuggets in the oven, but you make each other smile anyway.

Maybe epic love is when there's no one else in the world you'd rather have a million mundane Tuesdays with.

41

Dad can tell when he picks me up at the airport that something is wrong.

"Why couldn't the psychic stop crying?" he asks when we finally gets me into his car. Maneuvering in the snow with crutches is not an easy feat.

"I don't know, why?"

"Because she wasn't a happy medium!" he says, snickering to himself.

I snort, despite myself. "How long have you had that one locked and loaded?"

"Oh, for weeks. Was waiting 'til you were home to use it," he informs me, eyes on the slush-filled road as we pull out of the airport parkade. "When you asked me to pick you up, I thought for sure you'd have Caleb with you."

"Nope," I say dully, fastening my seat belt.

"Is he coming to visit soon?" he prods.

"I'm not sure," I say.

Caleb will be backpacking around Indonesia for the foreseeable future. At least, that was the plan as of twelve hours ago when we said goodbye. The way we parted wasn't angry, or sad, or anything in between. It was more of a quiet understanding that we were taking a break. For now.

Walking away, even temporarily, from my soulmate is one of the hardest things I've ever had to do. Even as we said goodbye, I thought about what would happen if I just stuck it out longer; maybe things would have been like they were in the beginning. Taking space after this long feels suspiciously like giving up. Because despite what Mei says about finding our way back to each other, I can't help but wonder, *What if we don't? What if I'm abandoning my soulmate? What if I'm setting myself up for a lifetime of loneliness?*

Still, when we parted at the train station, we made vague plans for me to join back up with him once I'm healed. Though it felt more like a noncommittal "Let's get together soon." The kind of plan you make with an old friend that may never come to fruition.

I also can't ignore the surge of relief I felt when I left—and when the wheels touched ground at home. And if there's anything I've learned from Mei and Ellen over the years, it's to trust my gut.

Admittedly, I do miss Caleb already. After spending that many months with someone, it feels weird to suddenly be apart. It's kind of like when you get gel nails removed and your natural nails feel weird and stubby, entirely changed.

Dad swings me a look. "I'm guessing things didn't go as planned?"

I sigh. "They did and they didn't." I tell him all about having the absolute time of my life—until I got injured.

Being out of commission is temporary, but who knows what life has in store. There could be many times when I'm ill or unable to live life to the fullest. And whether Caleb would admit it or not, I think he's viewed my injury as a burden. I think he was relieved to fly solo again.

Dad nods, barely suppressing his delight. He's trying to hide it, but I know he's amped to have me back home after this long. He even offered me a third-wheel ticket with him and Scheana on the cruise, but I declined given my knee.

"You know, Aunt Ellen has a T-shirt that says 'IF YOU CAN'T HANDLE ME AT MY WORST, YOU CAN'T HANDLE ME AT MY BEST,'" he reminds me.

I sink down in my seat and try to erase that from my memory. "Please never say that again."

"But it's true."

I shrug. "I'm still scared I made the wrong decision to leave." I'm confused as ever—with myself, more than anything.

Aunt Mei assured me that if we were truly meant to be together, we would find our way back into each other's lives. But I'm not sure I want it to be true. There's something missing between us. A gap I'm not sure can be filled with time and perspective. If that's the case, is Caleb really my soulmate? And does ignoring my vision mean I'm doomed?

"Why would it be the wrong decision if coming home is what feels right?"

"Well, the vision is always right. It has to be," I say, watching the big fluffy snowflakes hit the windshield in globs.

A year ago, I'd have given anything to have my family's abilities. I'd have done anything to know I had a soulmate out there. And now, I feel constrained by it, constrained by the obligation of being with someone I don't think I love, and faced with eternal loneliness and bad luck if I choose not to be. Things were easier when I could be like everyone else and make my own choices. When I didn't feel forced onto a certain path.

Dad considers this. "Why does it have to be an absolute?"

My eyes well with tears. "Because if it's wrong, it means I'm cursed. That I'm going to be alone and miserable forever."

"I have a hard time believing that."

"And it would mean I'm not like Mom. Or any other woman in the family." My whole life, I've been so used to things being out of my control—Mom's death, not inheriting the abilities, not knowing what I want to do with my life. Having this vision meant something more than finding The One. For the first time, something was guaranteed, the course of my life set. I wouldn't have to worry or wonder. Fate was finally going to take over and I could sit back and enjoy the ride. Or so I thought.

Dad's face falls. "That's not true."

"It is, though. For years, I thought I didn't inherit any of her talent, and it killed me. And then I had the vision and it made me feel like I had a tangible connection to her. And then traveling, following her route, I've never felt closer to her." In a sense, I felt like I was traveling for her, going all the places she wanted to but never got the chance to.

"You have no idea how similar you are, even without the vision."

"Really?"

He shuts his eyes and lets out a long sigh before pulling over to the side of the road. "Did you know your mom and I met at a work meeting?" he asks, putting the car in Park.

"Yeah, you told me that." I take a deep inhale over the squeak and drag of the windshield wipers, frankly shocked he's brought her up.

"Well, I never I told you that it wasn't a meet-cute. It was more . . . a meet-ugly," he says. I'm afraid to move an inch for fear he'll stop talking. "I'll admit, I wasn't nice to her. She disagreed with me on the interpretation of evidence on a high-profile case. I was so embarrassed because she pointed it out in front of our boss. I didn't take it well. I'd already been on the case for over a year, and she was brand new. So I thought, what could she possibly know that I don't?"

"Sounds like male fragility to me," I point out with a wry smile.

"You're probably right. I realized later that she had a point. I needed a fresh perspective like hers. By the time I apologized, she'd already made up her mind about me. It took weeks of groveling for her to forgive me.

"We slowly started talking, and then we hung out at a work party— bowling, of all things. That's when I really fell for her. She was such a romantic, like you. So interested in people, in new places, in doing things she'd never done before, like playing bocce or learning new games—or traveling. One day, I asked her on a date and she refused, which shocked me because we'd been getting along so well and I thought she liked me too. I didn't know if I'd misread things between us, so I asked her why. She said she wished she could, but it wouldn't work for reasons she couldn't explain. For weeks, that went on. Eventually, I convinced her to go out with me. She tried to scare me off by telling me she was a psychic. I think she assumed I'd run for the hills, having such a scientific outlook on the world."

"So the psychic thing didn't scare you off?"

He shakes his head. "I thought it was strange at first, I'll give you that. But it actually made me love her more. I liked that she didn't have this narrow view of the world like a lot of our colleagues. Things weren't completely black and white, with logical, scientific explanations. In fact, it's dangerous to think you know everything, that you can logic out every situation. There are things in this world that don't always have an explanation. The Zhao women have proven that over and over. I've witnessed it firsthand. Your mom actually predicted my dad's heart attack a day before it happened.

"We fell in love—hard. But one day, I found her in tears after work. She told me the truth, about her family's abilities. About how she was destined for one specific soulmate. And that it wasn't me."

My world tilts. "Wait, what?" I ask, bracing myself against the window.

Dad nods his head, confirming that I heard correctly.

His meaning settles, heavy in my core. "Her soulmate wasn't *you*?" I ask, barely above a whisper.

His mouth presses closed before opening again. "No."

I draw my head back. "What do you mean? But what about her vision? The glasses? The hearts?"

"She'd had a vision. And it had nothing to do with me. At all," he clarifies.

"I'm so confused. The vision Mei and Ellen told me about. It wasn't true?"

He pinches the bridge of his nose and turns to me. "Here's the thing. Your mother's family never would have approved of us if they knew she was going against her vision. So we made it up. And she swore me to secrecy."

"Even Mei and Ellen don't know? To this day?"

"No."

What the hell? I crack open the passenger door, in desperate need of fresh air.

I've lived my entire life thinking my parents were soulmates—that I was some product of fate—only to find out it was all a lie.

"So that's why you were so cagey with me," I conclude. Snippets of conversation come flooding back, of asking questions about Mom's vision, Dad evading and changing the subject. Dad was always a bit blasé about the soulmate idea in general, but I just thought it was because there was part of him that didn't believe in it.

"Yes," he admits, tone heavy. "She made me promise not to tell anyone until you were older. I wanted to tell you for so long, but I never knew if it was the right time. And then you were so excited when you had your vision, I didn't have the heart to tell you."

My eyes widen. "So that means . . . you aren't technically her soulmate."

"Not according to the vision—"

"Did she ever meet the person in the vision?"

"No. Not that I know of. She said she didn't have to, that I was who she was meant to be with."

I rake my hands through my hair. "I don't know what to say . . . You're not Mom's soulmate," I keep repeating.

How must Mom have felt? Knowing she was defying her family's beliefs and lying to them for years. I wonder if she ever felt alone like I do right now, or worse, regretted her decision.

"I beg to differ. I know you and your aunts are really hung up on fate. But your mom and I fell in love not because of fate, but because we simply liked each other. Loved each other enough to put in the hard work. That's romance to me."

I can't wrap my head around it. Mom went against the grain. She fell in love with someone who wasn't her soulmate.

Maybe we do have something in common after all.

42

Being back home after so many months abroad feels like stepping into an alternate dimension. I can still smell the garlicky aroma wafting from trattorias, hear the echoes of bustling markets, smell the fresh air of the Alps.

Home is different too. The living room now has decorative throw pillows. Cute little tea towels and potted plants have replaced Dad's Marvel figures in the kitchen. All Scheana's doing.

I finally meet her the day after I get back. She looks nothing like a scientist, not that scientists need to have a particular look. If I had to guess her occupation based on appearance alone, I'd assume she's a children's librarian or schoolteacher, with her bright-Grinch-green dress and jingly, light-up mini-Christmas-light necklace.

She's also extroverted, if her massive hug tells anything. "I can't believe I'm finally meeting you in the flesh. Though I feel like I already know you. Your dad doesn't shut up about you," she squeals into my ear.

"Honestly, same. Dad says you write romance novels," I say.

She lights up immediately and we fall into a half-hour talk about her top ten romance book starter recommendations, her author friend's book that's been adapted on Amazon Prime, and how newer rom-coms just don't hit the same way. I could probably talk to her for hours about Hugh Grant.

I can't help but smile as Dad sneaks up behind her, placing his hand around her waist. It's strange to see him this way, smitten and starry-eyed, after all these years of him just being, well, my dad. But she's exactly the kind of person he needs. Someone to pull him out of his shell, force him out of the house. She also isn't afraid to poke fun at his corny humor without being too harsh. Most of all, I'm grateful Dad has someone to watch true crime with and who makes him so happy.

Dad and Scheana leave on Christmas Eve, so I head to Ellen's. She lives in the brownstone that used to belong to my grandparents—the house my mom grew up in. Ellen goes all out with the festivities to make up for lost time. Christmas in the Zhao family is a relatively new tradition. My grandparents didn't celebrate it until the girls were old enough to realize that other kids got visits from Santa. Ellen has festive headbands for all, reindeer antlers and little snowmen on springs. The house is an explosion of multicolored lights coiled around every banister and taped to each window. She even has two trees, both draped in sheets of silver tinsel.

Following Christmas Eve tradition, Hank has the karaoke machine out and everyone is fighting for a turn on the mic. This year is a little more chaotic than usual, with Ellen juggling five-month-old baby Rosie and shuffling after Maisey. Apparently, her newest thing is running full-steam around the house with her eyes shut. And this year, Ellen invited our extended family.

There's my sassy great-aunt, who's eighty-seven and doing shots of eggnog and Baileys with Hank in the kitchen. Then there are my two second cousins and their families, both of whom are in their forties and happily married to their soulmates, at least I think they are. The moment they start peppering me with questions about my vision and Caleb, it becomes clear they've come specifically to celebrate me finding The One. I suppose this is my fault for not telling Ellen and Mei that things didn't work out.

I provide quite a few half-hearted, noncommittal responses over the Christmas music blasting from the fireplace TV channel until it all gets to be too much. *It's time to tell them.*

I usher Mei and Ellen into Maisey's pink bedroom for some privacy. It's a strange place to have a serious family discussion; Mei and I are squished together on Maisey's polka-dot trundle bed among a sea of stuffed animals, while Ellen paces around the room, rocking a sleeping Rosie, expertly evading all the toys on the fluffy rug. We've insisted she sit down in the nursing chair by the window, but she's "feeling too Christmasy" to relax.

"What's up? You're not engaged already, are you?" Mei asks.

"I'm not engaged," I assure her, though what I'm about to say is equally outlandish. "It doesn't have anything to do with me. Well, technically it does. But—"

Ellen raises a brow at Mei. "Does this have to do with your vision?"

Mei gives her a warning look and shakes her head, like I wasn't supposed to know.

"Vision? What vision?" I ask.

Mei waves my words away like pesky flies. "Oh, it's really nothing, sweetheart."

I hold firm. "You're keeping something from me."

Mei sighs. "Fine. When you were in Italy, I had a vision about you. It's hard to explain, but you were in a forest. A dense forest that was closing in. You were panicking, trying to decide where to go."

I swallow. "That sounds intense."

"It was. There were two options. One lit pathway that felt familiar, safe. And the other path was dark, twisty, but felt exciting."

"Which path did I choose?"

Mei's eyes dart to the floor. "Um . . . the forest swallowed you before you could decide. That's the real reason I came to Italy. I knew you needed support. I called Ellen immediately and booked my ticket. Then, of course, your dad found out I was going and had to tag along."

"Wow" is all I can say. I think about what the rest of the trip would have been like if Dad and Mei hadn't shown up. While I might have handled everything alone, I wouldn't have done it well. Having them there meant everything to me.

"Anyway, what were you going to tell us?" Mei asks, snapping me back to the issue at hand.

I pause for dramatic effect before coming out with it. "Dad wasn't Mom's soulmate."

I'm met with two sets of blank stares.

"Dad wasn't Mom's soulmate," I repeat, as though the world just glitched and they didn't catch what I said.

Mei is the first to utter a word, which is a cross between "What the eff?" and "Are you kidding?" She crunches her face, hands steepled in front of her.

Ellen just stands there, blinking and still rocking Rosie. There's a stretch of silence so long that Mei actually clears her throat, stumbling on words to try to fill the space until Ellen cuts her off. "What do you mean they weren't soulmates? That's impossible. Kim had a vision of your dad."

I explain everything Dad told me, about how they met, fell in love, and lied about the vision.

Ellen shakes her head. "I just can't believe Kim would lie to us like that. And for that many years."

"Dad said she didn't want to, but she didn't think she had a choice," I tell them.

"We would have supported whatever she wanted," Ellen says, clearly offended.

Mei shoots her a look. "Would we have supported her? Mom certainly wouldn't have approved."

Ellen considers that. "True. Mom would have freaked out. She was always warning us about what would happen if we didn't abide by our destiny when we were kids, remember?"

"You end up like Cousin Lin if you not careful," Mei says in my grandmother's accent.

"Honestly, I don't blame her for lying," Ellen decides.

They go back and forth rehashing everything, from Mom's vision, to when she first told them about Dad, to their first interaction with

Dad at a family mahjong night. I get the sense they're treating it delicately, because what's done is done. If Mom hadn't deviated, I wouldn't be here, which Ellen points out before rushing into the kitchen to deal with an icing-bag explosion.

I drape myself over the tiny mattress, nearly smoking my head on the wood slated footboard. "I feel like an illegitimate child or something."

Mei chuckles. "Well, you are the first non-soulmate child in the family."

I blink, taking that in. *Non-soulmate child.* Suddenly, it occurs to me. "Do you think that's why I'm cursed and talentless? Maybe this is Mom's punishment for being with Dad. Me."

She gives me a swift swat on the knee. "First, you are not cursed. There's no such thing."

"Fine. Doomed to eternal loneliness. Whatever."

"No one is doomed. In my opinion, it's all been blown out of proportion, all this whole folklore."

"Really?"

"That's why I never told you about it. Why I didn't want Ellen freaking you out for no reason. I mean, let's think statistically here. This has only happened twice. First Great-Aunt Shu was a recluse and lived across the country. No one was close enough to her to know what was really going on in her life. Your grandmother used to tell her story, but it would change every time. Her cause of death, her occupation. She'd be a farmer one time, and next a fisherman."

"But what about Cousin Lin?"

Mei crosses her legs and leans forward. "Let me tell you about Cousin Lin. Everyone likes to talk about how miserable she was, but I disagree. Did she have a hard couple of years? Of course. Who wouldn't be a little depressed after getting hit by a bus and losing their house and money? But she wasn't miserable. In fact, she made the best of things. She enjoyed gardening and was even part of a bird-watching group. One time, your mom and I asked her if she wanted to get married. And you know what she said?"

"What?"

"She said she wanted to be alone. That she chose her life. That she didn't need one person to make her happy. She said her family and friends fulfilled her. And I don't think she was just trying to save face. I truly think that's what made her happiest. She knew no one else understood, but she didn't care. She wanted to live life on her own terms."

"Wow. So Lin was actually a super progressive badass?"

She nods. "A total badass. But the point is, there is no consequence. Or curse. Or whatever. You're free to live your life exactly as you see fit."

I lower my gaze. "That's exactly it, though. Even if I'm not alone, I'm a massive disappointment."

"How could you say something like that? You've had two visions."

"Okay, but you guys have visions daily. I've had *two*. In my whole life. And up until a few months ago, I was the only woman in our entire family not to have the gift. I know how frustrated you and Ellen were that summer you first tried to mentor me. And I already know my dad wishes I stuck with forensics. I've disappointed literally everyone."

Mei shakes her head. "I still remember the day you said your first word. Your mom put you on the phone and you said something that sounded like 'Bubhuh,' which your mom was convinced was 'Mama.'" She smiles toward the frosted window, face lit with nostalgia. "Between you and me, it sounded nothing like 'Mama,' but I let her have it."

I can't help but tear up, thinking of the photo of my infant self in my mom's arms.

"When you were born, your grandfather made a joke about you being a scientist like your parents. And you know what your mom said?"

"What?"

"She didn't care if you were dumb as rocks, as long as you were a good, kind person. Not that you're a dummy, or anything of the sort." Our teary eyes catch and she wraps her arm around my shoulder. "But you are the kindest, most good-hearted young woman I know. You have to stop being so hard on yourself. We love you for who you are, not what you do."

I blow the air from my cheeks, running my finger over a loose thread on the bedspread. "It's just, everyone used to talk about how talented Mom was. It felt like an unspoken expectation that I'd follow in her footsteps. And finally, when I had my vision, it felt like I might be. But after all those years of wishing to have these abilities and knowing who my soulmate was, it didn't feel like I dreamed it would. I felt . . . I feel . . . suffocated by it."

"I understand how you feel. There was a period when I had a lot of resentment toward the family gift."

"You did?" Mei has always struck me as so proud of our legacy.

"Well, you know I don't like being told what to do," she says with a wink. "When I was growing up, I hated the idea that there was someone predestined for me. Your mom and Ellen were so excited about the prospect, dressing up as brides and pretending to get married in the backyard. Meanwhile, I hated feeling like I didn't have a choice in the matter. Maybe it had to do with the fact that I was bi and didn't know it yet. I didn't understand why the idea of finding a husband—a soulmate—getting married, and having children felt so lackluster. I thought I had two choices: be completely alone and probably disowned by your grandmother, or destined for a life of unhappiness with some boring salesman in a bad suit named Dave or Larry."

"Larry! I can't even imagine that." We both cackle at the thought.

"Larry with a bad comb-over." Mei's whole body shudders. "That's why I was so frustrated. I dated a bunch but could never bring myself to get serious. There was always this cloud over my head telling me it wasn't going to work out in the long run. That Larry was out there waiting for me. But then I realized something."

"What's that?"

"Remember I told you about when our family first came over and started integrating Western psychic practices, right? All the drama?"

I nod, sitting up, propping my back against a pillow. "Great-Aunt was super against it. She didn't want Western practices to dilute tradition."

"Generally, yes. But her biggest issue was that there are some big differences in philosophy, one being the understanding of fate."

"Really? How so?"

"Western fortune-telling looks at fate kind of like a self-driving car. It has one destination, and regardless of the choices you make in life, you'll always wind up charting the same course. But in traditional Chinese fortune-telling, fate and fortunes aren't set in stone. For example, I could give you a reading right now, and what I tell you in this moment could be correct."

I nod, trying to follow her logic closely.

"But free will is equally important in Chinese fortune-telling," she explains. "It's all about maximizing strength and timing to achieve the best possible outcomes, all of which can change depending on the decisions you make."

My mind reels, attempting to revise everything I thought I knew. "So, what you're saying is, fate isn't necessarily predetermined?"

"If you were to survey our family, they'd all tell you something different. Everyone has a slightly different interpretation of how it works."

"What's your interpretation?" I ask, desperate for some guidance.

"I don't believe our lives have to be predetermined. They can be, but it's up to you at the end of the day. Ultimately, for me, fate is about trusting yourself, just like you did with college. With coming home. You knew that direction was wrong for you, so you changed course. And now, your life has a new path, a new fate, if you will."

It was terrifying to make that choice. To trust myself enough to know that it was more than just being lazy, or not adjusting to the level of difficulty. It wasn't even apathy or disinterest. It was this overwhelming sense that college and the forensics path wasn't the direction I was supposed to take with my life. And it took courage to finally do something about it. Even still, that pales in comparison to the decision

Mom made. "I can't even imagine how hard it must have been for Mom to choose Dad, to go against her family tradition. What if that was her consequence?"

"Absolutely not. The only thing it tells you is how much your mom loved your dad. And anything that's a product of that love should never be disappointing in the slightest." She squeezes my hand and my eyes sprout with tears, warmth brimming through my chest. I love my aunts.

Until now, I thought having the vision was my one tie to Mom. But now I know that's not true. I'm connected to her through my whole family. It's the way Mei looks at me with the same surprised look Mom has in all her photos. The way Ellen hums everywhere she goes. Apparently, Mom did just the same. It's in their care for me, picking up in Mom's footsteps.

"Thank you," I say. "For being here for me my whole life. For literally hopping on a plane and flying halfway across the world to be there for me when I needed it. I love Dad and all, but I couldn't have gotten through without you and Ellen. I haven't told you that enough."

"Of course, sweetheart." Mei plants a kiss on my temple, then gives me a playful shake, bursting our sentimental bubble.

"You have no idea how happy I am to be home. Even if Dad ditched me for a cruise," I tease, even though it couldn't be further from the truth. He felt terrible about leaving me on Christmas Eve and was about to cancel until I convinced him not to. Sure, I wish I were spending it with Dad, but being with Ellen and Mei is the next best thing.

"Do you think you'll go back?" Mei asks.

I think about that. "I don't know. Maybe? That's what I'm confused about. I was happy for a while with Caleb."

"Let's take fate out of the equation for a minute. If it weren't a factor, would you still choose Caleb?"

"No," I say, almost instantly. I'm surprised at how easily I answered based on pure instinct. "I'm not sure I ever truly loved him to begin with. Infatuation, sure. But I think what I loved most was the idea of him." I loved the adventuring, the discovery. But when all that was stripped away, when we were just in a room alone, there was this distance between us I couldn't put my finger on. It's like lactose-free cheese—it should work in theory, but there's something about it that isn't right.

Mei dips her chin. "There you have it. Fate shouldn't be a strait-jacket, Lo. You should never feel forced to love someone. It should be easy, like second nature. Like breathing, so natural, you don't even realize you're doing it."

I massage the moon tattoo on my finger. "Kind of like how I feel about—"

"Teller," Mei finishes knowingly.

"But what about the vision I had about him? If our friendship is doomed to end, what's the point in trying for a relationship?"

"Maybe it meant the end of your friendship and birth of a romance?" she suggests.

I shake my head. "No. It was too ominous for that. It felt like the end of us completely."

She contemplates. "Our visions aren't always representative of the future. Sometimes, they're there to send a message. Maybe, in this case, it was trying to make you see how terrible life would be without him."

And she's right. It would be more than terrible. Maybe Teller isn't my "fated soulmate." But fate or free will, I can't ignore how I feel about him. I may lack focus to stick with most things for very long, but Teller has been a steady constant since we met. He came into my life when I needed him most. He made me feel like I was someone. He managed to make every mundane and ordinary moment feel like magic.

Being with Caleb felt like being whisked away on life's greatest adventure, but Teller feels like coming home.

43

Ever since I was a little girl, I imagined I'd be the subject of a grand cinematic gesture. You know, that final scene in the movies where one person runs across crowded New York traffic to confess their love in a dramatic fashion. They are sweaty, out of breath, and disheveled, but it doesn't matter in the least. The other person finds it both bewildering and endearing because it's clear evidence of how much they care.

I always dreamed of standing on a Romeo-and-Juliet-style balcony while my soulmate declared their undying love from below. Maybe he'd buy a thousand-dollar plane ticket just so he can get past security, then dash to the gate as everyone's boarding and convince me to stay, moments before I'm supposed to depart the country forever.

I definitely didn't picture myself on crutches, with my aunt as chauffeur, blasting "Hark! The Herald Angels Sing" on Christmas Eve. But here we are.

"So you're still not sure if he's actually single?" Mei shouts over the music.

"He doesn't post on social media. Bianca told me Sophie's socials haven't been that active either," I explain.

She gasps. "Going dark on social is one of the telltale signs of a breakup!"

"Lots of people go dark around exam time," I point out.

Mei makes a *tff* sound. "Your generation has such an obsession with mystery and intrigue. I miss the days when people set their Facebook relationship status to *Single*. Or *It's Complicated*. That was always gold. That's how you knew it was messy," she adds.

I crack a smile. "For real?"

"After the relationship status, they'd drop passive-aggressive life quotes about self-love and narcissistic behavior. Then there'd be an onslaught of look-at-me-I'm-so-happy-living-my-life photos. On the beach. At bars. Usually, a new haircut thrown in there too."

I chuckle at the thought of Teller changing his relationship status to *It's Complicated* and posting one of those angled selfies.

"You sure he's home?" Mei asks as we pull into the driveway behind his mom's Subaru, snow crunching beneath the tires.

"I have no idea," I say, peering in the bay window. Someone is home, based on the lights inside. "He was here as of three days ago, when Bianca saw him at the coffee shop. But if he's still with Sophie, it's totally possible he could be with her family."

Mei helps me maneuver to the door with my crutches. Normally, I'd insist on going alone, but the ice is hazardous. Before she makes it back to her car, the door swings open. It's Kurt, Teller's oldest brother. He's all bundled in his winter gear, ready to head out.

"Oh, hey, Lo, Merry Christmas," he says casually, brushing past me.

"Merry Christmas," I call after him. "Wait, um, is Teller here?"

"No clue!" he says with a shrug, heading down the driveway. I take that as a positive sign. If Teller weren't in town at all, surely Kurt would know?

I poke my head inside. The house isn't as messy as it once was, probably because the boys have all moved out. But it's still chaos in the entryway, with boots everywhere, coats, mittens, and hats strewn all over the bench. Nick comes barreling past, unfazed by my presence.

Nick also has no idea if Teller is home or not. How does no one know if their brother is home on Christmas Eve? After I call a shrill "Hello" from the entryway, Doris comes zigzagging down the hall, little stub of a tail wagging a mile a minute. I can't bend down to pick her up, so I lean over and let her lick my fingers until Mrs. Owens hears me.

"Lo! I haven't seen you in ages!" She looks the same as last summer, although her sandy hair is a little grayer at the roots. She's small as ever, a little too thin from running herself ragged at the coffee shop. Her face (and voice) is obscured by a stack of Christmas gifts, topped with crocheted stockings she's balancing in her arms. She keeps talking (yelling) to me from the kitchen, even though I'm out of sight. "I hear you're quite the adventurer these days."

I stand there petting Doris, and we have a whole conversation through the wall about Italy and my knee before she finally says, "By the way, Teller is at Roasters. You might be able to catch him before they close up early for the holiday."

I thank her and hightail it (more like slow limp) to Mei's car. "He's at Roasters."

~

The scent hits hard. Fresh-ground coffee beans with sweet hints of espresso and warm pastries.

A gangly-looking teen girl in a Roasters apron eyes Mei and me up from behind the counter, where she's fighting with the blender. I assumed Mei would leave once she saw me safely inside, but instead she peruses the chalk menu and display of muffins and various Christmas cookies. "Oh, they have those jam cookies Layla likes. I'll take five."

"Um, I'm looking for Teller," I say to the girl, scanning around for him.

She takes far too long before jerking a lazy acrylic finger over her shoulder. "He's cleaning the bathroom. A customer ran in there not long ago and said they used the toilet *aggressively*. Whatever that means."

I'm about to find out.

I hobble down the hall past the BATHROOMS sign, my crutches clicking as I go. Roasters has unisex single bathrooms. I knock on the first two with my crutch—empty. Then Teller emerges from the third, back to me in his smock, mopping the floor, headphones on.

I tap my crutch on the floor next to him, and he looks over his shoulder, eyes wide. "Lo?"

"Hi," I say, taking him in. All the hard angles of his face, every dip, shadow, and line. Even the way his hair falls, all mussed, refusing to lie flat. Every detail I've cataloged in my mind and wasn't sure I'd ever see again. He's all there. And it's perfect. He's perfect. So perfect, I don't know what to do with myself other than gawk.

He leans his weight into the mop and removes his headphones. He doesn't say anything, although I think that has more to do with shock than anything. He hasn't blinked once.

"Coldplay?" I ask, hearing the familiar voice of Chris Martin filtering through his speakers.

"It's 'Christmas Lights'" he says, voice hoarse as he eyes my crutches. "What happened?"

"I twisted my leg on a hike. Hurt my knee. I'm totally fine, though," I assure him.

"Why are you home?"

"Because things weren't right. And it took me a while to realize that. To realize a lot of things. But deep down, I think I always knew—" I pause, letting my heart lead the way. "I always knew I made a mistake."

His jaw stiffens and his eyes narrow suspiciously. "I . . . Are you saying this because things didn't work out with Caleb?" Harsh, but fair.

"No. I know that's how it probably sounds. But I swear, you are not second choice. You never were." I lower my head, tightening my hold on my crutches, limbs suddenly feeling heavy. "Caleb and I weren't right for each other, and I'm sorry I didn't realize it sooner. I mean, I did in my gut, but I didn't let myself recognize it. I was scared because I thought I was beholden to this vision. That I couldn't deviate from it, or I'd be giving up this chance at true love, giving up a chance to finally prove to my family that I'm not a huge failure. I wanted to be like my mom, my family, so badly. And as it turns out, I'm more like my mom than I thought."

"What do you mean?"

I repeat the whole story, exactly as Dad explained it to me. Teller is unreadable. He seems to be contemplating.

"But what about the vision? Fate? Eternal loneliness?"

"The curse thing isn't real," I explain. "And yes, fate is important. But we still have free will. We still have the ability to alter the course of our destiny. And I choose you, regardless of the vision. I should have chosen you years ago, Teller. I love you. The truth is, I think I always have? Even if I didn't see it from the beginning. I convinced myself that we were too different. But I realized all the things that make us so different are exactly what I love most about you. I love that you keep me on schedule. And you know I need someone to make sure I don't walk around barefoot or let random animals lick my face.

"After Tuscany, I was in denial about my feelings for you. When I finally realized it in Amalfi, it scared me, so I avoided my emotions completely. Avoided thinking of you for months. And it worked temporarily, but in the end all it did was show me that I never want to be without you. I can't be."

He watches me for a few seconds, stunned. Too stunned to speak, move. He doesn't even seem to breathe.

I wait for his reaction, continuing on when he doesn't respond.

"I know I'm probably too late. I know you're probably back with Sophie and—"

"I'm not back with Sophie," he says firmly.

"You're not?" I ask, tone neutral, not allowing myself to celebrate until I know just how he feels about her. Because after everything, all I want is for Teller to be happy, even if that comes at my own expense.

He shakes his head, like it was a given. "Of course not. We talked and talked, but it was never going to work with us, especially after what happened between you and me. I couldn't be with anyone until I got over you."

"And are you? Over me?"

He smirks. "I've been listening to Coldplay on a loop for months, so what do you think?"

I can't help but laugh. And when we meet eyes, neither can he.

"How could I ever be over you?" He leans the mop against the wall. "You know I'm not the kind of person who believes in superstition and fate and all that. But the first time you walked into The Cinema, I thought, 'Holy shit, this girl can't be real. She's way too happy, way too friendly.' I thought that light would fade. But it didn't. Even with the rudest customers, you were still kind, giving everyone the benefit of the doubt. And knowing it was one of the hardest times of your life just proves how genuine you are. Your sunshine is the closest thing to magic I've ever experienced. You've completely ruined me for anyone else."

It's everything I've ever wanted to hear and then some. I may be on crutches, but this is a true cinema moment. Our version—mine and Teller's. My knees weaken and I want to cry happy tears, but instead, all I say is, "Except for Doris."

He tilts his head in admission. "True. Doris is the number one girl in my life. As long as you can handle that."

"Can you handle being number three after Brandon and Brian?"

"I am fully okay with that," he says softly, taking a step toward me.

"Seriously, though, I want to give this a shot. A real shot. I don't know how it will work living four hours away, but I figure I'll get a car and drive up—"

He takes another step forward and gently presses his index finger over my lips. "Let's figure out the logistics later," he says, which almost sounds like a foreign language coming from him. Knowing Teller isn't worried fills me with comfort. For once, he's not stressing and planning. He's with me, fully absorbed in the moment.

He sweeps a hand across my back, stabilizing me enough to ditch the crutches. He balances them against the wall and pulls me to his chest, pressing me to him. He threads his fingers through my hair, pushing a section of my unruly bangs away from my eyes, then tilts my chin up.

Due to my knee, I can't pop onto my tiptoes to angle toward him, so he has to make up the distance by bending down at an awkward angle. It's soft, quiet, this kiss. Understated, just like him. One kiss becomes another, then two, then three. I kiss him like we aren't standing in public—in his mom's coffee shop, no less. Like we aren't in plain sight of Mei and a handful of customers a few feet away. Like there's not a dirty mop at the base of our feet. I kiss him until I completely forget where I am.

The gurgle and flush of a toilet pulls us back to reality. I peer up at Teller, who's cringing. "This is peak romance. A romantic gesture outside a bathroom."

"It's like a throwback to plunging at The Cinema," I say with a smile.

He presses his forehead to mine. "Oh god. Don't remind me."

"I can't say I pictured this. But somehow, it's . . . right."

"The crutches. Did you hobble all the way here?" he asks, voice gravelly in my ear as he breathes me in.

"Mei helped me," I say, fanning myself as the barbs of heat prick me. It occurs to me I've been in my coat and mitts this entire time.

Teller notices and unzips my coat. And then it hits me. The sudden prick of heat in my vision. That nutty, earthy espresso aroma. The sensation of hot, liquid warmth unfurling through me. All at once, my world shifts.

"Teller," I say, gripping his forearm for support. The space between us feels charged, thick.

He takes my mitts and coat, folding them over his arm. "Mm-hmm? You okay?"

I was so sure it all pointed to Caleb. Venice. But this moment feels uncanny. I'm overcome with this tingly sensation settling along the base of my spine, just like in my first vision.

"You good, Lo?"

"Better than ever," I say, angling my chin up so he can claim me with another kiss.

I register the warmth of his body crushing against mine. The wool of his sweater brushing against my neck. The softness of his lips. The thud of two hearts beating against each other, glowing inside and out. I welcome it all, letting each detail etch itself into my memory.

My grandmother always told me I'd just *know* when I met The One. I don't know for certain whether the vision was about Teller or not. But maybe it doesn't matter. Whether by cosmic design or free will, or maybe a mix of both, being with him is exactly where I'm supposed to be.

I just *know*.

ACKNOWLEDGMENTS

With every book I write, I always declare it "the hardest one I've written yet." However, this time, I really mean it. I came up with the plot of this book in July 2022, but I wasn't able to start writing it until a few months after welcoming my first baby in spring of 2023. Thanks to mom-brain and sleep deprivation, there were many times I didn't know if I could string a sentence together anymore. That's why my biggest heartfelt thank-you goes to J, who's unwavering support and patience allowed me to put pen to paper. Thank you also to my family and friends (author and real-life friends) for all your encouragement.

Endless appreciation to my editor, Carmen Johnson, for your excitement for this concept from the outset. Your insight and suggestions have shaped the book into what it is today. I'd also like to extend my deepest gratitude to Laura Chasen for your keen attention to detail, understanding of the characters, and invaluable suggestions that have truly elevated the heart of the book. A huge thank-you to Tara Whitaker, Rachel Norfleet, Zhui Ning Chang, Steve Schul, and my entire Amazon Publishing team. You all have been tremendously kind throughout this whole process and have made me feel so valued as an Amazon author. I am so grateful for all your hard work!

I also want to extend a massive thank-you to my agent, Kim Lionetti, and the BookEnds Literary team for your support over the last four years. I can't believe we're already on book five (with so many more to come).

To my readers, you are rock stars for coming on this journey with me. I hope Lo's journey resonates, inspires, and brings you all a glimmer of joy and hope when you need it most.

And lastly, to C, who has taught me the true meaning of love, patience, and resilience. This book is dedicated to you. May you always know how deeply you are loved and cherished. When you're old enough to read this book, I hope it serves as a reminder of all the infinite possibilities that await you.

ABOUT THE AUTHOR

Amy Lea is the international bestselling author of romantic comedies for adults and teens, including *Woke Up Like This*, a Mindy Kaling's Book Studio selection; *The Catch*; *Exes & O's*; and *Set on You*. They have been optioned for film and sold to over a dozen foreign territories. Amy's writing has also been featured in *USA Today*, *Entertainment Weekly*, and *Cosmopolitan*, among others. For more information, visit www.amyleabooks.com.